Balzac's Cane

Balzac's Cane

by
Delphine de Girardin

translated, annotated and introduced by
Brian Stableford

A Black Coat Press Book

TABLE OF CONTENTS

Introduction

The first of the two short novels translated here, *Le Lorgnon*, was published anonymously by Charles Gosselin in 1831, but was reprinted twice in the following year with the added by-line "Madame Émile de Girardin, née Delphine Gay." It was the author's first-published work of prose fiction, but its success was followed by a steady trickle of further prose works. *La Canne de Monsieur de Balzac*, another exercise in the same genre as *Le Lorgnon*, here translated as "Balzac's Cane," was published by Dumont in 1836. Its success was less immediate, and the generic experiment was not repeated again, but following a posthumous appearance in association with the earlier story and one other in a volume entitled *Nouvelles*, issued by Michel Levy in 1856, *La Canne de Monsieur de Balzac* became the more popular of the two—doubtless aided by the fact that Balzac was even more famous by then than he had been in 1836—and the later novella went through several more reprints in the 1860s.

As the by-line added to the first volume takes care to emphasize, Delphine de Girardin (1804-1855) was already famous in 1831 as the poet Delphine Gay. She was the daughter of Sophie Gay (1776-1852) and the latter's second husband. Sophie Gay, baptized Marie-Françoise-Sophie Nichault, was a writer of some note; her novels, which she began to publish following her divorce from her first husband in 1799 and her second marriage shortly thereafter, included *Laure d'Esteil* (1802), *Léonie de Monbreuse* (1813) and *Anatole* (1815), although her theatrical comedies and operas won more acclaim, and the most successful of all her works was the play

7

La Duchesse de Châteauroux. Sophie Gay's salon, although not as fashionable as others that she attended, including those hosted by Madame Récamier and the Duchesse de Duras, was one of the cauldrons of the French Romantic Movement, perhaps as important in its own way as the *cénacle* founded by Charles Nodier at the Bibliothèque de l'Arsenal in 1826. Alphonse de Lamartine and Alfred de Vigny were core members of both, and Sophie Gay went to one of Nodier's meetings—taking Delphine with her—in order to meet Victor Hugo, who also joined her group as well as founding his own.

The precocious Delphine became the star of Sophie Gay's salon while still in her late teens, and was nicknamed by Lamartine—not entirely ironically—"the muse of the nation." Lamartine was exceedingly fond of her and de Vigny wanted to marry her. They were not the only ones smitten; numerous contemporary documents record the rumor that a plot was hatched at the court of Charles X to arrange a morganatic marriage between Delphine and the king (who was nearly fifty years her senior) but that nothing came of it. Several of the writers who mention it suggest, diplomatically, that Charles probably knew nothing about it and that it was the work of one of his favorites done behind his back, but whether that is true or not, Charles certainly awarded her a pension of 1500 francs, ostensibly for her first book of poems, *Essais poétiques* (1824). Her early appearances in society outside the genteel salon circuit, initially in the company of de Vigny, soon gave rise to scandalous rumors, but that was inevitable, given that Sophie Gay was widely calumniated in a similar fashion, as any successful woman tended to be at the time, especially if she was talented, popular and showed evident signs of mental independence.

Delphine began writing at an early age; a second collection of her early writings was issued soon after the first as *Nouveaux essays poétiques* (1825). In her collection of children's stories *Contes d'une vieille fille à ses neveux* [Tales of an Old Maid for her Nephews] (1833), she explained that the stories therein had been written in an era when she had firmly decided that she would never marry—which is to say, the late 1820s—but by the time of its publication, as the collection's by-line made clear, she had changed her mind and had married. Her husband was not one of her more famous suitors, but an up-an-coming journalist, Émile de Girardin (1802-1881), who had also published a novel, the quasi-autobiographical *Émile* (1827). *Le Lorgnon* was probably begun prior to the marriage, which took place on 1 June 1831, although some of the references in the story to datable events prove that it was not finished until afterwards, and the version of the text reprinted in *Nouvelles* dates the preface November 1831; at any rate, the marriage does haunt the text in a slightly peculiar fashion; Émile de Girardin is surely clearly reflected therein, in the relatively minor character of the ambitious journalist, who is a pale figure by comparison with the dashing hero.

Although of noble descent, Émile de Girardin also had a radical heritage—his grandfather, René-Louis de Girardin, had provided Jean-Jacques Rousseau with a refuge and paid for his funerary monument—and he was himself illegitimate, his paternity not being formally recognized by his father, Comte Alexandre de Girardin, until 1837. (When he had an illegitimate son of his own, in 1839, Émile naturally named him Alexandre.) After his marriage, Émile de Girardin swiftly became famous, founding numerous newspapers and periodicals, including the pioneering popular daily *La Presse* and the long-running "family magazine" *La Musée des Familles*. The former inaugurated the tradition of the *roman feuilleton* serials, which was widely imitated and transformed the face of French popular fiction—and, by virtue of further imitation, English popular fiction too. The influence he gained as a power in the press was swiftly translated into a more straightforward political influence; he was first elected as a député in 1834, and remained in the Chambre almost continually until the 1851 *coup d'État*, returning to it again after the fall of the Second Empire. A "progressive conservative" during the reign of Louis-Philippe, he became an important ally of his former adversary Adolphe Thiers during the Third Republic. He was married again soon after Delphine's death in 1855, to a daughter of Prince Frederick of Nassau.

Once she was married, of course, Delphine added her own literary salon to the contemporary circuit, which was attended by the same luminaries as her mother's and, by virtue of its connection with Girardin's various periodicals, became an even more significant source of stimulation during the heyday of the Romantic Movement, at least as important as Hugo's *cénacle* and Théophile Gautier's *petit cénacle*. Delphine had, inevitably, been present at the notorious premiere of Hugo's *Hernani* in 1830, in a box rather than the stalls, although she lent vocal support from there to the claque organized by Petrus Borel and Gautier. She had also contributed to the periodical founded by Hugo, de Vigny and others, *La Muse française*, but she became far more prolific after her marriage, writing extensively for the periodicals founded by her husband, most famously a weekly column signed "Le Vicomte de Launay" in *La Presse*, many of whose inclusions were collected in *Lettres parisiennes* (1843). She wrote for all of his experimental ventures, including those whose editorial duties he farmed out to other aspiring writers, including Jules Janin, the editor of a pioneering magazine of fiction for children, and S. Henry Berthoud, the first editor of the *Musée des Familles* and also of a short-lived reincarnation of the *Mercure de France*. Other friends of the family who helped fill their pages included Gautier, Honoré de Balzac, George Sand and Alexandre Dumas, all of whom wrote feuilleton novels for Girardin.

Among the literary heroes of the core members of the French Romantic movement was the German writer Ernst Hoffmann, the great pioneer of psychologically-sophisticated supernatural fiction. The French Movement's principal publisher during its heyday, Eugène Renduel, issued a fourteen-volume showcase of his works in 1830-32, and several of the writers active in the cenacles took some inspiration from his works, none more so than Jules Janin, who was one of Émile de Girardin's closest associates at the time; the other, Henry Berthoud, had a strong interest in the folklore of his native

Flanders, and wrote numerous supernatural stories of his own in a similar vein. Berthoud's close friend Balzac also wrote a good deal of supernatural fiction in that period, and it is therefore not surprising that Delphine Gay, who was in regular social contact with all of them, should have participated in the vogue.[1]

Le Lorgnon is exactly contemporary with Balzac's La Peau de Chagrin (1831; tr. under various titles, none of which are able to reproduce the essential pun linking the French word chagrin not merely to its English equivalent but to the kind of animal hide known in English as "shagreen"). Although it is far more modest than Balzac's masterpiece in designing a thoroughly modern moral fable with the aid of its supernatural motif—which, following precedents in Hoffmann's work, is credited with a quasi-scientific origin—Le Lorgnon is similarly intense in employing its mechanism for psychological delving. Skimming over conventional hypocrisies and prejudices relatively lightly, the heart of the novel is its analysis of the unusual, and somewhat paradoxical psychology of its two principal female characters, Madame de Clairange and her stepdaughter Valentine. Valentine's family circumstances bear no apparent resemblance to Delphine's, but it is hard to believe that her paradoxical character does not echo the author's notion of herself, at least to some extent. Even if one regards the character as a pure invention, she is nevertheless a fascinating study, which makes an interesting comparison with the author's much later, and wryly disenchanted, study of female psychology, Marguerite, ou Deux amours [Marguerite; or, Two Loves] (1852).

The vogue for supernatural fiction in the camp of the Romantic Movement proved relatively brief, although the desupernaturalized Gothicism of Hugo and Paul Lacroix (alias

---

[1] For more about Jules Janin, see Black Coat Press' edition of The Magnetized Corpse, ISBN 978-1-61227-248-1; for S. Henry Berthoud, see Martyrs of Science, ISBN 978-1-61227-229-0.

"P. L. Jacob the Bibliophile")[2] maintained its prominence in their prose works, and the supernatural never entirely disappeared from the works of Berthoud, Janin, Balzac and Dumas, even though they all strove with calculated determination to develop more naturalistic kinds of fiction. By the time Delphine de Girardin published *La Canne de Monsieur de Balzac*, therefore, the wave of fashionability had passed by, and the latter novella is much more obviously a *jeu d'esprit*, undoubtedly inspired by salon conversation.

The background to the story is simple enough. When Balzac had his first great commercial success, with *Eugénie Grandet* (1833), he immediately compensated for his years of poverty-stricken struggle by fulfilling his long-held ambition to become a "dandy": an elegantly-clad figure who could cut a dash in Parisian society. Unlike the characters in his novels who helped enormously to cement the image and the mythology of the dandy, however—the most notable early example being Eugène de Rastignac in *Père Goriot* (1835)—Balzac was by no means a handsome man, and he needed to offset that disadvantage by a particular flamboyance of presentation. In order to help him do that he commissioned an unusually heavy and ornate walking-stick with a capacious ornamental head, of which he deliberately made something of a mystery, offering veiled hints about what the hollow pommel might contain.

As intended, the cane in question became something of a sensation, and for several years, while Balzac's career was in a spectacular ascendancy, it became his badge and his talisman. Unlike his literary career, his career as a dandy was meteoric, and he was soon in flight from his creditors, so the cane disappeared from the Opéra and the other locations where it had functioned as his standard—he wrote many of his subsequently masterpieces while literally in hiding—but while it was in play, the object was legendary. (It still exists, available for

---

[2] For Paul Lacroix, see *Danse Macabre*, ISBN 978-1-61227-205-4.

public consultation as a relic; the cavity in the head is now empty, but what it might once have contained remains, of course, open to conjecture.) When Delphine de Girardin's novella was first published, the cane was still recent in memory, but it is not entirely surprising that the story obtained a second lease of life when the object itself had become a nostalgic memory, although the author's genius had by then acquired a distinctive legend of its own, and his reputation a markedly different coloration.

In several ways *La Canne de Monsieur de Balzac* follows the same narrative pattern as *Le Lorgnon*; like the earlier story it is an "intrusive fantasy" in which a single supernatural device in the possession of the hero permits him to obtain an unusual insight into the society that surrounds him. The comedic aspects of the situation are brought out more fully, elaborately supported by the preliminary establishment of the hero as a man of humble origin whose ambitions are continually thwarted by the curse of being (unlike Balzac) too good-looking—until he comes into possession of the magical object, which repairs the defect by enabling him to become invisible. The comedy turns to blatant farce in one sequence where the magical cane is mislaid, coming into the accidental possession of a series of characters who employ it without any awareness of its effect, thus establishing the story as a precursor of the kind of comic fantasy developed extensively by "F. Anstey" (Thomas Anstey Guthrie) in England and Thorne Smith in the U.S.A. Like its predecessor, however, it eventually sacrifices its comedic aspect to become a peculiarly intense and highly unorthodox love story.

La Canne de Monsieur de Balzac is by no means unusual in seeking to update traditional tales of devices that confer invisibility, one of which is featured in the first and most famous of all *contes philosophiques*, the story of Gyges in Plato's *Republic*. It was briefly preceded into print by James Dalton's anonymous three-decker novel *The Invisible Gentleman* (1833), although it is highly unlikely that Delphine de Girardin had read that work. As a good Victorian, however,

Dalton—unlike Plato—had ignored one potential use of a method of invisibility that would probably be the first to occur to any male in possession of one: to insert himself surreptitiously into women's bedrooms. That potential had not been ignored by the writers associated with the French salon culture of the 18th century, who had delighted in improving salacious *contes des fées* [usually translated as "fairy stories," although "tales of enchantments" would be more accurate]. Alain-René Lesage's *Le Diable boiteux* (1707; tr. as *The Devil on Two Sticks*), in which the eponymous demons grants the hero invisible access to numerous bedrooms, was one of the key models of that kind of fiction, and Delphine de Girardin was the living epitome of the culture in question as it extended from the 18th century into the 19th, so it would have been very surprising indeed if she had followed Dalton's prudish example, even though, as a female writer in a more modest era, she was obliged to observe much stricter standards of decency than Lesage.

In fact, as the brief preface to the published version of *La Canne de Monsieur de Balzac* reveals, one of the chapters dropped from the book at the publisher's insistence was "a scene of passion" thought to be "too sad and intimate." The author gives no further detail except the title of the missing chapter, "Un Rêve d'Amour" [A Dream of Love] but a consideration of the published text suggests that the chapter in question is more likely to have concerned the character of Malvina than that of Clarisse, probably as the dreamer rather than the object of the dream, if that word is to be taken literally.

If, in fact, it did feature Malvina, is not impossible that the deleted chapter was located between the extant chapter XVI, which describes the initial phases of the hero's seduction of Malvina after using the cane to get into her bedroom unobserved, and chapter XVII, which describes the aftermath of their sexual intercourse, but the likelihood is that that it came after chapter XVII, or perhaps a version of it with a less brutal conclusion, and that the text following that chapter was written considerably later than that the first sixteen chapters. Although the evidence is a trifle slight, it seems likely that the first sixteen chapters and at least the first part of chapter XVII were written in 1834, not long after the real cane first made its sensational appearance, whereas all the subsequent chapters—which are markedly different in tone and subject-matter—were definitely written in 1836. If so, then the removal of the text indicated in the preface might have been the result of an earlier submission of a substantially different text, in 1834.

Whatever the truth of the matter was, one assumes that the missing chapter would not have been any more physically explicit than the surviving chapter XVII, but if it was as psychologically explicit and distinctive as that chapter, then its loss is surely deeply regrettable, because the beginning of chapter XVII is by far the most remarkable passage in the story, and perhaps equal in the combination of its sadness and its intimacy to the saddest intimacies in Balzac's contemporary works; it justifies the overall endeavor more than the satirical chapters dealing with the potentially-disastrous effects of male beauty or the hero's intensely peculiar and morally dubious courtship of Clarisse, although they too have their particular merit and fascination.

In spite of the differences between them, which make the comparison between *Le Lorgnon* and *La Canne de Monsieur de Balzac* interesting as a study in methodical evolution, the core of the entire enterprise lies in what they have in common, which is a determination to carry forward the Voltairean prospectus of employing fantastic devices in order to obtain a clearer view of "the world as it is." Both of the magical devices function by providing their heroes with a means of penetration, offering a better insight into the truth that lies behind the sham of human appearances and performances. In consequence, as well as being "tales of enchantments," they are also, and quintessentially, tales of disenchantments—with the determined exception that they retain an unshakable faith in the possibility, if not the comfortable practicability, of salvation by means of amour. That species of defiant optimism remained typical of the work of female writers long afterwards, including those whose own love lives were even more tormented than Delphine de Girardin's seems to have been; her close friend and fellow gossip-target George Sand provided a cardinal example, and there is no shortage of 20th-century works following the same trend.

Although they are fantastic in terms of their literary devices, therefore, *Le Lorgnon* and *La Canne de Monsieur de Balzac* are both fundamentally skeptical works, as all great literary fantasies are, committed to the notion that one cannot see reality clearly without taking an imaginative step that allows it to be seen at a hypothetical distance, with a more clinical penetration.

It might be the case that one of the reasons why Delphine de Girardin did not write any more supernatural fiction after *La Canne de Monsieur de Balzac* is that her own skepticism and penetration were prejudiced by the strong interest she developed in spiritism—the French equivalent of the Anglo-American spiritualism—which led her to attempt to evoke spirits herself, as a medium.

When she visited Victor Hugo during the early years of his exile following the 1851 coup, she staged séances at his house in Jersey, and appears to have left him with a lifelong interest in the subject; when he returned to Paris after the fall of the Second Empire, he took a strong interest in Camille Flammarion's experiments in automatic writing and the summoning of spirits, although there does not seem to be any record of their ever having succeeded in channeling the spirit of poor Delphine, by then long dead.

Modest as Delphine de Girardin's contribution to the tradition of Romantic fantasy is, it is both notable and distinctive, and the two stories here translated remain highly readable today, all the more so if one can read them with an awareness of their ground-breaking qualities.

These translations were made from the versions of the texts reproduced on the Bibliothèque Nationale's website: the

16

second Gosselin edition of *Le Lorgnon*, published in 1832, and the 1867 Michel Levy edition of *La Canne de Monsieur Balzac*. The London Library's copy of the 1856 edition of *Nouvelles* was also consulted, although the microscopic text made that version unappealing for use in the actual process of translation.

Brian Stableford

THE LORGNON

Preface to the First Edition

This preface is unfashionable; the author is under no illusion about that. To begin with, she[3] has written it herself, a grave error into which people no longer fall; then again, it is not longer than the work, nor is it better and does not prove that it is excellent. It is not threatening, and does not announce half a dozen books in the same genre that one is incessantly proposing to the publisher. It does not insult any government, past, present or future; it does not classify the merit of contemporary authors while immolating all those who obtained success before our era. The author does not prove therein that only her friends know how to write, that they alone have originality and genius; it is not that she lacks wit, or is not proud of their talents, but unfortunately, they have made themselves illustrious by means of their sublime verses and their eloquent and poetic prose; their celebrity is so great that one can no more claim to be establishing their reputation than to be adding to it. The great charlatanism of proper names will not,

---

[3] In the original, the pronoun *elle* is used when standing in for *la préface*, and *il* when substituting for the masculine noun *l'auteur*, without any implication as to the author's sex; in substituting English pronouns, following the different conventions of that language, I have naturally used "it" for "the preface" and "she" for "the author", but it might be worth bearing in mind that readers of the anonymous first edition would not have known that the author was female.

therefore, be the concern of this preface; it will not even praise those who ought to take account of it in the newspapers; no vanity is implored here; it does not take pleasure in the hatred of any party or the malevolence of any coterie; it is sufficient to say that it is as insignificant as the work itself.

Nor is the objective of this preface to reveal a great or sublime philosophical afterthought that one has forgotten to make sensible in the work; the author does not have any pretention to found a school, invent a style or demonstrate great moral truths, political or literary. She does not intend to prove anything; she does not intend to depict anything; her method is not theoretical; her characters are not portraits. She has no intention of correcting society; she would, on the contrary, be desolate if she changed it, because she likes it as it is; it amuses her and inspires her, and she cherishes all the ridiculous aspects that she discovers therein, because they reassures her and authorize her to retain her own—ridiculous aspects at which she laughs herself, amiably, when she perceives them. As she writes without pretention, she wants to be treated without consequence. The objective of this preface is, therefore, to declare that she has written these pages for herself, for her own amusement, without planning to publish them, and without thinking that anyone might read them; that she does not attach any importance to them. That is the whole of her charlatanism; that is her only originality.

Thus, let those serious who minds only see in the appearance of a book an author to be judged, and who hold an ivory knife suspended over her work like a dagger above a victim, not attempt to read this book! It has not been written for them; they will not understand it. It is only addressed to those idle imaginations who follow the dreams of a poet and the marvels of a tale of enchantment complaisantly, who do not analyze that which makes them laugh, who do not experience remorse in having understood a word that the Académie's dictionary has not sanctioned, who will allow us to publish an unpretentious *nouvelle* without thinking us an author in consequence, without criticizing it scathingly, as one sends a friend a letter written in haste, which one has not taken the trouble either to reread or even sign—in sum, those intelligent and indulgent readers who always feel a little gratitude to a book that had helped them to pass an idle hour, between business and pleasure, between a farewell and a return. That category includes men who are bored and women in love; is that not almost half the world?

On the face of the flatterer he read the truth.
Delphine Gay, *Madeleine*, ch. IX[4]

I

"Have you seen Edgar since his return?" said Frédéric Narvaux to his friend Monsieur de Fontvenel, while strolling with him along the main pathway of the Tuileries.

"No—I'm told that he's much changed."

"Unrecognizable, my dear."

"What! Has he been ill, then?"

"No, he's marvelously well, and no one proves more than him the extent to which our visage and bearing depend on our humor."

"I conclude, then, that he's very sullen, and what's worse, that he's become quite ugly."

"No, truly; entirely to the contrary; women find him a thousand times more seductive now, for he has a sentimental air about him, and that's all that they love."

"What are you telling me? Edgar de Lorville has become sentimental! I'd find it more plausible that you'd become religious. That hearty fellow, so fresh and cheerful, suspicious of nothing, as presumptuous as an advocate and as confident as a husband; who wanted to fight a duel over a dancer; who asked my advice in a card game when I was betting against him, and who escorted his rival to his mistress's house one evening without recognizing it?"

"Well, yes, my dear, that ingenuous fellow is no longer anything but a melancholy diplomat. There's nothing like diplomacy for destroying a natural gift. Imagine a conceited

---

[4] In this instance, "ch." Stands for "*chant*," not "*chapitre*." The line is from the long poem "Magdeleine," published in *Le dernier jour de Pompei: poème, suivis de poésies diverses* (1828).

Werther: the mocking and discouraged expression, the distracted gaze, the incredulous smile, not listening to what people say to him; understanding everything obliquely and replying the same way; looking at you through his lorgnon with a disdainful expression, in an insupportable fashion—and, in parentheses, through the most villainous lorgnon that any vaudeville comedian, boulevard fop or provincial bumpkin ever carried in their life."[5]

"You astonish me. I grew up with Lorville; he had excellent eyesight, and..."

"Exactly: it's a diplomatic ruse. Words, it's said, were invented in order to hide what one thinks, and the lorgnon to hide what one sees."

"You're mistaken—Edgar isn't as profound as that. In spite of his success in Vienna and his marvelous travels in Bohemia, I'd never have believed that he could become a melancholy dreamer. Why, look—I'm right!" Monsieur de Fontvenel exclaimed. "That's him I see on the terrace, laughing madly!"

"It is, indeed him," said Monsieur Narvaux, "but what is he laughing at while peering through his lorgnon at that young blonde? We absolutely must find out what's amusing him so much."

With that, they both went up the stairway to the terrace. Monsieur de Lorville, having perceived them, hurried to meet them. His gracious visage seemed to light up with pleasure on recognizing Monsieur de Fontvenel, his childhood friend—but in spite of his politeness, he could not dissimulate a disagreeable impression as he shook the hand that Frédéric held out to

---

[5] Nowadays, all spectacle lenses are hooked on to the ears, but in 1831, when the mechanical design of such devices was still relatively crude, many individuals with problematic vision—especially those who developed presbyopia as they grew older—preferred to attach their lenses to a stick, which they could hold up to their eyes when necessary, and in high society such lorgnons became fashion accessories of a sort.

him affectionately; with an involuntary movement, he seized his lorgnon swiftly and hid it in his bosom, and his physiognomy soon resumed its habitual melancholy impression.

That movement did not escape the two friends, and after the initial rituals of a return—the questions repeated a thousand times, the compliments, the reproaches, the futile explanations of letters gone astray or unanswered, projected voyages, unexpected events and all the inconsequentialities of the past that cause the important facts of the day before to be forgotten—Monsieur de Fontvenel said to his friend:

"Since when have you been blind? People aren't talking about anything but your lorgnon and the manner in which you use it. Let's see whether it merits its reputation?"

Edgar blushed, and darted a disdainful glance at Monsieur Narvaux, who exclaimed: "I have it! It's a souvenir of some beautiful German woman." Then, mimicking a German accent he added: "It's a token of loff, a gift of peauty."

Edgar could not help smiling, and Frédéric exclaimed: "No more doubt! It's a pledge, a token of love."

"A token, indeed," said Edgar, laughing, having recovered somewhat from his disturbance. "It's also the last time that anyone will mention it to me; since it makes me look ridiculous, I won't carry it any longer."

Monsieur de Lorville had been the possessor of the mysterious lorgnon for some time. Its story will seem surprising; some might even doubt its truth, so I shall content myself with reporting it faithfully without explaining it.

As he was concluding his travels, Edgar had met, in a little town in Bohemia, a savant unknown to the world, because he had employed the time that one usually uses in building a reputation to his education. Simultaneously a physicist, a physician, a mechanician and an optician, he was everything except Bohemian.

By virtue of studying the various properties of sight and the different qualities of crystal, the mysteries of myopia and all the secrets of ocular science, after many years of toil and many late nights—those long days of discouragement that serve as the repose of science, and those intoxicating hours in which the imagination lights up with the first glimmers of a discovery—after having more than once consulted the celebrated Gall and Lavater,[6] and after having put to sleep and woken up more than one somnambulist, that astonishing man had succeeded in concocting a kind of glass so perfectly in harmony with the visual rays, which reproduced so faithfully the slightest expressions of the physiognomy, showing the imperceptible details of the fugitive contractions of our features caused by the various stirrings of the soul in such a marvelous fashion, that the eye, with the aid of that light, could penetrate the most profound thought, and translate, so to speak the most intimate falsity. In a word, the possessor of that antiprism, that moral telescope, could see as far into thought as an astronomer into the heavens; and whatever mask was covering your face, seen through that denunciatory crystal, you only had the physiognomy of your true sentiments.

Living in retreat and with good people who did not hide their thoughts, having no other passion than science and no other interest than study, the poor savant had little suspicion of the inconveniences of his discovery; thus, in order to recognize a few services that Monsieur de Lorville had rendered him, he revealed his secret to him, and made him a present of a lorgnon made of that inappreciable crystal, perhaps to thank him for all the noble sentiment he had in his heart. In sum, in their double simplicity—the naivety of youth and the candor

---

[6] Johann Kaspar Lavater (1741-1801) repopularized the ancient Greek pseudoscience of physiognomy, which purports to deduce a person's character from outward appearances, in the 1770s. The physiologist Franz Josef Gall (1758-1828) subsequently popularized a more specialized version of it focused on the shape and size of the skull, supposedly reflective of the development of areas of the brain devoted to particular mental functions, which later came to be known, and widely mocked, as "phrenology."

of science—one thought he was making a profitable gift, and the other that he was receiving a talisman of good fortune.

II

Full of marvelous ideas, Edgar was eager to return to his homeland. An instinct of delicacy told him that in Paris alone would that talisman have its full value.

Paris: the city of prestige, where the gaze is judge and the appearance queen; where beauty resides in costume, conduct in manners, intelligence in good taste; where prejudices distort, where the most distinguished man blushes at his primitive qualities and strives to imitate those impossible to his nature; where life is a long battle between a character of birth that one subjugates and a character of adoption that one imposes one oneself; where everyone is in the toils of hypocrisy, where a profound mind strives to be light and a light mind to be pedantic, where everyone sees others in terms of fortune, imitates those who copy, and often borrows a costume that has been stolen from him. City of grave follies and innocent falsehoods, no one can penetrate your bounds without sharing in your delirium, without being subject there to one of the metamorphoses of vanity.

Armed with his talisman, Edgar rapidly traversed Germany and France, without stopping in any of the large cities that he had already visited. He scarcely had any other occasion to employ the lorgnon than on the different species of innkeepers with which it was necessary for him to communicate along the way. There were the same subtleties and the same ruses intended to retain him or rob him, and the naïve Edgar said to himself:

It's singular that, whether German, Italian or French, all innkeepers have the same thought; as the wise man said, people are the same everywhere.

That was how a young simpleton of twenty-three, full of rectitude and confidence, was thrown into the midst of the tortuous society of Paris with everyone's secret.

Edgar's parents, attached to the old court, had retired to one of their provincial properties. His best friends were absent, and his penetration could only be exercised, to begin with on people of little concern. So, for the first few days after he arrived in Paris, that penetration amused him and threw him off balance. There was stifled laughter, misunderstandings and endless arguments, because the young diplomat did not have the presence of mind as yet that such an art requires, and as he never responded to the words that lied to him, but always to the thought that his lorgnon translated for him, the result was a series of misconceptions, risible susceptibilities, and sometimes confessions so comical that Edgar saw nothing in his fatal lorgnon but an inexhaustible treasure of amusements.

It was then that he encountered Frédéric Narvaux, his former comrade at college. His joy in seeing him again was great, and he expressed it cordially, but Monsieur Narvaux put such enthusiasm into his own testimony that the worthy Edgar, delighted by such amity, wanted to double his enjoyment by penetrating into his friend's heart. He was very surprised to read, instead of the words that Monsieur Narvaux was voicing with passion—"My dear friend, how happy I am to see you returned," etc.—"Curse his return; I'll wager that Esther will go running after him again."

Edgar was confounded; he had believed Frédéric to be a model of frankness, and many others had made the same mistake. He was one of those men on whom everyone thinks they can count. He was reputed to be brave because he was quarrelsome, frank because he was contradictory, and obliging because he was familiar. It is true that he only attacked timid individuals, only contradicted those who had no opinions and only offered his services to people who, by virtue of their position and the delicacy of their character freed him from any danger that they might be accepted; nevertheless, his brusque attitude was imposing, and in any case, how could one suspect such a noisy person of dissimulation?

Scarcely had Monsieur de Lorville penetrated the secret of his character than he acquired a horror of his old friend. His gaiety disappeared, and gave way to the most painful suspicion and the most somber discouragement. His behavior, in Monsieur Narvaux's regard, changed completely. He ceased to address him as *tu*; he no longer listened to him, for he could not reconcile himself to hearing his protestations of friendship, which, denuded of grace and coquetry, had only ever had any value in his eyes by virtue of the confidence their brusqueness inspired.

Gracious and elegant lies have the precious advantage of still being seductive when the illusion has passed. The lies of a soft voice still have harmony; it is as if the charm of the sentiments they affect gives them, so to speak, the right of expression. But a gross and loud expression of friendship that loses its frankness becomes insupportable; it is an indirect insult that irritates, and with which no accommodation is possible. One finds oneself drawn to dissimulate with an adroit and softly perfidious person, but with a gaudy Tartuffe, the fatigued mind cannot hide its scorn or its disgust.

As soon as it was politely permissible for him to quit Monsieur Narvaux, Edgar bid him adieu. As they parted, after a thousand recitations of pleasure to which Edgar had not listened, Frédéric added: "We're all having supper this evening at Esther's—come along, you'll delight us."

Monsieur de Lorville, penetrating the thought, replied to that, and refused.

"Why not?" asked Frédéric. "I'll make a celebration out of bringing you along."

"And I" Edgar replied, dryly, "a duty out of leaving you to it."

Monsieur Narvaux had no desire to take his friend to the home of the young dancer who had loved Edgar before him, and who would doubtless still prefer him; he understood that he had been divined, and could not pardon Monsieur de Lorville for the skill with which he had penetrated he falseness of his invitation, much less the insolent generosity that had made him refuse. That was why he traced such an unflattering portrait of Edgar when he met him in the Tuileries.

"We're speaking ill of you, my dear," he proclaimed as he approached him. That as another of his tricks—he told the truth, but while laughing, in order to render it dubious. The ruse ought only to be permissible to women, for their hilarity almost always stems from embarrassment—and are not all the ruses of emotion pardonable?

Monsieur Narvaux was, according to the expression of an old philosopher I know, a man of the third finesse. The first finesse, he says, consists of hiding one's projects, the second of feigning imaginary ones to hide those one has, and the third is to state them out loud while laughing, as if they had never entered one's head. That remark always pursued me thereafter; it sometimes happens that, involuntarily, I classify my friends in one of those three categories, and I confess that I place very few of them in the first. There is so much mental activity in France that mystery itself wants to be active there; few people limit themselves simply to hiding their ambition and their thoughts; it costs them less to lie, or, what is worse, to affect opposite ones.

III

Edgar, who was beginning to understand the danger of his fatal lorgnon dared not make the experiment with his best friend. He was so glad to see Monsieur de Fontvenel, so touched by his cordial friendship, and he would have suffered so much if it had been necessary to doubt it. Alas, that prudent precaution was already a suspicion. An illusion that is protected is like a fortune that is in disarray; on the day when the word "economy" has resounded in a confident heart, it is half way to ruination.

Edgar had lost the flower of fellowship, the virginity of error that had rendered his youth so brilliant and his character so amiable.

Farewell sweet and confident amity, a thousand times more dangerous than amour in your aberrations; the latter at least knows that it is blind, is wary, and takes a guide; but you, blind without knowing it, march proudly where you believe you are summoned; you are trustful in your coolness, restful in your weakness; you nourish yourself on importunate advice, lull yourself with disagreeable truths that reassure you; and, in your reasoned error, you think that your route will be free of pitfalls because you know it is devoid of prestige.

Poor amity, the most bitter of disappointments! Already, Edgar no longer knows your pure and entire enjoyment; he bargains with his faith, economizes with trials, and while he thinks he is abandoning himself to the charms of his friend's affectionate discourse, a veiled prudence watches over his responses; muted suspicion is working in his thoughts; he sets aside projects that he will not talk about, little adventures that he had resolved to hide, which he would once have confided with an open heart.

In sum, doubt, frightful doubt, had come to place itself between them like an implacable spy, and the two friends, without taking account of their malaise, resembled those prisoners who can only receive visitors when accompanied by a gendarme, and who are astonished at being unable to sustain a conversation with their best friends.

"Why, it's six o'clock," Monsieur Narvaux exclaimed, passing in front of the Tuileries clock. "I'm late—I'm dining with my uncle, the Minister—so I'll leave you."

"I'll see you tomorrow," said Monsieur de Fontvenel.

"Where?"

"At the ball at the embassy."

"What an idea!" Frédéric replied, with a self-important, almost indignant expression. "You know very well that I can't go there." He implied by his definite tone that his political position did not permit him such a pleasure.

Edgar, annoyed by that broad hint, abruptly took out his lorgnon, and saw clearly that the grave political obstacle that forced Monsieur Narvaux to disdain the grand ball was nothing but the want of an invitation that he had been soliciting for a fortnight but had not yet obtained. An ironic smile followed that discovery.

Frédéric drew away.

Left alone with Monsieur de Fontvenel, and holding in his hand the deadly mirror in which the truth was reflected, Edgar could not resist the temptation to look at his friend. He was, in any case, excited by the vindicatory indignation and active scorn that the needless lie had inspired in him, and which gave him such a great impatience as to disconcert him. He felt that one step more taken toward disenchantment would give him the right to declare war on society, and that, fortified by the advantages of his penetration, he might find in malign mental pleasure a compensation for the naïve joy he had lost,

Courage, he said to himself. *I shall at least be freed from the torture of semi-confidence; if this one is also deceiving me, I shall no longer believe in anything; my heart will be broken; I shall be free, and I shall amuse myself by avenging myself.*

Having decided to break the charm, Monsieur de Lorville looked for an opportunity to peer through the lorgnon at his friend without being seen. Continuing the conversation, he said: "You little sister must be very beautiful now? Does she resemble you?" And as if to assure himself as to whether that resemblance might be an advantage, he fixed the implacable lorgnon upon his friend while he listened to his response.

"Yes," Monsieur de Fontvenel replied, "Stéphanie resembles me a little, but she isn't as pretty as she promised to be."

Edgar knew from other people that Mademoiselle de Fontvenel had become ravishing. That deceptive modesty alarmed him, but he was gladly relieved on penetrating the generous motive that had dictated it.

No, thought Monsieur de Fontvenel, *I don't want Edgar to fall in love with my sister; she's not rich enough for him, and I don't want anyone to be able to accuse me of speculating on my friend's kind sentiments, to involve him in a bad liaison to my own profit.*

What delicacy there was on that thought, and how sensible Edgar was of it! With what delight he contemplated that noble heart, in which the purest and most devoted sentiments seemed to have taken refuge. His young heart was pleasantly moved, in passing so suddenly from the anguish of mistrust to the transports of a renascent faith.

In the delirium of his joy, Edgar rediscovered his natural bonhomie. He could not contain himself and, forgetting the Tuileries, the strollers, the elegant women, the sentries and all the apparatus that recalls society and singularly moderates the impulses of the heart, he threw his arms around his friend and hugged him, exclaiming: "My dear Alphonse, how I love you, and how happy I am."

Monsieur de Fontvenel thought that he was completely insane, because, in order to avoid talking about his sister, he had hastened to change the subject of the conversation to an absolutely indifferent matter, without perceiving that Edgar was not listening. He had been talking about the theater, the plays put on in Paris during his absence. He was telling him about *Monsieur Cagnard*, and the best jokes in that fine farce,[7] when Monsieur de Lorville hugged him so passionately and could not understand why the names of Odry, Vernet and Madame Vautrin inspired such transports in him.[8] Thus one often accuses of madness a man whom a sudden discovery has changed his opinion, and of caprice a woman whom penetration has just enlightened.

---

[7] *Monsieur Cagnard, ou les conspirateurs, folie du jour*, was a one-act comedy by "Nicolas Dumersan" (Théophile Marion) and Nicolas Brazier, premièred at the Théâtre des Variétés on 5 February 1831.

[8] Jacques-Charles Odry (1779-1853), "Vernet" (1790-1848) and "Madame Vautrin" were popular comic actors of the day, who might well have been in the cast of *Monsieur Cagnard*.

IV

Reconciled with his talisman, Edgar was no longer thinking about anything but enjoying the pleasure that it promised
him in society. It was certain that it would aid him to unveil
many amusing things.

No one enjoyed an evening at the theater more than him,
the auditorium and the stage offering a double pleasure. Illusion was difficult for him, however, and the thoughts he discovered with the aid of his lorgnon in the soul of the actor
often prevented him from taking an interest in the character he
was portraying. For instance, the good and honest sentiments
that he read in the heart of the savage Marat at the peak of his
wrath, and the reveries of toilette that he discovered in the
thoughts of Charlotte Corday at the moment of the assassina-
tion; the pretty hat that he saw her admiring in the second
boxes as she raised her eyes to the heavens, in order to listen
to her sentence; the burlesque reflections of the poor young
actresses whose whalebone corsets hindered them so much in
dying gracefully, à la Smithson;[9] the petty preoccupations of
the great Napoléon, who was so afraid of offending the de-
fenders of the *juste milieu* by representing too faithfully "the
father of the son of man"—in sum, all those secrets known to
him alone—disturbed him in his terror, and made him a poor
judge.

Comedy, even that of Molière, could no longer grant him
great illusions. Lisette and Scapin,[10] far from amusing him
with their folly, made him feel pity; their souls were so sad in

---

[9] i.e., in the manner of Harriet Smithson (1800-1854), the An-
glo-Irish actress who arrived in Paris in 1828 and rapidly built
a reputation playing tragic roles. The composer Hector Berlioz
became madly infatuated with her; she inspired his *Symphonie
Fantastique* (1832) and subsequently married him.

[10] In *Les Fourberies de Scapin* (1671)

the midst of their gaiety, on seeing the hall empty and jesting in a desert.

No one! Not so much as a cat in the hall, thought the poor soubrette, dolorously, bursting out into that comedy laughter so lacking in contagion.

Seven livres ten sols in receipts, Scapin said to himself, bitterly, as he gamboled around Géronte.

And Lisette, continuing to frolic, thought: *To make a dress and not even to be looked at!*

And Scapin, continuing his pirouettes, said to himself: *Deduct five hundred for the national guardsmen who come to sleep gratis, lying on the benches in the stalls!*

All of that was comedy to break the heart.

Opera was no more amusing to observe. The noisy companions of Comte Ory,[11] did not seem as joyful and as drunk as they wanted to appear. Nor was the somnambulist as unhappy as she strove to make him believe.

In sum, the regulars of the Opéra and the other theaters were often astonished to see on the balcony a young man who seemed so intelligent alone in remaining serious when the entire audience burst out laughing, whereas, on the contrary, he sometimes laughed like a lunatic at the most pathetic of the most beautiful despairs of our great actresses. Often, too, the spectators seated next to him abruptly moved away, unable to account for their malaise but as if magnetized by the gaze of the young man, who smiled without speaking to them.

One evening at the Opéra, in the three facing boxes, there was a stout lady, decked out in finery, who must have had a very singular idea, because Monsieur de Lorville nearly died laughing while looking at her.

On the day of the great ball of which mention has already been made, Monsieur de Lorville had already been at the ambassador's residency for an hour, wandering back and forth, peering and listening, and hiding himself in order to observe.

---

[11] Rossini's comic opera *Le Comte Ory* had its French premiere in 1828.

He already knew the history of all the adornments; he had already penetrated all the little secrets of coquetry, the meager efforts of avarice, the prudent ruses of economy; he knew the names of all the bouquets. One woman respiring the perfume of her own and simpering, seemingly dreading that someone might divine its sentimental mystery, had simply bought it that morning from her florist; another said frankly that she had bought it, who really had received it. Almost all of them were lying without suspecting that so many ruses were futile, and that one did not even need a Bohemian lorgnon to divine the fact. But it was not on those facile discoveries that Edgar founded the pleasure of the soirée. All his malice was reserved in order to enjoy the appearance, awaited so impatiently, of Monsieur Narvaux.

His father, the Duc de Lorville being closely linked with the ambassador of***, it had been easy for him to obtain the invitation for his old friend so humbly requested, of which Monsieur Narvaux had probably despaired. Edgar imagined in advance the excuses that Frédéric would invent to excuse the fickleness of his conduct and explain his appearance at a fête that his political opinions obliged him to deny himself.

Monsieur de Lorville watched for that entrance as anxiously as the most passionate lover lying in wait for the appearance of the woman he loves.

Finally, the moment arrived. Frédéric Narvaux advanced, arrogantly, head held high, but with the embarrassed preoccupation, the indecisive politeness, and the vague, tentative salutations of a guest who does not know either the host or the hostess. Frédéric combined with that embarrassment, familiar to the most ubiquitous socialites, with another perplexity of which the latter are unfamiliar—that of being completely ignorant of whence his invitation had come. On receiving it, the previous evening, he had quarreled with his uncle the Minister, who had told him frankly that he had forgotten to inscribe his name on the list of new admissions. He could not guess where that favor had come from, not to whom he ought to address himself n order to be introduced to the host and hostess.

Monsieur de Lorville was too amused by his strange embarrassment to put an end to it right away. He took pleasure in seeing Monsieur Narvaux trail from one room to another, adrift, so to speak, on an ocean of strangers, passing in front of the ambassador he was seeking twenty times over in the course of his peregrinations.

Finally, Edgar, judging that the torture had lasted long enough, went straight up to Monsieur Narvaux, with a surprised expression, as if he had only just perceived him.

Frédéric seemed so relieved on finally finding someone he knew that Monsieur de Lorville could not suppress a smile on seeing is haste to speak to him.

This time, he thought, *the joy of seeing me again is sincere!*

Feigning astonishment, he exclaimed: "You here! I thought that your position..."

"Don't talk to me about that," Monsieur Narvaux interrupted. "You see me shamed of it, but I'm no better than I am, and when a pretty woman says to me: 'I want it,' I would go to a ball at the house of my greatest enemy to see her dance."

Edgar marveled at the audacity of the lie, and promised himself to undermine it. However, seeing that Frédéric was obstinate in remaining close to him, be began to repent of having procured him the invitation, and, profiting from the pretext that was offered to him, he lost himself in the crowd and ran to join his dancing-partner.

She was a ravishing blonde, beautiful and melancholy: large dark eyes, half-veiled by long eyelids, an incomplete smile, an air of compliance in lending herself to pleasures that were no longer such for her. An attitude of languor, and even of suffering, gave her entire person an inexpressible charm. Edgar had only been able to obtain the fourth quadrille, so many of the ultra-fashionable individuals of the moment were pressing around her. Mademoiselle d'Armilly had put on a slightly sulky expression when Edgar had come to ask her for a dance. In order to know the cause of it he had peered through the lorgnon as he drew away.

It's very tiresome, she was thinking, *to dance with people that one doesn't know.*

That reflection pleased Monsieur de Lorville a great deal. He was beginning to weary of the continual coquetries that women addressed to him, seduced by his pretty face, his distinguished attire and the elegance of his manners. *This young woman*, he thought, *prefers her old friends to her new conquests; I like that character, and forgive her the lack of enthusiasm with which she accepted my invitation.*

The ritornello of the fourth quadrille had already been played. Edgar came to take the hand of her pretty partner, and as it would not have been polite to use the lorgnon while chatting to her he yielded entirely to the pleasure of listening to her and admiring her.

Mademoiselle d'Armilly had abandoned her slightly sulky expression; her pretty figure had straightened up, her face was reanimated, her step more assured; in sum, she had the satisfied ensemble that often gives women away when they are dancing with someone who pleases them: the confident pleasure of a female waltzer who encounters a good male waltzer, or of a savant whist-player to whom fate has give a partner worthy of her.

Monsieur de Lorville noticed that change, and initially attributed it to the effect that Mademoiselle d'Armilly's beauty produced, and her desire to appear beautiful to the numerous circle of admirers who surrounded her. Soon, however, he saw that the metamorphosis of her manner extended to him. Mademoiselle d'Armilly seemed to soften her gaze in order to attach it to his, and to choose the softest tones of her voice in order to reply to him. In everything she said there was such an intention to please that it was impossible not to notice it. All that coquetry, devoid of ostentation and full of good taste, delighted Monsieur de Lorville.

"You've recently arrived from Germany," said Mademoiselle d'Armilly. "Did you stay for long in Vienna?"

Edgar understood then that Mademoiselle d'Armilly knew who he was, and remembered having noticed that she had asked young woman sitting nearby for his name when he came to look for her in order to dance.

"Yes," he replied, "I spent more than a year there."

"Do people enjoy themselves greatly there?"

"It depends; there are people who don't enjoy themselves anywhere; I know an Englishman who claims that Paris is the most tedious city in the world, and I can assure you that, for his part, he's right. He only stayed here for a month, with tertian fever[12]—so he was unable to believe that anyone enjoys themselves here."

Mademoiselle d'Armilly laughed at that joke so pleasantly that Monsieur de Lorville was glad to have excited her gaiety, and was thus able to render the conversation easy, by talking to her about what she wanted to know about him.

While he was dancing, a an elegant man of a reasonable age with whom Mademoiselle d'Armilly had been chatting for a part of the evening came to stand behind her, but he did not stay there for long; she received him so coldly and so stiffly that the poor admirer, disconcerted by that unexpected rigor, soon went away. Edgar asked his name.

"That's Monsieur de Champléry," said Mademoiselle d'Armilly, with an expression of confidence and child-like malice. "He's a protégé of my uncle. I dance with him by order, although he bores me to death."

Edgar was delighted by the naivety of that response and the gracious manner of linking herself with him by putting him, so to speak, on her side. He had never experienced a more seductive emotion in the presence of a young woman.

The quadrille finished, and it was necessary to separate. Edgar escorted Mademoiselle d'Armilly back to her seat, next to her mother. As she saw him draw away she addressed a smile full of gentility to him, which said: *We're already old friends*.

---

[12] Malaria.

While dreaming about his new passion Edgar went to stand in the embrasure of a window in order to admire her in silence. Mademoiselle d'Armilly, who followed him with her eyes, saw from a distance that he was making use of his lorgnon attentively, and, giving her physiognomy all the grace of embarrassment, she lowered her eyes.

Eager to know the impression that he had made on her, Edgar was avid to read her heart. But alas, this is what that tender soul was thinking about him and his intelligence:

He's the son of the Duc de Lorville; he'll have an income of sixteen thousand livres when he marries.

Oh, what a bitter disenchantment! Of his mind, not a word; of his person, not a memory. In vain he had been amiable, in vain he had rejoiced in looking his best that day; she had not listened to him; she had not looked at him. What she liked about him was his aged father and the ancient Château de Lorville, where he was so bored.

How he pardoned then the women that only liked him for his frivolous attributes. Mademoiselle d'Armilly was incapable of experiencing such a simple weakness. Ambition renders blind; the advantages it seeks are the only ones it understands; it does not merely disdain the others, but does not see them.

Falling from the height of his illusion, Edgar yielded to an immeasurable contempt. Every time he went past Mademoiselle d'Armilly he responded to her engaging gaze by turning his head away in the most insolent manner. *Oh*, he thought, *if it's only my rank that pleases her in me, well, I'll make her sensible of it by disdaining her.*

Mademoiselle d'Armilly soon noticed that difference in Monsieur de Lorville's sentiments; she did not seem surprised by it, and her resigned attitude struck him. He looked at her again in order to see what she thought of the change.

She explained it thus: *Someone has told him that I have no dowry.*

And with the justice of calculating individuals, she found it quite simple that Monsieur de Lorville was experiencing for her, at that moment, the same disdain that she had felt for him before knowing who he was.

So much dryness in such a young person, of such a languorous beauty, inspired a kind of horror in Monsieur de Lorville. Now that he had her secret, that young woman appeared to him as ugly as she really was beautiful, so true is it that all of a woman's charm depends on the sentiments she experiences, or that one supposes she has. Physiognomy is a language; in order to be moved by it, it is necessary to have faith in what it expresses.

V

In a bad mood and discouraged, Edgar resorted to his malice for a second time as a distraction. He took pleasure in embarrassing the people to whom he spoke by revealing to them what they were really thinking at the moment when they were expressing the contrary. At other times he amused himself by replying to people who had not spoken aloud, and were confused to have their thoughts divined.

Near the fireplace of one of the numerous rooms there was a stout monsieur who was not speaking to anyone and was watching the clock attentively. Knowing what he was thinking, Edgar said to him: "We'll be having supper shortly."

The monsieur recoiled in astonishment, but then reassured himself, thinking: *There's a young man as greedy as me.*

Later, he nearly picked a quarrel with one of those grave politicians who lie boldly by nature and for the sake of prudence, who believe that they are only dissimulating out of duty. Their conversation was truly risible to hear. Monsieur de Lorville, who only attended to the hidden thought, seemed to everyone to be a contradictory individual who understood everything in reverse, and to his interlocutor to be a teasing individual whose conversation was insupportable.

"The Ministry will last longer than people think," the politician said. "I have good reasons for supposing so."

"Really?" said Edgar, smiling. "You think it will be changed tomorrow?"

"I didn't say that, Monsieur," the other protested, annoyed, and added: "Furthermore, I scarcely care to enter into that boutique, and since no one is thinking of me..."

"Oh! Approaches have been made to you?"

"You're not listening to me, Monsieur."

"Yes, truly: you've been offered a portfolio, which you'll accept on certain conditions; nothing could be simpler."

The statesman blushed at being divined, pretended to believe that Edgar was joking, and abruptly changed the subject. "I've just come from the Ministry of Foreign Affairs," he said. "There's no news from Italy."

"Aha! said Edgar, peering at the diplomat. "A courier arrived this evening."

"Monsieur, I had the honor of telling you that no news had arrived."

"Yes, I heard; and you now know that the Austrians are in Bologne."[13]

"Me, Monsieur! I know nothing at all."

The diplomat remained confused. That news was still secret, and he had promised the Minister to keep it so. Irritated by such a singular dialogue, he went away, saying to himself that there was nothing like ignorance and stupidity for disconcerting an intelligent man—for, not knowing Monsieur de Lorville's secret, he attributed the accuracy of his ideas to hazard and mental incoherence.

These young men of the Faubourg Saint-Germain, he thought, *are so conceited...*

"Those of the Faubourg Saint-Jacques don't please you anymore," Edgar said, knowing that the mere word "student" made the politician tremble. The latter turned round swiftly, alarmed by the voice that was responding to his thought. He reflected for a long time about that extraordinary circumstance, and, unable to understand it, explained it by a phenomenon that was perhaps even more surprising, believing that he must have thought aloud for the first time in his life.

On going back into the ballroom, Edgar perceived his friend Narvaux, chatting mysteriously in a corner with someone who resembled, at a distance, a Turkish ambassador or an

---

[13] An Austrian army entered Bologna on 23 March 1831, at the request of Pope Gregory XVI, who was trying to suppress a Republican revolt in the Papal States. The rebels, intent on the unification of Italy, appealed for help to Louis-Philippe, the French king, but did not get it.

old Englishwoman. In fact, it was one of those inimitable old Englishwomen who, after having had fourteen or fifteen children in their own land, come to Paris to learn French. She was wearing one of those three-tier turbans that only England produces: feathers, flowers, diamonds, steel, jet acorns, ribbons and golden studs ornamented the imposing cupola, beneath which a long and fleshless face was simpering, further enhancing its enormity.

Edgar had never seen a more fantastic creature, or such a sumptuously ugly woman, in his travels or his nightmares. Monsieur Narvaux, who had discovered that species of pretentious mummy the previous year at the spa of Plombières seemed embarrassed to be discovered chatting so coquettishly with her by the most sarcastic of his friends. He turned his head away, pretending not to have seen Monsieur de Lorville, but the latter was implacable.

Resolute in punishing Monsieur Narvaux for his lies, he approached him in a discreet fashion and, designating the old Englishwoman, whispered in a mocking tone: "It's her, isn't it? Oh, you're right, my dear, I'm with you: I'd go to a ball hosted by my greatest enemy to see her dance."

Subtle men who remember their lies always have one in reserve in case of surprise or misfortune. They expect to be disconcerted, and never utter a falsehood without perceiving the risks it might run. As soon as he saw Monsieur de Lorville, Monsieur Narvaux had anticipated that malice, and, far from taking exception to it, he smiled complaisantly and then, raising his eyes to the heavens, adopted a dolorous tone.

"Oh, don't joke; I'm fearfully anxious; she hasn't come this evening and I don't know why."

I know exactly why, Edgar thought, stunned by that imperturbable dishonesty—and he drew away, penetrated by a kind of admiration for so much audacity and presence of mind. He sensed that without the magical power of the lorgnon he would have been completely duped by Monsieur Narvaux, so much candor and naivety did he put into his lies.

Saddened by all the disappointments of the evening, Edgar was about to leave the ball when a young man attracted his attention because of an expression of preoccupation and anguish of which he was curious to know the cause.

The young man in question was one of those elegant Pylades who are constant victims of a brilliant Orestes, to whose destiny and caprices they are equally subject. Their life is an eternal self-abnegation; they have nothing of their own, are of no consequence to themselves and do nothing for themselves; they wait to act until Orestes has decided, are only hungry at his meal-times, only travel in order to accompany him, and only permit themselves to like the places he visits most frequently. They even go so far to retrench their name; no one any longer refers to them except as so-and-so's friend, and their idleness adapts so marvelously to that life of reflection as not to render them responsible for any of their actions. Pylades lodges with Orestes, and although they both pay the same rent to their common landlord, and, in consequence, are equal in the eyes of the impartial owner, one says, proudly "my place," while the other says timidly, "our place."

The elegant planet of whom the young man observed by Monsieur de Lorville was the satellite had left the ball more than two hours previously. An explosive chagrin, on the effect of which he was counting to ensure the success of an amorous intrigue commenced at the ball, had motivated that prompt disappearance, and, in his calculated fury, the noble dandy had forgotten to inform his companion in pleasure, and associate in the carriage that was supposed to take them home, of his flight.

The errant shadow was wandering hither and yon, in search of an object to which he could attach himself. Edgar, divining his trouble, approached the unfortunate young man, and, knowing that pronouncing the name of his friend gave him the right to speak to him, pretended an acquaintance with the latter, saying: "Monsieur de Guercey left very early this evening—is he ill?"

"I believe so," the Pylades replied, "for he's forgotten me; we were supposed to go together. It's pouring with rain, and..."

"I'm at your disposal," Edgar said, quickly. "Only too happy to oblige a friend of Monsieur de Guercey."

They both left the ball. Monsieur de Lorville's people were summoned, and they climbed into the carriage. On the way, Edgar smiled in thinking about the astonishment his neighbor would experience on discovering hat Monsieur de Guercey and he were unacquainted. He amused himself conjecturing what they would make of it.

Then, returning to his home, he said to himself, sadly: *So that's the only advantage that the art of divination has procured me at that brilliant fête: the pleasure of obliging a stranger.*

VI

The next day, as Edgar sat down at table to have a morning meal with two of his cousins, Monsieur de Fontvenel was announced. He was pale and his face was distressed; it was easy to see that he was dominated by a sad thought. Having an important favor to ask of Monsieur de Lorville, he had come to see him at an early hour, hoping to find him alone.

"You're very welcome!" exclaimed Edgar, on seeing his friend. "Come in, noble support of the magistracy, master of requests, candidate for the Conseil d'État for your extraordinary services—we'll vote you two cutlets and a cup of tea; come and sit down with us and share our labors."

"I've eaten, thank you," Monsieur de Fontvenel replied, slightly disconcerted by the jesting. Looking at the other guests, he went on: "Please don't disturb yourselves."

That politeness was unnecessary, for the cousins had no desire to disturb themselves; they did not like Monsieur de Fontvenel. The relatives of a rich man never like his friends. Not unaware of their malevolence, Monsieur de Fontvenel was not at all at ease in their presence, and Edgar not at all to his advantage.

"Well, serious thinker," the latter had to him, in the kind of ironic tone that keeps people at a distance, "you're not saying anything. What important work deprived us of your presence at yesterday's ball?"

"Something unexpected kept me at home."

"I'm sorry for you, in truth," said one of the cousins. "The ball was admirable and I enjoyed myself greatly there."

All three then began talking about the fête, disregarding the fact that Monsieur de Fontvenel had not been there and could not join in the conversation—but he was too preoccupied and anxious to be sensible of that impoliteness.

Monsieur de Fontvenel found himself in an alarming situation, which might compromise his honor and his reputation.

The failure of a bank had just lost him a considerable sum of money, on which he had been counting to repay a large debt. He needed to pay out fifty thousand francs that same day, and did not have them. Knowing Monsieur de Lorville's generosity, he had come to borrow that sum from him. convinced that, if he was accessible, he would not hesitate to oblige.

His discouragement was considerable when, instead of finding his friend alone, as he usually was in the morning, he discovered him with two people with whose malevolence and cupidity he was aware.

As soon as had he came in he saw that the atmosphere was not favorable to him, and he renounced the plan of making his request. To be refused by someone indifferent appeared to him to be quite natural, but to see himself rejected by a friend would be heart-rending. A great sadness took possession of him.

Alas, is it not already to be rejected to abandon the idea of asking? Is there not inspiration in that timidity? Would the man whom one has not dared to ask for a favor have rendered it? Perhaps...for everything depends on the moment, in France most of all, where hearts and minds are so mobile.

After the meal, the two cousins, far from thinking of going away, went to establish themselves on two comfortable sofas in Monsieur de Lorville's bedroom, each picking up a newspaper. For his part, Edgar went to sit at his writing-desk, rearranged a few objects, and ended up starting to write, without worrying about what was going on around him.

Monsieur de Fontvenel was so discontented with the visit that he dared not conclude it; he wanted to wait until sufficient notice was taken of him to be able to leave without appearing too susceptible, and without seemed ill-humored. He picked up the *Revue de Paris*, which was on the table, and pretended to read it in order to put on a brave face.

From time to time, Edgar smiled as he glanced at him, looked at him through his lorgnon, and then resumed writing without addressing a word to him. Finally, annoyed by his malaise and thinking about means of finding the assistance elsewhere that he no longer hoped to obtain from his friend, Monsieur de Fontvenel headed for the door and was about to go out when Edgar called to him: "Wait a moment, blockhead; you're forgetting to take what you came to seek."

"What do you mean?" asked Monsieur de Fontvenel.

"What? You dare to tell me that you did not have an idea in coming here?"

"I don't say that, but I'm sure that I haven't mentioned it to anyone, and..."

Edgar interrupted him. "No matter! What need is there for words in friendship. Have you read La Fontaine's 'Monomotapa?'"[14]

"Yes, but..."

"Don't you know: 'That a true friend is a good thing;/He seeks your needs in the depths of your heart,/He spares you the embarrassment/of revealing them yourself...'"

"I know the fable by heart," said Monsieur de Fontvenel, "but who can...?"

"A fable, blasphemer?" exclaimed Edgar, laughing. "Here, take this letter, and don't treat as a fable any longer what is the truest thing in the world."

Then, handing him the letter he had just written, which was a letter of credit for fifty thousand francs drawn on his bank, he added: "Skeptic! Let this teach you not to doubt your friends."

Monsieur de Fontvenel read the note three times, and his astonishment was such that it overwhelmed any other senti-ment. The joy of finding the sum that would liberate him from such a great anxiety, the salvation of his honor, and the emo-tion of gratitude, all gave way to the impatience to know how Edgar had penetrated his secret. He looked around, seeking mentally to divine what could have betrayed him, but no one knew as yet about the event that had placed him in sudden

---

[14] The reference is to La Fontaine's fable "Les Deux amis," in which the two friends are said to live in Monomatapa (a king-dom in Africa).

embarrassment; no one could have mentioned it to Monsieur de Lorville. How had he known?

That mystery tormented him like a torture, and he resolved to find the explanation. However, he was touched by such generosity, and even more so by such delicacy. Tears of affection formed in his eyes; he would have liked to divine in his turn what his friend desired, in order to acquire it for him at the risk of his life.

Edgar enjoyed his astonishment and his joy, but to prevent his cousins from observing it, he made a sign to Monsieur de Fontvenel to say nothing in front of them, and escorted him back to the staircase.

"Until this evening," said Monsieur de Lorville. "I'll drop in at your mother's house briefly, and I hope that, in spite of three years of absence, the lovely Stéphanie will recognize me. Until this evening."

"Any time," said Monsieur Fontvenel, emotionally. "How I look forward to seeing you again! Oh, my life will not be long enough to testify to all that I'm feeling at his moment."

With these words, they embraced with a brotherly affection, and Monsieur de Fontvenel left, overwhelmed by gratitude, the happiest of men, but also the most tormented.

VII

It was ten o'clock in the evening when Monsieur de Lorville called on Madame de Fontvenel. He soon perceived that his friend had betrayed his kindness. Madame de Fontvenel, dominated by a tenderness that she could not hide, came to him with tears in her eyes, and although she did not mention the service that he had rendered her son, everything about her demonstrated the extent to which she was sensible of it.

Stéphanie, although more restrained, also testified similar sentiments. Her brother seemed proud and joyful, and Monsieur de Lorville felt all the pleasure of a good deed, and that of seeing profoundly happy souls that are worthy of it. Oh, what pleasant moments he had spent with that family, so benevolent toward him, with his mother's old friend, who had treated him like a son; he was astonished to have neglected them since his return. But in Paris, the people one likes the most are those one sees the least; if they are not launched to the same extent as we are into the whirlwind of worldly pleasures that drags us away, one loses sight of them, and they soon become complete strangers, unless some great misfortune befalls them which brings us back to them.

It is a singular thing, but incontestable, that in high society, to be seen every day where it is appropriate to be seen, it is necessary to have, not the same friends, but the same casual acquaintances. The important thing is not to be hindered; in friendship, as in everything, one only does what is comfortable; so opportunity takes precedence in all projects, and a man often neglects his best friend because he lives some distance away, and spends his life in the company of neighbors he detests.

Edgar was struck by the beauty of Mademoiselle de Fontvenel. What a difference there was between the mischievous little girl he had left behind three years ago and the tall and beautiful woman he rediscovered, ornamented with all the seductions that a distinguished education gives to an elevated nature.

He no longer recalled, on seeing Stéphanie so beautiful and imposing, that a few years before he had addressed her informally, like a sister, and it was with an almost timid emotion that he kissed the pretty hand that she held out to him affectionately. Soon, on seeing her laugh as of old, he was reassured. His soft gaze went alternately from Madame de Fontvenel to Stéphanie and to her brother, and he felt, involuntarily, that since he had returned to that house, all his thoughts had a future.

Several visits having followed, one evening, Monsieur de Lorville ceded the place that he occupied next to the mistress of the house, and went to join Stéphanie on the far side of the drawing room. She was sitting at a table covered with an album, newspapers and caricatures. Another young woman was embroidering beside her, a famous artist was amusing himself drawing grotesque faces that a young officer was imitating scrupulously; one person was copying a ballad, another seeking to transcribe surreptitiously a poetic but nevertheless seditious song by Béranger. Everyone seemed busy, but that did not prevent the conversation from being animated.

When Mademoiselle de Fontvenel saw Edgar approaching, she said: "Here comes Monsieur de Lorville. Let's be careful; woe betide anyone who has a secret to hide; he'll quickly divine what each of us desires. He's the most perceptive man in the world."

"Don't worry," said Edgar. "This evening I don't want to divine anything."

"What! You're very disdainful. You have no desire, then, to know what we're thinking?"

"Not yet. It can't be favorable to me; I've just arrived. The forgotten are always wrong, aren't they, Stéphanie? Oh, pardon me, *Mademoiselle*—but I can't get accustomed to being treated here as a stranger, and passing for someone newly introduced. It's absolutely necessary for me to find a right to your preference. Are we not almost cousins?"

"Not at all," replied Stéphanie, laughing, "and I can't entertain the slightest illusion about that."

"No matter; I shall call you cousin; that will dispel the air of ceremony to which a childhood friend can't adapt. So it's agreed: you can call me cousin too." Maliciously he added; "It wasn't so very long ago that you called me by a sweeter name, but I've already perceived, unfortunately, that those beautiful days are far behind us."

At those words, Mademoiselle de Fontvenel blushed, and the man she had called in childhood her "little husband" was greatly amused by that embarrassment. The slightest emotion, in a person who seems cold, has a charm that one can rarely resist; it appeals to our self-esteem. It is a triumph obtained, a destiny accomplished, for we imagine that the person in question, insensible until then, was waiting for us to become animated.

Edgar would have liked to pick up his lorgnon and divine Stéphanie's thought, but he dared not attract attention to the talisman, for fear that someone might discover the marvel. In any case, he was not suspicious; he knew that his friend's sister, Madame de Fontvenel's daughter, could only experience noble sentiments. It would have required a very great change to diminish that heart, which he had known in his childhood to be so good and generous.

Abandoning himself entirely to a nascent affection founded on pleasant memories, Edgar did not quit Stéphanie's company all evening. She seemed to find he greatest charm in recalling with him the games of her childhood, and Mademoiselle de Fontvenel, ordinarily so calm and equally gracious to everyone, appeared that evening as he had never seen her before, full of gaiety and coquetry.

It is true that Monsieur de Lorville was one of those men with whom women are always coquettish, without any plan or amorous inclination, and sometimes even involuntarily. The desire to please is contagious in a handsome man, even if one thinks him disdainful or difficult, even if one regards him as an authority. The most honest woman cannot resist the temptation to appear seductive to him, and, without thinking of giving him a hope, is not sorry to leave him a regret.

In vain, several women came to interrupt Edgar's conversation with Stéphanie; he always found a means to stay close to her. In vain, stormy political discussions in the next room attracted his attention; he did not join in with them.

For a long time, in any case, politics had become indifferent to him. He was keenly interested in the affairs of his country, but on the condition of not listening to what people said about them. How, in fact, can one reconcile oneself to talk politics when one has the secret of all opinions, when one has discovered that personal interest alone inspires and sustains them; that everyone chooses in his principles of morality of government those that will bring him the greatest reward; that there is in all violent opinions a foundation of memories or projects, a hidden agenda of a position lost, obtained or desired? When one knows, in sum, that everyone judges the general interest by his own particular position, all discussion becomes futile. It is not that the opinions lack good faith—oh, everyone is committed to his interests—but that they lack stability; and, while contradicting the most exaggerated, one foresees the chances one has of modifying one's situation, and the risks one runs in change. So Monsieur de Lorville, who knew all ambitions, said, jokingly, that before combating a political principle, he would wait until success or despair had fixed it definitively.

Monsieur de Lorville had only been to the Chambre des Députés once; his talisman had certainly had a golden opportunity to exercise its power than day. If Edgar had been German or English he would have been greatly amused by that ant-hive of declaiming vanities and those feigned examples of disinterested nobility, of whose history and conditions he was aware—but he loved his country too much to laugh at the ridicule in which it was drowning, and retained a sad and discouraging memory of the session. He thus refused the greatest amusement that his lorgnon offered him.

He could have compensated himself for that privation by going to observe, in the brilliant salons of the Palais-Royal, where the pleasures hide so much sadness, the new vanities and the new pretentions of the new courtiers of the new court;[15] unfortunately for his gaiety, the former position of his father imposed duties upon him to which he remained faithful. The latest troubles of that year would also have furnished him with observations no less piquant; he could have amused himself greatly watching the "mob" as it passed by, but the same sentiments that made him shun the Chambre des Députés turned his eyes away from a spectacle so afflicting for a veritable lover of his country.

Everyone, however, was astonished by his tolerance and his marvelous sympathy with all the different exaggerations. In his eyes, when he had his lorgnon, the two parties that divided France at that moment were designated as "the regretful" and "the hopeful," and in order to chat harmoniously with his interlocutor, it was sufficient to know to which of those two parties he belonged. Then, in accordance with his observation, he approved or criticized at hazard, sure of falling the right way without taking the trouble to listen.

Monsieur de Lorville pardoned everyone for choosing and devoting himself to the order of things that offered him the most advantages. He understood marvelously the love of

---

[15] March 1831 was only eight months after the July Revolution of 1830, which had replaced the old monarchy of Charles X with the constitutional monarchy of Louis-Philippe. Edgar seems to be neutral in his own opinions, but his father's Carlist affiliations compel him to shun the representatives of the new order. Most of Delphine Gay's friends were radical Republicans, but if the rumors were true that she had once been courted by the aging Charles himself, and given that he had certainly given her a pension, she probably felt that her own loyalties were a trifle divided.

good bourgeois individuals for Louis-Philippe, the regret of devotees for Charles X, and the dreams of the young for Bonaparte. He found it quite simple to hear the daughters of Ducs and peers regretting the old court, and the wives of bankers enthusiastically praising the new one; everyone, he knew, prefers the government that suits him, and as he knew that he was not devoid of personal interest himself in those universal questions, and that everyone judges the whole from his own point of view, he changed his position mentally, and thus found himself in agreement with everyone, without deceit and without effort.

VIII

A pompous visitor came to interrupt his pleasant conversation with Stéphanie. Madame de Clairange was not a woman to pass unperceived in a drawing room, and Mademoiselle de Fontvenel, although slightly annoyed, was obliged to get up to go and seek news of her health.

Edgar was left alone; a sentiment full of charm had taken possession of him. Astonished that an amour so prompt had already obtained so much empire over him, he sought to explain it by his memories.

I've known her for such a long time, he told himself, *that I love her; all the pleasant impressions of my childhood are associated with her. How many times has she consoled me when I was sad! How kind she was! And now she's ravishing!*

He contemplated her tenderly, almost religiously. He admired the pure forehead whose paleness was heightened by a fringe of black hair, the gaze full of nobility and honesty, the well-proportioned figure, to the elegance of which a simple costume in good taste gave full value.

Delighted to find so much intelligence and gentleness in a person of remarkable beauty, and proud of being favorably welcomed by her, Edgar dreamed about the happiness of spending his life with Stéphanie, and, flattering himself that he might be loved by her some day, rejoiced in advance in disconcerting, by that brilliant marriage, the humble delicacy of his friend's projects.

But he wanted to know exactly to what point she might share his ideas, and to read what was present in her heart. The arrival of Madame de Clairange was attracting everyone's attention, so Monsieur de Lorville, seeing that no one was observing him, chose that moment to satisfy his curiosity and confirm his hopes. He had been sure of Stéphanie's affection for a long time, and he also knew that no calculation of interest or ambition could enter a soul so pure, or arrive to disenchant it.

Finally, full of confidence, and seized by a joyful emotion, he looked at her...

What a surprise! What a discovery, crueler than any disenchantment!

Stéphanie is not thinking about him. Stéphanie is in love. Stéphanie's heart is no longer free. Her affectionate tone is only one of friendship, her coquetry merely a petty vengeance against the man she loves, the vulgar punishment of a minor slight.

Monsieur de Lorville looks around, seeking his rival; the young officer that he has not previously noticed, gives himself away by his attitude of resentment and is silence.

Poor Edgar! It is all over; his beautiful future evaporates. He experiences all the torments of jealousy, all the discouragement of a final adieu...

Another amour extinguished at birth, alas! Another fine dream destroyed.

Desolate, his heart devoured by regret, Edgar decided to leave; but before then, he promised himself to punish Stéphanie for the deceptive hope to which she had given rise. He wanted, at least, to console himself for the chagrin of having divined her secret, by proving to her that he possessed it and that it was in his dependence.

She came back toward him more gracious and more coquettish than she had been before.

"I warn you," she said, laughing, "that a plot is being woven against you; you are going to be introduced to Madame de Clairange, so prepare yourself to be amiable."

"Is there a destiny in being introduced to Madame de Clairange?" asked Edgar, ironically.

"No, but an introduction is a solemnity for which one cannot be too prepared. What can one say to someone that one does not know?"

"Oh, what one says to others; it hardly matters." Edgar pronounced the last words with a visible chagrin.

"How somber you've become," Stéphanie said. "What's the matter with you? What can have saddened you so suddenly?"

"The sight of a needless torment; I detest seeing suffering. Yes, truly, and I'm capable of going to tell that poor jealous fellow"—he pointed at the young officer who was facing her—"that you only love him, and that I don't merit his anger."

Mademoiselle de Fontvenel's embarrassment was extreme. She blushed and lowered her eyes. After a moment's pause, she said: "My brother is right. You're a very redoubtable observer."

"Yes, if I were malevolent," said Edgar, "but don't worry; I have no vanity, and no matter how modest the place is that I'm granted, I'm able to resign myself to it." He added: "However, I would like always to be allowed..."

The affectionate tone in which he pronounced those words moved Stéphanie visibly, and Monsieur de Lorville, divining that she was about to experience a few regrets and that the young officer had just lost his advantages, drew away, consoled by his superiority, as a great general consoles himself for a defeat, calculating the enemy's losses.

Edgar was soon introduced to Madame de Clairange, as had been threatened. He saw a woman who was still young, dressed artfully, whose face would have seemed completely insignificant without a continual benevolent grimace that composed a physiognomy of sorts.

Madame de Clairange had no soul, no mind, no qualities and no faults; only being drawn or retained by some primitive sentiment, good or bad, she had been able to choose all those that embellished her—and with exquisite taste, it must be said, in all fairness. The most natural emotions were, for her, mere adornments; she preferred generosity to malice as one prefers blue to pink, according to which suits one more. It cost her nothing to acquire a seductive virtue; in her, decency was a study, sensibility an ornamentation, mildness a system. By virtue of moderating it, she rendered her voice so faint that one could hardly hear it.

That preoccupation with moral attire was evident in his speech; all her sentences began with "Nothing is more fitting..." or, "Nothing is more becoming..." One imagined that she was about to talk about some fashionable hat or fabric, but not at all, it was piety or benevolence. Having decided on generosity in her charitable zeal, she did, in fact, a great deal of good, but all without charm, without making herself loved. Her bounty was, so to speak, lifeless; her consolations did not reach you; everything that she said to calm your distress proved that she did not understand it at all; and even those on whom she lavished her benefits, while thanking her gratefully, treated her as a stranger. That is because, in order to relate to the unhappy, it is necessary either to have suffered or to have dreamed.

There was not one person in Madame de Clairange's society to whom she had not rendered a service. So, as soon as she arrived, people pressed around her; everyone wanted to compensate her, by an apparent preference, for the sentiments that she did not inspire; without taking account of the scant sympathy that she inspired in them, people reproached themselves for remaining indifferent to such an obliging person, and soothed that remorse by praising her extravagantly. Thus, she had a reputation for devotion, for angelic bounty, that her nature did not merit but that her actions justified.

Mediocre souls and small minds were passionate in her favor, and willingly cited her conduct in order to humiliate other women. Distinguished people, on the contrary, elite souls, were wearied by so much studied virtue, and just as Monsieur de Florian's continual shepherdesses and perpetual sheep provoked the desire for a ferocious wolf,[16] the constant

---

[16] Jean-Pierre de Claris de Florian (1755-1794) was always overshadowed as a fabulist by La Fontaine, but was popular nevertheless for his works in that vein; he doubtless thought more highly of his plays and pastoral romances, but they made

perfections of Madame de Clairange provoked an aspiration for a good defect.

Madame de Clairange had acquired from a former marriage a daughter that she treated as her own; she even affected, in order to avoid the sins for which stepmothers are commonly reproached, to prefer Valentine, her husband's daughter, to her own children. The emotions of nature rarely recur in a character falsified by sentiments of convention, and in any case, heroism is easy for indifferent individuals.

One of the considerations that had engaged Madame de Clairange to adopt that system of imperturbable generosity was the difficulty she found in advantageously succeeding Monsieur de Clairange's first wife, one of the most remarkable celebrities of the century, whose brilliant reputation for intelligence was a painful burden for a woman who bore the same name.

Madame Clairange rendered herself justice, and, knowing that her intellect did not have the strength to struggle against the memory that everyone still retained of her rival, sought to combat that inconvenient memory by means of contrasts, studiously developing opposed qualities. She made herself modest and good because Valentine's mother was brilliant, and the vivacity of her wit had been thought for a long time to be malevolent.

Valentine, brought up until the age of fifteen by her mother, knew the extent to which that reputation was unmerited, and applied herself ever day to its destruction; she saw that duty of filial tenderness as a pious mission that had been confided to her. Her mother, like all superior women, had enemies and even more friends who feared her eagle eye. They knew that their weakness and their ingratitude could not be hidden from her, and took their revenge by speaking ill of her, of the

---

little impact on the public, although they got him elected to the Académie in 1788, while his aristocratic heritage was still reckoned an advantage.

empire she had over them, and from which, by virtue of compulsion or affection, they could not abstract themselves.

The principal trait of her character was an honesty of impression that was often misconstrued. She did not have the indulgent hypocrisy of people to whom everything is indifferent. Falsity, calculation and baseness inspired a noble indignation in her, which she could not dissimulate. Her passionate intellect revolted, and in its just scorn, the wittiest remarks and the most piquant quips escaped from her eloquence.

There was no lack of stupid people around her to pick up the crumbs that fell from her table, and her witticisms were soon repeated from one drawing room to another, debased and distorted by malice, and, above all, stripped of the generous sentiment that had inspired them—for when she employed her weapons, it was always to defend a friend or to absolve an innocent of a suspicion merited by another; no personal sentiment ever provoked her malignity.

Unfortunately, her jokes were good, they made an impression; they were imprinted, so to speak, with the poetry of humor that colors and renders it vivid; they had a lasting effect; those they struck did not recover—and thus, the first Madame de Clairange obtained a reputation as a malevolent woman, whom it was necessary to fear. Well, undoubtedly, it was necessary to fear her, and even to avoid her, if one lived in turpitude or exhibited a vice.

Valentine lamented that injustice of society toward her mother, and even more so the reputation for angelic bounty that the same society, always deluded and ever fond of mediocrity, accorded to the second Madame de Clairange.

How many times Valentine compared that artificial and sterile bounty with the noble and sincere generosity of her mother; with the boundless devotion and the enlightened zeal of a vivacious amity that is not stopped in its impulsion either by the certainty of self-injury or the dread of displeasing.

Valentine recalled the warmth with which her mother had paid tribute to the intelligence and advantages of her friends; the urgency she had put into being of use to them; the aged relatives who lived on her gifts; the misfortunes that she had prevented by her benevolent skill; the families she had reconciled; the many enemies she had brought together; the benevolent advice she had give to her own prejudice; the suspected women rehabilitated thanks to her; the rejected children who owed their brilliant existence to her; the misunderstood talents that owed their prompt reputation to her eulogies.

Valentine also recalled how often that woman, so lively in her gaiety, had been able to find consoling words for dolor, and she asked whether that active and intelligently directed bounty, that lifelong generosity, was not worth more than the studied benevolence of her stepmother, her futile and tedious consolations and the poor broth that she sent on fixed days to unknown indigents.

Madame de Clairange had acquired a status in society by her tenderness to her stepdaughter. She talked about her incessantly, heaped cares and attentions upon her which always concluded with the words: "I'm not very severe, for a stepmother, am I, Valentine?"

In spite of all the ostentation of that tenderness, it was evident that Valentine did not share it. How could she love a woman who made herself a living satire of her mother? She had never been able to forgive her for having dared to replace her. Every time that the name of Madame de Clairange, which no longer referred to her mother, was pronounced before her, Valentine was seen to shudder, and tears of regret and resentment escaped from her eyes.

Society in general reproached her for her coldness toward her stepmother, and the haste with which she had separated herself from her by marrying, at the age of seventeen, the Marquis de Champléry, already old, only in possession of a mediocre fortune, offering her no other future than a monotonous and remote life in the depths of the mountains of Auvergne.

Madame de Clairange had employed all the means at her disposal to prevent that marriage, which removed her most beautiful ornament and her most advantageous attitude, the striking proof of virtues that she had worked so hard to acquire, and which, by its importance, dispensed her from less extraordinary demonstrations—but she had no empire over Valentine, and the marriage was accomplished.

Soon, however, all her hopes were reborn; Monsieur de Champléry died. She immediately set off to join the young widow and to implore her to come back to her. Valentine resisted for a long time, but finally, vanquished by her persistence, she promised to come every winter to spend three months in Paris with Madame de Clairange, on condition that she was left free to live in the Auvergne for the rest of the year.

It was the epoch fixed for Madame de Champléry's return, and her stepmother had come in haste to share her happiness with Madame de Fontvenel, and especially with Stéphanie, whom that news interested keenly.

"When I have a joy, it is necessary that my friends share it," said Madame de Clairange; "I fatigue them so often with my anxieties that it is only just. But today, I want them all to be as happy as I am."

"What!" said Stéphanie, who knew where that preamble was leading. "Is she going to arrive soon?"

"How well we understand one another!" exclaimed Madame de Clairange. "How clever she is! How she divines me! All those who know me know that only the return of my poor inconsolable child could cause me such rejoicing."

"Who is the poor inconsolable child?" Edgar asked Monsieur de Fontvenel, in a whisper.

"Her stepdaughter."

"And for what is she inconsolable?"

"The death of her husband."

"What day are you expecting Valentine, Madame?" asked Stéphanie.

"Tomorrow," replied Madame de Clairange. "Yes, tomorrow—imagine my joy!"

"Tomorrow! Oh, how glad I am!" All of Stéphanie's features were animated by the most gracious emotion.

"Look!" cried Madame de Clairange. "See how well amity becomes her, how charming she is! Oh, if my merry child[17] were here, she would make fun of us, of our impatience, for she has no understanding of sentiment."

"Who does she mean by her merry child?" asked Edgar again.

"Still her stepdaughter," replied Monsieur de Fontvenel, smiling. "The inconsolable child."

"What! The same one. Is she, in fact, so merry and so inconsolable?"

"She's a singular person, whom, in spite of all your penetration, you wouldn't understand."

"Who are you talking about?" asked Monsieur Narvaux, who had just come in.

"Madame de Champléry."

"Oh, I don't like her!" he relied, loudly. "She's so prudish and sarcastic."

"Prudish!" retorted Monsieur de Fontvenel. "On the contrary. And she often says very amusing things..."

"I don't refuse her wit, but it's not a wit that pleases me; I like her stepmother much better, who is an angel of bounty, and I can't forgive Valentine for her ingratitude toward her."

While he was speaking, Stéphanie, after having offered tea to everyone, went to take a cup to her mother, carefully prepared according to her taste.

"How touching that attention is!" exclaimed Madame de Clairange, looking at her. "Nothing embellishes a young woman as much as the care that she devotes to her mother; it's the surest of coquetries. I was never able to persuade Valentine of that. She has no concern for me, and Heaven knows how hurt I am by her coldness."

---

[17] *Petite rieuse* [merry child] could also be construed as "little seagull," and if that were construed as a pet name it would make Madame de Clairange seem less self-contradictory, but the subsequent dialogue suggests that those listening to her assume that she is being paradoxical, and with reason.

"You astonish me," aid Madame de Fontvenel. "A year ago, when Stéphanie was ill, I witnessed the concern Valentine had for her friend, and I would be an ingrate mother if I allowed her to be accused of negligence."

Edgar listened with the greatest interest to that entire conversation, apparently quite insignificant, and when he left, he was astonished to think so much about that Valentine, at once so sad and so merry, so prudish and so frivolous, so cold and so loving—and he felt that her two greatest entitlements to prejudice in her favor were having displeased Monsieur Narvaux and being Stéphanie's friend.

IX

The impression that that soirée had left on him was soon effaced. Edgar, deceived twice in the emotions of his heart, resumed the course of mundane life; but, always disenchanted in his illusions, always punished in his hopes, he ended up conceiving such a rancor against his fatal lorgnon that he resolved not to make use of it any longer. He shut it away in a drawer in his writing-desk, and the day when he went out without carrying it on his person, he felt relieved, as if he were liberated, having rid himself of an importunate friend.

In his discoveries of the previous days everything had discontented him; he had learned to be suspicious of everything, even the caresses of a child—for self-interest, the leprosy of the century, attains us in infancy, and it is frightening to see little heads calculating before they are able to think.

The day before, Monsieur de Lorville had gone to see Madame de ***. Her granddaughter, as soon as she recognized him, came to him, leapt on to his knees and lavished caresses upon him. Edgar, surprised and touched by that enthusiastic welcome, wanted to know why the pretty child was so affectionate toward him; he looked at her through the lorgnon.

Caress him a lot, she was thinking. *He brought my cousin such lovely toys from Germany.*

Involuntarily, Edgar pushed the child away, and, disgusted to find in all ranks, at all ages, the same thoughts of interest and vanity, he decided to renounce a science that had become so monotonous, and admitted that the talent of penetrating all idea was not worth as much as the pleasure of being deceived.

Rid of his talisman, he rejoiced in becoming a good dupe, and thought that he was about to rediscover his former credulity. But there are secrets that one does not possess with impunity, and one can no longer rediscover ignorance.

His mind, accustomed to divining, made observations regardless, explained his suspicions, translated what was said to him, reestablishing vitiated verities. In sum, Monsieur de Lorville without his lorgnon was as we are in the absence of a friend who has empire over us. We act by memory; to every event, every object, we react by asking ourselves: *What would he do? What would he think? What would he say to that?* And we remain under the yoke of that despotic character, even when we believe that we are librated by his absence.

While returning from the Opéra, Monsieur de Lorville passed Madame de Fontvenel's door; he saw several carriages parked outside, and the idea occurred to him to call in briefly, even though it was already late.

He found that there were still a great many people there. As he came in, he heard Madame de Clairange pronouncing, with solicitude: "Valentine, don't drink orgeat; you'll make yourself ill."

She's here, Edgar thought, remembering everything he had been told about Madame de Champléry. Curious to see her, he looked in the direction of the round table around which Stéphanie and her young friends usually gathered—but he was too far away for him to be able to distinguish any woman in particular.

Obliged to remain with the mistress of the house in order to listen to the friendly reproaches that she was addressing to him for his negligence, Edgar became impatient at not being able to join Stéphanie. He did not doubt that Valentine was with her, and, thinking about what Monsieur de Fontvenel had said about the impossibility of his divining the character of Madame de Champléry, he began to repent of having abandoned his lorgnon.

Finally, he was permitted to approach the terrible round table, against which he already had a certain resentment, remembering all that he had experienced for Stéphanie in the same place. Mademoiselle de Fontvenel greeted him with her usual benevolence, and sat him down next to her, and he soon saw that his presence had caused a great sensation in the group of your women surrounding her.

His talent for penetration had evidently provoked rumor in socicty, and all the women were afraid of him. A very pretty young woman was sitting on the other side of Stéphanie; Edgar presumed that it was Valentine, and set about observing her. He found her cheerful and mocking, as announced.

Conversation was easily engaged, and, seeing the coquetry that was put into replying to him, he yielded to the pleasure of having an audience listen to him. He recounted some piquant anecdotes of his travels, and, knowing that Madame de Champléry liked intelligent wit, he flattered himself with having proved that he did not lack it; his self-esteem felt satisfied.

As he was enjoying the intoxication of a man glad to please, Madame de Clairange's voice resounded: "Come on, Valentine; it's past midnight and you're suffering. We have to go home."

Edgar murmured at being separated so soon from his pretty neighbor, but was astonished to see a tall, beautiful, cold and serious young woman stand up on the other side of the room in response to Madame de Clairange's voice, who was quite different from the idea he had formed of Madame de Champléry. It was, however, really her. He had not seen her because, until then, several people placed before her had hidden her from his view. He stood up in order to see her more clearly, but she left without giving him time to consider her.

Annoyed by his mistake, Edgar no longer found any pleasure in chatting to the young woman he had believed to be Madame de Champléry. He held it against her that he had been deceived, and thought, ill-humoredly: *I should have known that it wasn't her. Madame de Champléry must have more intelligence than that.*

In vain, Madame de Cilleray, unaware that she had owed Monsieur de Lorville's attentions to an error, continued her gracious coquetries, but Edgar was no longer listening, and drew away from her with a sullen expression, leaving her utterly disconcerted by that caprice.

Valentine's name, which he had heard pronounced with a sort of indignation, drew him into the next room, and, having been unable to talk to Madame de Champléry, as he would so much have like to do, he hoped to obtain compensation by hearing people talk about her.

"Valentine prudish and pretentious! Oh, Monsieur, you don't know her!" cried an old general, hotly. "I can assure you, on the contrary, that there are few women more straight-forward, and who think less about producing an effect."

"You'll grant me at least that she's capricious," said Monsieur Narvaux. "What an affectation to spend the whole evening chatting to one side with an old German diplomat, instead of mingling in the conversation of people of her own age and nationality. Why this sudden attitude of melancholy that she adopted this evening, when she stayed here yesterday until two in the morning and made us all die with laughter telling us about all the follies that go through her head!"

"But that's quite simple," said the general. "She'll suffer-ing today."

"That's not a reason; I've seen her like that a hundred times. She's an inexplicable woman; she's never the same two days running. Ask Fontvenel," Monsieur Narvaux added, "he'll tell you the same."

"I'm not as severe," replied Monsieur de Fontvenel. "I confess that Madame de Champléry has always appeared to me to have an incomprehensible character, but I know her too well to accuse her of being affected or capricious; she rather gives me the impression of a person dominated by some hid-den thought that troubles her, which she dreads that someone might divine—in sum, a person who has a secret."

"I tend to agree with you," said a woman endowed with a redoubtable observational intelligence. "Her gaiety is that of agitation, her silence that of constraint, and those are all symp-toms of..."

"What an idea!" said the general, ill-humoredly.

"No, I swear to you that it's not madness; the young woman has some secret thought that is tormenting her."

"Perhaps she has an aneurism of the heart," said a young man who was studying medicine. "That would explain the sudden melancholy."

"She has nothing at all," said the general, irritated by these conjectures. "Or rather, if you absolutely must know what's tormenting her, I'll tell you. Well, it's because…it's…it's her stepmother, who is, in my view, the most frightful torment and the most annoying malady that anyone could have."

"What injustice!" was exclaimed on all sides. "Madame de Clairange, who is so good, who overwhelms her stepdaughter with such care and attention!"

"Yes, she overwhelms her—that's exactly the right word."

"General," said Monsieur Narvaux, "I don't recognize in that your habitual benevolence. A woman so perfect, so generous, can't make those who depend on her unhappy, and I believe that her stepdaughter's preoccupation has a much more vulgar cause."

"Which is to say, Monsieur, that you think she has…"

"A lover!" completed the general, angrily. "You'll agree, then, that she hides him well, for no man in Paris, I think, can boast of compromising her."

"In Paris, no, but…"

"I know what you man: she has a provincial lover! In Clermont, doubtless—an Auvergnat."

At those words everyone stated to laugh. The anger of a good man almost always has something comical about it, firstly because one does not fear it, and secondly because it is exaggerated; only malevolence is able to exhale wrath in a measured fashion, and to conserve sufficient composure to choose the place where it ought to strike; indignation strikes at hazard, at the risk of failing to wound.

Monsieur de Fontvenel, seeing that Valentine's old friend was beginning to get seriously upset by the manner in which people were talking about her, wanted to put an end to the conversation, which he repented of having encouraged,

"Let's be patient," he said. "We have here someone who can easily enlighten us. If Madame de Champléry has a secret, as we think, there is a man whose piercing gaze will be able to discover it."

All eyes were then fixed on Edgar, at whom Monsieur de Fontvenel had pointed, and it was necessary to submit to the recitation of the marvelous discoveries that had been attributed to his penetration. He pretended to see nothing in those true stories but a fanciful tale, a joke, but undertook, laughing, to put all the ruses of his science to work in order to divine Madame de Champléry's secret, and promised to render an exact account of his observations in the near future.

Although he did not have his lorgnon about his person that evening, Monsieur de Lorville had no difficulty divining the interest that the old general had in Valentine, and, by virtue of a motive that he could not explain, he felt the need to prejudice him in his favor. So, seeing that the general was observing him attentively, he said: "Before engaging in this great enterprise, I ought to confess that I am already a suspect judge, and I have lost my impartiality somewhat."

"Why is that?" said Monsieur Narvaux. "You don't know Madame de Champléry; who can have given you such a favorable idea of her?"

"The very evil that you're speaking of her. She made you laugh yesterday until two o'clock in the morning, so she is witty and amusing. This evening, her crime is to have talked for a long time to an aged scholar, and not to have been able to hide her sadness; so she has a solid mind and a feeble heart. That, it seems to me, is what composes a very amiable woman. You see that I shall be a poor judge, and that, without wanting to, you've won me to her cause."

The old general lost his ill-humored expression; he approached Monsieur de Lorville and talked to him about his father and family, whom he knew, and questioned him benevolently about his projects. As he listened to him, Edgar wondered why he was so glad to have recruited a friend of Madame de Champléry to his side.

He attributed that preoccupation to curiosity. The power that he alone possessed to penetrate the secret of such a distinguished woman was sufficient explanation, in his view, of the impatience he experienced to find himself in her presence. Madame de Fontvenel had invited him to dinner for the following Thursday; Edgar knew that Madame de Clairange and her stepdaughter would be at that dinner, and he promised himself that he would take his talisman out of its hiding-place for the occasion. He had already pardoned it for all the torments that it had caused him, so proud was he of possessing it in such an important circumstance.

In fact, the mystery that surrounded Madame de Champléry, and the eccentricity of her character, combined with the advantages of her wit, were bound to inspire interest. Monsieur de Lorville formed a thousand conjectures about the secret that he was about to divine, while promising himself in advance not to betray it. A secret that imparts defects to such a perfect individual, he thought, could not be vulgar; there was not, in that mystery, any calculation or interest, since there was no hypocrisy.

Edgar thought about the great encounter with a childlike joy, and congratulated himself for having prepared for it in advance, recalling his last awkwardness—but destiny had other trials in store for him.

X

On Monday evening, Edgar ran into Monsieur de Fontvenel.

"Ah, it's you!" cried the latter. "You won't escape me—I'm taking you with me."

"Where?"

"To the Odéon."

"Oh, my friend, what have I done? Why you want me to go so far?"

"First of all, *La Maréchale d'Ancre*, whom it's absolutely necessary to see,[18] and secondly, the Marquise de Champléry."

"Ah! She's there?"

"Yes, with her stepmother and Stéphanie; there's only Narvaux and me to accompany them, and that's not sufficient; you know that woman are only amused at a play when there's a fashionable man in their box. Besides which, you haven't forgotten our engagement, and the secret that you're going to reveal to us."

"But I don't have..." Edgar was about to say "my lorgnon," but fortunately stopped himself in time.

"You don't have a seat," Monsieur de Fontvenel finished for him. "I'm offering you two; Monsieur de S*** has given us his box, or rather, his room; it's a front-of-stage box, and it's immense. You can accept without scruple; you won't inconvenience us."

---

[18] Alfred de Vigny's romantic drama *La Maréchale d'Ancre*, premiered at the Théâtre de l'Odéon on 25 June 1831, is based on the life of Léonora Dori, alias La Galigaï, the foster-sister of Marie de Medicis, who was burned as a witch. Marguerite Georges (1787-1867) played the lead; she was notorious for her claim to have slept with both Napoléon (when she was a teenager) and the Duke of Wellington.

Edgar yielded to his friend's insistence; he climbed into his tilbury in order to make the eternal journey with him, and they resumed their conversation about Madame de Champléry.

Edgar was like those people who have such a perfect knowledge of the place where they live that they are able to move about there without a light. By dint of reading thoughts with the aid of his magnificent lorgnon, he had ended up by studying them and deciphering them without its aide. He soon saw that his friend was talking about Valentine with a sort of resentment, and, recalling the extreme intimacy of Madame de Champléry and his sister, which gave them so many opportunities to meet, he thought that Monsieur de Fontvenel must have sought to please her, and that he only seem so scantly benevolent toward her, although he never spoke ill of her, because he had not succeeded.

Edgar also remembered that his friend had been the first one to suppose that Valentine had a secret. Now, that idea only ever occurs to a suitor who has been poorly received, and who, believing himself to be sufficiently seductive to be loved, attributes his defeat to some mysterious obstacle, some rival thought that prevents him from succeeding in spite of his advantages. Edgar regarded Monsieur de Fontvenel's observation as the ingenious explanation for his failure that he offered to his wounded self-esteem. He resolved only to judge Madame de Champléry for himself, and not to share in any of his friend's prejudices.

When they arrived at the Odéon, Monsieur de Lorville felt excited at the thought that he was about to spend the evening in the company of the strange woman who preoccupied him in such a strange manner, and, perhaps for the first time since his return to Paris, experienced embarrassment.

The science that he had brought back from his travels had given him so much assurance! His entire personality had changed in the meantime. His manners had acquired an aplomb astonishing for his age. In the attitude of a man who knows and divines, there is something calm, a security that is imposing; one senses that he has an advantage over us, and that however young he is, as the aplomb in question is not that of ignorance or that of stupidity, one is forced to recognize a sort of power in him. Besides which, when one has everyone's secret, one becomes so indulgent, and indulgence in youth is already a superiority. Thus, Monsieur de Lorville passed for one of the most intelligent young men in Paris: a reputation that he owed in part to his talisman, but which he was not incapable of sustaining.

At the moment when the two friends went into the box, Mademoiselle Georges was on stage; Madame de Clairange and Stéphanie were content to salute them without saying anything, in order not to attract the offended *shhs* of the stormy stalls of the Odéon. Madame de Champléry, sunk in her reflections did not turn her head to see who had come in, and Edgar, unable to see her face, was reduced to admiring her beautiful blonde hair, artfully arranged, and studying all the details of her elegant costume.

When he had contemplated the light scarf of embroidered tulle that surrounded her gracious neck for a few moments, the pretty blue belt that designed a slim and elegant waist, and the expertly-tailored white muslin dress, he began to get bored; then, in order to force Valentine to look in his direction, he imagined launching, in such a way that she could hear it, one of those revolting stupidities that provoke scandal and force the most distracted person to look up in order to see who the imbecile is that might have said it.

"In truth," said Edgar, Looking at Mademoiselle Georges and pretending to be mistaken. "Mademoiselle Mars is admirable in that costume."[19]

---

[19] "Mademoiselle Mars" (Anne Salvetat, 1779-1847) was Marguerite Georges' great rival, if only in the sense that both continued to portray supposedly young and beautiful heroines when well past their prime. If their portraits are trustworthy, it would have been difficult to make the mistake, although both had run to fat by 1831.

"Mademoiselle Mars! Mademoiselle Mars! What are you saying?" exclaimed everyone, immediately, mocking the mistaken simpleton.

The ruse had all the success he had expected of it. Valentine turned swiftly to look at Monsieur de Lorville. She recognized him, and blushed. Knowing full well that he had too much intelligence, and was too accustomed to Paris to be so grossly misled, and also warned by Stéphanie of his resolution to observe her, she divined that the stupid remark had been made deliberately, and the disdainful gaze that she darted at Monsieur de Lorville soon published him for his malice.

During the entr'acte, Monsieur de Fontvenel introduced his friend to Madame de Champléry. She greeted him coldly, and after having addressed to both of them a few insignificant comments on the play that was in performance, she began looking away, into the auditorium, with the attitude of a person who does not want to engage in conversation.

Madame de Clairange was not so disdainful toward Edgar; she took possession of him, heaped him with flatteries regarding his powers of perception, and ended up telling him that she was very glad to have nothing in her heart to conceal, for it would be very painful to be obliged to avoid the most amiable man she had ever encountered.

"I believe, in truth," she continued, "that Valentine is only so sulky this evening because she has some malign thought that she fears seeing you divine."

"What I think," interjected Valentine, with a hint of impatience, "is of interest, at the most, to the author of the play, and I wouldn't even hide it from him."

"You would be right, Madame," for he has enough talent and intelligence to listen to you," said Edgar, astonished by that malevolence.

Madame de Clairange made signs and employed the language of the eyes, eyebrows and shoulders—the pantomime of aunts and mothers scolding their daughters in public—to reproach Valentine for being so ungracious toward Monsieur de Lorville, but she persisted in her bad mood. Edgar could not help laughing at the despair that Madame de Clairange was experiencing. He suspected her of having said too much in his favor, and he already knew Valentine well enough to know that a eulogy from her stepmother would be lost on her.

Madame de Champléry did not appear to her advantage that evening; she seemed less beautiful than the day when he had seen her for the first time; her manners were graceless and her voice had a hard quality that was unattractive. The noble symmetry of her features, not being softened by any expression of gaiety or melancholy, gave her visage an air of severity that lacked charm. Monsieur de Lorville, seeing her thus, wondered how Madame de Clairange had ever been drawn to name such a grave and imposing person her "merry child."

While he was chatting to Madame de Clairange, Monsieur de Fontvenel said to Valentine: "Don't I see facing us your marvelous cousin Adolphe de Champléry?"

"Yes, it's him," Valentine replied. "He's doubtless here with his so-called beauty, Mademoiselle d'Armilly."

At that name, Edgar shuddered; he remembered his first trial and his first disappointment.

"Is she going to marry him?" he asked, curiously.

"Yes," said Valentine, "she's going to marry my cousin, Monsieur de Champléry."

"It's said that she loves him madly," said Monsieur Narvaux, "but he's scarcely seductive. " He added: "It's a cruel verity to admit, but the tedious please pretty women."

"Not all of them," said Edgar, insolently, "but it's certain that they often mistake assiduity for obsession. Besides which, tedium is a magnetism that takes away reason and numbs the will; it's the philter of the importunate."

At that moment Madame de Champléry leaned forward to look at someone in the auditorium.

"Who are you greeting, my dear?" asked her stepmother.

"Madame d'Armilly and her niece," Valentine replied.

"Where is she?" asked Stéphanie, excitedly. "She's said to be very beautiful; I'd like to see her."

"Oh, she's ravishing!" exclaimed Monsieur Narvaux. "She's the loveliest woman in Paris, isn't she, my dear?"

Edgar not wanting to praise Mademoiselle d'Armilly, nor speak ill of her, found it more convenient to say that he did not know her.

"Look at her, then, my dear—she's adorable!"

"She would have to be very pretty," said Monsieur de Fontvenel, in his turn, "to dare to take the name Madame de Champléry."

"People will always confuse the two of you," Stéphanie said to Valentine.

"No," she replied. "To distinguish us, people will call my cousin 'the beautiful Madame de Champléry.'"

"And they'll call you the good, which is much better."

As one can guess, that touching and novel thought was due to Madame de Clairange. Delighted to have found it, she added: "I see, my dear child, that you'll be obliged to remarry in order to avoid mistaken identity."

"It's an interesting motive," said Edgar, seeing the embarrassment that her mother's joke had caused Valentine. "It reminds me of a young woman who decided on the serious act of marriage in order to have the right to wear a beret that suited her marvelously, which someone had had the ingenious idea of making her try on, as if by chance."

"What!" exclaimed Monsieur Narvaux. "Is a husband absolutely necessary in order to dare to put on a hat?"

"Undoubtedly," said Madame de Clairange. Don't you know that in France, young women don't wear toques, bonnets or turbans?"

"Very fortunately," said Edgar. "Otherwise, how would one recognize them in drawing-rooms, since the mothers of families persist in ingenuousness? The custom is well-contrived; furthermore, it's a language, for on the day when an old maid renounces the prospect of marriage, she displays a white feather in a black toque, and it's as if the president of the Chambre had put on his headgear; the discussion is terminated."

Everyone laughed at that folly. The conversation regarding Mademoiselle d'Armilly's marriage having continued, Edgar left the box in order to go and admire her, and was soon seen to place himself on the balcony facing her, in such a fashion as to be able to contemplate Valentine at the same time.

He experienced a sentiment of sadness on seeing Mademoiselle d'Armilly again, the beautiful individual who had so cruelly punished his presumption that he had pleased her, and he felt a kind of aversion for her on remarking the tender gazes that she was addressing to the same Monsieur de Champléry of whom she had spoken to him with so much disdain, while she was employing all her skill to marry him. Then his eyes fell on Stéphanie, and then on Valentine, and he thought that it was singular so see those three women, the only ones who had preoccupied his heart since his return to Paris, gathered in the same place. The others had only been caprices, so far as he was concerned, and no idea of a future had troubled the pleasures of the present. But Stéphanie! And Valentine! By what right had the one he did not know occupied his thoughts so vividly?

That evening, however, she had lost her power, and Edgar experienced a pleasure that was not free of chagrin in admitting that she seemed the least beautiful of the three. Soon, that chagrin was augmented, for he saw her suddenly become animated and talk to Monsieur Narvaux with an expression of benevolence, almost of coquetry, which completed his irritation. He thought he could still hear all the nasty remarks that Monsieur Narvaux had made about her, and the falsity of the one and the dupery of the other revolted him equally. That is, however, very common in society; the man who speaks ill of a woman because the superiority of her mind humiliates him is often the one who appreciates her suffrage the most and goes to the greatest expense to obtain it, which he does without too much falsity.

If Edgar had had his talisman he would have been less severe on Valentine; he would have seen that she had not become animated because she was talking to someone else, but because she had noticed that he was looking at her. At close range, that gaze embarrassed her, but at a distance, it enlivened her; it was for him that she had become reanimated, and all her words, which he could not hear, were addressed to him.

There are women who are embellished by embarrassment, others who are neutralized by it, or entirely metamorphosed. Valentine was one of the latter; embarrassment was a torture for her; she would rather deny her good sentiments, hide her pure emotions, than risk the disturbance of expressing them. There was no subterfuge to which she would not resort in order to get out of difficulty. The most glacial quip, the most disenchanting politeness, was worth more from her than thanks that she would not have been able to pronounce without softening in consequence. So she feared amour, its dreads, its modesties and its disturbances, as the greatest of torments, and the man who might inspire it in her could expect in advance to be regarded by her as an enemy.

At the exit from the play, at the foot of the great staircase, Madame de Champléry found herself next to her future cousin, and the troubled manner in which Mademoiselle d'Armilly greeted Monsieur de Lorville, who had said that he did not know her, inspired some suspicion in Valentine. Edgar was somewhat disconcerted on seeing his lie discovered.

As a result, the evening was not at all the success for which Madame Clairange—whose projects Monsieur de Lorville had divined without difficulty—had hoped. Valentine had appeared to him to be lacking in grace, and worthy of finding Monsieur Narvaux amiable. As for Madame de Champléry, she judged Edgar to be false and conceited. And Madame de Clairange, seeing her clever plans going awry, said to herself, sadly: *My beautiful daughter will never be the Duchesse de Lorville.*

XI

It was the middle of summer, the season unbearable in Paris, when, without taking account of the sanitary instinct that is guiding us, we go for preference to see those of our friends who have gardens, in the same way that in winter, those most sensitive to cold see more of us.

"It's stifling this evening," we say, "why are there no squares in Paris where one can breathe easily, without being crowded as in the Tuileries? The people who have gardens attached to their houses are lucky at these times."

"Madame So-and-so's must be charming," someone else says.

"Is she in Paris?"

"Yes, she's staying for a few days with her mother, who is ill."

"Oh, the poor woman—let's go ask for news of her."

And soon, we are in a charming garden, surrounded by flowers, breathing pure air, without having gone to any other expense than asking one of our friends for news of her health.

That was how Edgar found himself in the home of one of his relatives, who possessed one of the most beautiful gardens in Paris, in the Rue de Varennes. The solitude of the quarter was so great that year that one could almost believe one was in the country. It was already dark when he arrived at Madame Montbert's house; the drawing rooms were illuminated, but everyone was still in the garden. Edgar advanced into the shadows toward the mistress of the house, chatted briefly with a few of his friends whom he recognized by the sound of their voices, and then, approaching a group of women sitting under the tall orange trees, he joined in their conversation.

From time to time he discovered a person of his acquaintance in the gloom by the uncertain gleams that the lamps shining in the drawing rooms spread over the lawns and through the foliage. "Oh, it's you!" he exclaimed—and everyone laughed at that species of blind man's bluff. At any rate, that conversation in the shadows, those anonymous quips and jokes launched into the darkness, unconfirmed by physiognomy, mysteries of wit, had something piquant about them that Monsieur de Lorville found very amusing.

One woman, in particular, had attracted his attention by means of a few witty remarks made with grace, and deft observations full of the benevolent gaiety that disdains epigrams, nourished by a lively imagination, which has no need of malicious sallies in order to shine. If the conversation turned to serious matters, the person in question, who seemed to be very young, launched ideas without pretention of astonishing precision and profundity, all in a soft voice and a warm tone that was enchanting.

The woman, whom Edgar could not see, had to be pretty. To begin with, she had the simultaneously noble and idle attitudes of a woman who knows herself to be agreeable and who has no need to be observed to be good, and furthermore, she spoke about the beauty of other women with justice and without envy, as if contented with her own share. Her costume was elegant; the pretty hood of white moiré silk that was the only thing distinguishable in the obscurity hid her face entirely, but her gracious movements and the indolent fashion with which she enveloped herself in her capacious shawl, without regard for the lack-trimmed sleeves that it was crumpling pitilessly—all that nonchalance—gave her an appearance of aristocracy perfectly in harmony with the grace and free expression of her mind.

Edgar waited with impatience for everyone to go into the drawing room in order to see the mysterious beauty who piqued his curiosity so sharply. He would have liked to ask her name, but he did not dare, because the woman, whom he was sure that he had never met, spoke to him like an old acquaintance, and might have made fun of him if she seemed not to know who she was.

Finally, the mistress of the house felt cold; she claimed that a mist was falling and that it was necessary to return to the drawing room. Everyone stood up; the women went first. Monsieur de Lorville followed them hastily, but when he searched among them for the white hood that was the sole object of his occupation, he found that it had disappeared.

The sound of a carriage was heard leaving the courtyard of the house, and the mistress of the house came back in, saying: "She's left us very early this evening."

"How pleasant she is," said a man standing nearby. "She's ravishing, and it's impossible to have more intelligence."

After that, the conversation turned to other subjects. Edgar, full of chagrin, and not daring, for reasons of pride, to appear to be ignorant of the name of a woman so much in fashion, whose reputation seemed so well-established, went home even more irritated than the previous evening, convinced that destiny had condemned him never to love, since it took such pleasure in disconcerting all his amorous hopes.

XII

The following day, at six o'clock in the evening, almost all the people who were to dine at Madame de Fontvenel's had arrived; they were only waiting for the old general and Monsieur de Lorville.

"Did you remind Edgar that we're expecting him today?" Madame de Fontvenel said to her son. "He's quite capable of having forgotten us—he gets so many invitations."

"Who? Monsieur de Lorville?" asked the young officer who was going to marry Stéphanie. "I can guarantee that he'll be here; I saw him yesterday and I'm expecting him here to tell him that he's won his bet."

"What bet?" asked Monsieur de Fontvenel.

"Oh, it's the strangest thing in the world—that Lorville is a sorcerer."

Everyone drew closer to the young officer, and he was bombarded with questions. Only Valentine said nothing, but she was not the least attentive.

"We were in the Café de Paris yesterday, sitting at a table near a window, waiting for our meal to be brought. I was reading the *Journal des Débats*, while Monsieur de Lorville was amusing himself peering through his lorgnon at the passers-by on the boulevard. From time to time I saw him laugh surreptitiously; at other times he laughed frankly, and so heartily that I was infected by the laughter without knowing why. In the end, impatiently, I asked him to share his hilarity by telling me what was exciting it.

"'Nothing,' he said. 'It's just that I see these smiling faces passing by, and I wonder where all those people are going; I try to divine it from their gait, and such singular ideas come into my head that...' And then he started laughing again.

"'That labor doesn't seem to me to be very difficult,' I replied. 'For instance, it's easy to divine that those two women who are running so rapidly with lorgnettes in their hands are going to the Opéra, and even to the fourth boxes, and that monsieur marching with his nose in the air isn't expected anywhere, and is only strolling for the sake of strolling.'

"'Well,' said Monsieur de Lorville, 'since you're so adept, tell me what that little fat man is thinking, who's leaving here with a contented expression and shaking his head like a thinker.'

"'He's a speculator,' I said who has made a profit on the Bourse and is calculating the chances of a favorable gamble tomorrow.'

"'Wrong!' he cried, confidently. 'He's not a stockbroker, he's a simple gourmand who's reliving his dinner in memory. Look: at this very moment he's saying, word for word: *that little melon was exquisite.*'

"At that moment, the waiter brought our soup. 'Do you know that short gentleman who was dining here,' I asked him, pointing through the window at the man in question, who was just going past.

"'Oh, yes, Monsieur,' the waiter replied. 'He's one of our regulars, a great lover of melons. He often tries five or six before finding one to his taste.'

"Monsieur de Lorville looked at me triumphantly, and I was amazed. As I found the game diverting, I continued it. I began to have confidence in Monsieur de Lorville's judgments, which, true or imaginary, were sometimes so comical that I was delighted to excite them. I didn't leave him time to prepare, but his replies were always ready.

"'What is that tall blond fellow thinking,' I asked him, 'who looks to be in a bad mood, walking between those two well-dressed young women?'

"'He's saying to himself: *Sixty francs for a box at the Opéra. It's ruinous!*'

"'And that handsome young fellow giving his arm to that thin and faded woman?'

"'*She's really not pretty at all; if her husband weren't my colonel...*'

"I started laughing. 'Let's see,' I went on, showing him a fat cab-driver who was putting on a show of whipping his horses while his agitated clients were putting their heads out of the windows.

"Monsieur de Lorville looked at him attentively, and smiled at the worthy man's thought, which he expressed in his own language: *Are they stupid! They're in a hurry and they're hiring me by the hour.*

"I laughed. 'Is it really possible that he's thinking that?' I said—but Monsieur de Lorville seemed so sure of his penetration that I wanted to confound him. I searched for an opportunity to prove that he was mistaken, and promised myself to choose a person of common enough appearance for me to dare to go up to him boldly, and who was walking at a sufficiently moderate pace for me to be able to catch up with him. As I was thinking about it, we saw a little seamstress go by, who was carrying a piece of taffeta that she was holding by the four corners, containing several pieces of fabric for dressmaking, which were visible through the gaps in the poorly-closed parcel.

"'What is that young person thinking?' I said to Monsieur de Lorville. 'Is she thinking about the way she's going to tailor those fabrics?'

"'Undoubtedly,' he said. 'This is the letter of what she's saying to herself: 'I'll never have enough taffeta for Madame Charlier's dress, and Ernest wants to make him a waistcoat on top!'

"I confess that I laughed at that supposition. But as he maintained that it was the truth, we struck a bet. I left him right away in order to run after the little seamstress, and caught up with her at the corner of the Rue de Grammont. Having followed her almost all the way home, I asked her, not without a great deal of difficulty keeping a straight face, whether she didn't have a dress to make for Madame Charlier. 'Yes, Monsieur,' she replied, 'a loose-fitting dress in black Naples.'

"I nearly died wanting to laugh at that response, but I persisted and asked her to tell me whether, by chance, Monsieur Ernest was coming to see her that day. She seemed a trifle embarrassed by the name, but eventually replied that Monsieur Ernest was indeed coming to see her at her mother's house, but that if I was one his friends would I please not say anything about it, because her master would scold her for leaving the shop early.

"I can't tell you how astonished I was to see all Monsieur de Lorville's predictions realized in that fashion. I made all the suppositions imaginable to explain the extraordinary aspects of the adventure, and ended up telling myself that it was probably more natural than I thought, and that, the girl being very pretty..."

At that point, Monsieur de Lorville was announced. Everyone smiled and looked at one another in silence. As the old general had also arrived, however, after a few polite words, they went into the dining room and sat down at table.

XIII

Edgar was seated facing Madame de Champléry, and although he no longer obtained great pleasure from observing her, he was struck by the glow of her complexion. He has so far only seen Valentine in the evening. *Very young women*, he said to himself, disdainfully, *generally having little in the way of physiognomy, are only truly pretty in the morning. In candlelight, the least piquant face is a hundred times preferable to theirs.*

Edgar also noticed that Valentine had pale and well-formed hands, but red arms; and that beauty of young girls did not please him in a woman.

For two days, his talisman had not left his person—he had been punished too much by having been without it for several days—but he only dared make use of it rarely.

During the dinner, the young officer, placed some distance away from Monsieur de Lorville, reminded him of the bet that he had won, adding that he was ready to hand over his ten louis.

"Keep them," said Edgar. "It would be theft; I was betting on a sure thing."

"Ah! That's what I said—you knew her."

"No...not her," said Edgar, slightly disconcerted by that interpretation, which he had not anticipated.

"In that case, it's Madame Charlier."

"Exactly," replied Edgar, laughing. "She's one of my best friends."

And everyone, taking that response as a joke, remained convinced that Edgar had been Monsieur Ernest's fortunate rival.

That is how the extraordinary incidents to which the marvelous talisman gave rise always ended up being explained, in a sufficiently natural manner.

Valentine, chatting with the general, who was sitting beside her, was incessantly interrupted in that conversation, which she was enjoying, by the questions, the pretentious remarks and tormenting attentions of Madame de Clairange.

"I'm sending you olives, Valentine, I know that you like them... Don't drink Madeira wine, Valentine, it makes you ill..." And Valentine, who did not like olives and never drank wine, responded to all these attentions in an impatient and curt manner that did not embellish her.

It's a pity, Edgar thought, *that that beautiful individual doesn't desire to please; she truly has admirable features, but it's all spoiled by her sulky expression, which doesn't even have the grace of gaucherie.*

Scarcely had they left the table than Madame de Clairange got ready to leave, and went through the drawing room to say goodbye to Valentine, promising to come back to find her later, if possible.

"Where are you going so soon?" Madame de Fontvenel asked her.

"Oh, my God, to visit the unfortunate, as always," replied Madame de Clairange. "I have poor friends in mourning, I have to go to console them; I also have a young invalid, and promised to keep her company."

"Always the same," said Madame de Fontvenel, offering her arm to Madame de Clairange in order to escort her to her carriage. "Always the model friend."

As the carriage drew away, the astonished general exclaimed: "Is she going to the theater?"

"No, not this evening," said Madame de Fontvenel, "But she went three days ago, for the first time in a long time."

"Ah!" said the general. "She's no longer so devoted, then? Since when, if you please?"

"Probably since the last revolution," said Edgar.

The general approved of the quip, and added: "It's always the fashionable virtue she chooses. Last year she was only occupied with young seminarists; I'll wager that now she's in quest of the July wounded."

Valentine having drawn nearer, the conversation was interrupted out of respect for her.

A few more people arrived. The evening papers were brought; the men started reading them and discussing politics. The women, after chatting between themselves for a little while, retired to the music room, and asked Stéphanie to sing. Edgar recognized the fresh, light voice that he had heard so often in the past, and was glad to listen to its gracious tones while continuing his reading.

Soon, the voice changed; one of Madame Duchambre's most melodious ballads succeeded a pretty ditty by Monsieur de Beauplan.[20] Monsieur de Lorville, moved by the tones full of charm that he could hear, and gripped by the profound melancholy of the beautiful voice, wanted to see who it was that had replaced Stéphanie. He wanted for the end of a verse to approach, and, having reached the piano, saw that it was Madame de Champléry.

Edgar was astonished that a person so cold in appearance, who spoke in such a curt manner, had such a soft and soulful voice when she sang. He was also struck by the gracious expression that Valentine's face had taken on, and wondered what the reason for the change was.

He picked up his lorgnon and looked at her; he saw then that the emotion that rendered her so beautiful was a memory of her mother. Valentine was never able to sing without remembering the pleasure that her beloved mother had experienced in hearing her voice, and without being troubled by the regret that she could no longer listen to it.

As Edgar was contemplating her in that touching emotion, Valentine perceived him and suddenly quit the piano.

"There's another verse!" someone exclaimed.

---

[20] Pauline Duchambge (1778-1858) was a successful composer and pianist, who supported herself by that means following her divorce from the Baron Duchambge. "Amédée de Beauplan" (Amédée Rousseau, 1790-1853) was also a painter, but is only remembered for his musical compositions.

"Yes," she said, "but I've forgotten the words."

Then, finding in the very excess of her embarrassment a kind of courage to hide it, she bravely approached Monsieur de Lorville, to whom she had thus far avoided speaking, and asked him whether he had stayed for a long time at Madame de Montbert the previous evening.

"What! You were at my aunt's house?" he said, astonished. "I didn't have the honor of seeing you there."

"That's simple enough," she said. "It was completely dark; besides which, I left shortly after your arrival."

"Do you know all the people who were there?" Edgar asked, slightly troubled.

"Yes, almost all of them."

"Well, I beg you, Madame, tell me who was the charming young woman sitting next to my aunt, who was wearing a pretty white hat, a large shawl..."

"That young woman!" Valentine interrupted, laughing. "But that was me."

"It was you!" exclaimed Edgar, enthusiastically. "That's wonderful!" He repented of that joyful exclamation, which had slipped out, and added: "How is it that I didn't recognize you?"

"Don't be astonished," Valentine replied. "It's my fault. I'm sometimes so different from myself. It sometimes happens that I'm not recognized in the evening at a ball by people who are looking for me, and who were introduced to me in the morning. Security and embarrassment make two different people of me, absolutely opposite, so I'm never amiable with those who displease me."

In Edgar's place, any other man would have replied to that remark with a compliment, but that was not his way. "Truly," he said, "I must have displeased you the other night at the play."

Valentine smiled at that slightly insolent conclusion, and gave him credit for having spared her the banal compliment she had expected.

"I confess," she said, "that I did not form a very good impression of you that evening…and if I hadn't been obliged to see you again…"

"I can believe it," said Edgar. "How could one not think badly of a man who confuses Mademoiselle Georges with Mademoiselle Mars?"

"Oh," said Valentine, with finesse, "it's much more pardonable than mistaking Madame de Cilleray for me."

Edgar recalled his first mistake, which he had not confessed to anyone, and was astonished to see that Valentine was aware of it.

"In truth," he said, "I'm extremely unfortunate; my incompetence is inexcusable. I spend an entire evening next to one woman, thinking that she's you, and then, when I'm lucky enough to encounter you, I don't recognize you."

"Don't be alarmed by those grave faults," said Madame de Champléry, with an even more malign expression. "They're compensated by the grace with which you greet women you've never seen. Although," she added, "one is not obliged to consider that one knows a woman when one has only danced with her once."

Edgar could not get over his surprise. *She divines everything*, he thought. *Does she too, perchance, have a lorgnon like mine?*

Well, no, in fact; she had no talisman but her perspicacity, but what talisman can equal the penetration of a woman who has an interest in divination?

In spite of his astonishment, Edgar was flattered by having been observed so attentively by Madame de Champléry, and thinking with pleasure that, in order to be so well instructed as to his slightest actions, she must have questioned Stéphanie. He knew, moreover, that irony is often the coquetry of intelligent and sensitive women, in the same way that languor is that of women who do not love anything. Proud of those first advances, he wanted to take advantage of them and pretended to take that malice, so gracious that it resembled a preference, seriously.

"You're very severe on me, Madame," he said, sadly, "and yet no one can have more pretentions than I have to your benevolence—perhaps even a right."

"Why is that?"

"My father," Monsieur de Lorville continued, in a penetrating tone, "was one of the closest friends of..."

"My mother," said Valentine, swiftly. "I know. I remember having seen him often in her home when I was a child—but I didn't know that he had a son."

"She was well aware of it," said Edgar, "and more than once..."

He stopped, as if he feared having said too much; but the sound of his voice, his gaze, and everything in his facial expression, completed the insinuation of an idea that he had not dared to articulate.

It was probable that Valentine's mother, linked for a long time with the Duc de Lorville, had dreamed about a marriage between their children that would further tighten their amity; but Edgar did not know anything about that, and if he allowed Valentine to believe it, it was in order to discover how far that belief might act in his favor.

No one excelled as much as he did in the delicate charlatanism of skillful individuals, which consists of insinuating an idea that is advantageous to them without compromising themselves by expressing it; they would be incapable of a lie, but they are able to profit from an error—and how can we have the courage to destroy an illusions that favors us?

Edgar did not yet have Madame de Champléry's secret, but he already knew the weaknesses of her heart. That young woman, so surly in the company of her stepmother, recovered all the grace of her spirit when she was apart from her. The memory of her mother still agitated her in the bosom of the pleasures of society; thus, to please her, it was necessary to speak ill of the one and regret the other—and Monsieur de Lorville, armed with that simple means, believed that he was sure of success.

Edgar and Valentine had already felt more emotion that evening than Stéphanie and her young suitor had experienced in the two years that they had been in love. What a difference there is between the agitations of a nascent love, irritated by intelligence and ignited by a brilliant imagination, and the gentle and untroubled sentiment, the patient hope of a certain happiness, of an amour untested by any obstacle!

Since Edgar had discovered that Madame de Champléry was the same woman that had charmed him a few days before, she had recovered all her empire over him, and his joy was great when, as he left, Monsieur de Fontvenel, who had been observing the two of them all evening, said to him resentfully: "I don't know, my dear, whether she had a secret, but I fear that she'll soon have two of them."

Jealousy already! Edgar thought—and he was right to rejoice; there is nothing more encouraging to pleasure than the prompt jealousy one inspires.

XIV

The Duc de Lorville was forever pressing his only son to marry. Edgar, disenchanted with the society that he knew too well, experienced the desire himself for a life of seclusion and affection, the need to have a home in which he was certain of being awaited impatiently and always received with pleasure.

Preoccupied with that vague project and an even vaguer choice, he desired to make the acquisition of a house in Paris and to establish himself in advance, imaginatively, with the wife of whom he dreamed. One morning, he went to the Rue de Bac to look over in detail a large and beautiful house that was for sale, and whose owner he knew.

It was eleven o'clock; at that intimate hour of the morning, for peaceful tenants, nothing is more annoying than the unexpected visit of a prospective purchaser, who, under the pretext of buying a house that he does not always have the means to do so, comes to disturb the household or business in their occupations, observing their mores and habits, and sometimes discovering their secrets. It is a propitious hour for family quarrels, in which a mother scolds her children and her domestics, or a husband rebukes his wife, his secretary or his salesman; a fatal hour in which memoirs are checked, projects of economy declared, annoying visits to be made in the evening decided, or the most fatiguing duties finally accomplished, even for a coquette—trying on a dress or replying to a love-letter.

Scarcely had Monsieur de Lorville, accompanied by the owner, come into the antechamber of the ground floor than the rumor of his arrival made itself felt, not only in the apartment in which the landlord had himself announced but on all the upper floors. The magic words: "This is a monsieur who wants to view the house," is sufficient to cast alarm into any household. A cry of fright rapidly rose from the ground floor to the first, from the first to second, the second to the third, and the third to the fourth. There, it died away in a modest and laborious retreat where life began with the day, and where that frightful hour, so early for the rest of the house, was a suitable hour for morning visits.

The inhabitants of the ground floor were eating their morning meal when they were told of the arrival of Monsieur de Lorville. They were all speaking loudly at the same time, like people quarreling, but the voices suddenly died away, and the greatest silence followed the family clamor.

Edgar and the owner went into the drawing room, where they were asked to wait for a moment.

"This apartment is large, as you can see," said the landlord. "It's rented to the Marquis de Châteaulancy, a peer of France; he spent a great deal of money on it last year and hosts admirable parties here. Three hundred people can fit in here without being crowded, but he's sulking now; he no longer wants to give balls, his pretext being that the 'glorious days' have ruined him. He's put beds in all my drawing rooms to accommodate his children, whom he's taken out of school. He's a Carlist; you can see that by his newspaper." He pointed to the *Gazette de France* that was open on the table,

"Indeed," said Monsieur de Lorville. "There's a very courageous bust on that sideboard."

At that moment the Marquis came in; he was as pale as a man who has just been very angry, but as gracious and polite as a man who knows how to constrain himself.

"A thousand pardons, Messieurs, for receiving you in such a disorderly room."

"It's me who owes you apologies," said the landlord. "I fear that we're disturbing you, but Monsieur de Lorville"—he indicated Edgar—"desires to buy the house, and I took the liberty of bringing him. Perhaps we've come too early?"

"No, really," said the Marquis, without looking at the landlord. Addressing himself to Monsieur de Lorville, he spoke to him with the benevolent air of a man of god society talking to one of his equals, whereas he treated the owner with the affected and distancing politeness that seems to say: *You're not one of us.*

They visited all the rooms of the vast apartment in succession. As they went through the Marquise's bedroom, Monsieur de Lorville perceived a woman sitting at a writing-desk, attentively occupied in writing a letter whose rough draft was in front of her.

Curious to know what she was writing, and what was the cause of the trouble he had remarked in the family, Edgar looked at the Marquise through his lorgnon, and read in her thoughts the words she was about to trace:

My husband and I would be very honored to have a man such as you for a son-in-law, but previous engagements...

Edgar could not read any more, the Marquise having stood up to greet him; but, suspecting that the letter must have been concerted with the Marquis, he directed the lorgnon at him in his turn.

No, in truth, he was thinking, *my daughter will not be the wife of a miserable parvenu. I've lost a great deal in the revolution, it's true, but so long as I live, no Châteaulancy will ever call herself Comtesse Chapotier!*

A few moments later a young woman went through the drawing room, weeping, and Monsieur de Lorville then knew all the family secrets, and all the inconveniences of the apartment too, for, if it had been better organized, the poor child would not have been forced to go through the drawing room in order to return to her own room, and show her tears to strangers.

On the first floor lived a former prefect of the Empire, the very same Comte Chapotier whose eldest son, an intelligent and distinguished young man, had pleased Mademoiselle de Châteaulancy so much, and had just been so cruelly rejected.

Comte Chapotier, who knew nothing about his eldest son's amours, was very worried about those of his second son, a lively and determined young man who appeared to be difficult to steer. When Monsieur de Lorville and the landlord came into the Comte's study, the young officer, sitting in a good armchair, was tranquilly reading his newspaper—*Le Temps*—without appearing to be listening to the sermon that his father was delivering to him gravely, standing in front of the fireplace in a pose that was simultaneously paternal and prefectorial, entirely appropriate to the circumstance. At the moment when the door opened he was saying:

"You can't think of it, my son; it's impossible..."

Seeing someone come in, he stopped. Then, after having addressed an insignificant comment to the landlord, in a patronizing and insolent tone, he was about to resume his sermon where he had left off when Monsieur de Lorville's name attracted his attention. His manner changed then, and he showed the son of the Duc de Lorville all the rooms of his apartment personally, with a politeness full of enthusiasm and a desire to oblige.

"This house is very fine, and we'd be very happy to have you as our landlord," he said without paying any heed to the actual landlord, who was there, and to whom that can scarcely have sounded amiable. "The apartments are superb, the drawing rooms vast; the antechamber can contain a large number of lackeys; everything here is grandiose, but it's necessary to be rich to live in it."

The Comte talked for a quarter of an hour; Edgar, astonished by such a singular familiarity, was not listening; he was entirely occupied by the discovery that he had just made. During the father's speech, he had aimed his lorgnon at the son.

My father is mad, the rebellious young man was thinking, *to prevent me from marrying Angeline, just because she's the daughter of an advocate, telling me that an advocate is nothing but a loquacious individual who sells his words, who lies for money, a merchant of phrases, a fabricator of paradoxes, and that all advocates are bunglers, who have doomed France with their political jargon—and a thousand other extravagances of that sort, as if our most celebrated magistrates and the majority of our great men hadn't started out by being advocates; as if advocates hadn't shown themselves, in every epoch of our history, to be the most redoubtable enemies of the arbitrary and the abusive, and as if eloquence weren't the primary power of parliamentary government!*

Very good, Edgar said to himself. *The Marquis refuses his daughter to the prefect; the prefect refuses his son to the advocate; let's see how far this will go, and to whom the advocate will refuse his daughter.*

XV

The advocate lived on the second floor; for, as will doubtless seem surprising, all the projects of marriage were being woven in the same house. The advocate received the landlord like a friend, but at Monsieur de Lorville's name, so well-known at the old court, he made a scornful grimace, which Edgar understood marvelously.

"I've been waiting for you impatiently, my dear," said the advocate to the landlord. "I am, alas, obliged to quit your apartment; I cannot live here any longer."

"Really?" asked the landlord, Alarmed by that declaration, although its tone was more one of chagrin than positive resolution. "What motive can you have for leaving me before your lease expires?"

"I'll tell you," replied the man of law,, and then addressed Edgar: "Pardon me, Monsieur Lorville, if I leave you, but I have a few words to say to Monsieur." Then he took the landlord into the next room and spoke to him for a few minutes in a low voice, while Edgar scanned the newspapers that were on the mantelpiece, the *Sténographe* and the *Gazette des Tribunaux*.

The discourse of the tribune, the pleas of the bar! he thought: *the reading of a true advocate.*

A conversation in a low voice was not sustainable for long by the man of eloquence, and the speech dictated by paternal indignation resounded in the ears of Monsieur de Lorville, proving that his talisman was unnecessary on this occasion.

"I hesitate to repeat it to you, my friend, but it's no longer possible for me to live in this house. You know my Angeline—a tender flower whom I've seen grow up in the shade, whom I've cultivated with all the *sollicitude* of a father. Intelligence, talent, grace, beauty, youth—what can I tell you?— she has it all; nature seems to have ornamented her since birth for the fêtes of the future, for the most brilliant destiny. I myself, by my assiduous cares, by my numerous endeavors, have been able to combine the gifts of fortune with the prodigalities of nature; I have been able to choose a spouse for her worthy of ensuring her happiness.

"Charmed by so many virtues, perhaps also seduced by the idea of allying himself with an honorable family whose head has spent twenty years in the noblest of professions, devoting his existence and talents to the defense of the oppressed, reparations of injustice and the reconciliation of families—in sum, to all the most sacred duties in life—happy and proud at the same time, that young man pressed by his desire to fix a date for that happy union, only needed to see it accomplished the consent of his father, a worthy magistrate who, as you know, lives under the same roof as us."

He raised his voice as if pleading in court. "That consent, Messieurs, was indubitable; my most ardent desires would have been fulfilled; happiness was already surrounding me with its prestige; my Angeline..."

Then, suddenly, the indignant father, rendered by wrath to the reality of language, cried vehemently: "Well, my friend, can you imagine what that silly girl has done? She has refused such a brilliant marriage, such an advantageous match. She has taken it into her head to fall in love without consulting me, without confessing it to her parents! She's in love! In love! And guess with whom, if you please...!"

The proprietor was unable to guess and appeared to have no hope of ever succeeding in it.

"What can I say!" cried the father, transported by rage. "Who could have divined such turpitude? She's in love with...I can't even pronounce the word...a *journalist!* A journalist, my dear! A miserable little journalist, a *collllumnist*, a *satirist!* Do you know what a journalist is, my dear? He's a man who lives on insults, caricatures and *callllumnies*, for whom nothing is sacred, who makes fun of your wife, your nose, your wig, your actions and your infirmities, who never sees anything in an event but the witticism it inspires, who unveils the secrets of your household in order to mock them, who makes jokes about disasters, puns about scourges, quips about your death and writes skits about your funeral: a monster, in sum, who ought to be banished from the social order, and I'd rather give my daughter to a galley-slave—yes, my dear, a galley-slave—than see her marry a journalist!"

Better and better, thought Monsieur de Lorville. *Now I need to know who the journalist disdains.* And, although he had decided not to buy the house, he expressed the desire to the owner to visit the other apartments.

The landlord seemed embarrassed then. "It's the same distribution everywhere," he said, in a constrained manner. Seeing that Monsieur de Lorville was determined to go all the way to the eaves, however, he added: "Pardon me; with your permission, I'll ask the porter to accompany you up there. It's just that a woman lives on the third with whom…I'm in a slightly delicate situation, and I don't care to see her at the moment." He continued in a confidential tone "But I can tell you that she's the widow of a master mason, who wants to marry again, you understand; and in truth, she's rather beautiful, and doesn't lack a fortune, but as you can imagine, an honest solicitor, a businessman like me, can't succeed a master mason."

Amazed by that fourth, quite unexpected disdain, Monsieur de Lorville had difficulty keeping a straight face, and in order to dissimulate his merriment he rapidly went up the staircase to the third door, without paying any heed to the owner, who was calling out to him to wait for his guide.

Edgar only stayed for a few minutes in the apartment of the mason's widow. The visit offered him nothing remarkable, except for a sky-blue velvet beret and a coral necklace, which the coquettish widow hastily put on in order to welcome him, and the care she put into calling him *Monsieur le Duc* seven times in ten minutes.

He soon reached the fourth floor, and paused for a moment at the journalist's door, reflecting before going in, searching for an easy way to engage him in conversation and prolong his visit. As he was standing there, hesitantly, the door opened and a ten-year-old child, coiffed in a paper bonnet and holding a parcel of books under his arm, came out abruptly. Monsieur de Lorville stopped him and asked him whether the journalist was at home.

"Yes," replied the child, brazenly, in English, delighted to know a word in a foreign language. Then, leaping on to the banister of the staircase, the boy went down in a rush, singing *La Parisienne*, and making as much noise as possible.[21]

The child having left all the doors open on his way out, Monsieur de Lorville went in without fear of being noticed, and darted a glance over a suite of apartments whose disposition was beginning to become perfectly familiar. The dining-room was papered with engravings and lithographs; the drawing room, which served as a library, was cluttered with books; the table was inundated with newspapers; there was a bust of the emperor, ad several portraits of illustrious authors, including Chateaubriand, Madame de Staël, Lamartine and Victor Hugo. Precious paintings could be seen here and there, which would have been admired in the finest gallery, which proved that the inhabitant of the modest redoubt had some of our most celebrated artists among his friends.

As he went further, Edgar perceived two épées suspended on the bedroom wall,[22] along with daggers, arrows and weapons from various countries. Further still, he saw a young man sitting at a desk, who seemed to be plunged in profound meditation or great despair. Several dictionaries and history

---

[21] *La Parisienne* was composed by Casimir Delavigne after the July Revolution as a celebration of the event, fitting it to the tune of a German military march; it served as the French national anthem until 1848.

[22] All journalists were routinely called out by people they had offended, but Émile de Girardin was notoriously pugnacious, ever ready to issue challenges himself; his papers once made much of the fact that the mild-mannered Alphonse Karr had refused to fight him.

books, which he recognized by their ponderous form, were open on the table in front of him, announcing that he was working on one of those long works that require research.

The young writer slapped his forehead from time to time, impatiently, and Monsieur de Lorville was amused to contemplate that intelligent man in search of a phrase and at grips with thought.

If Edgar had been able to see the young author's face he would have been glad to follow on that physiognomy, with the aid of his talisman, all the adventures of his ideas, to see them grow and collapse, reappear, perhaps to be rejected again, and then sustain themselves on the surface like swimmers in water, advancing audaciously, struggling with objections as if with the waves, agitating, battling courageously, and finally arriving at the shore, shaking themselves thoroughly, drying themselves off and discovering...a desert island!

Monsieur de Lorville would have delighted in that observation, but it was presently impossible; he had to advance further toward the young writer in order to read in his eyes whether he merited an investigation of his thoughts.

XVI

"I fear that I'm disturbing you, Monsieur," said Edgar to the journalist, who turned round abruptly. "I can see that you're busy."

"No, Monsieur, I wasn't doing anything. I was thinking."

He called that nothing. Seeing that his host was in a bad mood, Edgar began to repent of his visit and decided to cut it short.

"I'd like to know, Monsieur..."

"The author of the article against the new play? It's me, Monsieur; I've been expecting your visit. It couldn't be more timely, for I'm weary of life, and I'd be happy to risk it..."

Edgar smiled at the interpretation put on his visit, and replied: "I haven't come in search of a quarrel, Monsieur; I'm not an offended party demanding a reckoning. I've only come to look over the house with a view to buying it—but if you're absolutely determined to fight a duel this morning, I can render you that service."

The journalist smiled in his turn at that response. Monsieur de Lorville's cheerfulness having inspired confidence, he invited him to sit down for a while, and he conversation was engaged.

"You have a distinguished advocate for a neighbor whose daughter appeared to me to be very pretty," said Monsieur de Lorville, who had not seen the advocate's daughter but who knew that he could get the journalist's attention by praising her.

"Isn't she?" replied the latter, failing to hide a satisfied expression. "She's charming, but her father doesn't have as such intelligence as is generally believed.

"In fact, he seemed to me to have prejudices that..."

"Him? No! Oh, he has no prejudices!" said the journalist.

Monsieur de Lorville smiled. "You might think so," he said. "However, he appeared to me more than malevolent regarding everything touching the old court, and for the nobility in general."

"Oh, as to that he's right; those people have done us enough harm for one to have the right to speak ill of them."

At those words, Monsieur de Lorville could not suppress a twinge of pride, and seized the opportunity for a small vengeance.

"I also found him," he went on, maliciously, "very severe toward men of your profession, very unjust to journalists."

"Oh, my God, don't I know it!" cried the young writer, shuddering like an injured man whose wound has just been touched. "All these fine talkers, who think us worthless, are disdainful of us. I'm the pariah of the house. But it wasn't always like that; they were less proud in time of danger! Would you like to know where all three brave politicians of this house were during the 'glorious days?' That Marquis, instead of helping his king, that député-prefect, instead of being in the Chambre, and that advocate, instead of being at his post, were in hiding, Monsieur—yes, hiding in this very room. They took refuge here, under the pretext of having news, but, in reality, to be secure.

"All three of them were united here by fear, while I signed protests, came under rifle fire and became the improvised aide-de-camp of a well-known general in order to reestablish order in Paris—and they called me their liberator, a brave young man, and cried honor to journalists, said that journalists had saved France, in the fifteen years they'd been enlightening the country, that everything was owed to their zeal, their courage—and today they despise me!

"For they alone have gained from this revolution, which has ruined me; the former prefect has just been appointed to one of our foremost prefectures; the advocate is a counselor; and the court has already made advances to the Marquis; an embassy has been offered to him, which he'll soon accept—I know his fortune; he doesn't have it in him to be faithful for a year. And I, Monsieur, have obtained nothing, and they treat me as a petty journalist; they hold it against me that I hid them, and if they still greet me politely when they met me on the stairs it's because they're afraid of my paper, and dread reading their story in it one day."

The young journalist became increasingly animated on seeing that his listener was interested. "Well, undoubtedly," he went on, "it's a miserable condition to be obliged to blacken paper to make oneself known, and to criticize the government every morning in order that it will pay attention to you, and finally discover what you're worth. But it's necessary, you see, to be a journalist, because the only actual power nowadays is in the press.

"Under a Bonaparte, I'd have become a soldier; I'm twenty-four years old, I'd already be covered in wounds, and perhaps a colonel; but today, when all careers are obstructed, one can only acquire a reputation by scandal, it's necessary to have oneself put in prison, to attack ministers, to reveal abuses, denounce pretended injustices—in sum, shout in order to make oneself heard. The liberty of the press, Monsieur, is the sun, the daylight; its illuminates everything equally, without choice; so much the worse for those who have stains—let them stay in the shadow; it displays them, I agree, but it also protects from ambushes, and, if it makes defects stand out, it often gives credit to qualities. The fact is that it reigns, that it alone is omnipotent, and that it's necessary to have recourse to it to succeed."

Ever more animated, he went on: "Oh, Monsieur, if we had a Bonaparte, a man with an eagle eye, to distinguish us, to select us, to divine our faculties, to exalt them, to disrobe affairs to everyone in accordance with our talents, to understand our ideas, to conceive our plans and carry them out; a skillful man, who knew how to make an illiterate peasant into a great general like himself, and recognize a sage administrator in a man of twenty-five, we wouldn't be reduced, we representatives of young France, to living on teasing and insults, to risking our liberty and our life every day without glory, being imprisoned for our opinions, fighting for our writings, and dragging out a wretched existence between the Bois de Boulogne and Sainte-Pélagie!

"You don't know, Monsieur, what a torture it is for a young man without a protector and without a fortune to have abundant, fertile, ingenious ideas; to sense their facility, to see their luminosity, and not to be able to make them understood to those who would have the power to put them into practice! The means that one senses within oneself are a remorse when one can't employ them; mental capacity is a torment, a poison, a devouring fire, when it's inactive.

"Alas, I admit, Monsieur, that idle and turbulent youth will be deadly to the country, but whose fault is it? Is it not the responsibility of those who ought to direct it? We're calumniated because people aren't able to guide us; we're called revolutionaries, blood-drinkers, petty Robespierres, but we're only ambitious! If we dream of the republic it's because with that one has war, with war one has glory, and with glory fortune. Instead of being frightened of our dreams, let them give us hopes; instead of being irritated by our ardor, lest it turn to dangerous dementia, let them make it into heroism! Nothing is easier!

"Young France is like those young chargers fatigued by a long repose, who chew at the bit, foam at the mouth, and buck, throwing off the unskillful; rider, trampling him underfoot and crushing him, but which, steered by a sure hand, would arrive first at the post and win the prize. Oh, if I only had a little glory, a little fortune; if I could say 'do this,' instead of 'do you approve of this,' nothing would stop me in my career; I'd brave all obstacles, cross every step; I'd soon be a prefect, a député, a peer of France, an ambassador, a Minister... President... King!"

"In truth, Monsieur, I believe that you will be all that," said Edgar, struck by the young man's imperious attitude and his gaze full of inspiration and genius, "And I'd like to put myself in your favor in advance. I too claim to be one of you, and if by chance your newspaper has a few shares for sale, be good enough to let me know; here's my address."

The journalist took Monsieur de Lorville's card, but, after having read his name, he seemed embarrassed and repented of having said so much. The Duc de Lorville was known throughout France as an 'ultra' imbued with the most Gothic prejudices.

After a moment's silence, the young writer said to Edgar: "Pardon my astonishment, Monsieur, but I didn't expect to find in the son of Monsieur le Duc de Lorville so much sympathy for new ideas, and..."

"I know," Edgar interjected, "that bourgeois prejudices against the nobility are as ridiculous as ours."

"You agree, then, that your prejudices are ridiculous, and that one can be a distinguished man, a worthy man, without having five hundred ancestors?"

"Yes," replied Monsieur de Lorville, "But you'll grant me in my turn that one isn't always forced to be an imbecile because one has them."

"I'll agree to that wholeheartedly," replied the journalist, "and I confess that you've entirely cured me of my prejudices against the sons of Ducs."

"As you've destroyed mine against journalists," replied Monsieur de Lorville, cordially.

Then Edgar invited the young writer to come to lunch the following day, with some of his friends, and added in the most gracious manner: "A man like you, Monsieur, cannot remain unknown for long; I like all honorable celebrities, whom I seek out in advance."

They parted, charmed by one another, and it is worth comparing and contrasting the disharmony between three men of a reasonable age resident in that house, all of whom exercised honorable employments, with the sudden understanding of two young men who seemed to be widely separated by the difference in their fortune and condition.

Monsieur de Lorville, who sensed that the young man was his equal, began to believe in equality as a possible thing, and meditated the means and the chances of seeing its established universally one day. Having met the landlord again at the bottom of the stairway, he followed him into the garden, and, after having strolled briefly, they both went out through a small door which opened on to a peaceful street.

Edgar was preparing to leave, believing that the day's observations were complete, when he perceived, a short distance away, a cobbler whose modest workshop was sheltered and supported by the thick garden wall. The seeming ill humor of the worthy man attracted his attention, and he wanted to know why that workman in such a sedentary and tranquil trade, seemed so keenly irritated, and was waving his fist threateningly at a plump and attractive girl who was recognizable as a fruit-seller by virtue of her tray of peaches and pears.

Having moved closer to them he overheard these words:

"I tell you, Virginie, that you shan't be his wife; that I don't want an *organ-grinder* for a son-in-law, a vagabond without a domicile. The daughter of a man who has a boutique can't be the spouse of an *ixtrion*, a *paladin* who shows magic lantern slides, or whatever![23] I swear to you, as true as my name's Grichard, as true as this is a boot, that you shan't marry him!"

And the cobbler, inflamed with righteous anger, and penetrated with the dignity of his estate, raised his noble work, the fine ruin that he was repairing, to the heavens, like an august witness of the oath that he had just sworn.

"Oh, this is too much," said Monsieur de Lorville, bursting out laughing. "Adieu my beautiful dreams of equality! What is it, then, that our great philosophers understand by that word? How can it be defined? How about this: despising everyone who is beneath oneself, and only recognizing one's superiors as equals?"

From that day on, Edgar could not walk past that house without recalling the various observations that he had made

---

[23] One presumes that the cobbler means to imply *histrion* (actor) and *baladin* (strolling player) by the words that he mangles.

there. In fact, that house with its many floors was the emblem of society, except that the disdain was distributed in opposite directions; in society, it is directed downwards; in that house it was directed upwards, and then downwards again, for the young journalist, from the height of his mansard and his philosophy, paid everyone back with interest, despising impartially, in the pride of his genius, the old Marquis and the new Comte, the advocate and the mason, and the cobbler, and everyone else who lived beneath him.

XVII

Monsieur de Lorville carefully sought out opportunities to encounter Valentine. They were frequent, Madame de Clairange having asked him to come to see her often, and in any case, Valentine went to Madame de Fontvenel's house almost every evening, the latter's delicate health rarely permitting her to go out.

Edgar did not neglect, either, the days on which his aunt received visitors, and Madame de Montbert, astonished to see her nephew suddenly become so assiduous, and not attributing the honor of attracting him to her home to herself, sought to divine for which woman he came so frequently.

She isn't here yet, she said to herself, one evening, on seeing Monsieur de Lorville's irritated expression. *Let's hope that she comes, or he'll hold it against me, and I won't see him again.*

Madame de Montbert would have been sorry about that abandonment, firstly because her nephew amused her, and secondly because she was proud of him.

Suddenly, the two battens of the door opened, and the Marquise de Champléry was announced. Edgar's face seemed to light up with pleasure.

It's her, thought Madame de Montbert.

Monsieur de Lorville drew away immediately, and went to mingle with a group of men chatting to one side, in order not to intimidate Valentine with his sight, the power of which he was already well aware, and in order not to trouble her at the moment, so terrible for a young woman, when she enters a brilliant drawing room alone, after having been pompously announced.

Madame de Champléry advanced gracefully, with an air of assurance that surprised Monsieur de Lorville.

Why is it, he wondered, *that a woman with so much aplomb in her manner, with such a great familiarity with society, can sometimes be so easily embarrassed?*

It was because Valentine, unarmed against unexpected embarrassment, was full of courage in surmounting anticipated difficulties.

Not daring to approach her, Edgar admired her in silence; she had never seemed so beautiful to him as she did that evening. A woman is always at an advantage in a house whose mistress is her protectress. Madame de Montbert was full of benevolence for Valentine, and, which was even better, did not receive her stepmother.

But a confidence even firmer also embellished Valentine; a joyful emotion rendered her ravishing, even for those who did not know its cause. What was that, however, for the man who could read her heart?

Monsieur de Fontvenel loved Edgar like a brother, and remembered the touching grace with which he had anticipated his desire in an important matter; he dreamed incessantly of means to serve his projects, and of recognizing the delicacy of his methods by imitating them.

He had seen Edgar's nascent love for Madame de Champléry, and as he knew that Valentine was suspicious and easy to discourage in her hope of pleasing, he had applied himself to reassuring her as to Edgar's sentiments in her regard, and to exalt him in her nascent tenderness by all the eulogies of a passionate amity.

"He loves you, believe me," he said. "I've never seen him so seriously attached. Besides which, I know him; you alone can suit him."

Those confessions, made on another's behalf, undoubtedly cost him, but Monsieur de Fontvenel, in his devotion, dared not love the woman that his friend had chosen, and it pleased him to make a sacrifice worthy of both of them, in silencing the resentments of his self-esteem and the regrets of his heart.

It was shortly after that conversation that Valentine had come to Madame Montbert's, brilliant in the most beautiful adornment of all, the hope of being loved.

Edgar soon appeared as happy as she was, on divining her thought. And is it not to be twice as fortunate to owe to the devotion of a friend the tenderness of the woman one loves?

"You've come from Madame de Fontvenel's?" said Edgar, approaching Valentine. She seemed troubled by the name, as if it signified: *I know what has just been said to you.*

Indeed, there was a hint of that in it.

"Yes, I've seen her this evening," replied Madame de Champléry, and, fleeing the embarrassment of an emotion, she drew away precipitately. In her confusion, she went to sit down next to one of those tedious women who are always solitary or errant, to whom one only talks in winter, when they want to give a ball, and who remain in desperate abandonment the rest of the year.

Love has singular terrors, painful caprices; it alone, in its bizarrerie, could inspire in Valentine the idea of preferring the conversation of that woman devoid of intelligence, who she hardly knew and always avoided, to that of a charming man with whom she was in love. How strange that passion is, whose first impulse is to flee the one that one seeks, and whose second is to regret having fled!

Scarcely had Valentine realized who it was next to whom, in her distraction, she had come to place herself, than she understood the full extent of her imprudence. To remain for a whole evening, confined in a corner of a drawing room with a person one finds disagreeable, is a frightening future. She also feared having offended Monsieur de Lorville by quitting him so abruptly, and she looked at him to see whether he was annoyed—but the joy that was shining in Edgar's features reassured her, and even irritated her.

All men are conceited, she thought. *He believes, I'm sure, that I avoided him because I'm afraid of loving him*—and then, laughing at her own pride, she added: *Well, if that's what he believes, is he not right?*

While she was indulging in those reflections, a "fashionable" man, Monsieur de Salins, came toward her.

"What coquetry," he said, "to retire to a corner when one is sure of being sought! Why put yourself in the shadow like this when the light suits you so well?"

Satisfied with that poetic image, the young man pronounced the words in a manner to be heard by everyone, and attention was focused on Madame de Champléry. Several people came to sit with her, and group of elegant young woman formed. The conversation, sometimes individual and sometimes general, became animated.

In spite of her beauty and her intelligence, women liked Valentine, because she knew better than anyone else how to make the most of their advantages, and they forgave her for her amiability because she added to theirs.

Edgar, seeing Madame de Champléry so surrounded, did not want to approach her. Pretending to be dominated by a political subject that was being discussed heatedly, he applied himself to observing her, recalling the different impressions that she had caused him to experience before knowing her—which is to say, before he had focused his lorgnon on her attentively.

As for the secret of which there as so much talk, he thought, *I haven't yet discovered it. Perhaps she has none, or at least, if she has, it scarcely occupies her thoughts, for I haven't yet caught a glimpse of it there.*

At that moment, loud laughter burst out in the group where Valentine was. Edgar cast a glance at her; her embarrassed blush made him feel pity.

She had just spoken, without realizing it, one of those phrases that has two meanings, one simply witty, the other lewd; the men, only attaching the latter meaning to it, were laughing in an embarrassing fashion. Valentine, trying to put on a brave face, continued speaking and tried to repair her blunder, but everything she said added to it, which often happens in such cases, and the laughter was further augmented. Several women looked at her in astonishment, while others lowered their eyes with expressions of savant and indignant modesty.

Edgar picked up his lorgnon, and soon knew the cause of all the fuss. Oh, what joy there was for him in that discovery! It completed his intoxication. *So that's it,* he said to himself, smiling, *the strange secret.* Never had Madame de Champléry appeared more seductive to him than at that moment, ornamented by her gaucherie, and her disturbance, her impatience and her blush.

As soon as that first emotion had calmed down, he approached Valentine, determined to come to her aid and her get her out of her embarrassment into which her ignorance and naivety had led her.

"I recognize there the penetrating Lorville," said Monsieur de Salins. "He didn't hear what Madame said, but I'll wager that he understood it."

"Better than you, no doubt," said Edgar, with a sort of stiffness, "for when a woman does me the honor of speaking to me, I only ever understand what she means to say."

"It's certain," said Valentine, hastily, "that these messieurs have credited me with more wit than I intended to have."

The dignified way in which she pronounced those words caused all the jokes to cease, and the conversation, thanks to the cares of Monsieur de Lorville, having taken another course, Valentine sought to understand how Edgar, placed so far away for her, had been able to understand the disturbance that had agitated her and to come to her aid in such a timely fashion. That generosity, in such a mischievous man, inspired a keen gratitude in her. She knew that Monsieur de Lorville could only be so charitable for her, and that he always showed himself devoid of pity for the embarrassment of women he did not like.

Toward the end of the soirée, Edgar came to sit next to Valentine, with the air of a person intending to converse for a long time.

"Do you permit your friends to give you advice?" he asked, with an involuntary smile.

"Yes," said Valentine, "but I don't permit all those who desire to draw morals to believe that they're my friends."

"No matter; it's a right that I shall usurp, and between the two of us, I advise you never to converse with Monsieur de Salins."

"Why?"

"Because he has more intelligence than you on certain subjects—or, at least, a kind of intelligence that you do not have. It's true, believe me; his conversation does not suit you at all. There's no man more dangerous to you, except perhaps me."

"You," said Valentine, smiling. "Why is that?"

"A man who divines is always inconvenient—but don't worry; the secrets I divine are as sacred as those confided to me."

"But then," said Valentine, in an emotional tone, "it's necessary to have a secret to fear you, and..."

"No false vulgarity, please," Edgar interrupted. "Don't seek to deceive me; it would be futile—and don't fight the power of penetration that you have rendered so dear to me. If you knew how all your thoughts embellish you, how they sometimes compensate for your words and render you likeable, you would pardon someone who divines them."

"So," said Valentine, seeking to vanquish her agitation, "you believe that I have a secret."

"Yes," Edgar replied, with a sort of embarrassment.

"And you believe that you have divined it?"

"Yes...oh, don't blush."

Monsieur de Lorville's gaze was so full of tenderness as he spoke those words that Valentine was deceived as to their significance.

He has divined that I love him, she said to herself, *and he thinks that he has my secret.*

They chatted thus for a few minutes, each pursuing a different idea, but as their emotions were fundamentally similar, they heard one another without understanding one another. Valentine would have liked to punish Edgar for the overly prompt confidence he had in pleasing her, but he seemed so glad of that assurance that there was no means of reproaching him for it.

That evening decided Monsieur de Lorville's fate. Valentine had just acquired in a moment more rights to his affection than years of devotion and sacrifice would have assured her.

Poetic imaginations find treasures in an idea; exalted hearts are sometimes only smitten by circumstances, and an ugly woman, in a romantic situation often inspires more amour in them than a ravishing beauty in a vulgar situation.

XVIII

Preoccupied and delighted, Edgar was no longer thinking about anything but recalling the events that explained Madame de Champfléry's situation. He understood then the cause of the sudden embarrassment that was observable in her behavior and had often seemed suspect to him. He knew why Valentine's conversation was so lively and jovial with individuals whose good taste reassured her, and became, on the contrary, so cold and restrained with those whose poor taste was redoubtable. He remembered several equivocal things that she had said, which had shocked him, but were now justified so easily. In his eyes, now, Madame de Champléry had new graces, which he cherished as proofs of her candor.

This time, he said to himself, *I'm recompensed for my tenderness; I haven't been punished for daring to divine. I deserved, in the end, a fortunate discovery; thus far I had chosen so poorly. Mademoiselle d'Armilly's secret was her ambition, Stéphanie's her love for someone else, but Valentine's...! O charming mystery! How, too, could one suspect that a woman might take so much trouble to hide her innocence?*

Valentine had been only seventeen at the time of her marriage, which was decided promptly and in a singular manner.

One morning, Valentine was alone and weeping in her mother's old apartment. She had just been informed that Monsieur de Champléry wanted to talk to her, and was waiting in the drawing room to bid her adieu. She hastened to him.

"You're leaving," she said, in an emotional voice. "What will become of me? No one here loves and understands me, except you."

"Truly?" said Monsieur Champléry. "How amiable she is! No one loves you, you say—is that possible? I thought that your stepmother was so good and so kind to you."

"Oh, she's very good," said Valentine, sadly. "I have no complaint to make against her, but you know…it's not the same thing…"

"Of course—I understand," Monsieur de Champléry interjected, seeing that Valentine's tears were about to flow. "But your father?"

"Oh, since he's remarried, my father no longer looks at me with pleasure; he holds it against me that I've been mourning my mother for such a long time; my regrets offend him; he avoids me because I'm sad, and I can see that he no longer loves me. If you knew how I suffer in this house, in the room where my mother died, which I see inhabited by someone else; in these places filled for me with sweet and heart-rending memories. Oh, I sense that if I stay here much longer, I'll die of it."

Monsieur de Champléry looked at Valentine, and was struck by the distress in her features. For some time, her languor had been augmenting in a disquieting fashion, and he feared the effect of such a long dolor on the young woman.

As he contemplated her sadly, she said: "You see, it's to you alone that I dare to complain, to you alone that I can talk about my mother, whom you loved so much—and you're leaving me. Where are you going, then?"

"To Italy. The physicians are sending me there."

"What!" said Valentine. "You're ill—you who are always so cheerful?"

"Child," said Monsieur de Champléry, "insouciance is a virtue when there's no more hope; that's what I call true philosophy. But it's not a matter of me, poor Valentine. Is it true that you're so unhappy?"

"Oh, yes," she said, sobbing. "I've very unhappy! Anything would be better for me than this life of regret and isolation, my mother's house from which they want to expel her memory, this tomb in which they've imprisoning me, saying: *Forget her!*"

Moved by Valentine's despair, Monsieur de Champléry reflected on the means of taking her away from the existence that was so frightful for her. He remained motionless for a few moments, as if dominated by an idea whose risks he was weighing up.

Suddenly, his face became animated; his resolution was made; a thought of which he seemed to be proud had just taken root in his mind. The hope of a noble action that would repair the follies of his youth smiled in his imagination. The certainty of inspiring in Valentine a boundless gratitude and esteem; the joy of usurping, by the elevation of his sacrifice, the first exaltation of that young heart prior to amour; and finally, the pride of finally being the providence of a distinguished woman, of whose brilliant destiny he had a presentiment, determined him to consecrated his life—or at least the little time that remained to him—to her.

Monsieur de Champléry, who had fought in all the campaigns of the Empire, in consequence of his wounds, had been afflicted with a mortal malady that left him no hope of a cure. The death that he had confronted so many times as a soldier on the battlefield, did not frighten him any more than it had before, and the knowledge of his desperate state had not changed his humor; perhaps he was a little more cheerful, for he no longer had any anxiety about the future. The certainty of an imminent death seemed almost welcome at that moment, when it offered him the chance of a generous sacrifice that would ensure the happiness of another. The memory of Valentine's mother further encouraged him in a project of which her tenderness would have approved, and Monsieur de Champléry felt that in devoting them to the future happiness of the daughter of his best friend, his last moments would be free of bitterness.

By marrying Valentine, he said to himself, *I shall render her independent of her stepmother, and my imminent death will leave her entirely free to love and to choose. I shall cherish her like a father; I shall not, like an egotistical and ridiculous old man, talk about love to a young woman whose beautiful dreams are so respectable, whose chimeras are so imposing; I shall leave her pure for the man that she will one day*

love, and when, after my death, an amour worthy of her will
assure her happiness, she will name me respectfully to her
young husband; she will understand the nobility of my sacri-
fice then, and in her gratitude, will bless the memory of her
old friend. Smiling, he thought: *It will be the first time that a*
young widow will remarry without chasing away the importu-
nate memory of her first husband.

Valentine consented without difficulty to that project,
which delivered her from her present chagrin, and accepted
gratefully a sacrifice of which she did not understand the full
extent, and which she alone could have inspired.

Individuals endowed with an elevated mind exercise, unknown to themselves, a mysterious influence on those who
surround them. They throw, so to speak, a perfume of poetry
into the atmosphere they respire, and which intoxicates others
with them. There are paltry sentiments that one does not dare
express to them, vulgar actions that one never has the idea of
proposing to them. A noble character is a dignity that one
praises involuntarily. For elite souls, one chooses that which is
noblest and finest, as one presents to princes the most delicate
dishes; one changes oneself for them, one assumes the qualities that they esteem; one grows taller in order to reach them;
and one is surprised to conceive in their presence ideas and
projects entirely opposed to one's nature.

Society was astonished by that marriage; but, seeing
Monsieur de Champléry joyful, full of concern for his young
wife, no one divined the scant happiness that he expected.
Valentine and her husband spent a year in Italy, after which
Monsieur de Champléry, sensing his fatal hour approaching,
wanted to return to his beloved mountains of Auvergne, in
order to die there.

It was a difficult situation for a nineteen-year-old widow
to find herself launched into high society with all the liberty of
a woman and all the ignorance of a young girl. With her intelligence and her good taste, Valentine handled it easily, without
any fear that her secret would be penetrated by her stepmother.
She feared the romantic dividend that Madame de Clairange's

affectations might extract from such a singular situation, and to avoid the ridicule that her elegies would cast on her innocence, she fell into the contrary fault, and sometimes pretended to understand matters of which she was completely ignorant.

Thus, all Valentine's defects came from that pretentious and irritating woman, the mere sight of whom was sufficient to distort her character. The monotonous kindness of Madame de Clairange was so intolerable to her that she made herself brusque and impatient in order to avoid resembling her; the continual spectacle of an artificial sensitivity caused her to affect a culpable indifference to everything that ought to have moved her. She thus became a hypocrite in reverse, and strove to hide her virtuous sentiments with the same falsity that others put into dissimulating those over which one ought to blush.

How such a character was bound to please Monsieur de Lorville! What charm it had for the man who was able to divine it! Edgar sensed then that no other woman could be more agreeable to him.

Fine and delicate minds are more difficult to fix than others. Deceptive women disenchant them; naïve women who hide nothing of what they are experiencing annoy them. It is necessary that their penetration has something to divine: an honest character complicated by circumstances, an incessantly-renascent mystery that is always explicable in terms of a pure and generous sentiment.

XIX

Intoxicated by hope and full of gratitude for his talisman, Edgar employed it to divine Valentine's wishes and desires and to accommodate them before he had thought of expressing them.

If someone proposed a pleasure trip that he knew was bound to bore her, but which she would have accepted out of complaisance, he rejected the idea promptly. The play that would amuse her was always the one to which he offered to go, and Madame de Champléry was continually astonished by the conformity of their tastes.

It often happened that Valentine refused a pleasure that was offered to her for reasons of delicacy, fearful of depriving someone else. One day, when she persisted in refusing a place in Madame de Fontvenel's box at the Opéra, Edgar amused himself by observing her in order to discover the cause of her obstinacy.

"A thousand thanks, but no," she said, "you know that I detest premières; the music is usually poorly played, the actors don't know their roles, and there are always two interests: that of the play and that of the success; personally, I can only follow one at a time; I have a very exclusive mind."

"Invariably," said Edgar, and started to laugh at Valentine's thinking, which was:

I don't want to accept the place, because they'd force me to sit in the front of the box; Madame de Fontvenel wouldn't be able to see anything, and would put herself out for me. It's a pity, thought; I would have liked to see Le Philtre *and hear the music, which is said to be delightful.*[24]

Edgar immediately went out, ran to the Opéra, and by dint of intrigue succeeded in hiring a box already promised,

---

[24] *Le Philtre*, with music by Daniel Auber and a libretto by Eugène Scribe, had its premiere at the Opéra on 15 June 1831.

and the next day, Valentine received a note from Madame Montbert:

My nephew has obtained a box at the Opéra for me, for the first performance of Le Philtre, *telling me that you would like to go. He knows that it would delight me to have the opportunity to give you pleasure, Believe, however, my dear Valentine that I am not as much of an "old aunt" as I would like to appear—or, rather, that I am not yet enough of one.*

That deliberately complicated note caused Valentine to think. That evening, on seeing Edgar at the Opéra, she experienced one of those fits of embarrassment that rendered her so awkward.

Monsieur de Lorville took pleasure in adding to it. "You see," he said, "that I like to punish bad faith, even when it is inspired by a good sentiment—so be careful."

Disconcerted, Madame de Champléry only replied with a smile; how can one be resentful of malice that seeks to please?

On another occasion, Monsieur de Lorville granted Valentine's wish without he giving any indication of it, even by expressing the contrary. She had just been admiring the new paintings ornamenting the Musée that year, and, remembering her of one of the charming views of Naples painted by Smargiassi,[25] she promised herself to acquire the painting, the moderate price of which authorized that caprice.

Smargiassi's paintings, she thought, would be worth twice as much in two years' time, and to buy them now was, in fact, a good investment. That is how a reasonable woman always finds a pretext to indulge her fantasy.

As she was meditating that project, her caleche was stopped at a street corner by a traffic jam; she raised her head and perceived a young man some distance away examining her through a lorgnon; it was Monsieur de Lorville—and the following day, when Valentine came home from mass, she

---

[25] The Italian painter Gabrièle Smargiassi (1798-1882) had briefly served as tutor to Louis-Philippe, and had important patrons in France.

was very surprised to find, on going into her apartment, the painting she had admired so much the day before, and which she had thought of acquiring.

"Who sent this painting?" she asked, immediately.

"A commissionaire brought it, Madame, without saying of whose behalf."

"There was no letter?"

"No, Madame, but he gave me this paper on which Madame's address is written, to prove that he was not mistaken."

Valentine read the address; the handwriting was elegant, but it was unfamiliar. She remained immobile for a long time before the beautiful landscape, which reminded her of one of her favorite locations in Italy; then she started reflecting and meditating, wondering how it came to be there.

Monsieur de Fontvenel discovered her in that contemplation.

"How right you were to buy that landscape," he said. "Like you, I noticed it; it's enchanting."

"Isn't it?" said Valentine, distractedly—but, making an effort to compose herself, she showed him the address that she was holding. "Tell me, do you know this handwriting?"

"Oh, certainly—it's Edgar's. Why are you blushing? Is it him, then, who sent you the painting?"

"I don't know," said Valentine, embarrassed. "I liked it a great deal; I planned to buy it, but I hadn't yet mentioned it to anyone, and I can't imagine..."

"Oh, you know Edgar," Monsieur de Fontvenel interjected. "He'll have divined all that—he's an astonishing man. Do you know what he did for me?"

"No."

Monsieur de Fontvenel told her how Edgar had given him the fifty thousand francs that he had gone to borrow from him, before he had had time to make the request.

"I explained that singular adventure by thinking that Edgar had been warned by my valet, who, seeing me in despair, had gone without my knowledge to ask my friend for help, asking him to keep the step secret. That appeared natural to me, but I've seen the phenomenon of penetration renewed so frequently since then that I'm lost in conjectures. In truth, the wily Lorville must have a talisman, or spies all over Paris, in order to know what everyone is thinking. Has it been a long time since you've seen him?"

"I met him yesterday," Valentine replied. "Perhaps he was at the salon, like us, and noticed how much I admired the painting."

"No matter," said Monsieur de Fontvenel. "You won't dislodge my conviction that there's something extraordinary underneath it all."

"But I have scruples, I confess," said Madame de Champléry. "Although Monsieur de Lorville is the son of one of my mother's friends, perhaps I don't know him well enough to accept..."

"Oh, don't attach too much importance to such a simple thing, and don't afflict him with a refusal—he's be so unhap-py."

"Do you think so?" said Valentine, smiling.

XX

Touched by that amiable intention, Madame de Champléry presumed that Monsieur de Lorville would come to her stepmother's house that day in order to discover how it had been welcomed.

Madame de Clairange was expecting a great many guests that evening, and Valentine went down to the drawing room early, carefully dressed and gracious, like a woman satisfied with her adornment, and animated by the confident coquetry that always renders one benevolent and lovely.

Few people had arrived as yet, and her stepmother exclaimed, as soon as she perceived her: "Oh, Valentine, I've been waiting for you impatiently. I'm counting on you, my dear, to do the honors of my salon, for it's absolutely necessary that I leave. I'm running right away to the home of poor Monsieur Laréal, who broke his leg this morning. His cabriolet collided with an omnibus, in such a frightful fashion that he was nearly killed, with his horse and his domestic. Say all that, my dear, to anyone who notices my absence.

"But everyone will notice it, in your own home, Madame," said Valentine, trying not to smile, and surprised by her mother's haste in going to donate her care to someone she scarcely knew. She wanted to make that observation and say a few words to retain her, but seeing Madame de Clairange, committed to her good deed, draw away without listening to her, she resigned herself to playing the role of mistress of the house, and prepared herself patiently for the tedium of explaining to two hundred people, one after another, why Madame de Clairange, who had invited them, was not at home that day.

Valentine also sensed that her stepmother must regard as fortunate that opportunity to make a brilliant display of her charity. In fact, was it not a marvelous idea on the part of Madame de Clairange to have gather the most distinguished people in Paris in her home in order to demonstrate to them all, at a stroke, how devoted and benevolent she was, ready to sacrifice the pleasures of society to the kindness of soothing the unfortunate.

At the commencement of the soirée, Madame de Champléry recounted with sufficient exactitude, to the first ten people who questioned her, how Madame de Clairange had been obliged to go to the home of one of her friends who had broken a leg, and the story of the cabriolet, the horse and the omnibus—in sum, everything that she was able to say—but she had not anticipated the number of questions that such an event would attract to her.

"Who is the unfortunate friend?" someone asked, anxiously.

"Monsieur Laréal."

"Monsieur Laréal, you say? I don't know him. Perhaps he's one of her relatives?"

"No, Valentine replied, embarrassed. "He's...he's a Monsieur...who has broken his leg." Then she passed on quickly to someone else, in order not to laugh.

The latter immediately said: "Is Madame the Clairange ill? I don't see her anywhere."

"No, Madame; she's very well, but she's gone to visit one of her friends, who is ill."

"Oh, my God! Dangerously ill?"

"I hope not, but there was an accident...a crash...his cabriolet overturned and...he broke his leg."

"Who's broken his leg?" exclaimed Monsieur de Fontvenel. "That blockhead de Guersey, I'll wager. He has a mania for having horses so spirited, so untamable, that it doesn't astonish me."

And Monsieur de Guersey, who was in the next room, came in person to reassure those who were deploring his imprudence.

Everyone wanted to know to whom Madame de Clairange was so generously devoted, and poor Valentine was again obliged to articulate the name of the Monsieur Laréal, whom nobody knew. Finally, weary of endlessly repeating the adventure of the unknown individual who had broken his leg, she determined to respond that her stepmother would back soon. As for those who did not address themselves to her, convinced that they would find the mistress of the house in the next room, she let them wander from room to room without troubling their research.

Soon, however, having accomplished the politeness of asking for news of Madame de Clairange, forgot that they had not seen her. Even Valentine lost the memory of the accident, and devoted herself entirely to the gracious duty of welcoming everyone benevolently, talking to everyone about their interests, and animating, by her intelligence and the generosity of her manners, a gathering of pretty women and men remarkable for their talents or their celebrity.

The conversations were brilliant; everyone enjoyed themselves. For her part, Valentine, who was never amiable in her stepmother's presence, had no regrets. She sensed all the advantages conferred by the liberty in question, and, proud of the good grace with which she was carrying out her role, she waited impatiently for Monsieur de Lorville, in order to appear in his eyes in her full value.

She was a trifle confused at the thought of speak to him about the gift of the charming painting, but she had so many things to say to him and so many question to ask him, in the attempt to find out how he had been able to discover that she desired it, that she hoped in her joy and curiosity to be able to handle such a difficult situation easily.

If Monsieur de Lorville had arrived at that moment he would have been delighted by all the affectionate things she would have said to him in her gratitude. Unfortunately for Valentine, he came too late, and—an even more annoying circumstance—it was Madame de Clairange who brought him. She had encountered him just as she was coming back.

"Here he is! Here he is!" she cried, addressing her stepdaughter. "Tell him how happy you are with his amiable souvenir. How enchanting the painting is, and how gracious it is of you to have divined that Valentine had chosen it! You can't imagine how much pleasure it has given her. She was weeping with joy when I called in on her; I found her in contemplation before the souvenir." She looked at Edgar in a knowing fashion and added; "In truth, you're a very seductive man, and I'm no longer astonished that you're thought of..."

That declaration, made in a loud voice, displeased Valentine so much that she interrupted dryly, in her most disdainful tone; "The landscape is charming; I admired it a great deal; but I didn't know that it was Monsieur..." and she indicated Monsieur de Lorville.

"Who had chosen it," finished Monsieur, extremely annoyed in his turn to see that mysterious attention become a public matter. "And you're right," Madame, he added. "I don't merit the honor of being suspected."

In spite of the tone of chagrin with which he pronounced those words, he put on such a good show of telling the truth that Valentine ended up believing that Monsieur de Fontvenel had been mistaken in recognizing Edgar's handwriting in the address that had accompanied the painting, and that, in sum, someone other than Monsieur de Lorville had sent it. The disappointment that that idea caused her threw her into a sadness that she could not conceal.

Edgar was discontented himself to see that Madame de Champléry no longer suspected him of having thought of her, and finding himself constrained, by her stepmother's loquaciousness to deceive her.

Although they were both innocent of that annoyance, they punished one another for it. Edgar became surly, and Valentine adopted a coldly ironic tone with him by which he was wounded. Thus, the painting offered with so much grace, the ingenious attention that ought to have brought them closer together, served on the contrary to drive them apart.

Monsieur Narvaux, always in haste to do Edgar a disservice, was pleased to augment Valentine's chagrin.

"You're very disappointed," he said, maliciously. "You hoped that gallantry was Monsieur de Lorville's. It's natural to attribute that which causes us so much pleasure to those who please us!" And, seeing that Madame de Champléry was pretending not to have heard him, he added: "Moreover, when one does the honors of a fête so well, one ought to have an income of a hundred thousand livres—and you'd make such a pretty Duchesse! It's a pity that Edgar has a horror of marriage."

"No more so than me," replied Valentine, finally forced to respond to the determined malevolence.

"Who mentioned marriage?" someone asked.

"We were speaking ill of it," replied Monsieur Narvaux. "Madame doesn't understand how a widow can remarry."

"But if she's in love?" said Monsieur de Norville, moving closer to her.

"It would be necessary to be in love to lose one's head," replied Madame de Champléry, "And still nothing would excuse the sacrifice."

Valentine spoke those words so calmly, and with such a profound conviction, that Monsieur de Lorville seriously believed in her repugnance for a second marriage. He was astonished to see her converse in such a natural manner on a subject that ought to have embarrassed her. Edgar did not know the extent to which pride can paralyze the most sensitive heart.

Valentine was sincere, then, in the distancing that she was testifying for a second marriage, in the coldness that she was showing to him; he was no longer for her that amiable man, in haste to please her, whose conversation had so much charm for her, and whom she preferred to all others, because he responded to her thoughts, that she would otherwise by too embarrassed to express. He was no longer anything but an heir whom she was suspected of wanting to seduce, out of ambition, in order to be a Duchesse. Her coquetry toward him was deflowered; it was no longer, as before, out of the fear of loving him that she avoided him, it was with sincerity, as one avoids a difficult conversation, a friend that one no longer sees except with constraint, and whose presence causes more embarrassment than pleasure.

Edgar soon remarked that change, and as verity has a power that one cannot escape, he sensed all that he had lost in Madame de Champléry's heart, and was profoundly afflicted by it. Sad and discouraged, he compared Valentine's cold and simply polite manners with the emotional voice, the gaiety full of agitation and the coquetry full of tenderness that he had once remarked in her—and in the excess of his sadness he forgot the talisman that could have revealed the cause of that cruel difference, and perhaps consoled him.

Thus, Edgar no longer thought his life marvelous; the reality of all his bitterness overwhelmed him. Valentine no longer experienced any pleasure in being near him; that was evident; he felt it, and suffered from it. How could he imagine that the change that rendered him so unhappy could be explained in such a favorable manner?

Monsieur Narvaux, seeing him somber and pensive in solution, pointed it out to Madame de Champléry. "Do you know," he said, "he feigns sentiment marvelously. In truth, he creates the illusion."

Valentine looked at Edgar, and was struck by his pallor. "Doesn't he?" continued Monsieur Narvaux. "If I didn't know him so well, I might be deceived by it. At any rate, that attitude of despair is very appropriate, after the way you've treated him today."

At those words, Valentine smiled disdainfully, and Monsieur de Lorville, having observed that smile from afar, wanted to know what Monsieur Narvaux had said to provoke it. Finally, he remembered his lorgnon, and summoned it to his aid. It was necessary to put an end to it.

This is what Valentine was saying to herself:

What a pity that Monsieur de Lorville is so rich that one cannot love him without appearing to be ambitious; it would be so sweet to spend the rest of one's life with him, in retreat!

All of Madame de Champléry's conduct during the soirée was then explained. Edgar divined what his perfidious friend had been able to say to make Valentine's pride revolt and chill her heart. Suddenly relieved of his pain, he resumed a joyful expression that astonished everyone.

Madame de Champléry, most of all, was wounded by it; she had said nothing to give rise to that sudden cheerfulness, and had a right to be offended by it. A woman never pardons anyone she loves for the joy that she has not caused.

Having penetrated the sentiment of pride that was distancing him from Valentine, Edgar understood that his attentions for her would be futile henceforth, that the evidences of his affection would be poorly received, and he formed the strange project of engaging Madame de Champléry in spite of herself, of constraining her to a marriage that her pride would make her refuse, but which she desired in the depths of her heart, without admitting it to herself.

She detests embarrassment, he thought. *Well, I shall spare her that of a difficult confession. What good is my talisman to me, if not to prove to a woman that one does not believe everything she says, and to make her happy in spite of herself?*

Entirely occupied by his new project, he went away, smiling, without speaking to Madame de Champléry, and leaving her indignant at the sudden good humor that had succeeded such an ostentatious sadness.

That soirée, commenced in a brilliant manner, ended listlessly for Valentine. She no longer believed herself to be loved; everything irritated her. On returning to her apartment, however, and finding the painting that reminded her of all her hopes, the impressions of the morning were reawakened; her faith reappeared; she examined the address again, and the emotion she experienced at the sight of that handwriting proved to her that it was Monsieur de Lorville's.

He had to deny that he had sent it to me, she thought, *before all those people that my stepmother's exclamations had attracted. But it was him, I can no longer doubt it!*

Even the smile that had offended her appeared to her to be quite natural.

Perhaps, she said to herself, *he presumed that Monsieur Narvaux was attributing to himself the honor of that attention, which he called so elegantly a "gallantry."*

And, laughing in her turn at that idea, she promised herself to talk to Edgar the following day, and to prove to him that she had not been taken in by his lie.

Alone with her love, she no longer thought about the interpretation of interest that society might attribute to her, for the heart, left to its own devices, quickly forgets all the ambitions and all the vanities of life, which are unnecessary in a beautiful dream.

Valentine waited in vain for Monsieur de Lorville the next day. In the days that followed he did not put in an appearance at Madame de Fontvenel's house, and an entire week passed without anyone hearing any mention of him.

Alarmed, Madame de Champléry thought that he was angry with her, and decided to visit Madame de Montbert, hoping that she might give her news of her nephew.

She was received so coldly that she was disconcerted, Madame de Montbert, full of zeal for the interests of her friends, regarded as so many insults the secrets and sentiments that were not confided to her. Still young, and irreproachable in her conduct, she was resigned to the role of confidante, but she insisted on it, all the more so because it was a compensation. Wanting to punish Valentine for hiding her affection for her nephew from her, she took pleasure in repeating an item of news that had been given to her as certain, and which she knew was bound to disappoint her.

"Have you seen my nephew lately?" she asked Valentine, in a manner calculated to trouble her.

"No, Madame; I haven't seen him for some time."

"What! You haven't seen him since his return?"

"I didn't know that he'd left."

"Oh, he was only gone or a week. Madame de Montbert fixed her eyes on Valentine and added: "But I thought you were better informed. How can you not know that he has gone to Lorville to seek his father's consent?"

"His father's consent?" repeated Valentine, with visible anxiety.

"Of course—for his imminent marriage."

At those words, Valentine felt herself going pale. She found enough courage, however, to reply in an ill-assured tone: "I didn't know that he was to marry so soon. Who is he going to marry?"

"Mademoiselle de Sirieux, it's said." Taking note of Valentine's disturbance, Madame de Montbert added: "I can affirm nothing positively, myself. I even confess that I had another idea, and that when his imminent marriage was mentioned to me, knowing that he was very occupied with you, I thought at first that it was..."

"Me, Madame?" Madame de Champléry interjected, swiftly. "I haven't given any thought to remarrying, and Mademoiselle de Sirieux, who is very beautiful and very rich, will suit him much better than me."

"Don't worry, my dear," said Madame de Montbert, ironically, wounded by that feigned indifference, "you did not have to fear that danger. My nephew declared to us the other day that he had an invincible prejudice against widows, and that a woman who had belonged to another would never be his."

Valentine did not give evidence of any chagrin in response to that opinion, given to annoy her, and Madame de Montbert, astonished to see her malice go to waste, added: "I don't know whether it's necessary to believe the rumor, but what is certain is that for two years, my brother has been extremely desirous of seeing his son married, and that I received a letter from him this morning in which he expressed his delight at Edgar's happiness, and the pleasure he anticipated in seeing his old château rejuvenated by the presence of an amble daughter-in-law. The letter is on my desk and I can show it to you; but it doesn't name anyone, and perhaps it isn't Mademoiselle de Sirieux that Edgar is to marry. Perhaps that's nothing but a chagrin, and there might be a sudden change of mind."

"Why should there be?" replied Madame de Champléry, with dignity, replying to all that the words implied. "If the marriage suits his family, there's no reason to deflect him from it."

Fortunately for Valentine, someone came to interrupt that painful conversation, which she no longer felt the strength to continue. She left Madame de Montbert's house feigning a gracious and indifferent air, but as soon as she was in her carriage, her tears flowed in abundance.

The news of that prompt marriage seemed to her to be certain; the aversion that she had expressed for a second marriage was sufficient, in her thinking, to have discouraged Edgar, and to have decided him in favor of someone else. She knew that the Duc de Lorville keenly desired that his son should marry, in order to be able to keep him with him, having found himself very isolated since the loss of his place at court, and the interests and vanities that had taken the place of affection. She also knew that Monsieur de Sirieux was an old friend, and that the alliance would suit them both; and she found it quite simple that, despairing of her love, Edgar might seek to make his family happy by a union they desired. In any case, Edgar's journey to go and seek his father's consent proved that the ceremony was imminent, and Valentine admitted to herself, painfully, that she had no more hope to conserve.

Knowing that he had returned, she thought that he might perhaps come to Madame de Fontvenel's house that evening, but the entire evening went by without him appearing. Every time the door opened, poor Valentine shivered, a glimmer of hope awakening in her heart; then someone else came in, and she fell back into her depression.

Stéphanie dared not speak to her for fear of adding to her distress, for she was beginning to be distressed herself by Monsieur de Lorville's capricious conduct.

"That's how you all are, you young widows," Madame de Clairange said to her, as they were going home. "You disdain the men who occupy themselves with you, and then, when they decide on someone else, you regret them."

"Who am I regretting, then?" said Valentine, proudly.

"Monsieur de Lorville," aid Madame de Clairange, ill-humoredly. "I'll never console myself for your disdain toward him. It's not my fault; I did everything I could to get you to treat him better, but you never wanted to listen to me; I suppose that it's because of you that he hasn't come to tell Madame de Fontvenel about his marriage."

"Perhaps he isn't entirely decided."

"Yes he is—he talks about it himself as a concluded affair; no one has any doubt about it, and you're the only one not to be convinced. Oh, you can boast of having missed out on a fine destiny there!"

With those words they separated. Valentine, left alone, reflected on Edgar's conduct toward her. Sometimes she hated him, and accused him of the cruelest falsity; sometimes she justified him by the apparent coldness that she had always put into her behavior toward him.

Alas, she said to herself, tearfully, *how could he divine that I loved him? I hid all my emotions from him, I avoided him incessantly, and I responded by laughing and replying with levity to everything affectionate he said to me. Oh, if he knew how I'm suffering now, he'd doubtless feel pity for my dolor. Perhaps he'd even be happy about it?*

That thought plunged her into a chagrin that she had not yet experienced. How she found herself punished, then, for the dissimulation that had made her hide the sentiments that are uniquely capable of reassuring and seducing! How she detested her proud and timid character, which had cost her the love of the only man that she would ever be able to love.

She also imagined the amiable Edgar in the company of his new wife, attentive, witty and emotional, as she had seen him so many times. *He has chosen her out of chagrin*, she thought, *but soon he will love her as tenderly, alas, as he would have loved me!*

To lose happiness by one's own fault is the bitterest of disappointments for individuals possessed of imagination. An event that destiny inflicts upon them, frightful as it might be, seems less dolorous; a desperate misfortune has, by its very excess, something calming about it, but a golden opportunity, lost by their own fault appears to them incessantly, ornamented with the most brilliant images; they resuscitate it continually, in order to lose it again with more bitterness, and recompose their dreams in order to see it vanish again.

Thus Valentine tantalized herself with the image of a future for which she could no longer hope; she recalled to memory the words she should not have spoken, or which must have been misunderstood; the sentiments and the emotions that she repented of not having allowed to be divined—and all her thoughts plunged into the abyss of that futile and despairing labor.

XXII

Valentine spent the entire night sleeplessly, shedding tears of regret, of love, and sometimes of anger. The nest day, she was suffering so much that she wanted to stay in bed later than usual, but she was told that an old monsieur had come to talk about matters of business, but, having learned that she was not yet available had offered to return at midday.

Madame de Champléry got up and went into the drawing room to receive him.

"I beg Madame la Marquise's pardon for disturbing her so early," he said, with a smile, "but it's a matter of urgency, and I'm intent on concluding everything by this evening."

So saying, Monsieur Tomasseau, notary, placed several pieces of paper n the table, while Valentine wondered what the purpose of his visit could be.

"I have called on Madame's notary," Monsieur Tomasseau continued, riffling through his papers. "He told me that the birth certificate that we need is in her home, and I beg you to confide it to me before..."

"Pardon me, Monsieur," Madame de Champléry interrupted, "but I don't understand..."

"Madame can be perfectly tranquil; we have prepared everything to spare her the ennui of these formalities. Women are right to leave that vexation to men. So I only need to tell you what is indispensable. The contract has been drawn up in accordance with what we have agreed. Following the instructions that Madame la Marquise has given, her notary has furnished us with all the necessary documents, including the Marquis' death certificate and the will; nothing is lacking. Since yesterday we have had Monsieur le Duc's consent, but Madame must know that."

"What!" said Valentine. "What consent? What Duc?"

The notary looked at her in astonishment. "Why, that of Monsieur le Duc de Lorville," he replied.

At that name, Valentine shuddered, and repeated, in a troubled voice: "The consent of Monsieur le Duc de Lorville?"

Monsieur Tomasseau, bewildered by Valentine's surprised expression thought that he must have made a mistake.

"Is it not to Madame la Marquise de Champléry that I have the honor of speaking?"

"Yes, Monsieur."

"Is it the case, then," he continued, "that Madame did not know that we have the Duc's consent? Oh, he didn't have to be asked twice, I can assure you, for the young man told one of his friends this morning, in my presence, how happy his father was about the marriage, which had been the object of his desires for a long time."

Valentine thought she was dreaming; without listening to the notary's chatter, she scanned the various documents that were on the table, and her name and that of Edgar struck her eyes continually, as an inconceivable reality.

The notary, tenacious in his duty, interrupted the reverie by reiterating his request and asking Madame de Champléry to let him have her birth certificate. "Unfortunately," he said, "that document is still in Madame's hands; otherwise, I would not have been obliged to disturb her." He added, smiling: "For the young Duc and I agreed to deal with all of this between ourselves."

"It seems to me that that is what has been done," said Valentine.

"Are you lamenting, Madame, the care that has been taken to spare you that annoyance?"

"No, of course not, Monsieur. I'm very grateful for the trouble that you've taken. I thank you for it…but I'd like to know…" She searched for a pretext, to give her time to explain such a singular adventure. "I don't remember exactly where the document you're requesting is. I think I confided it to my stepmother before my departure, and as soon as she returns…"

"I will leave you time to find it, Madame, but I need to have it today, for the signature of the contract is fixed for Thursday, and we only have tomorrow to draft…"

"Already!" exclaimed Valentine, involuntarily.

"What! Madame had forgotten? But Monsieur de Lorville assured me..."

"No, truly," she said, sensing how ridiculous she must seem. "But I've been so troubled lately..."

"That's quite understandable," said the notary, in a grave tone. "One does not decide on such a solemn act without a great deal of emotion."

That reflection made Valentine smile, recalling how little her decision had embarrassed her. Then she became pensive again, and delivered herself to a thousand conjectures to explain the strange situation in which she found herself.

Then Monsieur Tomasseau, perceiving that she was no longer listening to him, rose to his feet, saying: "I shall have the honor of returning tomorrow to seek the indispensable document. However, if Madame finds it sooner, I beg her to give it to Monsieur de Lorville himself, who will be calling here today."

Those last words woke Valentine up again.

"He's coming here today?" she asked, urgently. "You're sure of that? He told you that?"

Then she stopped, thinking how singular that question must seem, and, recalling the strange fashion in which she had received Monsieur Tomasseau, she felt that it was necessary to redouble her politeness toward him, in order to prevent him from taking away too poor an impression of her. She escorted him to the door, addressing a host of obliging remarks to him—but all her cares were futile, and she saw him draw away shaking his head with the notarial scorn that signifies: *That woman has no understanding of business.*

XXIII

Valentine did not have time to deliver herself to her re-flections. The chambermaid ran to say, anxiously: "Come quickly, Madame. Madame your stepmother is ill; she has an attack of nerves. She's desolate; she must have learned of a great misfortune.

Valentine immediately went to Madame de Clairange's apartment, where she did, indeed, find her in despair.

"It's an indignity!" she cried. "She's a monster of in-gratitude! Me, who loves her so much; me who has always had a mother's solicitude for her; me, who preferred her to my own children; me, who would have sacrificed my fortune and my life to spare her a chagrin! To treat me as a stranger! To let me learn of her happiness from an indifferent individual whom I encountered by chance; to prove to me that I count for noth-ing in matters that concern her, and count for nothing in her life! Oh, it's frightful! It's unforgivable!"

All that wrath is directed against me, Valentine thought. *My God! What can I say to justify myself?*

Perceiving her stepdaughter, Madame de Clairange sud-denly struck a dignified pose appropriate to the offense.

"You dare to present yourself before me!" she said. "You don't blush at your falsity? What! When I talked to you yes-terday about Monsieur de Lorville's imminent marriage, you pretended ignorance, and you did not feel able to relieve my regrets by confiding to me that it was you that he had chosen? If it weren't for that notary I met just now as I came seeking news of you, I still wouldn't know. 'I haven't seen Monsieur de Lorville for ages,' you said, 'I don't know what's become of him.' And all your lies were only invented in order to be able to say to society: 'That stepmother who pretends to love her so passionately isn't anxious for her future. She counts for nothing in this fine marriage; she only found out the day be-fore!' Oh, Valentine, I didn't believe that you were so ungrateful, and I thought, at least, by virtue of my care and my tenderness, that I deserved more respect."

Valentine would have liked to be able to respond to these elegies in the form of reproaches, and to calm her stepmother's resentment, to which she was not insensible, but everything that she might attempt to say to justify herself was so improbable, so ridiculous, that she preferred to pass as culpable of a lie than to reveal a truth that she did not understand herself.

How, in fact, could she say that she knew nothing about her marriage, that Monsieur de Lorville had never mentioned the project to her, that she had not been asked to consent to it, and that he had drawn up all these grave documents that were so little conducive to pleasantry without having informed her, without even enquiring as to whether she had any opposition to it? No one would want to believe her, she would seem to be a woman who was being mocked, and Monsieur de Lorville would seem to be a madman. She, who was aware of Edgar's penchant for extraordinary actions, had confidence in him, but how could she share that confidence with anyone else, and attempt to explain an adventure without parallel?

Valentine commenced a whole series of phrases in her defense, but stopped immediately, in the impossibility of pronouncing them, so ridiculous would she have seemed.

Suddenly, the great indignation of her stepmother, the incomprehensible situation, the appearance of the notary—all the morning's events—seemed to her to be so comical that she started laughing in spite of herself, and fled like a child from her stepmother's apartment without having been able to find a single word with which to console her.

On returning to her own apartment, she found her table covered with lace ribbons, jewels, flowers, shawls and all the treasures of a wedding-basket. Having looked at one of the jewel-cases, Valentine recognized the coat of arms of the Duchesse de Lorville, and understood that Edgar had put his mother's diamonds into the basket.

It really is from him, she thought, *and it really is for me! What a strange man!*

At every moment she was interrupted in her reflections by the exclamations of her chambermaid, who could not weary of admiring so many beautiful things.

Thanks to Madame de Clairange's moans and the notary's visit, the entire household was already informed of Valentine's marriage

"How beautiful Madame will be in these diamonds!" cried the worthy girl, who was fond of her young mistress. "How they shine! The beautiful shawls! The pretty bracelets! Oh, my God! How beautiful all of it is, and how well-chosen!"

She suddenly stopped in her admiration on opening one of the boxes that was on the table; she could not suppress a smile, of which she repented immediately, and she could not help murmuring: "For a widow!"

Madame de Champléry, curious to know the cause of that smile, ordered her chambermaid to go away. As soon as she was alone she picked up the box. It appeared to be more elegant than florists' cartons usually are, even those in wedding baskets. She opened it, and blushed like a culpable discovered on seeing what it contained.

It was a marriage bouquet, and the head-dress of orange blossom that only maidens have the right to wear on their wedding day. The flowers were so beautiful, the box lined with white satin was so plush, that it was impossible to believe that it was a mistake—and in any case, Monsieur de Lorville had too much tact and intelligence to be suspected of poor taste on such an occasion. Trembling, Valentine perceived a note among the flowers. It was very brief:

Have I not divined it?

XXIV

Valentine's emotion was so profound on reading those words that tears escaped from her eyes. She sensed her happiness so keenly that she no longer thought of seeking an explanation. In spite of all that was marvelous about it, her excessive joy, the hammering of her heart, the fire that colored her face, the entirely natural emotion, were for her irrefutable proof of a real happiness that she could not doubt. For hearts that feel intensely, everything that moves them is probable; thus it is that they believe in dreams, and weep again on wakening for the friend of whose death they have dreamed.

Lost in the most intoxicating thoughts, Madame de Champléry was recalled to herself by the voice of her chambermaid, who was asking whether she wanted to get dressed, saying that everything was ready for her toilette. Valentine remembered then that Monsieur de Lorville was coming at four o'clock, and hastened to go into her bedroom, in order to get ready to receive him.

That morning, on waking up sad, suffering and discouraged, when Mademoiselle Angelique had come to take her orders, she had told her to bring one of those inconsequential dresses, loose and very quickly fastened, which one chooses for preference on rainy days, or when one has a headache or a chagrin—in sum, when one wants to be at ease in order to endure ennui. Such a costume was not, however, appropriate to the circumstances; Mademoiselle Angelique had sensed that, with the instinct of chambermaids, which is only comparable to that of beavers or elephants. She had divined that the garments readied for despair could not be appropriate to the expectation of such a great joy. Already, an elegant dazzlingly white dress, a brand new canezou from *Chez Mademoiselle Latouche*, a new belt in the very best taste, one of those seductive ribbons that the most economical of women cannot refuse herself, had been silently laid out by Mademoiselle Angelique, without any order from her mistress having evoked them.

Valentine perceived that complete change, and as she no longer had any desire to put on the paltry outfit that she had ordered, she did not have the bad faith to demand it; she was grateful to Mademoiselle Angelique for having spared her the appearance of a caprice—and there was, in any case, something touching in the joyful expression of the worthy girl that pleased Valentine by confirming her own happiness.

The future of that brilliant marriage rendered Mademoiselle Angelique almost as happy, on her own behalf, as her mistress. She rejoiced in the depths of her soul to see her acquire enough fortune no longer to be obliged to spend part of the year in the tedious Auvergne, where she had so often groaned in accompanying her, and imagined in advance the fine role that she was going to play in the château of the Duc de Lorville, fêted, courted and admired by the valet de chambre, the maître-d'hôtel, the huntsman—in sum, all the dignitaries of the antechamber. Thus, in her intoxication, never had she dressed her mistress with so much care and coquetry.

Valentine, charmed by those cares, which she might not have dared take, allowed herself to be ornamented, meekly, for she was so emotional, and her hand was so tremulous, that she could not have attached a single pin without pricking herself.

That small torture terminated, Valentine remained alone—alone with her thought! Oh, how sweet that thought was! Edgar was to arrive shortly; he was waiting for him. A dubious wait is already such an intense pleasure! How intense it is, then, when one is certain that he will come, when he has promised?

Madame de Champléry went into her drawing room. The painting by Smargiassi struck her gaze. She suddenly remembered the address that had come with it, and compared that handwriting with that of the note accompanying the bouquet of orange-blossom. She saw that it was the same, and raised the note to her lips saying: "How he must love me, to divine everything that I think!"

Then, arranging various objects on the shelves of her elegant and modest drawing room, she thought that Monsieur de Lorville had never been there, and wondered how it was that she had never received the man she was going to marry in her own apartment.

Then all the improbability of the situation became manifest to her, and doubt began to torment her—but it soon dissipated. Edgar could not be toying with her, In spite of his eccentricity and his humorous inclinations, his manners did not permit him to be suspected of an offensive stupidity. At twenty-four, Monsieur de Lorville already enjoyed the consideration of a mature man; no one had the idea of treating him lightly; the expression of severity on such a young and gracious face was a remarkable thing; it was a problem marvelously resolved to be imposing at his age, with a fashionable jacket, a waistcoat from Blain's and a cane from Verdier's. Nevertheless, the most distinguished men spoke to him deferentially. Beneath that elegant envelope, they divined a judge, an impartial critic—and impartiality is so imposing!

Time went by, and Madame de Champléry felt her emotions crowding her heart. She shivered at the slightest sound. The idea of seeing him again—the man she loved, the man she had been so afraid of losing, the man who had decided her fate without consulting her—although so sweet, cast an indescribable disturbance into her.

Any other woman in Valentine's place would have been extracted herself from the embarrassment of that first meeting by feigning the chagrin of an astonished petty pride, demanding whether he had the right to dispose thus of her future and her heart before having been authorized to do so by her consent—but Valentine was too honest to complain about a presumption that made her so happy and quibble over a union she desired. In any case, Edgar could not be duped by that finesse; how could Valentine think that she could abuse the man who had penetrated her secret in such an inconceivable fashion?

Four o'clock chimed. Agitated, Valentine felt her thoughts stir and her ideas become confused. Seeking to pull herself together, she picked up a book, and tried to read in order to return to one reality by the imagination of another. She thought she had chosen a collection of poetry, but after reading for a quarter of an hour she discovered that the work she was holding was an essay on the heredity of the peerage. She threw it on to the table immediately because she had just heard a tilbury stop abruptly outside the door.

The ear of a waiting woman recognizes the step of the beloved's horse as easily as the voice that is dear to her, and Valentine, who had lain in wait so many times for Monsieur de Lorville's arrival at her stepmother's house and Madame de Fontvenel's house could not doubt that it was him. Her anxiety redoubled; the emotion of joy has its anguish and its stifling effect, like that of pain.

She heard the door of the antechamber open, and then Edgar's voice, asking whether Madame de Lorville was visible. He corrected himself immediately: "Madame de Champléry, I meant to say." He had intended to ask whether Madame de Champéry was at home, and then give his own name in order to be announced, but in his haste he had confused the question and the response, and Valentine could not help smiling at his mistake.

That smile soothed her. Soon, all the seriousness of her happiness returned. Monsieur de Lorville was announced, and the door closed again behind him.

Oh, who could describe the charm emanating from the entire person of that amiable young man, adorned with the most touching emotion, ennobled by the most generous sentiments?

What a gleam there was in that face, so gracious, sad by dint of happiness, calm by dint of agitation—but inflamed by such a passionate gaze! What sweetness, what dignity in his bearing, what an air of caressant protection, or tender superiority! Whence came so much assurance?

An assurance of love! It came from a conduct pure and devoid of calculation, a devotion of which he was proud. A noble action gives us such aplomb, such authority and such grace.

Valentine had tried to stand up in order to receive Monsieur de Lorville, but she was so tremulous that she was constrained to remain seated on her sofa. Edgar came to sit beside her, and remained still for a few moments, contemplating her silently. Magnetized by that gaze, she raised her eyes; never had she seemed more beautiful than in that instant. Her complexion, dazzling in its freshness, was still animated by so much emotion; her inspired eyes were both soft and shining; there is always so much charm in the joyful face of a woman who was been weeping!

Edgar contemplated her with adoration.

"Valentine!" he cried, in an emotional voice. "How happy I am! You love me!"

At the sound of that dear voice, which she had not heard for such a long time, and which was pronouncing her name for the first time, Valentine's emotion was so sudden that she could not hold back her tears. In order to hide them, she leaned her forehead on Edgar's arm, and he hugged her tenderly to his heart.

Oh, how swiftly that young heart was beating, in which joy was unalloyed: ecstasy, sympathy, enchantment, the unknown delights of dreams.

Such a moment is worth an entire lifetime!

Then they talked about their love, like all those who are in love, like all those who are loved; they talked with confidence, like old friends, like new lovers—which are similar— and Valentine was astonished to find herself so much at ease with Monsieur de Lorville, who frightened her so much; for she was gradually reassured, perhaps in seeing that Edgar's tenderness was even more intense than her own; and then, as even the most fearful souls have experienced, a profound emotion triumphs as promptly over embarrassment as a great peril over timidity.

"What happiness," said Edgar, "to spend our lives to-gether! What a sweet harmony will exist between us, who understand one another so well, who have the same ideas, the same sentiments, the same tastes. I know all that; I know your heart so well. Will you forgive me for having had so much presumption, for having dared to divine my happiness?"

Those words reminded Valentine of all the marvels of Edgar's conduct, and reawakened her curiosity, which such a great emotion had dissipated momentarily.

"It's necessary that I forgive you," she said, "but explain the mystery to me, I implore you."

Edgar smiled, and anted t answer her—but how could he find words to explain the past coldly, when she was there, so beautiful, so close to him! In any case, what man would ever be imprudent enough to distract the woman he loves from his tenderness, by telling her marvelous stories?

Meanwhile, Valentine's eyes were questioning him.

"What does it matter?" he said. "Admit that I'm not mis-taken, that you love me; let me hear it from your mouth, and one day..."

"Oh, tell me," said Valentine, "by what prodigy you di-vine all my thoughts, even the one that I tried to hide. The mystery has something frightening about it, which troubles me. Speak, I beg you; tell the truth, please, or I shall lose my mind."

"I can't; I've promised to keep the secret—but don't you trust me?"

"No," said Valentine, sharply. "For some time your mar-velous penetration has tormented me; there's magic in that penetration, which no one escapes." In a supplicant tone, she added: "Don't laugh at my anxiety. I admit with joy every-thing that you're read in my heart; I love you; I'm happy; I admit it; I repeat it with delight; but in your turn, have pity on my reason—reveal the mystery to me."

Edgar was, so to speak, jealous of his talisman, and the effect that it would produce on Valentine's excited imagination. He tried to distract her curiosity by speaking about the prodigy as an indifferent matter.

"The mystery is much less extraordinary than you imagine. I'll explain it to you soon, and you'll see that it doesn't merit your occupation for such a long time."

Monsieur de Lorville pronounced these words in the soft but definite tone that leaves no hope, and Valentine, who was in one of those dispositions in which the mind, exhausted by the heart, incapable of analysis and contradiction, blindly accepts all beliefs, contented herself with that response, which would not have been sufficient at any other time.

Despairingly, she then questioned Monsieur de Lorville about his pretended marriage to Mademoiselle de Sirieux.

"There had been question of it," he replied, "but my father did not know that I loved you; he was delighted to learn it, and is waiting for us impatiently at Lorville. You know that we're leaving on Saturday, after the mass."

"I don't know anything," replied Valentine, blushing. "It's Saturday, then?"

"Yes, Saturday. We'll arrive at Lorville the same day. Oh, my father will be glad to see you again. He's making a fête of calling you his daughter."

"My poor mother!" exclaimed Valentine, then. "How happy she would be today! How she would have loved you, Edgar!"

And Valentine started weeping again, and Edgar embraced her again, for her tears.

"Dear Valentine," he said, "don't trouble my happiness with such bitter regrets."

"I lost those who loved me so young!" she replied.

"Alas, yes—but remember that I also love you, and am jealous of our memories."

"There is, however, one that I ought to remember on the day of my happiness," said Valentine, blushing. "It is a name that I only ever pronounce with respect, and which I've promised to make you cherish..."

"I've guessed it," Edgar interjected, seeing Valentine's anxiety. "That of Monsieur de Champéry. Oh, believe that no one blesses and reveres his memory more than I do."

"My old friend" cried Valentine, "you were right to count on my gratitude! I know today how much you loved me!" And she resumed weeping for the third time. Poor Valentine had probably not shed as many tears in her entire life as on that single day of happiness!

XXV

Monsieur de Lorville had succeeded in calming Madame de Clairange's despair and indignation by persuading her that she alone, by ingenious insinuations, had convinced Valentine to remarry, and that it was to her maternal skill that they owed all their happiness.

"Society knows that," he had said, to win her over, "and everyone has rendered justice to your zeal, and above all to your expertise, in this entire affair." And he had added, in the false tone that seduces all mediocre women, which he knew to be omnipotent in her regard: "As for me, you cannot doubt my gratitude!"

That ruse of Edgar's had reconciled Valentine with her stepmother, who, never letting an opportunity to shine in a sentimental manner escape her, saw in the ceremony of her marriage a future of appropriate emotions to model, notable attitudes to imitate to her embellishment, and touching sentiments to parody—in sum, a fine role for a mother intent on displaying, before an audience worthy of her, the eminent qualities of her heart.

The insistences of Edgar and Valentine had not been able to prevent her from hastily inviting her relatives, friends and acquaintances for the day of the signature of the contract. It was the day after the next, and it certainly required a great diligence to assemble such a crowd in so short a time. Only vanity is able to deploy such activity.

Valentine reminded her in vain that Monsieur Laréal was not yet better, that he was even worse than on the evening when she had sacrificed everything for him; Madame de Clairange was not listening. What did Monsieur Laréal and his broken leg matter to her now? That misfortune was no use to her, on a day when she could appear sensitive at home, and make an effect without going out of her way.

Monsieur Laréal, his malady and charitable cares were, therefore, set aside that evening. Madame de Champléry was condemned to the torture of seeing her happiness observed, weighed, commented on, and what was worse, disturbed by a hundred people for whom her marriage was of no interest, or were even put out by it.

Edgar tried to console her for that annoyance with the most amiable words; while he was alone with her in the drawing room waiting for her stepmother to get ready and for the guests to arrive, he addressed the most gracious flatteries to her beauty and her adornment, but Valentine did not seem resigned.

"How tedious I'm going to find this evening!" she said. "How am I going to respond to all those compliments that people will believe they're obliged to address to me; how am I going to avoid appearing too embarrassed or ridiculous? When I've looked at my fan two or three times while bowing, I'll no longer know what pose to adopt—that means of maintaining an appearance, already worn out, will no longer serve."

She pointed at Edgar's lorgnon, and added: "If I at least had a lorgnon like that one, I could amuse myself peering this way and that, and I'd feel more assured."

She smiled, and continued: "The habit of employing a lorgnon gives one a malevolent air that takes away the impression of gaucherie, and it's for that reason, I suppose, that you always wear that lorgnon, although you have excellent eyesight."

"Would you like me to lend it to you this evening?" said Edgar. "I was just thinking about offering it to you."

"No, thank you," she said. "I see more clearly with my own eyes."

"You think so?" said Edgar, having difficulty dissimulating a smile. "I affirm to you that if you had this lorgnon to observe everyone, you wouldn't be bored for an instant."

"What!" said Valentine. "Is it so very extraordinary?" Then, suddenly gripped by an idea, she went on: "In fact, now I think about it...Monsieur de Fontvenel and Monsieur

Narvaux have often remarked on that lorgnon as a singularity whose mystery they wanted to penetrate, and which..."

"Really?" Edgar interjected, anxious and becoming serious.

"Yes," said Valentine. "We even formed the project of demanding its sacrifice, and giving you a more attractive one. I don't remember all the details of the plot, I only know that there was one."

"If that's so," said Edgar, somewhat troubled, "it's necessary, in order to thwart their plot, that you should be in mine, and for you to promise me all the discretion that an important secret demands."

"Oh, I swear to you that I'll be discreet," said Valentine, seeing that Monsieur de Lorville was serious.

"I can trust you?" he went on, still hesitant.

"I could take offense at that question, but I'd rather respond simply: yes."

"Well," said Edgar, "now that our interests are the same, it's time to reveal to you a secret that will explain all my conduct."

"Speak," said Valentine, impatiently, already hearing several carriages coming into the courtyard of the hotel, and anticipating that Edgar would not have time to finish his story. "People are coming—speak."

"It's too late to explain the marvel to you," he said. "Try not to let anyone notice it, and above all hide your astonishment when..."

Edgar could not say any more; Madame de Fontvenel was announced, with her son and her daughter, and Valentine hastily hid the lorgnon in her belt, resolving to put it to the test as soon as she could do so without appearing extraordinary.

Knowing that several people were already gathered in her drawing room, Madame de Clairange came down immediately. She was pale, not having applied ant rouge, as she usually did, not out of forgetfulness, because she had decided not to put any on. The sad appearance of a woman evidently emotional seemed indispensable to her that day.

Valentine would have liked to try looking at her through the lorgnon that preoccupied her so intensely, but there were not enough people in the drawing room as yet for any of her movements to pass unperceived. In any case, everyone was talking about her, occupied with her, and when one is the object of everyone's observation oneself, one is poorly placed for observation.

The members of the two families admitted to hear the reading of the contract arrived.

Madame de Montbert, who was coming to Madame de Clairange's house for the first time, was received by her with an urgent politeness difficult to reconcile with the impression of affectionate languor that she had planned for the entire evening.

"I caused you a great deal of trouble the other day, my dear Valentine," Madame de Montbert said to her future niece, "but I didn't do it deliberately, and that's my excuse; in any case, Edgar has been so happy because of the chagrin that I caused you that you'll forgive me, won't you?"

As Valentine was about to reply, Madame de Clairange came to talk to them, and then Madame de Champléry's torture began. The quantity of inappropriate things that her stepmother could say in ten minutes to embarrass her was a veritable problem. Nothing could explain that absolute lack of tact and good taste in a person that no intense sentiment ever carried away, and who had the habit of always choosing the best things so say and do. It was difficult to conceive how, having acquired all the virtues most difficult to put into practice, she had never attained that quality. It is because good taste is, so to speak, the modesty of intelligence: that is why it can be neither imitated nor acquired.

"Are you feeling ill?" Madame de Fontvenel asked Madame de Clairange, who appeared to be expecting the question.

"A day like this is always so difficult for us," she replied, pretending to suppress an emotion that she did not feel. "I can't accustom myself to the idea of separating from Valentine. The first time that I married her I suffered a great deal, but I'm experiencing even more sadness today. Since the death of her husband she had been returned to me, and I hoped to keep her with me for longer."

Valentine, sensing the ridiculousness of recalling her first marriage at that moment, made every effort to interrupt an elegy so awkwardly commenced, but it was not easy to stop Madame de Clarange when she had launched into a sentiment that she thought appropriate, and once the parallel between the two marriages had been established, it was necessary to submit to it until the end.

By virtue of her singular situation, Valentine then experienced all the genres of embarrassment, the trouble of a young woman about to marry and the embarrassment of a widow marrying again. Fortunately, Monsieur de Lorville, whose presence added further to that torment, took pity on her and put an end to the conversation by asking Madame de Clairange whether the notary had arrived.

"He's in there," she said, pointing to the door of the second drawing room. "He's waiting for us."

They went into the next room then, and everyone took their places solemnly to listen to the reading of the contract.

At the moment when the notary began reading, the pompous arrival of a relative interrupted him. It was a newly married woman, dazzling with gold and jewels. Monsieur de Lorville, whom the appearance of the woman in question ought to have troubled in such a circumstance did not recognize her. He could not divine under that cloud of white feathers, those staged blond tresses and heavy adornments the young and beautiful person whose simple costume had once seduced his eyes; in sum, he could not recognize in that grandmotherly costume the sylphide Mademoiselle d'Armilly. It was, however, really her; she had fallen into the common error of newly married women, who, in their haste to wear the adornments forbidden to young maidens, decked themselves out like old women.

Having married a cousin of Madame de Champléry, Mademoiselle d'Armilly had only been invited for the signature of the marriage contract, and it was evident that she had hastened her arrival in order to hear the reading. That curiosity of suspicious relatives did not surprise Monsieur de Lorville at all; no interested sentiment, no narrow calculation could astonish him on the part of that languorous nymph, with whose sordid weaknesses he was familiar. In spite of her dissimulation, Valentine's first rival could not hide, beneath her compliments and her offensive eulogies, the resentment which seemed to threaten the happiness for which she expressed so many good wishes.

Valentine had never liked Mademoiselle d'Armilly, perhaps because Madame Clairange always cited her as the model of young women, exaggerating her sweetness and modesty; thus, by a instinct conservative of her illusions, Valentine, who had not wanted to attempt to test the magic lorgnon on her dear Stéphanie, wondered whether to try it out, without fear, on her new cousin, whose brilliant and showy adornment motivated a particular attention.

The notary continued the reading, and, as everyone was listening attentively to the different clauses of the contract Valentine judged that the moment was favorable. Mademoiselle d'Armilly was paying such great attention to the reading that one could peer at her for a long time without her noticing it.

Suddenly, Valentine saw her start with surprise at a certain article in the contract to which she had not listened herself. She seized the lorgnon and peered through it.

At first, Valentine stood there stupefied, as if frightened by the marvel. Although Monsieur de Lorville had warned her, and she had promised not to give any sign of astonishment, it was impossible to hide her surprise. She suddenly put her hand to her eyes, like someone who believes himself to be dreaming, and everyone, seeing her thus moved, imagined that she was wiping away tears of emotion and gratitude, touched by the sacrifices that Monsieur de Lorville was making in her favor, of which the document had informed her. But Valentine knew nothing of that, and the talisman that Edgar had just entrusted to her occupied her far more than the fortune of which she was assured. She only knew about the clause in the contract by virtue of her cousin's thought.

The latter was saying to herself: *He's giving her five hundred thousand francs! He's very generous. If I'd known that...* Then attaching to her husband a gaze full of tenderness that seemed to say "I love you," she thought: *I wouldn't have been reduced to marrying such an ugly man for so little!*

There was such a comical contrast between that tender gaze and that reflection full of disgust, that, in spite of the solemnity of the moment, Valentine burst out laughing...

A glance from Monsieur de Lorville, recalled her to an appropriate seriousness. Then she tried to recall all of Edgar's conduct, and to explain it by means of the talisman that had been confided to her.

In Valentine's place another woman might have shivered at that discovery, and would have swiftly searched her own memory to see whether, since she had known Monsieur Lorville, she had had any thought that she would have desired to hide from him, but Madame de Champléry, who knew very well how much she had gained by being divined, had nothing to fear from the past.

That's why he loved me, she thought. *This lorgnon seems to have been invented to give value to my character—for me alone, in fact, who has such visible faults and only ever hides my good sentiments.* Then she lost herself in conjectures regarding the history of the marvel, and it was only after a certain time that she felt sufficiently recovered from her trouble to try a second proof.

Madame de Clairange, placed facing her, had lowered her eyes; her head was slightly tilted, her arm was resting limply on the cushion of a sofa, and she seemed determined to remain for some time in that attitude, commanded by melancholy. Valentine took advantage of that moment to aim the lorgnon at her thoughts.

Yes, it's exactly like this, Madame de Clairange was saying to herself, that *Valentine's mother would have been today.*

In the same way, Mademoiselle Mars might have said to herself, while studying a new role: *it's exactly like this that Mademoiselle Contat would have played it.*[26]

In spite of the sad memory that the thought reawakened in Valentine's soul, she smiled at it disdainfully, and in order to distract herself, she fixed her eyes on Madame de Montbert, whose discontent air preoccupied her.

I really don't know what's wrong with Valentine this evening, she was thinking. *She does nothing but laugh in the most inappropriate fashion.*

That lesson recalled Madame de Champléry to herself; she renounced the pleasure of studying her friends in that fashion and immediately became grave and sad, as it was appropriate to be during that solemn reading.

The reading was concluded, however; each of them came in turn to sign the marriage contract, and conversations began. That evening, which she had expected to be so redoubtable, Valentine found very amusing. As soon as she had a moment to herself she began to use the lorgnon, and the interest and pleasure she found in it is comprehensible.

The principal members of the family having signed, Monsieur de Fontvenel's turn came. Valentine noticed that the pen was trembling in his hand, and observed him curiously. His thought moved her profoundly.

Courage, he said to himself. *She has never loved me, and has no idea how I regret it. I ought not to be sad; my friend will be so happy.*

Touched by that noble sentiment, she went to him and extended her hand to him. "You will always be our best friend," she said, in the affectionate tone that heals all wounds.

---

[26] Louise Contat (1760-1813) made her debut at the Comédie-Française at the age of sixteen, and was the star of the Parisian theater in the years before the Revolution, setting the standard to which the actresses of the Empire and the Restoration had to aspire.

Monsieur de Fontvenel kissed the hand gratefully, touched to see that she had understood him. It is so pleasant to be witnessed in a great emotion by the one who has caused it.

After Monsieur de Fontvenel, a young man whom Monsieur de Lorville had just introduced to Valentine approached the table to sign. It was the journalist that Edgar had met in the Rue de Bac, with whom he had formed a close friendship. Madame de Champléry, struck by the young writer's intelligent physiognomy, peered at him through the lorgnon while he signed.

Poor Angeline, he was thinking. *Our marriage is very uncertain.* Then, ceding the pen to someone else, he drew away, saying to himself: *How gracious all these women are! The Duchesse de *** is ravishing. Angeline is pretty, but she doesn't have the bearing, the easy manner of the women of high society. Her letter this morning caused me a great deal of pain; she's weeping night and day, poor child! But no matter, I ought not to write to her any longer; her father opposes the union... it would be lacking in honor. And besides, it's folly at my age to want to marry. In four years, if my great work is successful, I'll be on the Conseil d'Etat, and I'll be able to choose.*

There's a young man who doesn't lack ambition, Valentine thought. *Oh, if he possessed this talisman...*

In the meantime, Edgar took pleasure in contemplating Madame de Champléry's astonishment at each new revelation furnished by the lorgnon, and smiled at all the ruses she employed in order to look without being seen. Nevertheless, he experienced a confused sentiment of chagrin, holding against Valentine the fact that she seemed to have forgotten him, and he wondered why she was not seeking to divine his thoughts.

"Because I know them," she said, passing rapidly before him—and Monsieur de Lorville was shocked in his turn to hear a reply to an idea that he had not expressed.

"A thousand compliments, a thousand compliments, my dear Edgar," exclaimed a voice familiar to Valentine, then. "Receive all my sincere good wishes, oh, very since, have no doubt. It's not Frédéric Narvaux who has ever deceived any-one—his friends, at least; I can't answer for women; I don't want to make myself out to be any better than I am."

"Sincere good wishes are always welcome," replied Monsieur de Lorville, in a sarcastic tone. "Believe that I appreciate them fully, my dear—I owe you more than you suppose."

"You heard that," said Monsieur Narvaux to a young woman with whom he had just arrived. Then he began chatting to her in a confidential manner that excited Valentine's curiosity. She lent an ear, and heard Monsieur Narvaux saying in a low voice:

"But for me this marriage would have failed; Edgar left suddenly, and didn't want to hear talk of it. I ran after him and made him see that things were too far advanced, that he couldn't break it off; I talked to him about poor Madame de Champléry's despair. In the end, I did enough to ensure that he's marrying her today."

Valentine, ignorant of the extent to the extent to which Monsieur Narvaux was skilled in the art of lying, believed, in fact, that someone had calumniated her to Edgar, and that without the talisman, which had permitted him to read her heart, he might perhaps have ceased to love her—so she felt grateful to Monsieur Narvaux for having sought to justify her, and looked at him through the lorgnon, not suspecting that the thought whose envelope was so plain would not gain from being penetrated.

What he was thinking was: *It's not my fault if this marriage is taking place; I've done everything I could to prevent it.*

This time, Valentine was so surprised and alarmed at such an excess of dishonesty that she sought Edgar's eyes, in order to find, in the heart where she was loved, a refuge against such malice. Then, as if fascinated by evil and the curiosity it inspires, she peered at Monsieur Narvaux again.

What's that I see? he thought. *Edgar's lorgnon in the hands of his intended. There's some mystery there. If I could steal that lorgnon from her for a moment...yes, I'd like to know what it could do for me.*

Valentine shivered; she understood then all the danger of such a talisman in the hands of a wicked man, and appreciated more than ever the nobility of Monsieur de Lorville's character, recalling his conduct since he had been in possession of it. Oh, how dear that idea rendered him to her.

Dominated by the sweet sentiments to which that reflection gave rise, Valentine scarcely responded to the compliments and adieux of relatives and friends who were leaving,

When everyone had gone, Edgar asked her the cause of her profound reverie.

"I was thinking about the talisman," she replied, "and the noble usage that you have made of it."

"I was not wrong, then, to make you that confidence," Edgar said.

"On the contrary; how could one not love you more in thinking that that supernatural penetration only served to divine my tenderness and the misfortune of your friend—that with such a redoubtable power, you have only employed it for two generous actions!"

"Since the talisman makes me loved, keep it; I have no more need of it. The thoughts of people indifferent to me are beginning to bore me, and you will tell me yours."

"I accept it," Valentine said, tenderly, "but I'll return it to you if ever you doubt me."

Monsieur and Madame de Lorville are still the possessors of that lorgnon; they hide it carefully from the wicked and the ambitious—a needless prudence, as the talisman would be powerless in their hands. It requires an open mind and a pure heart to judge the world as it is; it is necessary to have nothing to desire to gaze without illusion, and nothing to hide in order to observe without malevolence.

BALZAC'S CANE

Preface

There was once, in this novel...

"But it isn't a novel."

In this work...

"But it isn't a work."

In this book...

"Even less is it a book."

In these pages, then, there was once a rather piquant chapter entitled "The Council of Ministers," but someone said to the author:

"Be careful; there'll be lawsuits; people will be recognized. Don't publish that chapter."

And the author meekly withdrew that chapter. There was another entitled "A Dream of Love." It was a rather tender love scene, as any scene of passion in a novel ought to be. But someone said to the author:

"It's not appropriate for you to publish a book in which passion plays such a large role; that chapter isn't necessary. Take it out."

And the author timidly removed that second chapter.

There were also two pieces of verse in these pages. One was a satire, the other an elegy. The satire was thought to be too mordant, the elegy too sad and intimate.

The author has sacrificed them, but it remains evident that a woman who lives in the world ought not to write, since she will only be permitted to publish a book if it is perfectly insignificant.

Fortunately, this one contains a letter from Monsieur Chateaubriand, a note from Béranger and verses by Lamartine; it has for its patron Monsieur Balzac. All of that can surely serve as *justificatory documentation*.

1836.

I. A Fatal Gift

It is a misfortune of which no one complains, a danger that no one dreads, a scourge that no one avoids. The scourge, it is true, is only contagious in one fashion, by heredity—and even then its succession is not at all certain—but even so, it is a scourge, a fatality that always pursues you, throughout your life, an obstacle to everything. It is not an obstacle that you encounter, but much more than that; it is an obstacle that you carry with you, a ridiculous slice of luck that simpletons envy you; a favor of the gods that makes you a pariah among men; or, to put it more simply, a gift of nature that makes you a fool in society.

In sum, that misfortune, that danger, that scourge, that obstacle, that source of ridicule is...I'll wager that you won't guess, and yet, when you know what it is, you'll say: "That's true." When the inconveniences of the advantage have been demonstrated to you, you'll say: "I don't envy it anymore." That misfortune, then, is male beauty.

Take note here of a difference in gender. We say "the good fortune of being *belle*" but "the misfortune of being *beau*." We shall demonstrate the difference shortly.

Someone said somewhere: What is the disagreeable thing that everyone desires? That someone replied to himself: old age. We are saying: What is the scourge that everyone envies, and we are replying to ourselves: male beauty. But by beauty we mean veritable beauty, perfect beauty, ancient beauty, fatal beauty. What is generally known as a handsome man is not a beautiful man. The former escapes the fatality; he has a thousand conditions of happiness. Firstly, he is almost always stupid and smug; secondly, estates have been created expressly for his handsomeness. Being a handsome man is a métier.

The handsome man, properly speaking, can perhaps be happy as a hunter, with a green uniform and a feather in his cap. He can perhaps be happy as a master of arms, and find a thousand ineffable enjoyments of pride in his poses. He might be happy as a hairdresser. He might be happy as a drum major—oh, then he is very happy! He might also be happy as a general of the Empire at the Franconi theater,[27] and play King Joachim Murat delightfully. He might, finally, he happy as a model in the most famous studios, playing his part in the successes that our great masters owe to him, legitimating, so to speak, the gifts he has received from nature by consecrating them to the fine arts.

The handsome man can tolerate life; the handsome man can dream of happiness.

But the beautiful man, the Antinous, the Greek Amour, the ideal man, the man with the pure face, with correct lines and an antique profile, the young and perfectly beautiful man, angelically beautiful, fatally beautiful, must drag out a miserable existence on earth among the prudent fathers and the fearful husbands who proscribe him, and—which is more terrible still—the noble and aged Englishwomen who run after him.

For it is an incontestable and unfortunate verity that a beautiful young man is not always seductive, but is always compromising.

Perhaps, in a country less civilized than ours, beauty is a power; but here, in Paris, where advantages are conventional, real beauty is unappreciated; it is not in harmony with our customs; it is a splendor that has too great an effect, an advantage that causes too much embarrassment; beautiful men have gone out of fashion with historical tableaux.

Nowadays, our apartments only admit paintings that fit on an easel. Nowadays, our women only dream of the love of pages, and politeness has stolen a march on beauty.

---

[27] Antonio Franconi (1738-1836), the founder of the equestrian theater named the Cirque Olympique, had retired by 1831 and the original Cirque Olympique had closed in 1816, but his sons and grandsons followed the family tradition of staging spectacular military plays, invariably featuring dashing cavaliers.

Woe betide, therefore, the beautiful man!

Now, there was once an exceedingly beautiful young man who was sad. He was not at all proud of his beauty, and, unfortunately, he had intelligence enough to sense all its danger. He knew the world; he had judged it wisely, and he experienced what every man experiences who knows the world: a bitter disgust and a profound discouragement. In maturity, that is known as repose, a return to port, a mild philosophy, but at twenty years of age, when life is beginning, to know where one is going is terrible.

What does it matter to a traveler who is reaching the end of his journey if he is robbed at the moment of arrival? What does it cost him? His baggage was useless, his purse exhausted, his cloak ragged, his provisions had run out. The loss is slight; he laughs at it. In any case, he is expected at home and the voyage is over. But woe betide the man who is robbed in the middle of his journey, who finds himself obliged to continue his journey devoid of help, with no cloak, no staff and no money! Oh, that man is miserable; he is discouraged; he stops; he forgets the goal of his journey, and if Providence does not come to his aid, he will allow himself to die of hunger in a ditch beside the road.

There are young men of twenty who have gout; there are others who have experience; the latter are the more unfortunate.

How, then, had that young man come by that elevation of thought, that sadness of mind? All of it stemmed from his beauty.

Intelligence coming from beauty! Oh, that's new!

It's true, though. Everything that isolates us magnifies us; sublime beauty is a superiority like any other, and every superiority is a exile.

I'll tell you this: that poor young man found himself isolated because he was too beautiful; he felt sad because he was isolated; and by degrees, he became an intelligent and distinguished man because he had been sad and misunderstood. Dolor is the culture of the soul, it is what fertilizes it; a heart irrigated by tears is fecund. A generous chagrin is omnipotent; it gives genius to patience, courage to weakness, and reason to youth; it can also give, in its munificence, intelligence to a beautiful man.

II. The First Obstacle

There is another misfortune that no one talks about, but which nevertheless does harm in the world, and that is to be saddled for life with a pretentious baptismal name.

The poor young man had that source of ridicule too. His name was Tancrède![28]

His father, a brave officer on half-pay and a Voltairean of the first rank, had given him that name in honor of his God, and that man's sole regret was that he did not have a daughter to call Aménaïde.

Tancrède Dorimont bore simultaneously a name of tragedy and an old name of comedy, and furthermore, was made like the hero of a romance![29]

Recommend to a banker, a notary, or the chief bureaucrat of some Ministry or other, a gentleman named Tancrède Dorimont, who is as handsome as an angel? I ask you, is that reasonable?

---

[28] *Tancrède* (1702) is the title of an operatic tragedy by André Campra, with a libretto by Antoine Danchet, based on an episode in Tommaso Tasso's *Gerusalemme liberata* (1581), which was further adapted as a play by Voltaire in 1760. The latter, in its turn, formed the basis of Rossini's opera *Tancredi* (1813). *Gerusalemme liberata* was a standard text in French schools through the 19th century, which helped to maintain the appeal of all three works. The author undoubtedly has the 1760 play in mind; it introduced the name Aménaïde, cited in the next paragraph along with Voltaire, as that of the hero's inamorata.

[29] There is more than one character named Dorimont featured in French theater of the period, but the character the author has in mind is probably the one in Emmanuel Dupaty's 1806 comedy·*La Jeune mère ou Les Acteurs de société*.

"We can't do anything with that self-infatuated fop," those honest men would say—for prejudices against beauty and intelligence are as strong now as prejudices against nobility, and a man of intelligence finds himself forced nowadays to take as much trouble to hide his advantages as he would once have taken to show them off.

If Tancrède had had a fortune he would not have perceived his misfortune. Everything is permitted to a rich man. Except for being rich, he is forgiven for everything. But for someone who has to make his own fortune, certain sources of ridicule are misfortunes.

How can an unsavory, ugly individual who is bald, with tinted spectacles and black teeth be persuaded that a young man as beautiful as Apollo, whose name is Tancrède, is not a fop, an impertinent fellow, a bit of a devil, a dandy and an idler? And how, then, can one make one's fortune when one is as beautiful as Apollo and has to deal, all the time, with unsavory, ugly men who are bald, with tinted spectacles and black teeth, and, what is more, all kinds of prejudices against you?

When he arrived in Paris, Tancrède had gone in person to Monsieur Nantua's in order to hand in a letter of recommendation to the rich banker in question, which someone had given to him. He had added to that letter a visiting card bearing his address. The following day, Monsieur Nantua had written him a very amiable note with his own hand, in which he invited him to call on him in the course of the day. The most obliging offers of service made that note a pledge of honor; to be protected by Monsieur Nantua was already an honor.

All was going well. Radiant with hope, Tancrède had a bath, had his hair cut, put on his best suit and headed for the dwelling of the man he was already calling his benefactor. The imprudent fellow was counting on his beautiful face to capture the benevolence of the banker, not because it was beautiful but because it was reminiscent of the charming face of his mother, and Tancrède knew that that resemblance would not be indifferent to Monsieur Nantua, an old admirer of Madame Dorimont.

Monsieur Nantua had just received some very important news that had disrupted all his plans when Tancrède came in, but Monsieur Nantua, like all men who engage in important affairs, did not like to seem busy.

It is a remarkable thing that futile people, who are only involved in miserable, petty affairs, have the pretention of never having a moment to themselves; they are buried by enormous stacks of paper, they cannot sleep, they eat on the run, they kiss their wives while putting on their gloves and only trim their beards once a week; in brief, they exhaust themselves in appearing to be occupied, in order to give themselves credit.

Very busy men, on the contrary, have the pretention of always being free; they behave like idle aristocrats; they pose as little Caesars dictating several letters at the same time in a nonchalant and distracted fashion, while taking a cup of tea or chocolate. Their mania is having no idea how they came to be millionaires.

We are not talking about those whose activity is indefatigable, who undertake more projects than they can possibly handle. Those men do not even have the time to have pretentions.

The man with whom we are concerned was one of those who does not want to appear busy. He was searching with a great deal of attention for a piece of a paper—a note, a report, what do I know?—riffling anxious through the documents in a file, but he did not want to appear to be attaching too much importance to that search. Nor did he want to be interrupted for a moment. All that was difficult, and this was the consequence:

His eyes were avidly pursuing, through all those various pieces of a paper, the name, the date or the figure that he wanted to find, while his semi-attentive ear strove to follow the conversation.

Monsieur Dorimont was announced.

"Show him in."

"You're punctual," said the banker to the young man, without raising his head. "Very good—that's a good sign. I said eleven o'clock; eleven has just chimed, and here you are. That's good; I like precision. In business, precision is a virtue."

"I wouldn't have pardoned myself for making a man whose moments must be precious wait for a minute," replied the naïve Tancrède, who thought he was saying something agreeable. Not at all: it was a blunder twice over, firstly in supposing that the millionaire would have deigned to wait, and secondly in suggesting to Monsieur Nantua that he thought he was always busy.

"In truth, my moments are no more precious than yours. I'm never doing anything. But warm yourself, I beg you. I'll be with you in an instant."

Tancrède went to the fireplace and remained silent.

"Is Madame your mother still in Blois?" asked Monsieur Nantua, still reading his papers.

"Yes, Monsieur."

"Do you know English?"

"Yes, Monsieur."

"She hasn't remarried? A widow at twenty-six!"

"No, Monsieur."

"And German? Do you know a little German?"

"Yes, Monsieur. I know a little Spanish too; I speak it well enough to travel agreeably in Spain," said the wily young man, who was aware of the extent to which money men have abused the peninsula.

"Oh, you know Spanish too? How knowledgeable you are! You haven't been brought up in Paris?"

Tancrède could not help smiling at the naivety of that epigram. "No, Monsieur," he said. "I was brought up in Geneva. I've only been at the Collège Henri IV for two years."

"How old are you?"

"Twenty-one."

178

The banker looked up at those words, and darted a rapid glance at Tancrède, but Tancrède had his head turned at that moment, and his face was not visible.

"You're tall for your age," said Monsieur Nantua, laughing. Then he thought: *The young man has a very distinguished appearance; I like him. Besides which, I'd like to oblige his mother...oh, the lovely woman...if I'd been rich in those days...!*

"Well, it's agreed," he said. "Tomorrow you'll come here as a member of the household. You know Spanish? That's good—very good; I believe I can use you. That's very good..." He suddenly interrupted himself, and cried: "Ah!" Then he fell silent, and started running an anxious eye over the piece of paper he had just found.

In the meantime, the young man said to himself: *I'm astonished that Monsieur Nantua, such a great admirer of my mother, hasn't been struck by my resemblance to her.*

In the modesty of his attitude, Tancrède had not perceived that the banker had not yet looked at him.

Finally, Monsieur Nantua stood up. His face was radiant; he had found the information he wanted, and everything whose accomplishment he was meditating would become possible with that document.

Hope produces benevolence and generosity in noble natures; it is only envious and mediocre hearts that tighten and close up at the approach of good fortune.

Monsieur Nantua, suddenly rediscovering the chance of executing an important project that the sudden emergence of an obstacle had momentarily disrupted, felt that he was in one of those benevolent states of mind in which one likes to do good, not for the pleasure of doing good in itself, but in order to share with someone else the joy that one is feeling. It is not a happy man that one desires, but a mind excited to contentment in order that its disposition might harmonize with ours. It is a guest that we are inviting to a banquet offered to us, whom we are intoxicating in order that he might share our pleasure and that the meal might be more joyful.

"My word, you're in luck," said Monsieur Nantua, approaching the fireplace, "For here's the very affair..."

Monsieur Nantua suddenly interrupted himself; his gaze remained fixed, as if by enchantment, on Tancrède's face. For a few moments, the banker remained silent; immobile, he contemplated his young protégé.

That's the resemblance having its effect, Tancrède thought. *That's good; if the man takes me under his wing, I'm saved. How he's looking at me!*

Monsieur Nantua was still examining Tancrède, and a thousand diverse thoughts were passing through his mind.

To begin with, the appearance of the beautiful young man charmed him like the appearance of a beautiful painting: that perfect beauty, in the full flush of youth, had something delightful about it, which flattered the gaze. Then again, there was such a striking resemblance to a lovely woman that he had been afraid to love. All those impressions spoke in Tancrède's favor at first; noble and powerful nature had its rights, momentarily—but then came the reaction of society, and mundane considerations had their turn.

Damn! thought Monsieur Nantua. *I don't want an Adonis like that in my house. If my daughter, who is already so romantic, saw him...! Oh, good God, that's all I need. He's as poor as a church mouse—he's not the son-in-law I need...not to mention that these good-looking fellows are always stupid and idle.*

"I'm amazed," he said, in order to explain his long silence. "I can't weary of looking at you, so striking is the resemblance to your mother."

"People often tell me that," Tancrède replied—and he suddenly felt sad. His confidence vanished, but he could not tell what it was that had driven it away.

The fact is that Monsieur Nantua had not put into the pronunciation of those words the inflection that he ought to have put into them. His accent was cold, his manner embarrassed; in sum, everything about him betrayed the sudden change that had occurred in his plans with regard to his protégé.

"Half past eleven already!" exclaimed Monsieur Nantua, looking at the clock.

"I'll leave you," said Tancrède, immediately heading for the door. Then he stopped, not daring to say: *I shall have the honor of taking your orders tomorrow.*

Monsieur Nantua divined his thought. "Until tomorrow, at ten o'clock," he said—but he said it strangely; it sounded like a lie.

Tancrède went away discouraged. Why? He did not know; but he had a presentiment, divining that the protection of the rich banker was no longer acquired, that he was not going to be a member of the household, and that it would be necessary, in spite of his benevolence, to turn his sights in another direction.

And that evening, Tancrède received an infinitely polite and gracious letter from Monsieur Nantua, in which Monsieur Nantua expressed his regret at not being able, for reasons independent of his will, to give Monsieur Dorimont the employment that he had initially promised him, adding, nevertheless, that in the desire to be useful to him, he had recommended him to one of his friends, who would do for him all that he had desired to do.

The next day, Tancrède was introduced into the home of that friend, Monsieur Poirceau, the director of a new fire insurance company.

III. The Second Obstacle

"Monsieur Poirceau?"

"That's here; please take the trouble to come in."

The trouble! I swear to you that that really was the word, for, in order to get to that door, it was necessary to lay veritable siege to it.

The head of the staircase, vulgarly known as the landing, was barricaded with benches placed here and there in all directions, completely blocking the way.

After a great deal of difficulty, Tancrède succeeded in reaching the antechamber; there it was necessary to stop again.

An enormous rolled-up carpet obstructed the passage; behind that carpet was the large dining-room table, crenellated with all its chairs, forming a graceful edifice; then, to either side of it, more benches, then a step, a sideboard covered in porcelain, then rosewood flower-stands awaiting flowers, then candelabras awaiting candles, then a marble table-top, then straw mats, spades, tongs, stools, footstools and a so-called Levantine coffee-pot.

Tancrède traversed that chaos without misfortune, and reached the dining room.

Further difficulties: in the dining room, the furniture—bracket-tables, sofas, settees, armchairs, wing-chairs, divans—was in competition; and then came the precious objects: the clock with its incessantly threatened glass; flower vases so beautiful that one dared not put flowers in them; the bust of an uncle, a general; a sewing-table cluttered with embroideries; and then the piano. All these things being contained with difficulty in the dining room, the disorder was at its maximum.

Tancrède thought that he was moving over the debris of the world like another Attila. Having never been in an administration of this sort, he imagined that all these items of furniture had been saved from a fire the day before, and had been deposited here until their owner could find another dwelling.

He got his bearings, climbed over a row of chairs, and went around an enormous sofa as one goes around a mountain, encountering many things on the way, but he did not see anyone.

"Monsieur Poirceau?" he asked, for a second time.

"This way! Over here!" cried a distant voice.

Tancrède still could not see anyone.

He succeeded in reaching the drawing room door.

In the drawing room, where the bedroom furniture was on display, he was glad to feel more at ease—but there again, he could not see anyone.

As Tancrède headed for the bedroom door, the same voice said: "Why, Caroline hasn't taken the dust-sheets."

At the same moment a large package, thrown by an invisible hand, came to strike Tancrède in the face, and he was immediately stifled, lost, buried under a deluge of skirts of all colors and all sizes, from which he had all the trouble in the world disentangling himself. Some had a thousand little strings that hooked on to the buttons of his coat, others had little sleeves in which his arms got lost, all of it lavishly powdered with dust. It was an embarrassment such as he had never encountered.

After emerging from all that, Tancrède found himself face to face with a great simpleton of a domestic armed with a broom and a feather-duster. The latter was momentarily disconcerted.

"Pardon me, Monsieur; I thought it was the upholsterer's boy come to dismantle the beds and I was amusing myself, for a laugh. If I'd known..."

"Monsieur Poirceau?" asked Tancrède, interrupting the excuses. Then, seeing that the room was completely unfurnished, he added: "But I fear that I'm disturbing him in the middle of moving house."

"We're not moving house," the domestic replied. "As long as the Company stays here, we'll live here. I see that Monsieur finds the apartment a trifle topsy-turvy; that's because of the ball, and that accursed boy, who hasn't come..."

"A ball, this evening? I'll come back another time."

"Oh, it isn't the first ball we've given here. Monsieur can receive Monsieur; if Monsieur cares to go into Monsieur's study, I'll go inform Monsieur."

There are few nuances in the domestic population of Paris. Either they are insolent individuals who scarcely reply *yes* or *no* to you, or they are friends full of confidence, who bring you up to date with all the affairs of the household since day one.

Monsieur Poirceau received Tancrède cordially. "Monsieur Nantua is very interested in you," he said. "He recommended you very warmly." As he said that, Monsieur Poirceau examined Tancrède from head to toe, seemingly dazzled by admiration. "Have you been in Paris for long?" he added.

"Two days."

"Is it the first time that you've come?"

"No, Monsieur, I began my studies at the Collège Henri IV, and only left Paris five years ago."

"You stayed in the provinces?"

"At Geneva, at the home of one of my uncles, Monsieur Loindet."

"Monsieur Loindet is your uncle? I know him well. He had a very beautiful sister; might she be your mother?"

"Yes, Monsieur."

"Ah, of course—I can see the resemblance. I was just saying to myself: that face isn't unknown to me."

Good, Tancrède thought. *My face is having its effect again.*

Monsieur Poirceau continued: "I knew your mother when she was young. She was so beautiful. Oh, everyone admired her! And so intelligent, sensible and reasonable! She's a woman of merit. Where is she now?"

Tancrède replied to all the questions that Monsieur Poirceau asked him about his mother, and rejoiced in the benevolence and affection that his new benefactor manifested for her.

"The beautiful Amélie! She won't remember me—but no matter! I'm glad to be able to be useful to her. Her son is no stranger to me. I hope that we can reach an understanding. But before anything else, I want to introduce you to my wife. We're hosting a little ball this evening; we need dancers, and I couldn't bring her a more handsome cavalier!"

Tancrède dissolved in polite expressions of gratitude.

"That's settled," continued Monsieur Poirceau. "Come along this evening, and tomorrow we'll talk business. I have what you need. Until this evening! If you write to your mother, mention her old admirer Poirceau!"

Tancrède withdrew.

I hope my wife will be content, Monsieur Poirceau thought. *She's so keen on her dancers looking good. A handsome lad! I'll wager that one won't find a better-looking young man at all the balls in Paris. It's his mother; he's exactly like his mother! The boy pleases me. I'll be glad to have him with me. He must be a worthy young man, and Nantua appears to think highly of him.*

With that, the director of the fire insurance company went back to his apartment.

Tancrède returned to his lodgings, delighted by the welcome he had received.

In truth, I'm lucky. Everyone wishes me well. There's the banker who recommended me, the director of the Premium Insurance Company Against Fire—a little long-winded, that— who is taking me under his wing; I'm making progress. I like that old gentleman: he's frank, cheerful, and he hosts balls. I like that.

And Tancrède sat down to write a letter to his mother, in order to make her party to his hopes.

That evening, he went to the ball.

What a difference! He no longer recognized the house.

Where's the door? It seems to me that I came in here this morning.

No door! It had been replaced by a large mirror. There were flower-stands and carpets in the corridor. Tancrède could not understand how it had been possible to produce so many rapid improvements between morning and evening.

As he made his entrance, Monsieur Poirceau came to take his arm. Tancrède did not know why that person had come to meet him; he no longer recognized Monsieur Poirceau.

The gentleman had also been subjected to a few embellishments. He was no longer the cheerful, friendly individual that he had seen in the morning, entirely at home in his silk bonnet, dressing-gown and embroidered slippers; he was a busy host, lost in a cravat, sad in a formal suit, inhibited in a drawing room, tormented by a thousand trivia—but still good and benevolent.

"Madame Poirceau is over there; I'll introduce you to her."

Tancrède advanced toward the mistress of the house.

The introduction was effected in silence.

Madame Poirceau scarcely cast a glance over the good-looking dancer about whom she had been told so much, preoccupied as she was by the arrival of a stout German woman covered in jewels and flowers, who seemed to be an important individual.

Monsieur Poirceau was discontented by the slight effect that his protégé had had on his wife.

"Come on," he said. "I'll introduce you to my niece."

Monsieur Poirceau's niece was a pretty young woman who, by virtue of one of those hazards that one finds in works of fiction, Tancrède had already met in Geneva. Recognition followed; Madame Thélissier greeted Monsieur Dorimont very graciously. She was engaged for several waltzes and quadrilles, but she found a means of muddling up her engagements so effectively that she was free, and was able to waltz legitimately with him—which very rapidly attracted the attention of all the women to our Apollo.

"Who is that dancing with Madame Thélissier?"

"Do you know that man who is dancing with Monsieur Poirceau's niece?"

"Go ask Madame Poirceau the name of the gentleman dancing with Malvina."

"Monsieur Bénard," said one old lady, "try to find out who that gentleman is who is dancing with Madame Thélissier."

"No one knows him—he's a savage."

"I rather think he's an Englishman."

Then, in the next room, a young woman who painted in oils exclaimed: "What an admirable head! What lines! It's Endymion!" And her gaze attached itself joyfully to the beautiful stranger.

Painting is an emancipation for young women. It gives them the right to look young men in the face, and in detail; admiration purifies everything. If I had a daughter, she would paint landscapes.

Further away, a group of old women expressed themselves thus:

"It's a misfortune to be as beautiful as that."

"I'll wager that he's stupid enough to eat hay."

"Oh, there you go with your prejudices," said one elegant lady of the Empire. "In my day, the men were very handsome, and I can assure you that they had intelligence."

"You mean that one found it in them."

"There's Madame Poirceau—quickly, ask her the name of our Adonis."

Madame Poirceau did not know who they were talking about; she had not looked at Tancrède and had not been listening when her husband told her his name.

"What! You don't know that you have such a marvel in your home? Look over there—the handsome waltzer with your niece. No one's talking about anyone but him; he's making an event of your ball—which is, by the way, quite charming."

Madame Poiceau then repented of having paid so little attention to an individual who was giving her soirée so much glamour. She went over to her niece and took the opportunity to say a few obliging words to Monsieur Dorimont. In his turn, Tancrède seized the opportunity to ask Madame Poirceau to grant him a quadrille, and the sixth was promised to him as a favor.

Madame Poirceau was at an age when one still dances, for a woman's life is divided up as follows:

The age at which one dances, but dares not waltz: that is the spring.

The age at which one still dances, and when one waltzes: that is the summer.

The age at which one still dances, but prefers waltzes: that is the autumn

And finally, the age at which one no longer dances: that is the winter...the ever-rigorous winter of life!

Madame Poirceau was beautiful, in accordance with the principles of art, ugly in accordance with the rules of amour: beautiful in that her features manifested a perfect regularity, ugly in that they lacked harmony. She had one of those faces that is superb in description, but not at all to behold: the passport beauty that seduces the vulgar, with large eyes, an aquiline nose, a small mouth, a high forehead, an oval face and a round chin. In order to make herself loved via an ambassador, like a princess, Madame Poirceau could have sent her description, but not her portrait.

No matter: she is what is called a beautiful woman, a perfect doll with invisible springs, an impassive face of wax, invulnerable, never unkempt and never undressed; always adorned, tightened, pinched and corseted, with not a hair out of place or a ribbon astray. Madame Poiceau never sits on a chair; she seems ornamented in her dressing gown, armored in casual clothing, fully armed in her ball-grown.

She follows all the fashions, not with taste or pleasure, but conscientiously. Her hairdresser is the finest hairdresser in Paris—Charpentier, I believe—and whatever coiffure it pleases Charpentier to contrive for her, she respects, and is careful not to allow anyone to touch it. The coiffure is disadvantageous to her? No matter; that is not her concern. That garland is heavy? No matter; she is not responsible for it. A pin is sticking into her flesh? No matter; she allows it to remain, for fear of deranging the coiffure.

She has the same respect for her couturier. As I have said, Madame Poirceau follows all the laws of fashion blindly, the laws of society scrupulously, the laws of nature reasonably. She is severe, but not malevolent; she only smiles on days when she is giving a ball; she says, with a pedantic expression, that women ought not to occupy themselves with literature; she talks about household matters like a professor; she has a slow wit, and regards as indecent any joke that she does not understand.

Her presence casts a chill wherever she goes; her arrival has the effect of a door opening in a box at the theater. When she has to spend the evening at a friend's soirée, that friends warns her regulars; they do not come that evening. Men fear her as they fear tedium; women call her "the beautiful Madame Poirceau." She adds value to the ugliest, and yet she is rarely invited anywhere—not that she is importunate; she never occupies herself with the affairs of others; she is discreet and immobile. She is a statue, but a statue to which it is necessary to be polite, which is annoying.

Well, for women like that have the same follies as others would be revolting!

Madame Poirceau was only struck by Tancrède's beauty as the lady of the house. Such a beautiful young man had no dangers for her; in her position, Madame Poirceau would never have permitted herself to fall in love with such a remarkable man. Hide an intrigue with a hero like that, then! Prudes know how to impose great privations on themselves; in that they have more merit than virtuous women; at least they have virtue in their favor, the others do not even have love.

Madame Poirceau only paid tribute to Tancrède; she had found the man she needed a long time ago, and she left it at that.

Now this is the man she had chosen.

He was a man of about thirty-five, about four feet eight inches tall, an employee in the Registry Office. An honorable

189

position in the world, a comfortable fortune, success in several genres: none of that had been able to console him for the misfortune of being short. Since the age when he had admitted that he would not grow any taller, the man had been unhappy.

Everything that can be imagined for raising himself up in the sight of others he had employed: he wore a top hat, boots with high heels, and held himself as upright as a giraffe; he continually raised himself up on tiptoe, like a man who wants to see a cortege passing by. The idea of growing preoccupied him incessantly; he would have given half his fortune and several years of his life to be an ordinary man, to reach five feet two inches.

Small men who resign themselves to it sometimes have a good deal of grace; they have all the advantages of their height then: suppleness, agility and lightness; they can we what called "genteel." But little men who revolt against the mean fashion in which nature has treated them, who struggle madly against her, can never be genteel; they are ridiculous, ever ridiculous, like all pretentions afflicted with incapacity. Furthermore, they are ill-natured, malevolent, denigratory and envious.

When one speaks of a man one finds displeasing, one says that he seems content with himself; well, I say, personally, that I know something more displeasing still, and that is a man who is discontented with himself.

The latter will never forgive you for anything; you can never appease him; flatteries irritate him; politeness seems to him to be pity, a kindness a charity. He is despairingly humble, susceptible of getting on one's nerves; one does not know what to say to him. If you ask him to dinner, he replies: "Thank you, no; I must be honest; I'm too surly to be a guest." If you invite him to come to listen to poetry or music, he said: "No thank you, I'm too obscure a being to be part of such a brilliant company." If you propose a trip to the country to him, he replies: "No thank you, gaiety is required for those kinds of pleasures; invite amiable people, they're better than I am for that." The man in question does not enjoy anything; he is eaten away by modesty, but a frightful modesty, a hostile humility that puts everyone on their guard: an imaginary leprosy that causes his fellows to flee.

Fortunately, the malady is very rare in our country, and we only mention it in order to observe its existence.

Our monsieur was one of those individuals, not because he believed himself to be devoid of merit, but because he felt small, and incessantly said to himself that the older he grew, the stouter he would get, and the smaller he would seem.

For him, everything was embarrassment and suffering. That little body contained a big heart full of hatred: a hatred of Herculean proportions, always vivacious, ever renewed, universal and yet partial, for if he detested people in general, there were some he abhorred in particular:

Firstly, anyone of tall stature; he regarded anyone of that sort as an enemy, as a thief who had stolen six inches from him. A tall stature seemed to him to be a spoliation, for which he had a right to take vengeance;

Secondly, any schoolboy who surpassed him by a fraction of an inch and was not thought to be too tall for his age;

Thirdly, any child he saw growing, and who threatened to catch him up.

He avoided very tall men, because in their vicinity he seemed even more minimal. He also avoided beautiful women, because of their humiliating majesty. But what he detested most in all the world, was to encounter—which was very rare—a man of his own height!

Oh, then he suffered martyrdom, he felt matched; it was frightful. His ridicule was attached to that of another, and completed; he could not abide it. What did he do in such circumstances? He took his hat, put it on his head, and left.

Well, all of that was nothing; there was one torment more horrible than all those torments, one malediction that still pursued that man, a fatality that put the seal on his misery, and that was his name. Oh, that name was an exceedingly cruel hazard in his position. What a bitter irony! What a trick of

191

fate! What an epigram of nature! What a practical joke of destiny!

That little man was named Monsieur Legrand.

Monsieur Legrand arrived at Madame Poirceau's house at a quarter to midnight, as a true friend of the household. He was even surlier than usual. He did not like balls or ostentatious soirées, because on such occasions he had to forsake his high-heeled boots, and in varnished shoes he lost the best part of two inches.

"Always elegant," one mother, whose daughter was dancing, said to him. Everyone knows that those poor mothers, constrained to sit in the sidelines throughout the soirée, are avid for conversation. Anyone traversing the dance floor is quickly seized in passing, caught on the wing—they are so bored!

"How late you are!" this one remarked.

Monsieur Legrand did not reply. Two men standing in front of him were completely blocking his view of the ball. He was furious; he felt so small, so sadly lost in the crowd.

"You've just arrived?" continued the mother in the turban. "You haven't yet seen the phoenix that everyone is talking about?"

Then, having set up the joke, she added: "We already have the Phoenix Company; now we have the phoenix of the company."

Monsieur Legrand did not like wordplay. "I have no idea what phoenix you're referring to, Madame," he replied, coldly.

"The Apollo, the Céladon, the Adonis, the darling of all these ladies."

"I don't know what you mean with your Apollo, your Céladon, your Adonis and your darling, Madame."

The mother in the turban was wounded by the affectation that Monsieur Legrand put into repeating her words, and to avenge herself, said: "I thought you knew him, since he's *also* a member of the household."

That *also* was crushing. Monsieur Legrand went red.

"There he is," the malevolent individual went on. "What beautiful eyes! What a noble air! Do you see him?"

Monsieur Legrand could not see anything; he still had a gentleman in front of him who was hiding the entire ball. Finally, he rebelled, cut through the crowd and, insinuating himself hither and yon, eventually reached the mistress of the house.

Tancrède approached her at the same moment. Monsieur Legrand perceived him. He was petrified. Streams of bile ran through all his veins. Hatred and the most ferocious rage sparkled in his gaze. There are romances in which furious dwarves and wrathful gnomes are depicted—well, he was exactly like that.

Tancrède advanced with a serene and gracious air, having no suspicion that his destiny was being decided in that tiny unperceived body; and yet, solely by virtue of that presence, his entire future had just been changed.

In vain he had been rejoicing for an hour in finding himself so welcome, in having for a protector a man who could, by means of his connections, aid him in his fortune; in vain he was preparing a mild coquetry with the niece of the household, forming the most beautiful plans: all that was destroyed, overturned by a futile little being whom he had not even seen coming in, and whom he did not see leaving.

O fatality! That is life. A little stone that slips can bring down a fine charger; an indiscreet or malevolent dolt can abort the sublime schemes of a hero.

"You haven't forgotten me, have you, Madame?" said Tancrède to Madame Poirceau. "This is the sixth quadrille, which you were kind enough to grant me.

The little man heard that and started.

"You're not the kind of person one forgets," Madame Poirceau replied.

At those words, the little man started again. Never in her life had Madame Poirceau said anything so gracious, and that was alarming.

Monsieur Poirceau came to find Tancrède then, in order to introduce him to one of his friends.

"You're not going to dance with that fop," said Monsieur Legrand immediately, trembling with anger.

"Me! And why not, Monsieur?" Madame Poirceau replied, with dignity.

"Because I don't like him."

"It's necessary, however, that you grow accustomed to his face, since Monsieur Poirceau is taking him in, and he's replacing Monsieur Dupré."

"That cannot be, Madame. That fop won't replace Dupré; I won't suffer it."

"But Monsieur..."

"Be careful, Madame! It's necessary to choose between that fop and me. Do you hear me?"

He had spoken.

And the next day, when Tancrède presented himself at Monsieur Poirceau's house in order to take up his new employment, the respectable director of the fire insurance company received him with a melancholy expression, and, having looked at him sadly, like a friend to whom it is necessary to bid farewell, told him, approximately:

"My dear Monsieur Dorimont, you see before you a desolate man; it is impossible for me, quite impossible, to give you the position I promised you. I'm truly very sorry; I liked you so much! Everything that I know about you spoke in your favor. But I have been obliged to yield, to give in. My wife is a reasonable woman, very reasonable, you see; she is not one of those light-headed individuals who likes to drag elegant young men in her wake: dandies, or 'yellow gloves,' as people say nowadays. No, she's a simple woman, who doesn't seek to shine, and I won't hide it from you that your extreme beauty frightened her."

At these words, Tancrède started in surprise. He thought so little of his beauty, and of Madame Poirceau even less.

"'It's inappropriate,' she said to me this morning," the excellent director of the fire insurance company continued, "'for such a handsome man to be in our midst; it would give rise to gossip; with an old and infirm husband, a wife ought not to admit to her home a young man of such remarkable beauty; it would make people talk, make you look ridiculous, and I could never tolerate that.' What could I say to that? Nothing. All of it was true, and it was necessary for me to submit to it. Women, my dear chap, often have more tact than we do, and all those things, which hadn't occurred to me, leapt to her eyes immediately. What do you expect? Every advantage has its inconvenience; beauty is an advantage, but it's sometimes a misfortune."

Tancrède made no reply. The old gentleman, who had been talking to him for a quarter of an hour about his beauty, was beginning to annoy him—and all his hopes overturned for such a miserable reason! He had reason to be chagrined.

"It's astonishing," Monsieur Poirceau continued, "to discover that people have reason for complaint, precisely because one is tempted to envy them. It's necessary, too, that I make you another confession."

What is he going to confess to me now? Tancrède wondered.

"Monsieur Nantua, to whom you went the other day, and who recommended you so warmly to me, renounced the idea of taking you into his employ for the same reason."

"What! He thought me…?"

"Too good-looking, my dear chap, too good-looking. He was afraid for his daughter."

"But that's utterly absurd!" exclaimed Tancrède, beside himself.

"Not at all; it's very prudent, and in his place, I would have done the same. But listen: I'm interested in you. Achille Lennoix, the young engineer who has just obtained the concession to build a railway between Paris and Saint-Quentin, has asked me to recommend someone. He's young, he has no wife, no daughter to marry, and I believe that you're just what he needs. I've written him this letter for you; take it to him on my behalf, and you'll be well-received. Adieu, my handsome young man; don't lose heart, and don't hold the difficulties you're encountering against anyone but nature; she has been too prodigal toward you, and you're paying the penalty in life. *Au revoir*, I hope, and a thousand regrets."

It was thus that Tancrède, refused for the second time, separated from the worthy Monsieur Poirceau, the director of the fire insurance company.

IV. The Third Hope

Achille Lennoix was a man full of imagination and activity, always the prey of his ideas; he had a prompt glance and made up his mind quickly, at the risk of being mistaken, for he claimed that one loses less time in making and repairing an error than in hesitating between two courses and choosing the best one to take. He had been working so hard and soliciting so much for a month in order to obtain the concession for a railway from Paris to Saint-Quentin that he had fallen ill, and, as it was extremely inconvenient to be ill when such a major affair demanded his attention, by virtue of tormenting himself, he had rendered himself incurable.

Tancrède was admitted to his presence. Monsieur Lennoix looked him rapidly up and down, chatted with him for a few minutes, and his resolution was made.

This is the man I need, he thought. *The fellow has good manners; he'll do us honor; people will see that we don't only employ laborers.*

Then they talked mathematics; Tancrède was skilled enough in mathematics. They talked about England; Tancrède offered to travel to London, knowing English perfectly. He also offered to come and work with the invalid that evening, understanding how much annoyance Monsieur Lennoix must be experiencing by virtue of the idleness to which his suffering was condemning him.

Monsieur Lennoix seized that idea enthusiastically. The two young men understood one another marvelously.

After an hour of conversation, Tancrède withdrew, and his sudden friend gave him an appointment for seven o'clock that evening, after dinner.

On seeing him leave, Monsieur Lennoix rubbed his hands.

That young man will suit me, he thought. *He understood me immediately; he saw right away that what's making me ill is wasting my time. I divine that he's a man of intelligence, and only that.*

Monsieur Lennoix was far from being alarmed by his new employee's beauty; on the contrary, that noble and distinguished appearance seduced him It is possible to seduce people of merit by means of what is good; they are not among the petty minds frightened by advantages. Then again, men of imagination are never envious. They value their future more than anyone else; no one is marching where they are going, no one has ever arrived where they intend to be; they cannot envy what they see, because what they dream of is beyond it.

While Monsieur Lennoix devoted himself to these reflections, Tancrède got lost in a corridor.

It was the fatal hour, the hour of melancholy and mystery, when the sun, which is still the day star for the man of the fields, is no more for the sad inhabitant of the city than a half-extinct street-light, a dying and perfidious lantern that leads one astray in the shadows. In the large squares, on the quays and the boulevards, it is still daylight; in the streets there is a mild twilight, a quasi-moonlight; inside the houses it is gloomy; so what is there in the corridors? Darkness, profound darkness.

It is the hour of all sins, the hour of thefts and confessions; it is the instant when a blush is no longer visible, when one can say "I love you" brazenly—and, alas, one says it. It is the hour when the overworked seamstress persists in working, and makes a mistake, the uncertain light having deceived her eyes—she gets a knot in the thread, what do I know?—and she commits some trivial error whose consequences cause a great disturbance. It is, finally, the hour when antechambers are deserted, when domestics light the lamps; there are even prudent ones who have already closed the shutters before the lamplight has appeared.

Tancrède went astray in complete darkness as he left Monsieur Lennoix's apartment. He floated for a few moments in the dark corridor as on a narrow stream, holding on to the bank to either side of him; he was afraid of an unexpected staircase, his steps were anxious. On leaning his hand upon the wall he encountered a door that immediately gave way, and he found himself in an elegant little drawing room, which was adequately illuminated by a street-light outside the window.

A feeble light filtered through the crack of another door, for which Tancrède headed. He knocked lightly, out of prudence.

"Come in," said a rather soft voice.

Tancrède opened the door.

"Pardon me, Madame," he said, on seeing a rather pretty young woman advancing toward him."

"Monsieur," she said—and then stopped dead.

The sight of the beautiful young man seemed to her to be a divine apparition.

"Monsieur desires to speak to my…?" She was about to say "my son," but the word expired on her lips. She would have liked to be no more than sixteen years old.

"A thousand apologies, Madame," said Tancrède, but there's no light in the corridor…and..."

"Truly, Monsieur, that's incredible. Baptiste! Light the lamp! Baptiste is coming to light Monsieur's way."

Baptiste had too many lamps to light at that moment to have one to bring.

"He's not coming. I'll show you out myself."

As she said that, Madame Lennoix—for she was Monsieur Lennoix's mother—took the candle she had lit in order to seal a letter, and, in spite of Tancrède's protests, she escorted him to the staircase.

The she watched him leave.

That circumstance is apparently trivial, and yet it was terrible! O fatal encounter!

Madame Lennoix was at an age when one is beginning to admire handsome men again. At fifteen one admires them instinctively, at forty, by conviction.

What proves that the advantages of vanity and social convention are stupidities is that with age, one becomes scornful of them; it is that, in growing old, that which is true, that which is genuinely beautiful, has more attractions for us than the imaginary pleasures, the artificial qualities, that one previously found preferable to anything else. Thus, the woman who, at twenty, chooses a badly-turned out fop because he is a Duc or because he owns fine horses, at forty, if she is a widow, will marry a young man who has neither celebrity nor a fortune. Thus, a man who spends his youth running after false pleasures and false honors, retires at fifty to his country estate in order to breathe pure air there, sow fir-trees and black wheat, and feels happier for it.

Is it the case, then, that it is necessary to have studied society to learn to love nature? If young people knew that, how much annoyance they would avoid! How much disgust, how many bitter days they could spare themselves! They would remain in their native town, and how happy they would be there! It reminds me of the two charming lines that Monsieur de La Touche addressed to one of his friends,[30] in talking about the enchanted banks of the Creuse:

> *Happiness is there, under the same rock*
> *From which we both set out in search for it!*

Those lines ought to be engraved in letters of gold at the entrance to every village. What a sweet moral they contain! What a lesson?

Madame Lennoix had been brought back, by the effect of age, to the pure emotions of the heart. She could not see Tancrède without a disturbance full of charm, and his lovely image pursued her as she returned to her apartment.

No more rest for her henceforth. Cupid's perfidious arrows have wounded her, for the malign god still occupies him-

---

[30] The poet and novelist Henri de Latouche (1785-1851) was a significant promoter of Romanticism, publishing the work of the ill-fated André Chénier, who had fallen victim to the Terror, in 1819, and encouraging the young George Sand.

self with marriageable mothers. So she feels that she is in love…with whom?

That is the question.

Madame Lennoix's passions resemble her son's resolutions: they are prompt. A thousand corruptive and seductive thoughts immediately come to assail her.

I'm rich, I'm free, and I'm still young and pretty, since an architect mistook me for my son's wife the other day; what prevents me from marrying again? My son neglects me, absorbed in his business; he might go away at any moment and I'd be left alone. Why not profit from my advantages while there's still time?

That is it; she has made up her mind; she is a beauty who has no time to lose.

Trembling, she goes to see her son.

"Who is the young man," she said, "who came out of here just now?"

"He's a friend of Monsieur Poirceau; he was recommend to me by him."

"Is he a young man of good family?"

"Yes, certainly; he's the son of a distinguished officer, Monsieur Dorimont."

"Dorimont! That's a pretty name, which suits him very well. You've reached an understanding with him?"

"Yes, Mother, perfectly. He's full of intelligence; he seems to me to be very knowledgeable."

"To have intelligence, and to be so beautiful!"

"Yes, he is, indeed, good-looking."

"Good-looking?—but he's admirable! I've never seen a more seductive appearance, more distinguished features, a more expressive physiognomy: grace, nobility, delicacy, he has it all!"

"Oh, my God, how excited you are, Mother," said Monsieur Lennoix, laughing. "In truth, I believe you want to marry him."

At those words, Madame Lennoix blushed as redly as a young girl.

Now, do you know of anything more painful, or sadder, for a person who has delicacy in his heart than to see his mother blush?

At first, Monsieur Lennoix was sorry to have caused embarrassment to a woman he respected, but afterwards, that singular redness alarmed him. He had made a poor joke, with no idea that it might be applicable to Madame Lennoix's thoughts; but that redness, the emotion that he saw in his mother's eyes, inspired the dread of an event of which he had never dreamed.

Another incident soon confirmed his terrors.

Madame Lennoix's sister came in.

"Nephew," she said, "who is the young man who was coming out of your house, whom I've just encountered in the courtyard? I've never seen anything so admirable! Champmartin is coming to dine with me the day after tomorrow; it's absolutely necessary, my sister, that you bring that young man. He has what it takes to turn a painter's head—to put him on his knees!"[31]

Good—now my aunt's joining in! thought Monsieur Lennoix.

"Didn't you see him, my sister?"

"Indeed," replied Madame Lennoix, quite troubled. "My son scarcely noticed him."

"My nephew is having eye trouble, in that case!" exclaimed the aunt, who had loved an artist in her youth. "It's necessary to be weak-sighted not to see that he's the most beautiful man in Paris, in the entire world. Raphael, Carlo Dolce, Poussin and Murillo, do not have, in all their masterpieces, a specimen like that! Personally, I've never seen a finer head!"

---

[31] Charles-Émile Callande de Champmartin (1797-1883) built a considerable reputation as a portraitist after first exhibiting at the Salon of 1819. His best-known works include a portrait of Victor Hugo's mistress, the actress Juliette Drouet, costumed as the author's princess Smyrne.

Madame Lennoix did not say anything; she remained mute; she was being modest; it was her young man; she was the one who had admired him first. The prerogative of praising him was no longer hers. Had she not offered him, in thought, her heart, her fortune and her hand? She was waiting for him to respond; delicacy required, now, that she said nothing more.

The son, with his eagle eye, penetrated his mother's soul. In an instant, all the scourges appeared to him: an absurd marriage; a divided fortune; a tyrannical stepfather; lawsuits, quarrels, displacement, separation, perhaps children, unwelcome little brothers, teas, ruination, intimate dramas, family scenes, annoyances of every sort...

And his resolution was made at the same instant.

And that evening, when Tancrède went back to his lodgings to change, he was handed a note on behalf of Monsieur Lennoix.

Fever had gripped the young invalid, the perfidious letter said, and the physician had imperiously ordered complete rest; it was necessary not to think of returning to work for a long time.

A few days later, Tancrède went to ask for news of Monsieur Lennoix. The porter replied that Monsieur Lennoix was much better, and had gone out.

Tancrède perceived Madame Lennoix at the window; their eyes met...he divined everything. The conduct of the son was explained by a single glance on the part of the mother.

"Woe is me!" exclaimed Tancrède. "Always women!" And he drew away, furiously.

And as his despair had reached its extreme, he took the only possible decision for someone in his position. He went to spend the evening at the Opéra.

V. Monsieur Balzac's Cane

As we have said, extreme beauty is a misfortune for a man, especially a young man with his fortune to make. You will understand that now the words that appeared at first to be unintelligible: *there was once an exceedingly beautiful young man who was sad*, and you will also understand why he felt discouraged, and why he was cursing nature.

Three times, poor Tancrède had been rejected, precisely because of the very beauty that seemed to him to be a brilliant advantage, but which was nothing but a source of disappointment and chagrin.

What could he do? Make himself ugly? What man would have the courage? What woman would advise him to do so?

He went, therefore, to the Opéra. When a misfortune is without remedy, the wise thing is to forget it; when one does not know the route it is necessary to follow, one goes forth at hazard, and one does well. Hazard is only hostile to those who neglect their duties for it; for a man who has nothing to do, and has the right to go looking for adventures, hazard is always favorable.

Robert le Diable was playing that day.[32] Tancrède went to place himself in the orchestra stalls, but scarcely had he sat down than a strange object attracted his gaze.

On the ledge of a box at the front of the stage, a cane was displayed. Was it really a walking-stick? What an enormous cane! To what giant can that stout cane belong?

---

[32] The opera *Robert le Diable*, by Giacomo Meyerbeer, with a libretto by Eugene Sue and Germain Delavigne, was premiered at the Opéra in November 1831 and had a tremendous success, launching a vogue for "devil plays." Act Three features a magic branch that bestows magical powers, including the ability to become invisible, on the eponymous hero, who is the victim of a diabolical pact signed by his father.

Undoubtedly, it is the colossal cane of a colossal statue of Monsieur Voltaire. What audacious individual has arrogated the right to carry it?

Tancrède picks up his opera-glasses and begins to study that cane-monster. The expression is received: we have already had the concert-monster, the lawsuit-monster, the budget-monster.

Tancrède then perceives, at the top of that club of sorts, turquoises, gold and marvelous carvings—and behind all that, two large dark eyes, shinier than the stones.

The curtain went up; the second act began, and the man—the man who belonged to the cane—leaned forward to watch the stage.

"Pardon me, Monsieur," Tancrède said to his neighbor, "might I ask you the name of that gentleman with the long hair?"

"That's Monsieur de Balzac."

"What? The author of *La Physiologie du mariage?*"[33]

"The author of *La Peau de Chagrin, Eugénie Grandet* and *Père Goriot.*"

"Ah, Monsieur, a thousand thanks."

Tancrède resumed examining Monsieur de Balzac and his cane.

The cane preoccupied him. *How can such an intelligent man*, he wondered, *have such an ugly cane? Perhaps it contains an umbrella. There's some mystery behind this.*

---

[33] *La Physiologie du marriage* (1929, initially issued anonymously with the by-line "*Un Jeune Célibataire*") is a series of "meditations" analyzing and commenting on the state of marriage in France, which provided the theoretical bedrock for such cynical fictional analyses as *Eugénie Grandet* and *Le Père Goriot*. Its publication caused a scandal—as, of course, it was intended to do—although a considerable sector of high society reveled proudly in the depiction of its corruption and perversion.

The affectation that Tancrède put into not looking at the stage, always peering in the same direction, deceived a pretty young woman whose box was next to Monsieur de Balzac's box. The young woman simpered, believing that it was her that the young man was contemplating.

The affectation that the pretty young woman put into staring at the same place in the orchestra stalls deceived Tancrède's neighbor, who began focusing his opera-glasses exclusively at the young woman, not doubting that her gaze was addressed to him. Finally, the affectation of his neighbor in keeping his opera-glasses fixed on the same women attracted Tancrède's attention, who then divined clearly that he was the one at whom she was making eyes.

The proof is that as soon as his eyes met the young woman's, she stopped looking at him.

Glances; a blush; a little cough; a boa thrown back over the shoulder; a little glove taken off to reveal a white hand; a bottle of salts opened twenty times over and sniffed; pinched expressions; demi-sighs; obliques glances; furtive smiles—the entire infallible pantomime of feminine coquetry was employed simultaneously to inform Tancrède that he was loved.

He took that as read, and when, slightly before the end of the performance, he saw his pretty conquest stand up and quit the box she was in, he left the orchestra stalls and went to watch for his beauty at the foot of the main staircase.

She saw him, and did not seem astonished; she forgot to be emotional, but appeared to be meditating a project.

In the meantime, a député passed by whom she knew slightly. He was in a hurry, and walking rapidly. She stopped him, and said: "Are you going to the Italiens tomorrow?" As she spoke, she looked at Tancrède.

"Me?" the député replied. "Why do you ask? I never go there. The music bores me to death; I only like ballets."

The young woman did not care what the député liked. She had made use of him to hear what she wanted to say to someone else. His role was finished, and she set him free.

Meanwhile, the handsome stranger was also playing his little pantomime. His perfectly serous expression, his ultra-respectable bearing and his particularly languid expression expressed his thought sufficiently.

The young woman could no longer doubt her victory, so she did what all coquettes do: after having been scandalously provocative, they suddenly affect a superb dignity—but it is necessary for that to be very sure that they cannot be misinter-preted; they only affect dignity once it can no longer do them any harm.

So, the proud Célimène[34] of the Rue de Provence, seeing that her slave was submissive to her, drew away nobly, with the air of an empress, without deigning to glance at him, but saying to herself in a whisper, in her satisfied vanity: "He's understood."

---

[34] The reference is to a character in Molière's *Le Misanthrope*: a vain flirt who toys with the affections of several of the play's male characters, including the hero Alceste.

VI. Preoccupations

Tancrède went back home partly consoled for his misfortunes. Distractions have that agreeable effect; if they do not expel chagrin, at least they age it; even the indifferent events that are placed between the morning's bad news and the evening set it back almost a year; then it becomes an old annoyance, from which one no longer deigns to suffer. Our imagination resembles our domestics, who, in order to appease us when we show them something broken, reply: "Oh, it's been like that for a long time." It's absurd, and yet it consoles us immediately.

Tancrède had forgotten Madame Lennoix, her son and all the railways imaginable, preoccupied as he was with the Opéra, Monsieur de Balzac, his cane and is new conquest.

It isn't always a misfortune to be beautiful, he said to himself, *since...after all...that woman doesn't know me, and if...well, it's down to my nice face.*

He went to bed and went to sleep.

In the middle of the night, he woke up. He was agitated; he could not explain what was tormenting him. He thought about it, thinking hard, rapidly and involuntarily.

About the young woman who wanted to love him?

No, it was not a dream of love.

About Madame Lennoix, who wanted to marry him?

No, it was not a nightmare.

He was thinking—shall I tell you?—about Monsieur de Balzac's cane.

Madame Lennoix was a past danger. The young coquette was an adventure whose denouement was foreseen; there was nothing mysterious or marvelous about it—but that cane, that enormous cane, that monstrous cane, how many mysteries it might and must contain!

What reason had persuaded Monsieur de Balzac to load himself down with that club? Why did he always carry it with him? For reasons of elegance, infirmity, mania or necessity? Did it conceal an umbrella, an épée, a dagger, a carbine, an iron bedstead?

But for the sake of elegance one does not equip oneself with something so ridiculous; one chooses something more seductive. By necessity? I don't know that Monsieur de Balzac is lame, or ill; besides which, an invalid who can swagger around with that cane hardly seems worthy of pity. It's not natural; it conceals a great, fine, inconceivable mystery. I shall have to that enigma; I shall attach myself to Monsieur de Balzac, even if I have to go to his home to question him, pester him and torment him; I shall find out why he condemns him-self to drag that stout and ugly cane with him everywhere, which ages him, inconveniences him and seems to me to be good for nothing.

In sum, the proof that the cane conceals a mystery is that it preoccupies me; for after all, what does it have to do with me?

Thus Tancrède spoke to himself. That reasoning, which appears at first glance to be silly, does not lack justice, howev-er. When something is, by its nature, utterly indifferent to us, and yet we are singularly preoccupied with it, it is an indica-tion that ought to worry us. Our instinct is inspiring us, warn-ing us; our intelligence is sniffing something that our reason cannot see, for instinct is the nose of intelligence…a thousand apologies for that absurdity, but unfortunately, it expresses what I think.

After an hour of similar reflections, Tancrède went back to sleep.

In the morning, on waking up, he asked himself what there was to do: nothing; absolutely nothing. He had no pro-tector to go and test out, no letter of recommendation from which he could hope for a good result. There was the proud idleness of despair, and as he had no reproach to make to him-self, given that all his steps had failed without it being his fault, Tancrède set about savoring what he called his liberty.

In fact, that state would be liberty, for as long as the thousand francs his mother had given him lasted.

Poor mother! She had said: "It's necessary not to arrive in Paris without money," and then she had gone to work, and had succeeded in gathering together a thousand écus. She had found that for which the alchemists had searched for so long: the secret of making gold.

How many tiny diamonds, earrings, boxes, golden dice, rings, and even pairs of scissors it is necessary to find, gather and have weighed, in order to put together such a large sum when one's entire annual income is only two thousand écus! How many cruel petty sacrifices it had been necessary for the worthy Madame Dorimont to make to achieve that treasure! How many hesitations, and perhaps regrets!

What, that chain too?

I'll keep that; it came to me from... but it's very heavy; it will pass.

That pin, my uncle gave me that... it's all I have left of him...

That bracelet has come back into fashion, it's pretty, it's a pity; that necklace, how well it suits me... if I had a daughter, I'd give it to her...

Those earrings have always been too heavy.

That brooch? Poor Édouard...

That ring? Poor Alfred...

And the ring and the brooch go to join the rest, with a sigh, a tear; and then an old Jew takes it all away under his dirty overcoat. He carries away your past, your memories, the story of your life, divided into bracelets, fasteners, chains and rings. And for such a great sacrifice, you obtain a little money; joyfully, you give it to your son, who does not know what it costs you, who takes it as if it were his due, and which, almost always, he will go and lose in some Parisian gambling den.

And you will then have the most painful thing on earth, more bitter than a disenchantment, more poignant than a humiliation, more revolting than an injustice, more crushing than a regret: you will have made a *futile sacrifice*.

Oh, do you know of anything more heart-rending than that thought: *I might as well not have done that which cost me so much.*

A futile sacrifice! Like Mademoiselle de Sombreuil: to drink blood to save her father, and see her father mount the scaffold;[35] to sense all through your life the blood of another, the blood that you have drunk, running through your veins, and not to have saved the person you wanted to save! To have made a sublime effort of courage, to have vanquished disgust, and horror...for nothing! Oh, that makes you shudder. A great futile sacrifice...futile! It is almost a remorse.

Fortunately, Madame Dorimont did not know that torture. Her son was a good man, and when he had accepted the thousand écus heroically improvised by his mother, he had promised to return them to her with interest.

With a thousand écus and a room rented for a hundred francs a month, one can live well for a fortnight in Paris, and a fortnight is a long future at twenty years of age.

---

[35] Marie-Maurille de Sombreuil, Comtess de Villelume (1763-1823) became legendary when she was rumored to have struck a bargain at the height of the Terror with the Revolutionary Stanislas-Marie Maillard, alias *Tape-Dur*, who allegedly promised to spare her father from the guillotine if she would drink a glass of fresh blood shed by the recent victims. She was said to have done so, but only to have obtained a temporary reprieve. Several of the leading Romantic poets wrote versions of the legend, including Victor Hugo, and it was also repeated by the historian Edgar Quinet, although he was surely aware that the story was apocryphal.

VII. Finesse

Tancrède remembered, however, that he had a duty to fulfill: to wit, to go to the Théâtre-Italien that evening.

The first person he saw when he arrived was his superb conquest.

She seemed to be looking for someone; she saw him...and stopped looking.

The young woman was habitually much more expressive at the Théâtre-Italien than the Opéra. She raised her eyes at each of Rubini's notes; she shook her head in measure, in order to prove that she was a musician. The auditorium, being much smaller than that of the Opéra, permitted the details of that coquetry to be better appreciated, there, and she delivered herself to her advantages with an abandon that made the most of them.

Tancrède soon saw that he could not do otherwise than fall in love with her, but, in order to do that, he would require further information.

He questioned his neighbor politely. In order not to seem too stupid he put on an English accent when he asked the name of the pretty woman. Unfortunately, the neighbor was English, and replied in English that he did not know, but that he encountered her almost every day in the Tuileries. Fortunately, Tancrède knew English very well, and tolerated the manner in which the other pronounced the word *Thioulluourille*. It was certainly necessary to know English well to understand that.

After an evening of glances and roulades, Tancrède went home without any other incident.

He found his beauty in the Tuileries the following day.

The lady was very elegant; she was offering her arm to her mother, a rather badly-dressed old woman who was walking a dog.

She perceived Monsieur Dorimont and blushed.

That was in order.

There was a quarter of an hour of intelligent strolling.

The young woman appeared to search for her handkerchief in her sleeve and dropped a little portfolio containing visiting cards.

The mother did not see that, or was perhaps accustomed to her daughter's clumsiness. Tancrède saw the little portfolio fall, and approached in order to pick it up.

The lady increased her pace without paying any attention to him.

Tancrède did not understand that maneuver; at first he remained motionless, and reflected momentarily.

The strolling beauty came back in his direction.

Tancrède waited; then, advancing toward her very respectfully, he said: "I believe this belongs to you, Madame," presenting the portfolio to her.

"No, Monsieur," the audacious person replied. "It's not mine."

The mother was speaking to her dog at that moment, and had not heard. Then she saw Tancrède drawing away.

"What did that handsome young man want?" she said.

"Nothing, Mother; he had found a bracelet. But I'm cold...let's go home."

The two women left the Tuileries.

Tancrède stood there considering the portfolio, without understanding the profound ruse. At first he thought that he had been mistaken; he feared that he had made a blunder. He opened the portfolio, however.

Perhaps the cards conceal a note, he thought. The idea chilled him; it would be going too fast.

The portfolio did not contain a note, but visiting cards: lots of visiting cards.

Monsieur and Madame Montbert, Rue de Provence no.

Madame Virginie Montbert, Rue de Provence no.

Monsieur Isidore Montbert, Rue de Provence no.

Then it began again: Monsieur and Madame Montbert, Madame Virginie Montbert, Monsieur Isidore Montbert.

"Ah! I get it!" he exclaimed, laughing. "Good, it's in order for me to know her name. O Virginie! Charming name! I've got an idea...which is to take this little portfolio to number ** Rue de Provence myself. I'll say that I was strolling in the Tuileries, that I found it, and, the visiting cards having indicated to me that it belonged...Imbecile!" He broke off suddenly and slapped his forehead. "That's what she wants; that's what she indicated to you so clearly, and that you've taken such a long time to understand. And I, who thought I'd found that cunning means...which she had given me. Oh, women, women! They're superior to us in everything. We think we're strong, very ingenious, and we don't have a single good idea that doesn't come from them."

VIII. Fatality

"What a beautiful man! Oh, what a beautiful man!" said Madame Montbert's chambermaid, after having let Tancrède into the drawing room. "What a handsome fellow! She's lucky!"

"What's the matter with you, Adèle? Is it someone for my daughter?" said Madame Montbert's mother.

"Yes, Madame, and I was saying that I'd never seen such a beautiful man in my life."

Madame Pavart went into her daughter's room; she only stayed for a minute, not even wanting to sit down. Having been informed of Madame's plans for the evening, she left, but as she closed the door she said: "Be careful, my girl, be careful."

There was an entire past in those few words. What they meant was: *You won't always be so lucky; this one will be more difficult to hide.*

Tancrède wanted to resume his conversation. The progress he had made thus far in the heart of Madame Montbert had been sensible; it had quickly become obvious that she was unloved.

The mother's prudent words had, however, cooled the young woman down; she had sensed all the danger. Great difficulties appeared to her, difficulties without number, a happiness full of brambles and thorns. She was momentarily fearful.

Tancrède perceived that cooling; he redoubled his grace and amiability.

That seduction triumphed over a temporary dread, and Madame Montbert went so far as to invite Monsieur Dorimont to come again soon.

Tancrède went away very satisfied with that first visit.

Under the coaching entrance he perceived a man who was watching him very attentively. The man seemed to be waiting there for him.

There was nothing astonishing, however, in the fact that the man was there. It was the porter, whom the chambermaid had alerted, and who wanted to see whether Mademoiselle Adèle's eulogies were merited.

Tancrède therefore found him in front of him, and the porter admired him.

Another week passed in encounters, strolls, mute language, gazes—and love grew every day in Virginie's experienced heart; and, collating all her memories, she sensed that she had never been loved in this fashion. Tancrède was able to say, in the full force of the word, that he was preferred to all others—and that was very flattering, I can assure you!

Tancrède judged that he had languished for an appropriate interval, and that he might hazard a second visit to the lady. He therefore returned to her home.

On seeing him, the porter said: "Look, there's the handsome young man again. It appears that he comes frequently."

Take note of the misfortune! Tancrède had only been to Madame Montbert's home twice, but it counted as ten, so much had he been noticed.

Madame Montbert was alone. She was moved by the sight of Monsieur Dorimont, and Tancrède thought she was even prettier. They chatted briefly. They were reaching an understanding…when Monsieur Montbert came in.

Monsieur Montbert frowned on recognizing Tancrède. That frosty welcome was not encouraging. Tancrède bowed profoundly and withdrew.

As soon as he had gone, Monsieur Montbert said to his wife: "What does that fop want? He follows you everywhere like a shadow: to the theater, to the Tuileries. When we go out, I encounter no one but him.

Madame Montbert made no reply. *My husband has noticed him!* she thought.

Tancrède was discontented. However, as Monsieur Montbert was hardly ever at home, he was not discouraged, and a few days later, he went to see her again.

"Oh, my God!" she cried, when she saw him. "What imprudence! You can't come here again—my husband has discovered everything!"

Already? thought Tancrède. *But there isn't anything to discover!*

"It's impossible for me to receive you openly," Madame Montbert went on.

Those words, which were full of naivety and the future, reassured Monsieur Dorimont.

"My husband," she continued, "noticed you at the Opéra; the other evening, at the Gymnase, he was suspicious; I no longer recognize him, in truth." Tenderly, she added: "It's a great pity; it's never happened before. Until now, I've been so tranquil. I'm unlucky, for it's the only time I've been in love, and truly..."

Those words, which were full of foolishness and the past, cooled Monsieur Dorimont down again.

"And I too, am unlucky, Madame," he said, with extreme politeness, "since fate wants me to fail where everyone else succeeds."

Tancrède pronounced that adieu in a tone so perfectly respectful that Madame Montbert did not sense all its insolence; she took it for lacerating regret, and raised her beautiful eyes to the heavens, as a sign of sympathy. It was not until later, in consequence—Monsieur Dorimont making no request to return, avoiding looking at her at the theater and appearing to have renounced any conclusion—that she realized that he had been mocking her.

She consoled herself easily. It was a pity, she thought; he was very beautiful—but it would have been very difficult. And she forgot him. Now, you know what souls of that sort call "forgetting!"

IX. A Great Discovery

Poor Tancrède, however, was furious, not about the obstacles he had found, because one could say that he had profited from those obstacles, but about the difficulties that the adventure presaged for him.

Tancrède had not had time to divine the category of woman and the region of spirits to which Madame Montbert belonged. She was one of those perfectly pretty and insignificant sylphs whom one loves as much as is comfortable and one leaves at the first hint of difficulty. One comes to them with so much confidence, which the slightest difficulty discourages; one had not foreseen it, had not prepared for it, and it puts one off. Poor women! One has nothing against them; the snag never comes from them, but they do not have what it takes to produce the genius to overcome it.

It was not, therefore, because of Madame Montbert that Tancrède was so afflicted by the fatality that was pursuing him; he did not love her and could not regret her, but another thought, sweeter, more profound and dearer, had preoccupied him for some time.

The charming young woman that he had met at the ball at Madame Poirceau's house, Malvina, he had often seen again in society; he had been received more than once in her home, in her mother's home, and the memory of Malvina charmed him. Tancrède was working hard to please her, and, by a singular coincidence, his adventure with Madame Montbert had disrupted his plans for the seduction of Madame Thélissier; for, all things considered, if he found so many obstacles with regard to the former, who appeared to have so much experience in vanquishing them, how many would he find in regard to the latter, a young woman so candid, so well bought up, and so surrounded, who must have so much circumspection to maintain?

Thus it often happens that an unimportant event makes us unhappy because it is a warning for another, which interests us more and which seems unconnected with it. Our friends cannot understand our sadness, and say to us: "In truth, it's childish to be so afflicted over nothing..."

Nothing! It is sometimes our whole future.

Tancrède revolted against his destiny. *It's too much*, he said to himself; *it's enough to drive one mad; this can't go on. Husbands see me, porters admire me, women are afraid of me. I'm a pariah, a leper, someone accursed; there's a spell on me—but what can I do? To whom can I complain? Can I say that nothing I do succeeds, that I'm rejected everywhere, because I'm too beautiful? In truth, I'd like to be frightful; yes, in truth...or invisible. Oh, how charming it would be to be invisible, to penetrate everywhere without being seen, to love and never to compromise the one that one loves; to be near to her without anyone knowing, without her knowing herself. Oh, what joy! That's the gift I'd choose...*"

And his great anger evaporated in reverie.

Then he became cheerful again. "I'll go to the Opéra," Tancrède said, "expressly not to look at her, that stupid Virginie; we'll see whether her husband notices that."

Tancrède arrives at the Opéra.

Monsieur de Balzac isn't here his evening, he says to himself. *Too bad; that man and his cane interest me.*

Tancrède sits down in the orchestra stalls. He looks up. Monsieur de Balzac is in front of him, with his cane.

Oh! There's Monsieur de Balzac. I didn't see him come in. That's odd.

Mademoiselle *** is dancing a few steps with Monsieur ***. Monsieur de Balzac stands up.

Tancrède, well aware that the two dancers are not very remarkable, resumes watching Monsieur de Balzac.

Monsieur de Balzac has disappeared, and yet no one has left his box. The door has not even been opened.

219

Mademoiselles Elssler are dancing their pretty, fraternal sequence, so elegant and so gracious.[36]

Tancrède admires them at first, but then, preoccupied with Monsieur de Balzac's flight, he looks in the direction of the box again.

Surprise! Monsieur de Balzac is sitting in his seat. He is there with his cane, as if he had always been there. Tancrède thinks that he is delirious.

Mademoiselles Elssler are dancing, and then they fly away, their dance concluded.

O marvel! Monsieur de Balzac is no longer there. Has he flown away with them?

Tancrède is more and more intrigued.

To begin with he fidgets and stirs, all his being shivering as if at the approach of a great event; then he arms himself with resolution, places himself in front of the box where Monsieur de Balzac was, and stands there, motionless, arrested before the mystery in order to force it to reveal itself. He watches, he spies, he observes, he puts all of this might into his soul and his gaze. Oh, when a man is so dogged in pursuit of a secret, it's necessary that he should end up possessing it.

Where is Monsieur de Balzac at this moment? He hasn't come out of his box; he's there, but I can't see him. What does it mean? No one has come out of the box; the door had remained closed all the time, and yet a man has disappeared. If he's gone, how did he get out? If he's there, why is he no longer visible? He is, therefore, invisible...invisible!

That word plunged Tancrède back into his reveries.

---

[36] The Elssler sisters, Thérèse (1808-1878) and Fanny (1810-1884), became leading ballerinas of the Romantic era, arriving in the company that later became known as the Paris Opera Ballet in 1834. The younger sister soon eclipsed her elder as a performer and became far more famous; Théophile Gautier called her "the pagan danger" because she seemed so much more sensual and impassioned than her great rival, the light and precise Marie Taglioni.

How I'd like to be invisible! Oh, if I were invisible...

Gyges had a ring that rendered him invisible. Robert le Diable had a branch that rendered him invisible. Oh, if I had that branch...! In the fable, in all poetry, the ancients, the Arabs, imagined objects that rendered one invisible...

And Tancrède, while dreaming, was still watching. At the same instant, and suddenly, Monsieur de Balzac reappeared—and the door of the box had not opened! It was certain that Monsieur de Balzac had not left the box.

And Monsieur Balzac's hand was holding his stout cane...

Tancrède can see him, and can see that cane...

That cane, he thinks. *What if that cane were a ring, like Gyges' ring, like Robert le Diable's branch? What if that cane has the gift of rendering one invisible? That's it...yes that's it!* Tancrède is beside himself.

And he leaves the auditorium, repeating like a madman: "I know it, I know it. I said so, that there as a mystery; I know it, I no longer have any doubt about it..."

He arrives in the foyer, where Monsieur de Balzac is strolling with Madame ***.

Tancrède accosts him boldly.

What does it matter what he's going to say to me? He'll take me for an eccentric, and he'll address me as such; intelligent people are accustomed to bizarre things; he'll understand me.

"Pardon me, Monsieur," Tancrède says, striving to vanquish his embarrassment and emotion, "but you can render me an important service."

"Me, Monsieur? But I don't have the honor of knowing you," replies Monsieur de Balzac. "In what way can I oblige you?"

"By kindly lending me your cane for a few minutes."

At these words, Monsieur de Balzac becomes troubled. "My cane, Monsieur? And why?"

"It's a wager that I've made with some friends. I'm only asking you for five minutes...believe that..."

"It's impossible, Monsieur," says Monsieur de Balzac, dryly. "It's impossible. I'm sorry…Monsieur."

With these words, Monsieur de Balzac draws away. Addressing the person on his arm, he says: "What does this lunatic want of me? Do you understand any of this?"

"The Monsieur is drunk," replies Monsieur de Balzac's friend, mimicking Arnal in God knows what role.[37]

Monsieur de Balzac smiles, but he is anxious. *What idea can that young man have?* he wonders.

Meanwhile, the intrepid Tancrède has not yet despaired of succeeding; he returns to the attack, and, approaching the celebrated writer, whispers to him in an oracular tone: "That refusal is a confession, Monsieur; I have your secret; but believe that I shall respect it."

Monsieur de Balzac seems increasingly troubled.

"Reassure yourself, Monsieur," Tancrède continues. "I shall not abuse a discovery made by chance. I understand perfectly that you cannot consent to be separated from such a precious cane, especially in favor of a stranger: I know how indiscreet I have been in asking it of you, and I beg you to accept my apologies."

"Of course, Monsieur," Monsieur de Balzac then replies, evidently very agitated, "the request appeared singular to me; but if I knew the motive that made you address it to me, I might…"

"I can't explain myself here, in front of everyone; if you'd care to grant me a moment…"

"Tomorrow," Monsieur de Balzac interrupted. "Yes, tomorrow. Come to my house at midday; we'll talk about it."

Tancrède bowed gracefully and drew away.

"Do you know that young man?" Monsieur de Balzac immediately asked his friend.

"No, I don't know his name, but I see him often at the Opéra and the Italiens. He's some agreeable provincial."

---

[37] The reference is to the comic actor Étienne Arnal (1794-1872), who spent twenty years at the Théâtre du Vaudeville,

"He's handsome, but I think he's mad. What does he want of me?"

"Nothing," said the friend. "It's a pretext to see a great man at close range. He wants to be able to say, when he returns to his little village: 'I've seen Balzac, I've seen Lamartine; I've seen Béranger.' I tell you, he's some provincial simpleton who admires you."

"Thank you," replied Monsieur de Balzac, laughing. And he drew away—not without anxiety, because the young man's penetration was tormenting him.

X. A Marvel

Well, yes, that was it: that frightful cane was like Gyges' ring or Robert le Diable's branch; it rendered people invisible.

That cannot be, some will say.

Have they not said that about everything?

Has not every invention been denied at its birth? Has not every freshly-resolved problem been a lie until the day it passes into the condition of a vulgarity?

Industry, in our day, gives birth to marvels and makes miracles. Reread, I beg you, the *Thousand-and-One Nights*, and you will see that the most optimistic chimeras, the prodigies invented of old to seduce the imagination, have been realized and popularized nowadays without anyone being able to conceive that they were once impossible dreams.

Thus, for instance, in the story of Prince Ahmed and the fairy Paribanou, it is said that Prince Houssain, the brother of Prince Ahmed, possessed a carpet on which it was sufficient to sit down in order to be transported, almost instantaneously, to where one wanted to go, without being stopped by any obstacle, and that he had paid forty purses for that carpet.

Much noise was made about that marvel at the time. Well, today we have something better than that—yes, better! We have railways. They are a hundred times preferable to that carpet, firstly because by that means one goes more rapidly, one travels in numbers, and certainly far more cheaply.

It is also said that Prince Ali, the younger brother of Prince Houssain had bought for thirty purses a little ivory tube with which he could see everything that was happening among the most distant people.

Well, that tube about which so much fuss was made was nothing but a telescope, a marvel to which we very pay little attention; and yet, what is more admirable than to be tranquilly sitting at a window, seeing everything happening a long way away—ships arriving, men fighting—and thus witnessing all sorts of dangers that cannot reach us? But who has ever thought of admiring a telescope?

Finally, it is related that Prince Ali, the brother of Prince Houssain, had, for his part, purchased in the bezeistein[38] of Samarkand an artificial apple for which he paid thirty-five purses. That apple had the virtue of curing all kinds of diseases, by the simplest means in the world, since it simply consisted of having the person sniff it.

Well, I ask you, has not homeopathy made many others? Instead of an apple, it is a little bottle; you sniff it, and are cured. You are going to die…a little powder on the tongue, and are saved.

Let us admit that there is nothing more vulgar than prodigies.

In the Thousand-and-One Nights there is also question of an economical little pavilion which, deployed in a certain fashion, shelters an army of two hundred thousand men. I don't know that anyone has imagined anything similar as yet; perhaps we have no need for it. Bonaparte lodged his soldiers every evening, mentally, in towns that he counted on capturing during the day; we lodge them in our own homes temporarily; but if we went to war, I'll wager that we would replace the fairy Paribanou's parasol advantageously, and that what was a marvel in the Arab tale would merely be a highly ingenious economical procedure for us.

All of that explains to you how a rival of Verdier,[39] whose address we shall not give you for reasons that are pri-

---

[38] This esoteric term is appropriated from Jacques Savary des Brulons' *Dictionnaire universel de commerce, d'histoire naturelle et des arts* (1742), where it is defined as a kind of marketplace—effectively, therefore, a bazaar.

[39] Possibly the physician and educator Jean Verdier, who established an institute of orthopedics and a school of physical education in Paris in 1770 near the Jardin des Plantes, but more likely his nephew Pierre-Louis Verdier, who was notable for numerous orthopedic inventions to correct or ameliorate

vate, has found a means of making a marvelous cane that has the property of rendering in visible the person who is carrying it. Invisible, and invisible only: not insensible, not impalpable—I agree that the invention is not yet perfected. It is even necessary, for the cane to have all its power, that one holds it in the left hand. In the right hand it has no virtue: you can be seen, and it can be seen; it's very ugly, and that's all. But as soon as your left hand takes possession of it, you disappear from human eyes; people search for you in vain…you're there and you're no longer here…it's admirable.

In a year's time, everyone will have one of those canes; they will become commonplace and useless, for if everyone else is invisible, what purpose does it serve to be invisible oneself? What is the point of hiding in order to observe individuals that one cannot see? There will be a universal darkness devoid of interest. Fortunately, the procedure is thus far unknown. Monsieur de Balzac is the only one who has used it, perhaps even abused it—because, we say it with regret, perhaps he has lacked delicacy in unveiling as he has in his works the secrets that he has discovered with the aid of his invisibility. No matter—his talent is now explained; we know what he has done in order to be able to read the souls of his protagonists, of "La Femme de trente ans," of Eugénie Grandet, of Louis Lambert, of Madame Jules, of Madame de Beauséant, of Père Goriot, and of all the other souls whose sufferings he recounts with such palpitating verity.[40]

---

human deformities. Jean's son Jean-François and Pierre-Louis' brother Thomas were in the same line of work, and the reference might be intended to encompass the whole family.

[40] *La Femme de trente ans*, one of several portmanteau novels in the Comédie Humaine, only received that definitive title in 1842, but the third part, originally published in 1832, then had the title "À Trente ans," and Balzac was probably using the collective title in private conversations. Louis Lambert is the eponymous hero of an 1832 novella generally thought to be quasi-autobiographical. Madame Jules (Clémence Desmarets)

People say: "How is it that Monsieur de Balzac, who is not a miser, is so familiar with all the sentiments, all the tortures and enjoyments of avarice? How does Monsieur de Balzac, who has never been a dressmaker, know so thoroughly all the thoughts, petty ambitions and intimate chimeras of a young seamstress of the Rue Mouffetard? How can he represent his characters so accurately, not only in their relationships with others but in the most intimate details of solitude? That he knows the sentiments, so be it: art can dream and encounter them accurately; but that he knows the habits, the routines and even the most secret minutiae of a character so perfectly, the manias of a vice, the imperceptible nuances of a passion and the familiarities of genius...that is surprising. Private life, that is what he paints with so much authority, and how he has succeeded in saying everything, knowing everything and making everything visible astonishes the reader.

It is by means of that monstrous cane.

Like the popular princes who disguise themselves in order to visit the huts of the poor and the palaces of the rich whom they wish to test, Monsieur de Balzac hides himself in order to observe; the watches people who believe themselves to be alone, who are thinking as no one has ever seen them think; he observes genius that he discovers in a dressing-gown, sentiments in a night-shirt, vanities in a night-cap, passions in bedroom-slippers, furies in ear-muffs, despairs in camisoles, and then he puts all that in a book for you. And the book runs all over France; it is translated in Germany, pirated in Belgium—and Monsieur de Balzac passes for a man of genius. O charlatanism! It is the cane that wins him admiration, and not the man who possesses it; he has only one merit: the manner of making use of it.

---

is a character in *Ferragus* (1833). The Vicomtesse de Beauséant appears in numerous novels in the Comédie Humaine, but first became distinct in *Le Père Goriot*.

Now, this is what happened. Tancrède went to see Monsieur de Balzac, and told him how he had discovered the singular virtue of his cane.

"I was so preoccupied," he told him, "by the need to be invisible, that it isn't astonishing that I divined the marvel of which I was dreaming."

"You?" exclaimed Monsieur de Balzac. "It seems to me that you have less interest than anyone else in not being seen."

Tancrède then recounted, naively, all the failures that his excessively great beauty had caused him while he had been in Paris.

Monsieur de Balzac listened curiously. He was glad to observe that new situation; he wanted to link himself more intimately with a young man that he found to be distinguished and intelligent, and who, moreover, knew his secret. Thanks to his cane, Monsieur de Balzac very rapidly discovered what was contained in the character of his friends. Tancrède, for his part, did not neglect anything to capture the confidence of the illustrious writer. He got closer to him, rented an apartment in his neighborhood, and finally found the means to render him one of those services on which lifelong friendship is founded.

We shall not say what that service was, the sex of which merits tact; the individuals it would compromise will be grateful to us for that discretion. It is sufficient to know that Tancrède gave proof on that occasion of so much delicacy, presence of mind and reserve that Monsieur de Balzac consented to lend him his precious cane for a few days, without fear that he would ever want to abuse the power that it gave him.

Tancrède was delighted, transited, at the pinnacle of his joy; he finally possessed what he desired so much. He experienced, however, what sometimes happens to people who suddenly see their most extraordinary wishes granted: they find themselves thrown off course, the unexpected happiness deranges them; they are not expecting it, having amused themselves dreaming of something because they thought it impossible, which, when they obtain it, leaves them at a loss because they no longer know what to do with it. O humanity!

Tancrède was still charmed by being able to be invisible at will, but he wondered how that power might be of service to him.

How, he wondered, *unless I go to burgle houses, can the gift enable me to me fortune?*

Fortunately, circumstances replied to that question.

XI. A Stroke of Luck

While this was happening, Tancrède received a letter from his mother, who first begged his pardon for having made him so beautiful, and then recommended him, as a last resort, to Monsieur ***, the Minister of ***, in whom she had an omnipotent protector.

Tancrède went to seek protection in the establishment of the protector, who protected him—in which there is nothing extraordinary, for he had a bureau of benevolence established in his office on certain days at certain times; he routinely protected a dozen schemers every Thursday morning.

Thus recommended, Tancrède went to see the Minister, from whom he had received a letter granting him an audience. The Minister, who had been teased, tormented and hauled over the coals the day before by an opposition député—I believe it is called interpellation—was in a very bad mood; in addition, it was necessary that he appear indignant in his response to the Chambre, and he was working himself up into a state of wrath in order to prepare a violent speech. He treated his eloquence like a racehorse that one "trains" before the conflict. The Minister hustled everyone—that's a technical term—and he hustled Tancrède, not listening to him and replying absentmindedly; in sum, he abused his position in order to wound him without him having the right to complain.

Tancrède rebelled.

Ah, Monsieur le Ministre, he thought, *you're treating me like this because I'm an unknown young man from whom you have nothing to fear! You're crushing me with your power, because you believe me to be devoid of credit. Well, I too have a power, and since you're abusing yours, I'll use mine, and we shall see...*

Tancrède went through the reception rooms and down the staircase of the Ministry without having yet made a definite plan. Outside the door he went back to the cabriolet that

230

had brought him, picked up the cane that he had left in his cloak, paid off the cab driver and went back into the large courtyard of the building, braving the implacable guardsman, invisibly.

He walked back and forth for some time, invisible, seething with anger.

As he was walking, the Minister's carriage stopped outside the perron. A bizarre footman, dressed in livery that was not merely fanciful but, I will even say, fantastic, came to open the door of the vehicle.

The Minister came down the steps very slowly, followed by another individual who was speaking to him heatedly, while the domestic held the carriage door open, having lowered the footstep.

Tancrède drew nearer, like a schoolboy, and was then gripped by a crazy idea. Seeing that carriage gaping for a quarter of an hour, he was tempted to sit down and have a rest. Suddenly, he launched himself invisibly on to the footstep and went to sit inside the vehicle.

The movement that he imparted to the carriage caused the horses to move forward. The coachman retained them easily, but the noise had recalled the Minister from his conversation; he realized that he was late and hastened to climb into the carriage. Tancrède wanted to get out, and immediately got up, but the Minister, who had just sat down, leaned out of the window blocking the door completely with his girth.

Tancrède still hoped to escape, but the Minister stretched out his legs officially, and gave his orders; the carriage door closed and the horses set off.

Once established in his carriage the Minister spread himself out, extending himself and taking up as much space as he could. Tancrède, by contrast, squeezed himself, huddled up and hid as if he were not invisible. He felt indiscreet, and no longer want to be so with regard to the Minister. The wrongs that we do to someone who has offended us calm our resentments swiftly, especially when they are involuntary and we have not chosen to do them.

A noble character only imagines a noble vengeance; he only dreams of cruelties worthy of him. The wrongs of hazard, the unfortunate consequences of circumstance that he inflicts upon his enemy, seem beneath his hatred; he is ashamed of them. In the honesty of his reason he recognizes that his enemy has not acted as badly as he has, and, as he is disenchanted with his own hatred, he forgives out of humility. Tancrède reproached himself for his conduct; the Minister had simply lacked respect in welcoming him lightly, but he was lacking in delicacy in following him without his knowledge, like a spy.

Tancrède was devoting himself to these reflections when the Minister suddenly exclaimed: "Messieurs..." Tancrède could not help smiling; his pinched his lips and made grimaces in order to maintain his composure, not thinking that no one could see him. One has difficulty getting used to being invisible.

"Messieurs," the Minister continued, "the Minister has no difficulty in replying to the attacks of his enemies..." The orator paused, and the resumed: "We are in a position, Messieurs, to prove to our adversaries..." He paused again, and resumed: "It is not the first time Messieurs, that the opposition has..." He stopped again. "Very well," he said, "I'll find all that when we get there."

The Minister was right. He only found his ideas at the tribune—which was annoying. Needless to say, they stayed there.

It appears that we're going to the Chambre, Tancrède thought. *So much the better; I haven't been yet.*

The Minister resumed muttering between his teeth.

Now he's talking to himself, Tancrède thought.

But the Minister raised his voice. "Sire, that cannot be. I have already had the honor of telling the king that it would raise a cry of protest…people would also say that..."

At that moment the vehicle stopped, not at the Chambre des Députés, as Tancrède had thought, but at the Tuileries.

The Minister got out of the carriage. Tancrède immediately followed him. Fortunately, the footman was a bumpkin who gave him time to get down before he thought of raising the footstep.

Drawn by hazard and curiosity, Tancrède followed the Minister; he had never visited the Tuileries; all this was amusing.

He goes up the great stairway whose magnificence dazzles him, traverses the guard room and penetrates, still in the Minister's wake, into a grave room with blue walls, in the middle of which is a large table covered with a blue velvet cloth: a historic room that was once the Emperor's drawing room, and is now the diplomatic laboratory, known in Paris as the "ministerial boutique" and in Europe as the Cabinet des Tuileries.

Several men were already gathered in the room. The Minister, whom Tancrède was escorting like an invisible bailiff's henchman, was evidently late; with him that was systematic. If punctuality is the politeness of kings, lack of punctuality is, on the other hand, the skill of ministers—those, at least, who are influential. Firstly, it adds to their importance, and secondly, an ingenious man who has ideas loses nothing by allowing others exhaust words, arguing at length, turning over and muddying questions that he alone can resolve. It is an advantage for him to arrive mentally sound and fresh in the midst of weary individuals, shaken in their opinions by all the objections to which they have been subjected; it is a fine role to play; it always seems to rally the various camps; one is always the sword that tips the balance.

It is very clever, but in order to do that, it is necessary to be a man of importance; for necessarily, those for whom people will not wait, unfortunates for whom no one ever waits, and who never will be awaited for anything—oh, those we advise to be on time, or even to arrive a little ahead of time, if they want to obtain a share of anything whatsoever and to count for something in any decision, so long as they live.

Tancrède's Minister was, therefore, greeted as a man for whom people wait, and from whom an idea is expected.

An individual who seemed to have some sort of preponderance over the others came toward him, extending his hand cordially.

But I've see that face somewhere, Tancrède thought; *that man isn't unknown to me...*

"Does the king know?" said one of the Ministers.

How foolish I am! Tancrède thought, immediately. *It's the king. How did I not guess that immediately? I ought, however, have expected to find the king here.*

A few moments thereafter, the king sat down at the table, and the Ministers all took their places in the Council.

Tancrède was singularly embarrassed, torn between curiosity regarding what was about to be said and the shame of committing an espionage unworthy of him. Eventually, he capitulated with his conscience. *Espionage,* he said to himself, *consists of repeating, not of knowing.* And he disposed himself to listen.

Unfortunately, while walking in the courtyard of the Ministry, he had got cold. That chill had revived a cold in the head with which he had been battling for a week, and which had seemed to have forgotten him momentarily. It was one of those fine afflictions that causes a scandal in the theater and at the Académies, one of those stubborn coughs that are known as whooping cough in childhood but are respected toward the end of life under the more imposing name of catarrh.

At first, Tancrède struggled with the hostile cough; he choked and suffocated. Soon, however, the combat became impossible; he coughed and coughed boldly, relieving himself of all the frenzy of his infection.

The king was reading. He was scanning a work that one of his Ministers had just handed to him. He did not look up but he heard that frightful cough and had no doubt that it belonged to one of his Ministers. Judging a man of war, exhausted by numerous campaigns, more capable of beings its owner than the other Ministers, who were younger than him, he addressed himself to the Minister of War and said: "Do you have a cold, Monsieur de Maréchal?"

The Maréchal did not have a cold, but, being too well brought-up to contradict his sovereign, and in order to misappropriate a mark of interest that others might envy, he bowed respectfully and replied: "Yes, Sire, a bad cold. The other day, at the review..." And he started coughing enthusiastically.

Tancrède was saved. A flattery had rendered probability to that fantastic cough, by which the king might have been astonished. He coughed in concert with the Maréchal, who soon ended up surpassing him.

The latter's cough, flattering at first, had become sincere. That kind of ruse is facile at that age. He acquitted himself so well that Tancrède was tempted to say to him: *Thank you, worthy man, enough; one has no further need of you.*

At that moment an usher came in; he handed the Minister of Foreign Affairs a package containing dispatches.

· "Correspondence from London," said the king.

He broke the seal. "The Ministry has changed. Lord *** has handed in his resignation."

That news caused a sensation in the Council. There was agitation and alarm. The king spoke; a lively discussion began, and became very interesting...so interesting, in fact, that he has forbidden us to report it.

"That's going to send stock prices down," said one of the Ministers in a low voice, to one of his colleagues, while the others were holding forth.

That was what Tancrède understood most clearly in the entire discussion.

What if I were to take advantage of that circumstance? he thought.

Then he stopped listening to what as being said; he lost himself in schemes, meditated twenty projects, rejected some, weighed others, and ended up deciding to go and see Monsieur Nantua, in order to make him party to the news of which hazard had informed him.

An usher came in on some pretext or other; as soon as the door was open, Tancrède slipped out.

He soon arrived at Monsieur Nantua's house. It was his audience day, for even millionaires have days set aside for morning receptions.

Recalling the manner in which he had disappointed Tancrède in his hopes, Monsieur Nantua initially greeted him with embarrassment, but Tancrède rapidly put him at his ease.

"Monsieur," he said, "I've come to tell you something very important, and you can, for your part, render me a great service. A circumstance, which reasons of delicacy do not permit me to explain to you, has rendered me, before everyone else, the possessor of an item of news that will have a considerable influence on stock prices. I've come to inform you in all haste, only asking, as the price of my good will, for a modest interest in our operations.

"But my dear boy," said the banker, smiling, "I don't understand for, after all..."

"And that's the misfortune!" exclaimed Tancrède. "Oh, Monsieur, if I could explain myself clearly, if I could tell you the truth, so that you would see that there's no doubt about it, I would employ a different language, dictating the severest of conditions; but I need, above all, to inspire confidence in you, and as nothing is more extraordinary than the situation in which I find myself, I'm only preoccupied by one idea, which is not to pass in your eyes for a madman, even though there's reason enough to lose one's head. To hold in one's hands the means of making a fortune and not to be able to make it! And that because one is unknown! Believe me, Monsieur, if I had the slightest credit. I wouldn't have come to torment you; I would have handled the affair on my own, I can assure you."

"You're forgetting, my dear boy," said Monsieur Nantua, maliciously, "that your intention was to be of service to me."

Tancrède started laughing in his turn. "Undoubtedly, I also wanted to render you a service," he said. "Above all, I'd like to be able to speak to you frankly; but you know the world too well not to understand that there are twenty circumstances in the adventurous life of a young man that can put him in possession of a secret, honestly and even legally, without him

236

being able to explain how he has come to know it—but look, I promise, if I deceive you…yes, I'll sign at this very moment an obligation for fifty thousand francs, with which you'll be able to have me thrown in prison for a year, if the news that I give you isn't accurate."

"Well," said Monsieur Nantua, "I trust you; but trust me too; tell me the news and if I judge…"

"In fact," said Tancrède, I'll tell you anyway; alone, I can do nothing, and I'd like you to profit from it."

"Well?"

"Well, the English Ministry has changed. Lord *** has resigned."

That news produced even more effect on the banker than it had on the Council of Ministers.

"But…are you sure?" he said.

"I'm as certain as it is possible to be, and at this moment I would give all the money I'd like to make to be able to in-spire my conviction in you and tell you the strange events that gave it to me. I know, I tell you, I'm positively certain."

"Why hasn't the telegraph already…oh the fog has been so bad for three days that that's understandable[41]…but you give me your word of honor…?"

"My word of honor," said Tancrède, with a tone of sin-cerity.

"Well then, *au revoir*, my associate! Come back tomor-row morning."

Tancrède left, very agitated.

As he watched him leave, Monsieur Nantua thought: *It's some story of a woman; the handsome fellow was doubtless*

---

[41] The "telegraph" to which reference is being made is the Chappe semaphore system, of which Napoléon I had made such profitable use in administering his Empire, and which plays a key role in the plot of Alexandre Dumas' *Le Comte de Monte Cristo*. The author could not know that it would soon be superseded by the electric telegraph, which was not subject to disruption by fog.

hiding in a boudoir when the Minister read his dispatches. He has to be discreet. That's it.

The news was true, as we know. The fall in stocks was greater than might have been anticipated, and Monsieur Nantua made a larger sum than he had dared to hope.

Tancrède received a share in his profits, and that unexpected fortune was sufficient for his momentary ambition.

He had said to himself: *I can't live without money*—and he had gone to some trouble to obtain money. Now he said to himself: *I can't live without love*—and he set about trying to find love.

That is easier, some might think; I don't believe so, personally. The paupers of the heart are the most numerous in Paris, and as there is no hospice for them, one risks encountering them everywhere, and they are the ones who attack and rob you.

XII. The Cane is Endangered

Nothing is as dangerous as a first success. Every stroke of luck is a trap that destiny extends for us. At any rate, the inevitable result of the great application of intelligence that an audacious enterprise demands is a mental fatigue, a relaxation of all the faculties, a deviation in our senses, a negligence consequential to the very intoxication of triumph, which leads us to compromise the success that we bought with so much effort the day before. In battle, in love, in everything, the day after is a great day: *the day after!*

And yet, it is that day that one disdains; it is that day on which one goes to sleep. O danger, O folly! Day after, terrible day, decisive and solemn, the future depends on you; you make it; it belongs to you. In glory, what is a battle won without the day after that consecrates it? In amour, what is a day of happiness, without the day after that purifies it? The day after is the wisdom in the glory, the conscience in the amour. It is to the day after that history looks for its judgments; it is from the day after that the heart dates its memories.

And the proverb that says: *There is no festival without its day after*, does not mean that it is necessary to amuse oneself for two days in succession; it means that it is only on the following day that we know whether or not we were right to rejoice on the day before.

O wisdom of nations!

Tancrède owed to his cane a great success, which stunned him; it was that simple.

A few days before, he had been devoid of resources, rejected by all the establishments that had initially welcomed him with benevolence, tormented by the idea of not being able to repay his mother the poor thousand écus so dearly obtained; having been unhappy and discouraged, with no money and no friends, he suddenly found himself in possession of a considerable sum, and, what was even better, in a business relationship with one of the most highly-esteemed bankers in Paris.

His extreme beauty was now no longer an obstacle to his relationship with Monsieur Nantua. It was no longer a matter of making him part of his household and employing him in his offices; Mademoiselle Nantua had no chance of seeing him. Tancrède could, therefore, meet Monsieur Nantua at the Bourse, at the Opéra, and make business deals with him, without any danger to the young woman's romantic imagination.

In any case, the prudent father had fewer scruples since Monsieur Dorimont served his interests so well. Tancrède was therefore on a lucky streak, and he experienced the great joy of a soothed soul, the lightness of a liberated mind, the appreciated happiness that is fatal. For fate is generous in that it leaves us happiness as long as we are unaware of it, but if some imprudent individual dares to say: "How happy I am!" destiny revolts, the world cries scandal and some fine catastrophe immediately arrives to reestablish equilibrium in the heart—which is to say, regrets, dread and ennui—and the head that was raised is lowered again, the voice that was singing fades away, and everything returns to normal.

Tancrède was fatally happy. He had just reported the change in his situation to his mother, explaining it by means of a lie; he had also returned to her, with generous interest, the sum that she had given him on departure. That long letter, written with pleasure, had renewed his joy.

He could not keep still; he walked back and forth in his room, talked to himself, recounted projects to himself. Eventually, in order to employ his agitation, he picked up his cane and hat, and went out to make his visits.

His cane and his hat—take note of that; those perennially insignificant words are of great importance on this occasion, but Tancrède did not attach sufficient importance to them. He picked up his cane and his hat as any other man might pick up his cane and hat. Woe betide the treasure that falls into the hands of such a young man! Treasures are not made for youth;

at twenty one does not know how to be rich, or how to be loved.

Tancrède, therefore, went out like a numbskull, joyful and light, astonished that no one was complimenting him on a happiness to which he had not made anyone party,

Intense emotions have an instinct that would serve us as a thermometer to judge the people we love, if we consulted it more frequently. There are friends that we go to see immediately when something good happens to us; our happiness is only complete when they know about it; we run to their homes in order to tell them about it, and if they are out, we tell their porter about our happiness, in order that he can inform them of it when they return.

Those are the true friends; there are others about whom we think with trepidation, saying to ourselves: *How will they take it?* They are the false friends. There are others about whom one does not think at all. They are sometimes the best, but that is because we do not like them, and as that is not our fault, there is no need to talk about it.

The fact is that the instinct of the heart guides us toward those who ought to understand us, on the days when there is a need to be understood, just as the science of pleasure guides the Parisian toward the Théâtre Italien when he desires to hear music, toward the Vaudeville when he wants to be amused, or toward the Rocher de Cancale when he intends to dine.[42]

---

[42] The Rocher de Cancale was the most fashionable restaurant in Paris in the 1830s, where the members of the Jockey Club hung out there and all the dandies went to strut. Balzac, who was a regular in the days when he was showing off the cane, set scenes in several key works there, notably the components eventually assembled into the portmanteau novels *Illusions perdues* and *Splendeurs et misères des courtisanes*, which include an account of the career of the ambitious writer and dandy Lucien de Rubempré, and his manipulation by his Mephistophelean protector Vautrin.

Thus, a vague thought said to Tancrède that the person who would rejoice most in his joy, after his mother, was the genteel Madame Thélissier; he sensed that she was not indifferent to him; he already read in her eyes a disturbance of which she was far from divining the cause.

Malvina had never taken account of her impressions; her soul was still in the golden age of sentiments; those she experienced had not yet been named. Her heart had always been so occupied, so busy, that she had never had time to analyze and baptize her impressions. Her mother, always suffering, had taken possession of all her thoughts until the age of sixteen, when she had been married; then children had come, so rapidly and so numerously, that she had not had the time to perceive that she did not love her husband at all. She liked him, of course, because he was good and he helped her to care for her mother, but she did not experience any love—but then, love was something to which she had never given any thought.

She did not think, she lived; her heart was very sensitive, but her imagination was dormant. She loved her children because she was their mother, but she had never said to herself: "Maternal love is the passion of my life." In the same way, when she gave her mother such enlightened, such touching care, she did not say to herself: "Filial piety occupies all my days." She did not make a fuss about anything. When her mother had an attack of gout, she spent the night with her; when her mother was well, she spent the night at a ball, amusing herself like any young woman.

Too naïve and too natural not to be a coquette, she sought to please, but involuntarily; she liked hats, dresses, flowers and ribbons, without claiming to be a fashionable woman. She occupied herself with the household without believing that she was a good housekeeper; she fulfilled all her duties without knowing why it was that people called them duties. She had accepted all the roles that life had offered her, without knowing to what employment they belonged, with innocence and good faith; but everything gave rise to the fear that she might accept the most perilous adventure with the same innocence and good faith.

She was, in sum, what cold and romantic women call, disdainfully, "a good little wife." Unfortunately, those good little wives have more soul than great languorous women, and Malvina was all the more sensitive because she was not romantic. She did not believe in all the great events that are recounted in books; she thought that they must have happened in the fabulous times of history, not imagining that in the Rue Saint-Honoré or the Rue de Gaillon, anything extraordinary might happen to a woman who lived with her husband and children. Besides which, she read very little: a few pages in the evening, in order, as she said herself, "to put her to sleep"—and what is read with that objective is rarely made to excite thought and trouble the imagination.

She was, therefore, unprotected, either by foolish dreams or false ideas, and a veritable amour, a singular event, would have found her defenseless. People sometimes protest against romantic imaginations; I believe, on the contrary, that they are much less easy to carry away than others. The habit of living in an imaginary world inspires prejudices in them against everything that happens in the real world. The events of life never seem worthy to occupy their soul; none of that is what they are waiting for, in order to blossom. And I have always seen those young women with pale faces, a melancholy gaze and nebulous, sentimental utterances end up voluntarily marrying old men for money, while reasonable and cheerful women nobly risk their future in a marriage of inclination.

Yes, romantic chimeras preserve one from amour. I know a woman who, at the age of sixteen, told herself that she would love a young Englishman that she met in a meadow. Forty years later, that woman has never loved, because she has never encountered an Englishman…in a meadow! Without that dream, she might perhaps have loved one or several Frenchmen, encountered quite simply on the boulevards. That proves once again that the defects of the mind save the heart.

Tancrède found Madame Thélissier surrounded by children: not merely her own but all the children of her neighbors and cousins. That troop of demons was whirling, leaping and galloping in the drawing room, while Malvina played them quadrilles, waltzes and gallops.

On seeing Monsieur Dorimont come in, Malvina quit the piano, to the great consternation of the dancers. Some suddenly stopped, no longer hearing the music; others continued to whirl, and finding obstacles in those who had stopped, collided with them abruptly. Several of them fell down on the carpet.

Malvina's youngest child, a daughter, was one of those. She was scarcely three years old. She was one of those little balls, round and pink, whom the slightest shock causes to roll. She did not hurt herself, but she cried a lot. Tancrède, seeing her on the floor at his feet, hastened to pick her up before Malvina had time to reach her. He took the little girl in his arms and took her to her mother, and everyone tried to console her.

In the meantime, a villainous red-haired boy, a child of the neighborhood, had picked up the cane that Tancrède had left on the floor while picking up Madame Thélisier's little daughter.

He had taken possession of the marvelous cane!

The cane that...

The cane with which...

The cane by means of which...

In sum, Monsieur de Balzac's cane.

The frightful child strutted around the dining room, around the round table, astride that cane, and as he was holding the cane in his left hand, he was invisible, the frightful child! And Tancrède, not seeing him armed with his cane, did not think of taking it off him. O fatality!

Malvina, glad to see Tancrède consoling her daughter so kindly, left her in his arms. It was the only voluntary coquetry of which she was capable; she was drawn to it by the pleasure that she found in gazing at the two of them; it was a spectacle that charmed her eyes, the young man's beautiful face so close to the pretty face of the child.

For his part, he employed those indirect flatteries so familiar to young men—even novices in the seduction of innocents—addressing compliments to the little girl that only the mother could understand.

Tancrède smiled a lot, he made himself amiable, which was all very well—but when one wishes to seduce, it is necessary not to have anything else to do, and, whatever the wealth one desires might be, it is necessary not to neglect the treasure one possesses.

After playing with the child for some time, Tancrède went to pick up his hat—but imagine his alarm when he could not find his cane!

"It was Amédée who took it," said another child, jealous of not having had the idea first.

And everyone started calling for Amédée.

"Amédée, the Monsieur wants his cane."

"Amédée! Amédée!"

"Well, what?" said the invisible child. "Here I am—why are you shouting like that?"

"Why, he's here! Where are you hiding, then?"

"I'm not hiding—I'm here."

They looked under the table.

"Come on, Monsieur Amédée," said a furious aunt. "It's very naughty to have taken a cane that doesn't belong to you; it's very indiscreet. Why did you take that cane?"

The child, seeing that he was going to be scolded for having taken the cane, hid it rapidly in a corner and suddenly showing himself, arrived in the drawing-room empty-handed.

Tancrède, not having witnessed that scene, was searching for his cane under all the items of furniture.

"Well," said someone to the child, "what have you done with the cane?"

"Me? I didn't take the cane."

"Oh, the liar!" said the other little boy.

"What! You didn't take Monsieur's cane?"

"No, Madame."

"What were you doing in the dining room? We looked for you and couldn't find you."

"I was hiding under the table to frighten Jules," he said, audaciously—for the frightful child lied very well.

The aunt, who was exceedingly maladroit in her severity, was even more so in her indulgence. "In fact," she said, "I went to look for Amédée in the dining room myself, and I can say that I didn't see the cane in his hand."

"It doesn't matter—let's search," said Tancrède, gripped by the sharpest anxiety.

They raced into the dining room and looked behind the sideboards: nothing; beside the stove; nothing. Finally, someone shouted: "Here it is! I've found it behind the door."

Tancrède approached, joyfully.

"Here," the aunt said to him, presenting him with a cane.

O dolor! It is not his; it is not Monsieur de Balzac's cane. It is a stout umbrella-cane.

The frightful child approaches, examines the cane and, inexperienced as a thief, exclaims: "That's funny. That's not the one I was playing with—but that's where I put it. Someone's changed it."

"Oh, wretch! So it was you who took it!" cried Tancrède beside himself. Then, fearing that he might give himself away, he says: "Someone's made a mistake. Give me the umbrella—let's try to find out who it belongs to."

XIII. Without Knowing It

Monsieur Thélissier's study had a door that gave access to the dining room, and as Monsieur Thélissier lived in the heart of Paris, the business quarter, where the houses are so close to one another as to prevent daylight and air from penetrating them, Monsieur Thélissier's dining room was very dark at midday; it only had one window, set obliquely, and looking out on to a big wall, perforated here and there by loopholes, letting in light of sufferance, as it were.

It happened that a stout gentleman, emerging from Monsieur Thélissier's study after a long conference, had come into that gloomy dining room to pick up his umbrella-cane from the corner where he had left it. As he could not see, and was groping around, he made a mistake, and mistook Monsieur de Balzac's cane for his own—and as it was not raining, it was some time before he perceived his error.

ᵗ By virtue of one of those fatalities with which life is strewn, that stout gentleman had injured his right wrist a few days earlier and—as you will have guessed—had his arm in a sling. The right arm, do you see? He therefore picked up the marvelous cane in his left hand, and went out tranquilly, without anyone seeing him, invisible without knowing it.

He walked for a few moments along the boulevards pleasantly enough. So long as he was walking, all went well; he avoided people coming toward him of his own accord, and waked without encountering any obstacle. But curiosity impelled him to stop in front of some theater posters, and he scanned them attentively. The Vaudeville, the Gymnase and the Porte-Saint-Martin: he wanted to read them all, in order to make the best choice for his evening's pleasure. He had reached the Cirque-Olympique and was reading the remarkable advertisement: "Ascension, contrary to nature, of the mare named Blanche," when a young man in a great hurry, skimming the sidewalk at a rapid pace, slammed violently into the immobile and curious rock that was blocking his path.

The curious man received a terrible blow. "Look out, Monsieur!" he cried. "I'm not an imperceptible mite; you can see me perfectly well."

The young man had only one idea in his head: to avoid any quarrel that might delay him; and as he had not been looking where he was going, so preoccupied was he, he did not perceive that he had not seen anything. The marvelous was lost on him; so many things passed before his eyes, he relied so heavily on his distractions, that nothing, in any circumstances, seemed to him to be extraordinary. One is always invisible to absorbed minds.

The stout gentleman stood aside, in order not to block the path. He received several blows from elbows in the space of a quarter of an hour, but he attributed them to the narrowness of the sidewalk, and continued on his way, making a thousand reasonable reflections on the mania for imitation that makes us establish sidewalks in Paris in very narrow streets because they have them in London in very broad ones.

Good! he thought, on returning to the boulevard; *one can walk in comfort here.*

At the same moment, a commissionaire who was carrying a large rocking horse—the king of toys! sublime invention! the first emotion of childhood—over his shoulders emerged, not without difficulty from the famous Tempier store.[43] He hesitated momentarily before remarking on the boulevard, but, seeing an empty space, he advanced boldly. One might have thought that the wooden horse he was sustaining in the air was that of the siege of Troy. The stout gentleman, was strolling delightedly, unaware that the Greek machine was threatening him from behind.

---

[43] *Chez Tempier*, at 27 Boulevard des Italiens, sold "*bimbeloterie*"—fashionable knick-knacks.

As he passed in front of the clock of the Chinese Baths the commissionaire perceived that he was late and increased his pace.

Then a terrible shock jarred all the thoughts of the frightened idler. It is a great misfortune to be invisible without also being insensible—and it is quite common in this world. It often happens that people to whom no attention is paid could tell us a thousand things that would break our hearts.

The stout gentleman, having received a violent blow on the head, turned round furiously.

"Monsieur!" he said, indignantly.

He found himself face to face with the huge head of the rocking-horse, which was staring at him. Seeing that there could not have been any attention to offend in that attack, he turned his attention to the commissionaire.

"Clumsy oaf!" he cried. "Didn't you see me? As I said a little while ago, am I then an imperceptible mite, that you couldn't avoid me?"

The commissionaire, who had not seen anyone, had no idea to whom those words were addressed. He continued on his way without even turning round, for the horse did not permit him to do so.

The stout gentleman rubbed his head, picked up his hat and crossed over the boulevard.

The other side is more tranquil, he said to himself. And he advanced in the direction of the Café de Paris.

In fact, few people were walking on the boulevard, it was not yet the season when it becomes impracticable. A few women, here and there, were looking at the fabrics displayed in *Chinois* and *Sauvage*, or studying the new jewelry at Boulet's. Two or three députés, halted by an encounter, were exchanging news. Apart from that, the boulevard was almost empty.

The stout gentleman strolled on. Suddenly, however, a little laundress, bandy-legged and limping, came out of the Rue du Helder carrying an enormous basket suspended from her arm, dragging herself and her load along at an indecisive pace. The gentleman saw her coming toward him.

It's a pity, he thought, *to load that paltry creature down with such a burden.* And he changed course in order to give her more room.

The little laundress, however, vacillating in her march and fatigued by her burden, moved it from one arm to the other hand, drawn by its weight, made a detour and nearly collided with the prudent pedestrian, brushing his legs with her basket with all the strength of her frailty. He uttered an exclamation of surprise and fury.

"Be careful, Mademoiselle! Couldn't you avoid me? In truth, you'll make me believe that I'm an imperceptible flea..."

"The basket's too heavy," said the little laundress, without seeing the gentleman. And she continued on her way.

I'm having no luck today, thought the invisible man. *One slams into my midriff, another breaks my head and this one snags my legs. In truth, I'm unfortunate. And when one doesn't have the use of both arms, one is quite disorganized.*

He turned into the Rue du Helder, which he went along as far as the Rue des Trois-Frères; having arrived there he heard a window open over his head. A young woman leaned over the sill, holding a vase of flowers in her hand. They were autumn flowers: Bengal roses, Chinese asters, and red and white chrysanthemums; they were no longer fresh and were about to be renewed.

The young woman looked around. *No one*, she thought, *no one!*

But the invisible gentleman was underneath the window. *No one!*

And she tipped the flowers into the street. The gentleman received all the flowers, and their water—green and fetid water, which does not show any mercy to clothes, and which stained the stout gentleman's white waistcoat with surprising promptitude.

His anger was indescribable.

His face was risible. Fortunately, no one could see it. Green tears ran down his cheeks; asters separated from the bouquet had caught on the brim of his hat, giving him the appearance of a shepherd; chrysanthemums had come to rest on his broad shoulders and roses were hooked by their thorns on to his arms, in his side-whiskers and behind the collar of his jacket; he was like a flowering bush, unfortunately with dead flowers.

Ashamed and furious, he shook off all those bouquets, and, not being able to show himself anywhere in that state, went home—where no one was expecting him.

It was Sunday; that day, it was his custom to go out to dine with one of his friends; they was joy in the lodgings, because the master would not be back until late in the evening.

The cook, who was very pretty—an old gentleman's cook is always pretty—was due to go out to see a play. She was beautifully dressed-up, but, not seeing the domestic, her colleague, who was to give her his arm to escort her to the Gaîté, she went up to the apartment to find out what had happened to her cavalier.

The latter was occupied in choosing the waistcoat that he counted on borrowing surreptitiously from his master for the day.

When the choice was made, she helped him to make it tighter, and they amused themselves, joking, trying to fill the space that exited between his back and the fabric, by virtue of the difference in girth between the master and the servant.

The Frontin had taken two cushions; one stood in for the Monsieur's back and the other his chest and then the Frontin mimicked his master, and, what was worse, took delight in parodying him.[44]

---

[44] The valet Frontin, a precursor of Figaro, was a stock character in French comic opera of the 18th century, employed in numerous works by Marivaux and borrowed by Philippe Poisson, Jean-Baptiste Gresset and others.

"Put Monsieur's jacket on," said the cook. "Look, like this…one could believe that it's him. Oh, how ugly you are! Do the walk, then. Oh, that's it! Nose in the air! Oh, that's it! You look just as stupid as him."

Now, Monsieur had been there for a quarter of an hour, immobile, stupefied and invisible.

Finally, he found his voice. "Joseph!" he shouted.

The laughing cook, not seeing anyone, imagined that Joseph, in order to complete the resemblance, was also imitating his master's voice.

"That's exactly the way that he calls you," she said. "Ha ha ha! It's just like him."

"Rosalie!" shouted the master again, increasingly irritated.

And Rosalie, not seeing anyone and persisting in her idea, replied: "That's it. I believe I can hear him…what!"

Finally, the master, beside himself, threw down the cane that rendered him invisible, and came to grab his insolent valet by the collar with the only hand that was capable of expressing his anger.

"Monsieur!" cried the cook, flabbergasted.

"Monsieur!" said the disarmed Frontin.

"I'll throw the pair of you out!"

"But Monsieur…"

"I'll throw you out, you hear? Silence! Give me what I need to get dressed. Tomorrow, both of you will be out of here."

He got dressed.

The valet, seeing the verdure that was covering his master's garments, could not help saying: "Where has Monsieur been? What has happened to Monsieur?"

The master did not reply. All he said, as he left, was: "Take that cane back to Monsieur Thélissier's house this evening, and ask for my umbrella, which I left there."

"Yes, Monsieur."

And the cane remained in the hands of a sacked domestic!

XIV. Further Perils

Thus, it was running one more danger.

Rosalie, too upset to go to the play, gave Joseph his liberty.

Joseph prepared, sadly, to take the cane back to Monsieur Thélissier's house.

On the way, however, he meets a friend.

They chat. Joseph confesses that his master had sacked him; the friend is astonished; he knows of a vacant position that someone had mentioned to him. He suggests that they go into a wine merchant's in order to talk about it more comfortably. Joseph accepts; they drink a great deal.

Other people come into the wine-merchant's.

A joker wants the place where the two friends are sitting; the joke is taken amiss. Joseph is quarrelsome; he makes threats, making the most of the cane. The cane is scorned; the cane becomes indignant; it acts.

Insults, kicks, punches, thrusts of the cane; the combatants pursue one another into the street. The quarrel heats up to such an extent that the need for a Commissaire de Police is felt. Someone runs to fetch the Commissaire.

In the meantime, the two champions fight over the cane, one to keep it, the other to seize it, because it gives too much advantage to his enemy.

In brief, in the course of the struggle, they both grip it with their left hands.

The Commissaire arrives.

"Where are they?"

No more combatants.

"You told me that two men were fighting!" says Monsieur le Commissaire. "I can't see them."

"Oh, but I can hear them," says the maidservant. "They must be in the next street."

O mystery! Frightful oaths can be heard, but no one can be seen—no one except the bewildered witnesses, who are looking on without being able to understand.

Finally, the two enemies, exhausted by fury, both let go of the cane at the same time, and fall down at the feet of Monsieur le Commissaire, who is forced thereby to take a step back.

The cane has fallen with them. Monsieur le Commissaire, with a majestic gesture, picks it up. As he has need of all his eloquence, and he talks more fluently with his right hand, he picks up the cane with his left hand.

No more Commissaire!

Total eclipse of a Commissaire de Police!

"Ah!" says the wine-merchant to the two quarrelers. "Monsieur le Commissaire is here to reckon with you."

"Well, where is he, then, Monsieur le Commissaire?"

"He was here a moment ago."

"I can hear him speaking," says someone.

Indeed, Monsieur le Commissaire, although invisible, is no less conciliating; his pacifying speech is continuing its slow progress. His attitude is exceedingly noble, his manner very calm, but alas, his fine bearing is going to waste.

Finally, Joseph, having recovered his composure, asks for his cane; he cries that someone has stolen his cane, and Monsieur le Commissaire, in order to return it to him with more dignity, passes it into his right hand.

Monsieur le Commissaire reappears.

As there were two doors on either side of the tavern, which let out into different streets, these marvelous disappearances were explained away, and no one worried any more about the terrible quarrel.

Monsieur le Commissaire made a speech full of wisdom to the two enemies, who had become humble.

Joseph hastened to return the cane to Madame Thésillier, who hastened in her turn to send it back to Monsieur Dorimont—without suspecting, the poor woman, the torments that she was preparing for herself.

Let those who have found an amour they thought lost, who have saved a friend in danger, who have obtained mercy for a condemned man, who have seen a sick person cured, or who have remade their fortune, imagine what Tancrède experienced on seeing his mislaid treasure again. For ourselves, we recognize the impossibility of describing it.

XV. Seductions

Once having reentered into possession of his treasure, Tancrède gave no further thought to anything but his amours, and the cane was very useful to him in continuing his assiduities.

Tancrède went to see Madame Thésillier almost every day, but he went there so cleverly that he could not compromise her. As soon as he arrived in the Rue de Gaillon he passed the cane into his left hand and became invisible. He was thus able to enter the house unknown to the porter; he went upstairs and he rang. He had to wait for a moment; then the domestic came to open the door; not seeing anyone, he advanced toward the staircase to find out who had rung, and exclaimed: "They've gone!"

In the meantime, Monsieur Dorimont went in to Malvina's apartment. "I found the door open," he said.

"One of my children must have left it open. Pauline can't close it yet."

And the marvelous was explained again.

Tancrède stayed with Malvina for as long as she was alone; if he heard someone coming he got up and left quickly, passing the cane into his left hand—with the result that no one ever saw him leaving Madame Thésillier's apartment, or only rarely, even though he came almost every day.

Malvina did not suspect anything, and as she avoided pronouncing Monsieur Dorimont's name, because the name caused her to blush, she never noticed that no one ever talked about him; she believed that the silence came from her, and did not think it astonishing.

Tancrède was happy; he was beloved, that was not hidden from him, but it was still a long way from the chaste confession he had obtained to the cruel happiness for which he was ambitious.

That little woman, who seems so naïve, he thought, *will be very difficult to lead astray.*

He was right. Nowadays, there is nothing but candor that is reckless.

This situation is intolerable, he said to himself one day. *I can't live any longer in this uncertainty. At any rate, there's my cane—it's necessary to employ it.*

He reflected a great deal, and went to see *Robert le Diable* for a second time, in search of inspiration.

Madame Damoreau[45] was still at the Opéra; she sang the aria in the fourth act—"Mercy! Have mercy on yourself, and have mercy on me!"—so admirably, and was so pretty on her knees, that Tancrède was electrified.

He did not understand Robert's generosity at all; the music is so beautiful that it produces a result precisely opposite to the one that it ought to produce in the work; that is its merit. Tancrède emerged from the Opéra passionately pitiless, and headed for Malvina's abode armed with his diabolical cane.

And to that magic power, that prestige, poor Malvina had nothing to oppose: no talisman, no chaperon, not even that redoubtable defender of young women, the aegis that often preserves them in great peril, the presence of her children—for the natural protector of women is less often an old man or a big brother than a very small child. By virtue of a fatal hazard, Malvina did not have her sons or her daughter with her that evening; two days before she had confided them to their grandmother, for fear of the measles, which was in the house. It was a prudent measure, but, alas, it always brings misfortune to a young mother to be parted from her children.

It was midnight!

---

[45] The soprano Laura Cinti-Damoreau (1801-1863) played Isabelle, the female lead, in the initial 1831 cast of *Robert le Diable*, and reprised the role in several subsequent versions. Robert, equipped with the magic branch, is urged by the demon to employ it to seduce Isabelle, but cannot go through with it (and thus saves his soul).

"What, Monsieur, you here? At this hour? But that's frightful!"

"Malvina!"

"It's infamous!"

"Is it to me that you ought to speak thus, Malvina? I thought you loved me."

"Yes, I thought so…but…but how did you get here? Who let you in? If Joséphine is capable…"

"Don't accuse her. It wasn't her."

"I'll sack her!"

"Calm down, please; no one saw me come in."

"One o'clock in the morning! To come into the home of a woman who has never given you the right to act thus! To the home of a woman you love…who would have sacrificed her life for you, who trusted you. Oh, it's horrible!"

"Reassure yourself, Madame. I love you; you are free in my presence. I only wanted your love; my only error is to have believed that I had it."

"Who let you in here? Explain that mystery to me. Has François taken your money?"

"I haven't seduced any of your domestics, Madame, and if my presence irritates you to that extent, I can leave without your being compromised by any eyes."

"I don't understand—it's enough to drive one mad. Tell me, how did you get in?"

"Through the window," Tancrède replied, audaciously.

"Oh, my God!" she cried. "He might have been killed…"

Tancrède improvised a lie. "I was at the home of one of my friends, a young painter who lives nearby. The windows of his studio overlook your courtyard. I left him this evening at the usual time, but instead of going out by the door, I climbed on to the terrace, and from there to the roof. I was able to get into this house through the window of the attic, which had been left open."

The story was absurd, but for that very reason it had a good effect. The extravagant is the probable, in matters of amour.

Malvina was so alarmed by the danger that Tancrède had run for her that she forgave him for his temerity. "My God!" she said. "What folly! This house is so high..."

Seeing the heart of the woman reappear, Tancrède experienced some shame for having usurped that pity by a lie. He lost his audacity.

"Since my imprudence offends you," he said, "I'll leave you; but before sending me away so cruelly...forgive me, Malvina."

"You can't go. Getting down to that terrace would be more difficult than climbing up. It's necessary to wait."

"To wait until daylight, so that I'll be seen?"

"No, you have to hide."

"Where shall I hide?"

She reflected for a moment, and then said: "In the linen cupboard...yes no one will go in there. You can stay there until morning, and then, when everyone in the house is up and about, at a time when you can finally show yourself decently, you can leave..."

"No, I'd rather go now," he said, sadly. "I'm already repenting of having come."

"How wicked you are!"

He made as if to leave.

She shivered.

"Wait a moment longer," she said. "Perhaps there's another means..."

"If it's to spare me a danger that you're retaining me, Madame, don't worry: I have nothing to fear."

"You can't leave by way of that terrace; I don't want that."

"Oh, that's true," he said, bitterly. "If a man were found dead, fallen from a window of your house, that might compromise you."

She was so hurt by that idea that she made no reply. She was agitated; she was trembling. Finally, she made a decision.

"Stay, Monsieur," she said, coldly.

Then she went to the fireplace, reanimated the fire, lit more candles, closed the curtains of her bed and, having enveloped herself in a large shawl, came to sit in an armchair, making a sign to her importunate guest to take a chair facing her.

Tancrède then established himself as if for a visit, while she did so like a traveler resigned to spend the night in the common room of an inn, all of whose bedrooms are occupied.

Tancrède gazed at her in silence, so much did her calmness and firmness irritate him. *She doesn't love me*, he thought. *I was mistaken.*

That thought caused him to suffer. He wanted to avenge himself. He affected a great indifference, and played the role of a man suddenly cured of his love; he felt that his situation was ridiculous, Malvina had too much advantage over him by virtue of her coldness and dignity; he wanted to disconcert her by destroying that prestige, taking away from the scene all the solemnity that Madame Thélissier's grave manner gave it.

He started speaking, as if he were chatting in a drawing room, and said, in a perfectly serious one: "Did you know Madame, that Monsieur Guizot[46] has handed in his resignation?"

Malvina, who had not expected Monsieur Guizot at that hour, could not help smiling.

"It's a little late to talk politics," she said.

"Oh, I don't insist on it..."

---

[46] The Statesman François Guizot was Louis-Philippe's Minister of Education from 1832-37. He was the leader of the "Doctrinaires," and Émile de Girardin, who belonged to a more liberal rival party, loathed him.

He fell silent for a few moments, and then resumed, with the same aplomb: "It's rumored that Scribe is entering the lists for the Académie; it's believed that he's going to be nominated."[47]

She smiled again, involuntarily.

"What mania for conversation has got into you?" she said.

"What! You want me to sit here without saying a word, without sleeping, without making love, from two o'clock in the morning until two in the afternoon? For it wouldn't be appropriate for me to leave before the hour at which I might have come."

"Well, talk then—say what you please."

He searched for a few moments, after which he continued: "You have pretty candlesticks, Madame, but I notice several more items of the same sort on the shelves: those vases and jars. Are you very fond of the Chinese, then, Madame?"

The word "Chinese" has had the property of making people laugh for centuries—no one knows why—but pronounced in such a pedantic manner, at that hour, and in the romantic situation in which Malvina found herself, it was irresistible; she could not hear it without laughing.

Tancrède, seeing her less severe, added: "You haven't ever reflected, Madame, about the preference that draws you, without your being aware of it, toward the Chinese?"

"No, Monsieur," she replied. "It was necessary for a man to come to my room, at this hour, against my will..." She could not finish, and started laughing, frankly.

"You're mocking me," he said, graciously, "and with reason." But as he said that he moved closer to her, and tried to take her hand. She snatched it away swiftly.

---

[47] In fact, Eugène Scribe was elected to the Académie in 1834, so this scene appears to be set before his election, suggesting that this part of the novella's text might well have been written early in 1834.

"No, leave me alone," she said. "I'm angry with you. I'm laughing because the situation is ridiculous, and you're saying foolish things to me; but seriously, your conduct offends me, and I regret the confidence I had in you."

Poor woman! Those words were a great mistake, because they brought the conversation and all thoughts back to the subject of amour. When one is annoyed with a man one loves, it is a great weakness to talk to him about his errors; it risks allowing him to justify himself. It was a great imprudence for such a young woman to expose herself to listening to the excuses of such a beautiful young man at half past two in the morning. A pardon accorded at that hour can quickly turn into a crime for both parties.

Alas, he justified himself, by means of the sole excuse that explains similar imprudences: an excess of love—and it is a very good excuse, where a woman is concerned. He asked for forgiveness so humbly that she no longer dared hold it against him. He was so sorry to have displeased her that it was necessary to console him.

What can I tell you? Only a few minutes went by, and a notable change had taken place in the dialogue of those two people, formerly so irritated with one another. The conversation had become more in harmony with the hour, the place, the situation and the individuals; there was no more need, in order to sustain it, to talk about the ministry or the Académie, and there was not a single further mention of Monsieur Scribe's election or Monsieur Guizot's resignation.

XVII. Unknown Joy

There is for a woman a moment of delirium, of which the being she loves most is ignorant, and which would be the most beautiful secret of his life if he could divine it.

It is the moment of solitude that follows an adored presence; it is the instant when, returned to herself by the suspension of an overwhelming felicity, the soul expands and savors with enchantment a joy previously too potent, almost painful by virtue of its excess; it is the instant when timid thought launches forth, abandoning itself, delivering itself, when passion expresses itself, when ecstasy rediscovers its voice.

Then life lights up, our heart catches fire with a thousand glimmers, like a temple for a triumph, adorned with all its glories, shining as if for a celebration; it is the triumph of being loved, and in the transports of its gratitude, it raises toward the object of its worship a *Te Deum* of actions and graces, a hymn of happiness and love.

To remain alone with the intoxicating thought: he loves me! That moment is perhaps the sweetest of all moments for a woman, in whom the most intense passion is always veiled by a cloud of timidity. It is then that she loves, then that she dares to love. She is alone, with no witness—for even the one that one cherishes the most is still a witness.

In his presence, the soul is long constrained; the sight of him throws us into such profound disturbance, his voice makes us shudder, his gaze dazzles us, his thought absorbs us; an emotion so violent is almost a torment; we are then prey to our happiness; we do not think of savoring it—but as soon as a temporary adieu delivers us, our magnetic soul respires.

Then she exhales; she recovers her will-power; she understands herself; she knows that she is in love. She is no longer subject to her love; she accepts it, so to speak. Then she dares to recall the master that has just departed, dares to evoke him; she brings him back in imagination, retains him, speaks to him, confesses all her folly, recounts all her joy. As he is no longer there, except in dream, she is no longer afraid of him, she can be frank, she tells him everything. Alone, she has more love than in his presence; alone, she is more his than when her head is on his heart.

And Malvina believed herself to be alone.

When it had been necessary to part, trembling and at a discreet pace, she had led Tancrède to a kind of antechamber where he was to spend the rest of the night.

Tancrède had stayed there for a few minutes. But—there are always comical hazards in the most romantic adventures—it happened that a dog, an unfortunate dog, which lived in a nearby room, scented our hero and became alarmed; it started to bark, under the pretext that it was a good guard; it barked so forcefully, so obstinately and so faithfully that Tancrède understood that he could not stay in that place without attracting the attention of the whole house, for the gift of invisibility is no protection against the nasal divination of a dog.

Tancrède retracted his steps. Madame Thélissier had not yet closed the door to her apartment; the candle that she was carrying had gone out, and that had delayed her. At first Tancrède wanted to speak to her, to explain the danger, but he changed his mind.

Why worry her? he thought; and he went back into Malvina's room invisibly.

And Malvina thought she was alone—but he was there!

How emotional she was! She could scarcely stand up.

She leaned on a table, and then passed her hand over her face in order to collect her ides; she thought she was dreaming; but when she had cast her eyes around her, when she had looked at the place where he had been, still ornamented by his presence, she understood the truth; she understood that she was in love, that she had just given her life by way of love.

Then she thought about him, and nothing but him.

She does not think about the children she adores, her husband, whom she respects and has betrayed, of her mother, who was always irreproachable and who would curse her...she no longer knows anything of her past life; she has forgotten her birth, her name, her youth; her existence only dates from an hour ago; she could not say who she is; she has forgotten everything, I tell you—and that is her excuse.

She is in love! That powerful word fills her heart entirely. Tomorrow, she will remember; tomorrow she will rediscover remorse and fear, but this evening she is loved, and her entire thought is amour.

Alas, nothing has prepared her for amour. It has struck her like lightning, without her being able to think of avoiding it. Such a violent passion in such a young heart is terrible; Malvina is too young to have the idea of combating it, too honest not to be happy; but that joy is mortal, it intoxicates her, it leads her astray. Poor woman! In her joy, she is to be pitied.

Yes, but to him she gives pleasure; for him she is seductive thus.

What delirium! What fever! She speaks; he listens.

"How I love him!" she says, in a stifled voice "How charming he is! How beautiful he is! Oh, my God, how I love him!"

She is mad—but he finds her sublime in her dementia. He contemplates her; he adores her.

Suddenly, he sees her smile, and then, as gracious as a child, she gathers her long black tresses in her hand. She looks at them, she remembers how he kissed them; and, madly, she kisses them and admires them. She admires her arms, her beautiful white hands; she remembers what he said to her while caressing them; she repeats his words, so tender, the voluptuous flatteries that intoxicated her; she rejoices in being beautiful, is proud of herself, and loves herself like a memory.

One thought makes her blush, another softens her; she weeps; then the most intense joy returns. She appeals to him, to the man who loves her, pronounces his name with intoxication, reveals all her passion to him; and pale, trembling, vanquished by such a new emotion, she falls to her knees, exhausted, dissolving in tears and smiling with love.

And he is there...immobile...intoxicated; he is there, watching her love.

For a long time he has respected her delirium, in order better to discover so much love; but soon, that love carries him away; Malvina is so beautiful on her knees! His courage abandons him; he is about to launch himself toward her, to sustain her in his arms, and hug her to his heart.

Adieu, oaths! Adieu, mystery of the marvelous cane! Monsieur de Balzac, you will be betrayed; Malvina will know by means of what prodigy Tancrède has followed her, your secret will be revealed...tremble, then, Monsieur de Balzac...but no, you are the author of *La Physiologie du mariage*, and you will conserve all your rights...

Just as Tancrède, carried away by his tenderness, is about to reveal his presence, shuffling footsteps become audible in the corridor.

Malvina gets up...she listens...the key turns in the lock; the bedroom door opens...Monsieur Thélissier, clad in a floral-patterned dressing gown, coiffed in a black silk night-cap and holding a night-light, comes into his wife's apartment.

Although invisible, Tancrède recoils in fear.

Malvina shivers, but it is not remorse that is agitating her; remorse is already reason, it is strength; a remorse is already a distraction in love, and love in the heart is still omnipotent; the hour of remorse has not yet come; the sight of her spouse does not give it to her. It is not shame that she experiences at the sight of him, it is hatred. She is not afraid of his anger, she is horrified by the thought of his tenderness; her one thought is to avoid it. She is indignant; her entire soul revolts against him; she no longer belongs to him, she is free; she has been liberated by treason. O misery! Her duties have changed master; her fidelity is to the man she loves; the man she does not love is her enemy.

Monsieur Thélissier is far from divining what is happening in the soul of his wife; he believes her to be incapable of experiencing the slightest passion. He married Malvina so young that he still treats her as a child. The people who have seen us born never know us; they do not want to understand that one grows up, they always look at us through the lens of their prejudices; and in their stupid astonishment, they call "strange changes of character" the natural developments that age brings into our ideas, our faults and our sentiments. They cannot imagine that a woman they have seen playing with a doll at the age of six can die of the chagrin of love at twenty-five—and yet, it has been seen.

Monsieur Thélissier, moreover, had no understanding at all of the delicacies—or, to put it better, the corruptions—of the heart; he was what is known as "a good husband," easy to live with and generous, but professing the least romantic ideas about women, regarding a wife, in the final analysis, as a legitimate servant, made for raising children and maintaining the household, but unworthy of occupying seriously the thoughts of a gallant man—which did not prevent him, however, from finding Malvina very pretty.

"You're up already, Mina?" he said, on seeing his wife by the fireplace. "Did that accursed dog wake you up, as it did me?"

"I'm ill," she replied, in a tremulous voice.

"Ill, my child! What's the matter, then? Do you want me to go fetch Villermay?"

"I have a horrible fever; leave me alone."

"You're very grumpy this evening."

As he spoke, Monsieur Thélissier placed his night-light on a table and turned in order to go and close the door, which he had left open.

"Don't close the door," she said. "I need air; I'm stifling."

Tancrède was in torment; he wanted to go away, but a cruel curiosity retained him.

"I'm suffering badly," said Malvina, impatiently, seeing that her husband was establishing himself in her room with the intention of staying there. "I need to look after myself; go; leave me alone."

"No one can look after you better than me, Mina—but you don't look ill at all; you're pink, and if..."

"My head is on fire, I'm suffering horribly."

"You need to go back to bed. Put up your hair and go back to bed."

"I don't want to, I tell you; I got up when you came."

"But what's the matter with you? I no longer recognize you. You're calling me *vous*, like a monsieur! Come on, don't be capricious—come and kiss me."

Malvina shuddered; a mortal chill ran through her veins.

"You're sulking," said Monsieur Thélissier. "Well, I'm not proud, I'll come to you."

With those words, Monsieur Thélissier advanced toward his wife.

She tried to move away; he held her back.

"Come on," he said, passing his hand over Malvina's forehead, "let's see whether that little head is burning..."

And then he gave her, on the forehead, a frightful kiss...

That kiss reverberated in Tancrède's heart like a rifle-shot; he ran to the door and fled.

O disenchantment!

That kiss had awakened Malvina from her stupor; such a great danger rendered her perfidious; she softened suddenly, and in an almost gracious tone she said: "I beg you, leave me alone; go, I'll call you if it its worse, but go; if I can sleep, I'll be better tomorrow."

The good Monsieur Thélissier yielded to his wife's insistence; he was a little chilly, and he was not sorry to go back to bed.

Malvina, poor woman, left alone, wept all through what remained of the night.

She is weeping still, for the ingrate Tancrède has never returned.

The shock that he had received was so powerful that it had killed his love. Malvina always appeared to him in her husband's arms; he could not free himself of that image. Of all his memories, that alone remained.

Sometimes he said to himself: "Whence comes that disgust? I knew full well, though…yes, but I had not seen it." He cried in his fury: "Accursed cane! Is that the happiness I ought to expect from you? Was it really worth the trouble of making myself invisible for…? Poor fool! I loved her so much! I would love her still, but for that fatal gift. What a lesson!"

Why was he astonished? That's life. To glimpse the person who charmed our soul and our eyes in an unfavorable light, is that not what is known as a revelation? To discover that one was mistaken to love, to believe, to hope, is that not what one calls self-knowledge? There are people who take a great deal of trouble getting there! If a new mythology were to be made, we would demand that Eros would not be the son of Beauty but of Ignorance.

What am I saying? Is that not the moral of the misfortunes of Psyche, punished so harshly for wanting to know who it was that she loved?

One day, Tancrède made a terrible resolution.

I shall no longer love any but widows or young women, he said to himself. *It's a free woman that I need.*

And, like an apostle of Monsieur Saint-Simon,[48] he set forth in search of the "free woman."

---

[48] Disciples of the utopian socialist Claude-Henri de Rouvroy, Comte de Saint-Simon (1760-1825), especially the faction led by Barthélemy-Prosper Enfantin (1796-1864), were active in their propaganda throughout the 1830s, undeterred when their experimental community at Ménilmontant was closed down by the authorities in 1832.

XVIII. A Poetic Evening

One evening, when it was not raining, Tancrède was wandering the streets of Paris, not knowing which theater to favor with his presence.

The Vaudeville was putting on *La Croix d'Or*; the Variétés was staging *La Croix d'Or*; at the Théâtre du Palais-Royale, *La Croix d'Or* was playing. Always *La Croix d'Or*! Which to choose? The embarrassment was considerable.[49]

If each of the theaters had been putting on a different play, Tancrède would have been able to decide, but the same subject everywhere! He would have needed to be a veteran theater-goer to know which one he ought to prefer.

While walking along the boulevard, Tancrède perceived a kind of queue of carriages at the corner of the Rue Taitbout.

Is there a theater along there? he wondered—and, mechanically, he headed in the direction from which the queue was extending.

The carriages all had coats of arms painted on their panels; the horses were melancholy, the coachmen miserable; on the other hand, the footman were well-dressed and redolent of good houses.

From time to time, old or young women showed themselves, in turbans or bonnets, and it was a pleasure to see their ill humor.

---

[49] *La Croix d'or*, a two act comedy by Michel-Nicolas Balisson, Baron de Rougement and Charles Depeuty was published as a book in 1835, and cannot have been playing in multiple venues before that publication, so this reference and the one to Scribe's candidature to the Académie imply different temporal settings. This chapter was published separately in Berthoud's *Mercure de France* early in 1836, ahead of the book publication of the full text, and might well have been written—or rewritten—specifically for that publication.

Suddenly, the glass of one of the carriages came down, and a young man stuck out his blond head.

"What is it?" he said. "Why aren't we moving?"

"It's a queue, Monsieur."

"What? We're in a queue?" he exclaimed. "Oh, that's charming. Madame de D*** wrote to me: 'Come, it will be just us; I haven't invited anyone; it's an informal little soirée.' And now it turns out that she's assembling all Paris."[50]

"She couldn't do otherwise," said another voice emerging from the same carriage. "Everyone wants to hear Lamartine's verses, and Madame de D*** would have fallen out with all her friends."

Ah! thought Tancrède. *It appears that these Messieurs are going to a literary soirée. Well, I too am curious to hear Lamartine's verses. Why shouldn't I too give myself that pleasure. The cane owes me a reparation.* And Tancrède passed the cane to his left hand.

The carriage containing the two young men stopped outside the door of a pretty little town house in the Rue Saint-Georges, and the two superb dandies went into the antechamber, without suspecting that they were three.

They took off their overcoats. Tancrède, stupidly, was about to do the same, but fortunately remembered that it was unnecessary, so he kept his on, and replaced the hat that routine politeness had caused him to take off.

The two battens of the drawing room door opened, and Tancrède quickly passed through first while the newcomers were being announced, and were busy reestablishing an amiable disorder to the curls of their hair.

Tancrède was beginning to get used to being invisible; that day, however, privately, he felt embarrassed to be so

---

[50] In the 1830s Charles d'Outremont, who had married the Comtesse de Duras, a daughter of the famous salon-keeper the Duchesse de Duras (née Chaire Kersaint, 1777-1828), had a town house in the Rue Taitbout; he routinely styled himself Outremont de Duras, while his wife retained her title.

poorly dressed, with muddy boots and a morning suit, in a florid, gilded, perfumed salon ornamented by the most elegant women in Paris.

A great anxiety gripped him. *What if, by virtue of carelessness, I were to take my cane in my right hand?* he thought. *What if I were to be seen? What would become of me?*

He shivered. He experienced so much shame that he hastened to pass into another room, less richly-furnished and less brightly-lit than the first, which was more in harmony with his costume and his thoughts. Tancrède was timid and embarrassed by his appearance, as if he could be seen.

He was not yet at his ease in the second reception room; there were too many people there. He took refuge in a third, much smaller, where there was no one, and went to sit down at a table covered with books, newspapers and albums, in order to put his face straight. What do you think of that? An invisible man who feels he need to put his face straight! It proves that society always acts upon us, even when we are most independent of it.

It also proves that each of our advantages is a science, and that it is necessary to study it to get the best out of it. A cured mute has no idea how to talk; he has to spend years learning how to pronounce the words. A man suddenly enriched does not know how to spend money. In the same way, an invisible man needs experience and study to understand that he cannot be seen, and to turn that incalculable advantage to his profit; otherwise, it will only be one more embarrassment for him.

Tancrède amused himself, therefore, looking at the albums, without thinking that it was not for that reason that he had fraudulently entered the salon. All the great names of delicate painting radiated among the designs. There were flowers by Redouté, horses by Carle Vernet, bedouins by Horace, charming water-colors by Cicéri, those little landscapes that have so much space, which enable one to see so far and dream for such a long time…ravishing Spanish women by Géniole, caricatures by Grandville and Henri Monnier, two brigands by Schnetz, all minor masterpieces.[51]

While toying with the various papers that were on the table, Tancrède perceived a partly-open letter whose signature caused him to shiver.

Chateaubriand!

The letter, in which Monsieur de Chateaubriand offered his apologies for being unable to come to the soirée, had surely been forgotten on purpose, and left on the table intentionally. The mistress of the house was evidently counting on people being indiscreet.

Tancrède realized that intention, and read the letter curiously.

I have never been so tempted in my life. To implore in such an amiable manner an old beast like me! I need all my forty years of virtue to resist the double attack of your beauty and your intelligence; God knows how I can get out of it. Alas, I don't go out; I no longer go out and I no longer see anyone. If I last until next winter, I count on depositing my gray hair on the altar of the Fates, in order that they won't give anyone the trouble of cutting them, and I shall take my place among the most ancient perruques of your acquaintance. May your youth take pity on my catarrhs, influenzas, rheumatisms, gouts and so on. In depriving myself of the pleasure of seeing you and hearing you, I am more unhappy than culpable.

Chateaubriand

That gaiety, that coquetry, that pretention to old age in a man still so young, that still-poetic joke made by a genius so

---

[51] The reference are to Pierre-Joseph Redouté (1759-1840), Carle Vernet (1758-1836), his son Horace Vernet (1789-1863). Pierre-Luc-Charles Cicéri (1782-1868), Alfred-André Geniole (1813-1861), "J. J. Grandvile" (Jean Gérard, 1803-1847), Henri Monier (1799-1877) and Jean-Victor Schnetz (1787-1870).

imposing, had something original about it, which charmed Tancrède. What is more seductive than grace united with strength? Do you know anything lovelier than a soldier playing with a child?

Tancrède thought that note so gracious that he amused himself by copying it in pencil. It was an infidelity; it was a crime; but what is the good of being invisible if not to be indiscreet?

As Monsieur Dorimont was occupied in the execution of his crime, several people came into the room.

"Whose hat is that?" asked a young woman, laughing.

Tancrède turned round swiftly, and then perceived his hat on a chair beside him. He wanted to take it back, but attention was focused on the wretched hat; he dared not cause it to disappear by putting it back on his head—for the hat was only invisible when Tancrède was wearing it; apart from him, the hat ceased to participate in the marvelous; everyone could then admire it.

"Whose does the hat belong to?" exclaimed a young foreigner.

"To no one—there's no one here."

"It must belong to the piano tuner, who left it here this morning," said someone laughing.

"It's Madame de D 's hairdresser's hat. Hide it, Monsieur de Bonnard."

Suddenly, an elegant foot kicked the hat under the table.

Saved! thought Tancrède.

A rumor became audible in the salon.

"Here's Monsieur Lamartine!" someone exclaimed.

"No," said someone else. "Lamartine's gone to see his president this evening. Monsieur de *** saw him at Dupin's.[52] He'll come along later."

"Who's that arriving, then?"

---

[52] Lamartine's correspondence with the mathematician and economist Charles Dupin (1784-1873), a professor at the Conservatoire des Arts et Métiers, has been published.

274

"It's the Duchesse de ***."

"The beautiful Duchesse de ***? I don't know her. Let's go see her."

Everyone moved back into the large drawing room.

Since Lamartine hasn't arrived, Tancrède thought, *I might as well stay here.*

And he resumed his pillage.

A second letter was on the table; it was signed *Béranger.* Which one? There are several Bérangers.

The word "prison," which he found in the first lines of the letter, left no more doubt. It was obviously not the peer of France or the counselor to the court of cassation who had written it.

That letter too was a note of apology.

Alas no, Madame, it's not coquetry that you're employing with me but generosity; you once passed sweet consolations through the bars of my prison, or my dungeon, as we poets say. Today, you are taking pity on a poor voluntary recluse and you want to reattach him to the society that must seem to you so full of happiness, for it is grateful to you. Unfortunately, Madame, the recluse is suffering, and his physician has forbidden him society and its emotions. Deign to accept my excuses, and have a little compassion for the privation that is imposed upon me.

There was a tone of melancholy in the note that made Tancrède pensive. He smiled at a comparison that occurred to him.

It's a singular hazard, he thought, *that has enabled me to find such a cheerful letter from the poet of* Atala *and such a graciously sad note from the singer of* Lisette.[53]

---

[53] René de Chateaubriand's novella *Atala, ou Les Amours de deux sauvages dans le désert* was actually published in 1801; 1831 is presumably a misprint, but seems to appear in all the editions available for consultation. The oft-imprisoned Pierre-

Then he reflected, and, recalling the famous booklet by Monsieur de Chateaubriand, published in 1831, and the beautiful song by Béranger—"Tell me, soldier, do you remember?"—he replied that well-organized men of genius are able to unite the two genres: depth in sentiment and lightness in wit.

While reflecting thus, he copied Béranger's letter. He had just finished copying it when a great agitation became manifest in Madam de D 's drawing rooms.

Monsieur de Lamartine, who had arrived some time before, had consented to recite a few verses.

Tancrède hastened into the salon in order to listen to him.

Tancrède had never seen Monsieur de Lamartine, but he recognized him immediately; he was exactly as he had imagined.

Monsieur de Lamartine read the admirable poem of *Jocelyn*, or, rather, the scene of the archbishop's confession in the person of Grenoble; for the whole poem is a dramatic scene and would have a superb effect in the theater.[54]

Monsieur de Lamartine's voice is pure and sonorous; he recited the lines in a very simple manner, but with inspiration and dignity, with the profound and veiled emotion that is all the more powerful for being restrained: the suppressed emotion, so communicative, which seems to be taking refuge in the auditorium because the poet is rejecting it.

Everyone was delighted, transported. Tancrède, intoxicated by admiration, had forgotten where he was, who he was, Monsieur de Balzac's cane and all imaginable marvels; the

---

Jean de Béranger (1780-1857) wrote several ballads addressed to or featuring a mistress to whom he referred as Lisette, the most popular of which came to be known simply as "La Lisette". The line quoted is from an older popular song to whose tune Béranger fitted several new lyrics.

[54] Lamarttine's *Jocelyn* was published in 1836, although the author might well have heard the poem recited before publication.

necessity of being invisible was far from his thoughts. Along with everyone else he exclaimed: "It's sublime! It's the most beautiful poetry that has ever existed! it's a divine inspiration!" and all sorts of true things that we are far from contesting—but as he said all that, he raised his arms, gesticulating and applauding, and the cane became what it wanted to be.

Finally, as Monsieur de Lamartine arrived at the lines: "A divine change took place in my entire being, and when I raised my head I was a priest!" Tancrède, having moved forward in order to get a better view of the poet, whom everyone was thanking, perceived that several people were looking at him, and shivered.

A woman of respectable age demanded his name, in a scandalized fashion. He poor young scatterbrain hastened to become invisible again, but it took him a long time to recover from his disturbance.

To have been seen so poorly dressed in such an elegant company, to have remained in a drawing room for an entire evening in a morning coat, with his hat on his head—what shame! He was a man dishonored.

Admiration renders people indiscreet; they imagine they have rights over the object of their appreciation. After those beautiful verses, they wanted more, and tormented Monsieur de Lamartine for a long time.

"Have you written any new verses?" someone asked.

"Yes, addressed to me," said a young poet, proudly.

"Oh, recite them!" someone cried.

"I'm afraid that I might not be able to remember them…"

"Begin anyway—you'll find them."

Monsieur de Lamartine, who was in an extraordinarily obliging mood that evening, recited some lines that he had written the previous day, to Monsieur Léon Bruys d'Ouilly.[55]

---

[55] Léon Bruys d'Ouilly and Lamartine travelled to Italy together in 1832; they collaborated on the "roman en vers" *Thérèse* (1836), in which the poem reproduced here, dated

Children of the same hill
Drinkers from the same stream,
Like two nests in the hawthorn,
God put your cradle close to mine.

From our neighboring roofs the smoke
Melted into the same sky,
And from your perfumed herbs,
My bees stole the honey.

Often I saw your sweet mother
Treading he paths of my meadow,
Bringing you, like a young brother
Very small, toward me by the hand.

And lifting you toward my lyre,
In her slightly tremulous arms,
Teaching me to read in your verses:
A child playing with fire!

And I thought, by adventure,
In contemplating the moving gold
Of your silky tresses,
Where kisses often rained:

"Charming visage, happy childhood!
Devoid of foresight and forgetfulness,
May glory never hollow out
The slightest crease on that white brow.

Paris, April 1836, appeared as a headpiece. I have not attempted to reproduce the scansion of rhyme-scheme of the poem—
or any of the other translated verses—assuming that conserva-
tion of the meaning is more important than mimicking the
form.

Let no torch ever illuminate
Those lovely eyes with somber flame
Like a smoking firebrand
Reflected in a stream.

Let no predatory claws
Whiten before their time
Those tresses where my hand drowns,
Thick foliage of spring.

Let the hand that is vibrating
In my breast at every moment
Never tear a fiber from your heart
Like a string from an instrument.

If a voice sings in our soul
Let its melodious echo
Sound in a woman's ear
And its glory in two fine eyes."

I left; I wandered for years;
When I returned to the verdant valley
In search of our faded youth
I found nothing but your name.

The fire that made me a poet,
Jealous of your restful days,
Had descended upon your head
Like an eagle upon a flock.

The nascent star of your career
Had inundated your forehead,
Darting glints of light
Which presaged its fire.

Full of intoxicated anxiety,
Listening to your voice swell.

I thought again of your solitude,
Your childhood in the woods.

Weep for your son, my valley,
He will know the worth too late,
Of an hour of your flowing shadow,
A dream that one cradles apart.

The flight of the transient breeze,
Pure sleep to the sound of the stream
And the voices of sister and mother,
Which summon us to awake...

XIX. A Muse

There was a young woman in Madame de D***'s salon whom Tancrède had noticed, firstly because she was very pretty, and secondly because the extreme simplicity of her attire contrasted with the elegant luxury of the women around her.

That young woman's name was Clarisse Blandais. She was seventeen; she had left Limoges, her home town, and had come to Paris in order to be a poet, as Petit-Jean had come to Amiens in order to be Swiss.[56]

Her mother, a reasonable and philosophical woman, had said to herself: *Nowadays, the métier of poet is a very good one for women. Madame Valmore and Madame Tastu have a celebrity that does no harm to their happiness; they find in their talent noble enjoyments and pure consolations.*[57] *Mademoiselle G***, who makes verses like my daughter, enjoys a very agreeable situation in society. Mademoiselle Mercoeur, who is much lamented, received a pension from the govern-*

---

[56] The quotation refers to a line in Racine's comedy *Les Plaideurs* (1668): "Il m'avait fait venir d'Amiens pour être Suisse," from a tirade by the porter Petit-Jean. Eating or drinking "à la Suisse" [Swiss-style] means doing it alone.

[57] Marceline Desbordes-Valmore (1786-1859) was an actress and singer as well as a poet and novelist; her *Élegies et Romances* (1819) was a significant early contribution to French Romanticism; she was the only female writer included in Paul Verlaine's *Les Poètes maudits*. Amable Tastu, née Sabine Volart (1798-1885) published her first volume of *Poésies* in 1826, and also published items in *La Muse Française* and the *Mercure de France*; her talent was praised by Lamartine, Hugo and Sainte-Beuve. Chateaubriand also dedicated a poem to her. The "Mademoiselle G*** included in the list of female poets of the 1820s is presumably Delphine Gay.

ment of five hundred francs, which would be sufficient for my daughter and me.[58] *I don't see why Clarisse, who is incontestably a poet, should not obtain the same advantages; she has no fortune, I shall have difficulty marrying her off; let's try to make her a destiny by means of her talent.*

And the wise mother had packed her bags, bid farewell to the banks of the Vienne, booked three seats in the coupé of the diligence, and the Limoges mail-coach had brought one more muse to the capital.

The sixtieth, I believe.

Madame Blandais did not know anyone in Paris, and sometimes felt frightened by the boldness of her voyage, especially when her traveling companions asked her indiscreet questions; she got out of it by means of lies. How could she confess that she was going into that chaos in order to make herself known, and to seek admirers in that whirlwind of strangers in which she could not count a single friend? For her only introduction into that new world, Madame Blandais had a single letter of recommendation that the député of her arrondissement had given her for one of his colleagues—but that colleague was Monsieur de Lamartine!

That was a great deal.

Monsieur de Lamartine had greeted the young woman as a hope; she had confided a few verses to him of which she was proud; and in sum, Madame de D***, an old friend of the great poet, had taken responsibility for introducing the Corinne of Limoges into the literary world.

Clarisse was still trembling with the tender emotion that her protector's verses had caused her when the mistress of the

---

[58] Elisa Mercoeur (1809-1835) owed her meteoric reputation as a child prodigy and prolific writer largely to the publicizing efforts of her mother, Adélaide Mercoeur, who issued her complete works—including novels and plays as well as her poetry, the most important collection of which was *Poésies* (1829)—in 1843 and wrote an extravagant memoir of her life.

house approached her and told her that people wanted to hear her.

After him!" said Clarisse, with mild indignation.

"You promised me this morning," said Madame de D***, "that you would not have to be begged."

Clarisse took the hand that Madame de D*** was holding out to her, and went to sit down in the place designated to her.

At first, Clarisse was very red. Because everyone was looking at her; he she became very pale, because she was anxious, for what she was experiencing was emotion rather than timidity. Timidity sometimes disguises itself as a kind of misery; an invincible timidity is born of a defect; one only hides oneself sincerely when one has no interest in being seen. Madame de Lavallière would perhaps have been Madame de Montespan if she had not been lame. The pride of beauty is in nature; a horse poses as soon as it sense that it is being admired; even an elephant is not indifferent to success, and I don't see why we can't admit frankly the petty sentiment of vanity that we have in common with the elephant.

Clarisse was trembling, but she was brave; she had no self-assurance, but she had courage, and perhaps consciousness of her worth.

She began: "Why trouble my days in their finest year..."

"Wait, my daughter," said a voice emerging from a provincial that the color of a turtle-dove decorated with knots of red and green ribbons. "Let's say what the subject is, or these ladies won't understand."

"The mother doesn't have a high opinion of our intelligence," said a young woman.

Madame Blandais went on: "This is the subject: there was, in the vicinity of Limoges, a very respectable man who often came to see us at Chantelouve. He as a cousin of the president, and his first marriage had been the niece of a public prosecutor; he was a senior tax-collector himself."

Mysterious hilarity.

"My daughter pleased him; he asked me for her hand in marriage via the sub-prefect himself; I made my daughter party to the proposal, but he disproportionate union frightened her—the suitor was sixty-four years old. The child asked me for three days to reflect, and by way of reflection she wrote the lines that she will have the honor of reading to you."

"That woman speaks very well in public," said one of our great orators.

"I wasn't listening," said another. "What's the subject?"

"A young girl refusing to marry a tax-farmer."

"That's very poetic. Why? Was there a reason for the refusal?"

"We're about to find out. A few faults, a few vices, a few infirmities, perhaps."

"Oh, the horror!" cried several women, laughing.

"She's very pretty, the girl," said a young man. "She has charming eyes."

"Shh! Listen."

She's delightful, Tancrède thought.

The young woman, who had been smiling graciously during her mother's speech, then resumed in a soft voice:

Why trouble my days in their finest year,
My mother, by imposing a dolorous bond:
A union of hazard, profaned in advance
   In which the heart counts for nothing?

Fortune, at your age, is perhaps a joy,
But at mine, its favors are superfluous;
In our innocent days will its gifts give birth
   To a single extra smile?

Would you, then, hide my blonde tresses
Under velvet pleats and heavy jewels?
Do you find that white adornment, mother,
   Sufficient for my fifteen years?

I don't go to balls to be looked at;
Prideful fêtes my heart does not envy
I would weep as I donned an embroidered robe,
    A present from an aged spouse.

Reason, you say, bids me to marry
Should I be sacrificed to its law so young?
God bids me to hope; for the soul that prays,
    The true reason is faith.

Why withdraw your wing before time?
My face is still as timid and serene.
I'm happy here, mother; when I weep,
    It isn't from chagrin.

Far from the agitated world my blissful days flow
Why are you so fearful of a lot that that I love?
You say that wars are fought, that thrones collapse
    But I know nothing of that.

Dolor is still a mystery for my soul;
My banqueting lips have only tasted honey;
I see only the flowers and fruits of the earth
    And the azure of the sky.

I have placed my dwelling outside the storm;
I hear the wind moan, but feel it not,
I only take freshness from the torrent
    That ravages the plain.

The glacier rose that a black rock protects
Flowers fearlessly thus, sheltered from winds,
And in those accursed fields, those deserts of snow,
    Finds only a spring.

Thus, in these vales of misery profound,
In these fields of egotism where nothing can grow,

In this land of ingrates, this desert of society,
    I bloom in order to love.

I know not what instinct makes me cherish life,
A perfume of the future presaging kind fate,
Tells me: You shall know glory without envy
    And love without remorse.

I believe in happiness, my shining star;
A protective angel leads me by the hand,
And I shall go to God without tearing my veil
    On the brambles of the path.

As one believes in the spring that the winter sends,
As one waits in the bosom of night for the day,
Sad, I sense the advent of indescribable joy,
    Alone, I envision love.

One who will love me, whom I will love, exists
Invisible to you he enchants my eyes,
He appears charming to me, my life assists
    Like a spirit of the skies!

And I blush with dread at the thought alone,
As I am seen to shudder in his presence,
As if he were there, in my insensate joy,
    I fear to betray myself.

That dream of my heart is no chimera;
He will come; don't send me away from him
Keep me with you, mother, oh let me stay.
    To await him in our arms.[59]

---

[59] This poem, original to the present work, was reprinted under the title "La Jeune fille," signed "Mme de Girardin" in the periodical *Le Caméléon*, in 1837.

Those verses caused so much pleasure that the preface, which had caused laughter at first, was forgotten. Clarisse was charming in reciting them; her gaze was inspired, her entire person embellished. The harmony of beauty, youth and poetry was a seductive ensemble. Then again, there was a conviction of optimism in her entire soul that deflected criticism. Malevolence felt impotent against that young heart, so rich in hope, so well armed in joy for the future.

Clarisse obtained the most brilliant success. She was finally able to please.

Do you know who she resembled? Do you know Mademoiselle Antonia Lambert, the young woman whose voice is so beautiful, who sings with inspiration, as one would like to recite verses?[60] Well, she alone can give an idea of Clarisse. Like her, Clarisse was tall and slim; she had the same blue eyes, the same blonde hair, the same soft smile, the same graceful bearing, and the same blend of confidence and modesty in her manners that the combination of extreme youth and great talent provides.

If everyone was delighted, what must Tancrède have been experiencing, to whom those verses seemed to be addressed? *One who will love me, whom I will love, exists/Invisible to you he enchants my eyes...* There was an entire destiny in that hazard.

He spent the rest of the evening observing Clarisse, and that observation was dangerous. One could not know her without loving her. Clarisse had a great deal of intelligence, finesse and naivety; her simplicity was astonishing.

"She's not pedantic," someone said.

And why should she have been?

---

[60] Antonia Lambert's singing was complimented more than once in the *Revue de Paris* during 1836. She subsequently became Madame Labarre, but continued singing, often accompanied on the piano by her sister Honorine, but seems to have made little impact on history outside the salon society of the period.

Pedantry supposes difficult labor; it serves to call attention to a talent that has been costly. A pedant is a man who has paled over an idea that was not even his own; he wants people to know how much trouble he has taken. The savant always remembers the science, but the poet does not perceive the poetry; he does not search for his ideas, they come to find him of their own accord, and he expresses them in order to soothe himself. One makes verses as one falls in love, without being conscious of it, without willing it. The poet rhymes his dreams in order to staunch his soul, without pretentions, without asking to be admired, as the man who falls in love makes a confession to express what he is experiencing, and it never occurs to such a man to say: "I did well to say 'I love you' today; I must have been very seductive!"

Yes, the veritable poet is as simple as verity itself; he cannot be pedantic; pedantry lives on pretentions, and pretentions are incompatible with involuntary talent. In any case, poets are the aristocrats of intelligence; why would they have, as pedants do, the manners of parvenus?

XX. The Sibyl's Lair

Madame Blandais and her daughter, seeing that it was already one o'clock in the morning, looked at one another anxiously.

"We ought to think about going, my child," said the mother.

"Marguerite will think that we're dead," said Clarisse.

And they headed for the door.

A valet came toward them. "Who is it necessary to call?" he asked.

He imagined that he was about to received the reply: Michel, Louis or Simon—the name of some domestic.

"I would like a cab," said Madame Blandais, with satisfaction—because it was a great luxury for her to travel in a carriage. She was ready to make the most of it.

Tancrède, who had followed Clarisse, on hearing those words, was frightened by the idea that those poor women were about to find themselves, at two o'clock in the morning, without a protector, exposed to all the rigors of a fiacre-driver. Guided by a somewhat tender zeal, he resolved to escort them invisibly all the way to their abode.

I'll know their address, he thought. *There's always that.*

The fiacre arrived.

Madame Blandais climbed up first. When it was Clarisse's turn, the invisible Tancrède, placing himself between her and the coachman, helped her up the footstep; it was on his arm that she leaned. He was also careful to preserve her white attire from contact with the wheel, and was recompensed for his concern by hearing the young woman say, as she sat down in the carriage: "How polite these cab-drivers are!"

The vehicle moved off. Tancrède followed it, first with his eyes, and then, the ardor of the horses having relented, matching their pace. After a moderately long journey, he arrived at the same time as the fiacre and the muse in the Rue de la Bienfaisance where she lived.

Come on, Tancrède thought. *Courage! Better to be disenchanted right away*. And he went into the apartment with the two women.

"Ah, there you are, Mamzelle!" cried an old maidservant. "Oh, my God, how frightened I was! Oh, Mamzelle, let me embrace you."

"What's the matter with you, Marguerite? What's happened to you?"

"Nothing, Madame—but to you? How anxious I was! Did you get lost, then?"

"No, Marguerite," said Clarisse, with a glorious expression. "It's the soirée that finished late."

"Was it a celebration, then?"

"I'll tell you all about it. Is there any milk left? I'm hungry."

"What! You haven't eaten anything? At the home of a Comtesse?"

"Yes, truly, there were excellent dainties," said Madame Blandais, "but Clarisse refused everything. It was superb: the beautiful drawing room! It was very warm. This hat was stifling."

Madame Blandais began to undress.

For the sake of discretion, Tancrède went out with Marguerite, who went to look in her little kitchen for any provisions that might remain there. Tancrède took advantage of the time to observe the more-than-modest accommodation, and everything that he saw pleased him, with its mixture of bourgeois simplicity and natural distinction.

Marguerite had to go into Clarissse's room; she went in to look for two silver spoons, because the young muse was the custodian of all the silverware in the house, which consisted of six sets of cutlery, a saucepan and her old school mug.

Tancrède then amused himself studying Clarisse's little bedroom. What can I tell you? He fell in love with that room.

A very small, very young bed—if one can put it like that—veiled with white curtains, was situated at the back of the room. Near the bed was a pretty lacquered table; that had to be a new present, as it richness contrasted with the rest of the furniture.

Next to the window was a kind of desk; on the desk were books—an English dictionary, collections of poetry—a work-basket, a vase full of flowers, and a box of candy. A small bookshelf was attached to the wall; Tancred examined it rapidly; the books were all incomplete sets; he could not help laughing. On the mantelpiece there was a small watch, a rosary, a light purse and a flask. Tancrède observed all of it with pleasure, and yet with a voluntary malevolence.

I want to know her, he said to himself. *I want to be disenchanted right away. Clarisse pleases me too much; I shan't quit her until I no longer love her.*

And the memory of Malvina caused him to sigh bitterly.

Marguerite, having completed her search of the cupboard, returned to Madame Blandais' room.

Madame Blandais was busy stoking up the fire; Clarisse cleared a small space on the mantelpiece to take her frugal supper. The mother had put on a dark-hued dressing gown; the young woman had changed her muslin dress for a long peignoir in blue percaline. She looked charming. Tancrède thought her even prettier in that negligee, in perfect harmony with his own costume, which had nothing ceremonious about it.

"Here's the milk, Mamzelle," said Marguerite, "and a little bread."

"Ah! That's good—put it down there. Do you want some, Maman?"

"No, really; I only drink milk in Paris when I'm forced to do so. What a difference from the milk of our meadows! In Paris, the milk is detestable; it's falsified."

"No, Maman, this is excellent—anyway, I'm hungry."

Clarisse tasted the milk, and then got up in order to go in search of sugar.

291

In the meantime, the amorous invisible man, falling into the commonplace of amour, wanted to touch with his lips the cup that an adored mouth had just pressed. He picked up Clarisse's cup, but, either by virtue of distraction or real appetite, he drank much more milk than he intended. He put the cup down again, trembling.

Clarisse came back and saw that her cup was half empty.

"Who's drunk my milk!" she cried, like a schoolgirl.

"You did," replied her mother, laughing.

"Me? I scarcely sipped it. I'm sure of it—someone has drunk my milk. It's a mystery. Perhaps there's a cat here."

"No," said Madame Blanchais. "Is it your invisible being, do you think?"

"Seriously, someone has drunk my milk."

"It was you, scatterbrain—I saw you. You're mad; you never think about what you're doing. Go on, hurry up and finish your supper; it's late and Marguerite is sleepy."

"Marguerite's already asleep; I sent her to bed."

Clarisse sat down by the fire and started dipping her bread in the little milk that Tancrède had left her.

"It's very amusing, high society," said Madame Blandais. "I love Paris, staying in Paris suits me—it's a pity it's so expensive. Do you know that in the three months we've been here, we've already spent four hundred francs?"

"Four hundred francs!" repeated Clarisse, with astonishment. "That's a lot."

"It's enormous! It's a king's ransom—but the money won't be wasted if you're successful and make a name for yourself; that soirée has already gone well."

"Did I say my verses well, Maman?" Clarisse asked.

"Yes, very well, except that you don't speak loudly enough—they couldn't hear you in the other room."

"So much the worse for the people who were there! I don't want to shout—and then, I was scared. There were some nasty young women there; one of them made fun of my black shoes—I heard what she said—and another said, to excuse me: 'She hasn't been in Paris long.' She must be kind, the one who said that."

"The Comte de D*** is a very handsome man," said Madame Blandais.

"Yes, but I don't like him. I like Monsieur de Lamartine better. What a fine face!" Tancrède was about to be jealous, when she added: "But there was a beautiful young man there—did you see him?"

"No."

"You didn't see him? He was quite remarkable, though, because he was wearing his hat, which seemed singular to me."

"You're mad, my girl. A young man wouldn't be permitted to keep his hat on in Madame de D 's drawing room."

"I saw him! Only for a moment, it's true, but I saw him with his hat on his head. Perhaps he'd asked for permission to keep it on," said Clarisse, laughing, "like that old Monsieur de Livray, who was always too cold, and who came in saying: 'With your permission, Madame?'—meaning that he wouldn't take off his bonnet."

"Child!" said Madame Blandais.

"I can assure you, Madame, that I saw, in Madame de D 's home, a young man who had his hat on his head, that the man looked at me intently, and that I've never in my life seen such beautiful eyes. He had a gaze that one remembers, that one carries away; I'll never forget those eyes…I can still see them."

Tancrède could not resist an invincible temptation. He was facing Clarisse, behind Madame Blandais' armchair. Rapidly, he transferred his cane to his right hand, and became visible.

Clarisse screamed—but already the cane had returned to the left hand, and Tancrède had disappeared.

"What's the matter with you, girl?"

"Nothing, Maman," said the young woman, trembling all over.

"But you're so pale…"

"It seemed to me that I saw, again..."

"What?"

"The young man."

"You're having visions today, as you did when you were small; you were always talking to us about apparitions, nuns who came to sit next to your bed. You're still the same; just now you said that someone had drunk your milk, but it was you who drank it, and now you're seeing young men in my room!"

And Madame Blandais raised her eyes to the heavens, smiling.

"Well, all right," said Clarisse, gaily. "I too am having...what did you call them?"

"Visions, apparitions."

"No, that's not the fashionable word; it's longer than that...hallucinations. So, it's decided that I'm having hallucinations. Bonsoir, Maman."

So saying, Clarisse went to kiss her mother.

"Bonsoir, my daughter," replied Madame Blandais. And, pursuing her joke: "If you find your handsome young man in your room, call me."

"Yes, Maman."

And Clarisse went to bed.

XXI. A Phantom

Here are two characters invented expressly for my cane,
Tancrède thought. *A dreamy young girl who doesn't know
what she's doing, who doesn't listen to anything, who doesn't
look at her surroundings, who thinks herself scatterbrained
and always expects to be mistaken; and a mother who's rather
credulous, accustomed to the childishness of her daughter,
who is even pleased by her distractions, considering them as
evidence of poetry. The more the young woman says extravagant and incomprehensible things, the more poetic she's believed to be, to the extent that she could go mad without anyone perceiving it.*

Tancrède dared not follow Clarisse into her room; a sentiment of respect held him back. That delicacy also inspired
another sentiment in him; he thought he was too badly dressed
for a phantom. He dared not risk an apparition in a frock-coat;
he was not really elegant enough to be an ideal. In any case, he
was already too much in love not to be careful of himself; one
acquires a considerable importance in one's own eyes as soon
as one is in love, and one does not take risks lightly.

As soon as it was possible to slip out of the house where
Madame Blandais lived, Tancrède went home. The next day,
when he woke up, he remembered Clarisse, and admitted that
he had become as attached to her, in one day, as if he had
known hr since infancy.

He had found her so genteel, so simple, that he had forgotten that she wrote verses. It was out of vanity that he recalled her. The role of the ideal that he was preparing to play
was singularly flattering to his pride, and reconciled him to his
excessively great beauty, the advantage from which he had
suffered so much. In fact, it was a noble ambition to make
himself the Apollo of such a charming sibyl, to realize such
poetic chimeras, to appropriate such beautiful dreams, to dom-
inate such a pure imagination—in sum, to make himself

adored as an angel—when he possessed all the qualities of a bad lot.

However, as Tancrède was, fundamentally, a thoroughly honest man, he did not want to risk being loved before knowing whether Clarisse pleased him enough for him to consent to link her life with his, and he applied himself first to observing her mysteriously.

That observation did not leave him in uncertainty for long. Every time he saw Clarisse he loved her more; everything that he discovered in her candid and poetic soul charmed him; there was inspiration, discovered in its most sublime aspect; there was love, observed it its birth, in its primal purity, a love as vague and fresh as spring foliage; there was, in sum, the most gracious mixture, a passionate dream in a heart full of innocence, a gaze of genius with a child-like smile.

The situation of invisible observer had so much charm that Tancrède was content to prolong it, and yet he was already very much in love. The tenderness that a young woman inspires is more patient; one regrets on her behalf the holy ignorance of which a day of love will inevitably rob her; an adieu is always sad, even when it leads to happiness.

Clarisse was joyful without knowing why. She was living in an amorous atmosphere, which intoxicated her. The invisible Tancrède was often close to her; that veiled presence acted on her soul without her being aware of it. Sometimes, a rapid apparition enabled her to glimpse the gracious phantom; she smiled, she had become accustomed to those visions; she expect then; she counted on them; if they had been absent for several days she would have been unhappy.

Her life passed quietly, sometimes in writing verses brilliant with youth and hope, sometimes in running around in the rather large garden of the house in which she lived; she often sang familiar songs, for entire hours, and then others that she improvised n her joy.

Her mother, who heard her crazy roulades, asked her then: "What's making you so happy? What's wrong with you?"

Nothing was wrong; she was sixteen years old, and the weather was fine; that was sufficient to explain her god mood. The seductive phantom also had something to do with her joy, but Clarisse did not know that, since she believed that the extraordinary apparitions in question were an effect of her imagination.

Sometimes she talked about them to her mother, laughing.

"Oh, Maman," she said, "a strange thing happened to me yesterday. As I was arranging my hair in front of the mirror...you'll make fun of me."

"Well?"

"I saw my beautiful young man."

"In the mirror?"

"Yes. I turned round right away, thinking that he was behind me, but there was no one there—and yet I believe I heard laughter."

"Go on," said Madame Blandais. "Now you think you can hear him; before you were content to see him."

Clarisse told her mother about that apparition, but there was another, which she did not mention.

Tancrède had received a letter from Monsieur de Balzac, which announced his imminent return to Paris. The moment to return the cane was imminent; it was necessary to hasten to take advantage of its power.

One morning when Tancrède had come to see Clarisse, he had found her in tears; he was very sad then that he was invisible, seeing the woman he loved weeping and not being able to ask her what is wrong, not being able to console her.

The poor child wept for a long time. Then Madame Blandais arrived, and told her, in a severe tone, to put her hat on and come for a walk in the Jardin des Plantes. It was a long journey and the walk bore some resemblance to a punishment.

Madame Blandais relied on forced marches to calm Clarisse's over-excited imagination. It was obvious that Madame Blandais had scolded her daughter, but why? That was what Tancrède wanted to know. He followed Clarisse and her mother; he listened, but at first they walked in silence.

Finally, Madame Blandais spoke: "You'll repent of it later, my girl. All your dreams won't lead to anything. Besides which, the young man is very amiable, and since Madame de D*** is interested in him, he must certainly be a distinguished individual. If you refuse all your opportunities, you'll never marry; your invisible man won't marry you, and you'll remain an old maid. Truly, my child, it's unreasonable of you to refuse the chance of a good marriage for the sake of crazy dreams. It's my duty to enlighten you. I forgave you when you refused a man older than you, but this time I'll be more severe."

Oh, so that's it, thought Tancrède. *Poor thing! She's being tormented; it's necessary to give her a reason.*

Tancrède accompanied Clarissa as far as the Jardin des Plantes, then, surrendering her to the ferocious animals, he went back home to write to his mother about his marriage plans.

That evening, he returned to Clarisse; she had gone to bed early; fatigued by her long walk, she was sound asleep. Tancrède went into her room, opening the door as quietly as possible.

Clarisse did not hear anything. At that age, sleep is a lethargy.

Tancrède was astonished to find Clarisse already in bed and asleep. He approached the bed quietly; he heard the regular respiration that is evidence of a real slumber so profound that no dream is permitted to surge forth and no memory to survive.

How well she sleeps! Tancrède thought.

And that slumber, which he envied, inspired a great respect in him.

That's definitely the slumber of a poor young woman who has been weeping, he said to himself. *She must be very weary, after such a long walk in Paris! They don't dare go by carriage for the sake of economy, and Clarisse would rather come back on foot than risk a public vehicle. I like that, and I know that little pride is honest. Clarisse is too elegant by nature for her condition. What a joy it would be to be rich, and to be able to give her the position in society that she merits. Oh, my lovely Clarisse, how I love you!*

As he formulated these words, Tancrède leaned over the bed and imprinted a chaste kiss on Clarisse's rosy cheek. Clarisse did not wake up. Tancrède, stirred by the kiss, risked another, more affectionate.

Clarisse did not wake up. Then Tancrède started to laugh, and he sat down n an armchair beside the bed, and watched her sleep.

He remained there for a few minutes, contemplating that sweet image, and his entire future appeared to him. He imagined the happy days that he would spend with Clarisse, the pleasure that he would have in taking her with him, to introduce her to is mother. He was quite certain that Madame Dorimont would love Clarisse; the young woman would please her by virtue of her intelligence, and the delicacy of her sentiments.

He thought about the suitor with whom Clarisse was being menaced, and wondered why Madame de D*** wanted to marry him off; he reflected bitterly on the manias of great ladies, who always wanted to patronize, without recalling—the ingrate—that he owed the pleasure of having seen Clarisse to the mania in question. He was amused by the idea that the young woman had refused a real marriage for him, whom she did not know, whom she loved in a dream; he found that success very flattering.

He thought that his encounter with Monsieur de Balzac had been a very fortunate hazard for him, that he owed his fortune and his happiness to it, and he thanked Monsieur de Balzac, who had lent him is cane, with all his heart.

In his imagination, he bought a little country house near Blois, and prepared there, for his illustrious friend, a beautiful apartment in which he alone would have the right to stay. He also remembered Monsieur Nantua, the help that he had ob-

299

tained from him, and the brilliant fortune that he owed to him; he also prepared an apartment for Monsieur Nantua in his country house, in his imagination. The he thought about the pleasure of having a pretty wife all to himself, a very ignorant and naïve young woman, whom love frightened and a word caused to blush; an entirely fresh young heart that had never loved, whose first emotion, whose first joy he would have...

And as all these ideas were pleasant, they lulled him gently. By degrees, his morning walk, the silence, the half-light, the sympathy of slumber, and the purity of his sentiments, perhaps, acted upon his senses, and involuntarily, drawn by example, he ended up falling asleep himself.

His head slumped slowly on to the bed; it remained lying there; and the cane, which a dormant hand was no longer sustaining, soon slid on to the carpet.

At daybreak, Clarissa opened her eyes.

How astonished, how frightened, she was, to find herself looking at a man asleep beside her bed!

She was so frightened that she was unable to cry out; she remained paralyzed and stupefied for a moment.

Finally, when she found her voice, she shouted: "Maman!"

Tancrède woke up with a start. It took him a few seconds to remember where he was. He looked at the young woman; and Clarisse's eyes, staring at him fearfully, disconcerted him.

Am I no longer invisible, then? he wondered.

Then he remembered his cane, and, seeing it lying at his feet, realized how he had given himself away.

At first he experienced an intense chagrin, thinking about Monsieur de Balzac and the secret that he had promised to keep; but soon, remembering Clarisse's credulous character, he was reassured. He picked up the cane adroitly, and ceased to be visible.

Clarisse's eyes were still fixed on him, but as she could no longer see him, her gaze was no longer the same. Strangely enough, she had been frightened when he was there, but now that she was no longer there, she was sad.

She remained pensive for a long time, and, not seeing anyone in her room, noticing that the door was firmly closed, persuaded herself that she had not seen anyone.

"What a singular dream1" she said, aloud, with a sigh.

Then she put her head back on her pillow, perhaps in the hope of continuing the dream.

Tancrède loved that credulity.

She'll find that apparition quite natural, he said to himself. *She'd rather believe that she's losing her mind than imagine that an amorous man wants to seduce her.*

And that is why superior souls are so easy to deceive: because the most extraordinary things—fascinations, phenomena, miracles; everything, in sum—appears more probable to them than a malevolent action.

Tancrède went home laughing at that night of love spent so peacefully; at first he regarded himself as a fool who had not been able to take advantage of such a good opportunity; afterwards he judged himself as an honest man who would have blushed to abuse the innocence of a young woman; but finally, as he had a precise mind, he admitted that he was simply an egotist, who already respected, in the purity of Clarisse, the reputation of his wife.

Clarisse spent the day as cheerfully, but with a great emotion in the depths of her heart: the vague and burning agitation that has so many charms. She told herself that she had had a vision, an agitated sleep, as a consequence of fatigue, caused by an excessively long walk.

Doubtless I had a fever, a fever of exhaustion. She did not give it any further thought.

But when evening came, she felt more fearful; an instinct warned her not to trust herself. She dared not go to bed.

I'm not sleepy; I'll read...no, I'll copy out those verses of Madame Valmore's that I like so much, L'Ange gardien.[61]

---

[61] The poem in question was subsequently set to music by Pauline Duchambge, and is now best known in that version; it is mentioned in passing in Flaubert's *Madame Bovary*.

She sat down at her table, but at the slightest noise she looked up, and trembled.

What if he comes? she thought.

Suddenly, she imagined that there was a secret door in her room; she picked up a candle and started searching. Her chamber was so small that it was soon passed in review: no secret door, or trapdoor; there was no means of placing the slightest fantastic adventure in that bourgeois dwelling. Clarisse was ashamed of her search; she thought about all the jokes that her mother would make if she found her running around like that, in the middle of the night, after a phantom. She resumed writing, and stayed up all night, without getting undressed, without sleeping. She still told herself that there was nothing to fear, but she acted as if she were in danger.

Tancrède came to see her in the morning; he found her very pale, and, perceiving that she had not gone to bed all night, reproached himself for having caused her so much anxiety. He searched for a means to reassure her.

Poor thing! Tancrède thought. *Is she going to spend all her nights like that? She'll make herself ill.*

Then the strangest idea occurred to him. While Clarisse was with her mother, Tancrède picked up the pen that she had just put down, and after the last paragraph that was partly copied he wrote these words:

I shall not come tomorrow. Tancrède.

XXII. A Day of Inspiration

I shall not come tomorrow.

He comes every day, then! And he's going to come again! What a mystery! My God, what should I think?

Clarisse spent entire hours looking at that strange writing. Her mind lost itself in suppositions; her ideas were seething; there was an endless maze of conjectures.

To begin with, the name Tancrède worried her.

Someone's making fun of me, of my romantic character, she thought, *and they have chosen that name from a tragedy in order to make me feel that it's ridiculous to write verses.*

Afterwards, she became accustomed to the name, and even ended up liking it. She remembered the noble bearing and the soft gaze of its bearer; she told herself that such a perfectly beautiful being could not be wicked, and would not toy in a cowardly fashion with an innocent young woman who had no protector.

She was reassured—and as soon as she was reassured, she was madly in love. Doubt having been effaced, there was a reaction of confidence; she abandoned herself to it naively.

Yes, she said, *I believe in him; it's someone who loves me; he doesn't want o deceive me. He'll come; I'll give him my life; I'll never love anyone but him. So much the better if he can see me, so much the better if he can hear me: he'll know everything that I think, he'll know that he's my only hope, that I love him like the guardian angel who watches over my days. From now on I shall only speak and act to please him; I won't do anything that might afflict him. Oh, what happiness if he accompanies me always! He'll see that I love him, and he will love me. I know that my dreams will be accomplished!*

While thinking thus, Clarisse was inflamed by the most poetic sentiments; involuntarily, her emotions were formulated in harmonious verses; the memory of the guardian angel who presided over her days inspired her. She spent the whole night working—which is to say, soothing her soul by means of the naïve expression of her sentiments.

And the next day, when Tancrède, invisible, returned to her presence, he found her at grips with the Muse; he saw that the means he had employed to calm her imagination had only served to excite it further. That was bound to happen, so it was not very astonishing, but it did not matter; he congratulated himself for the mad idea: the agitation of dread had given way to that of inspiration, and that was much better.

Beehives can be made of glass, through which one can watch the bees at work; the rooms of poets ought to be made transparent, in order to observe them in inspiration. What a fine spectacle it would be to see rich thought awakening! Thanks to his invisibility, Tancrède had been able to observe a woman at grips with passion, prey to her memories of amour; now he observed a young woman at grips with her genius, prey to her involuntary desires, her pure hopes of love.

How charming Clarisse appeared to him thus! How beautiful her eyes were, ornamented with their genius! Her blonde hair descended in golden waves over her white shoulders; her complexion was dazzling; her mouth was inspired; her smile was radiant. Tancrède contemplated her with delight. They had changed roles; it was no longer him, but now her who seemed an ideal being; she was the one who was the celestial apparition, the divine image that fascinates the gaze.

Dazzled and transported, Tancrède thought that he was seeing the angel of poetry; he was already searching for her white wings; Clarisse appeared to him to be ideal, sublime, so beautiful that he ceased to love her momentarily...and admired her!

But she recited the verses that she had just finished. The verses were for him, and when he understood that his love had inspired them, he forgave her for having had the talent to compose them.

My Guardian Angel[62]

Like the immortal being of whom Marceline sings,
His forehead is not ornamented with dazzling rays;
He does not have the freshness and infantile grace
    Of the roses of spring.

His veil is not golden, his robe is not white
As the nenuphar, the friend of deserted waves;
Over my heart, entirely his, he never leans
    Repeating my verses.

I never hear his slow and sonorous voice,
Softly murmuring these sweet, confused words.
A harmonious language that one can still hear
    When one no longer hears it.

Never, never has his hand trembled in mine!
Once only, his dark gaze encountered my eyes,
And yet he holds my life enchained to his
    Like the earth to the skies.

At the poetic hour when the declining day
Extends a red veil over the horizon's rim,
When a bird singing joyfully upon the hill
    Falls sleep in the bush.

My angel appears to me, but as in a dream,

---

[62] Author's note: "These verses are by Mademoiselle Élise
Moreau, who has kindly given me permission to publish them
in this novel." A second note identifies the "Marceline" to
whom the first line of the poem refers as Madame Valmore.
Élise Moreau (1813-1876), also known as Élise Moreau de
Rus, another protégée of Lamartine's, who later became Madame Paulin Gagne, published *Rêves d'une jeune fille* in 1837
but this poem does not appear therein.

His features are covered in white mist;
It seems to me then that he lifts me in his arms,
  And sometimes I'm afraid.

And I pass my hand over my burning brow
My emotional voice becomes tremulous,
And I say to my angel: "Oh speak, speak to me,
If it is only required to die to be your lover,
You can dispose of my life as you will,
  For my life is yours.

But alas, I am only a child of the earth,
And you, whose existence is a divine mystery,
Whom the breeze puts to sleep in an azure palace,
Can you really love me? I have the hope,
Son of heaven, my love perfumed with innocence
  Ought to please your pure heart.

Without you I would be solitary, uncomprehended,
In this vale of tears where the poet breaks
Her soul at every step toward the immortal abode,
I would often turn my eyes full of sadness
And I would see the flowers of my youth grow pale
  Before the end of the day.

Be blessed! But to flee to the eternal spheres
Are you already deploying your transparent wings?
Your absence is a hurt from which I suffer so much!
Oh, give me your hand, let us rise to the skies together!"
Rapidly he vanishes, and then it seems to me
  That my heart will die.

But suddenly I sense, penetrating my soul
A memory softer than a woman's voice;
For my angel has said: "One day you shall see me!
When the noble children of the sacred harmony
Place on your head the palms of genius

I shall open my arms..."

He is not abusing me? I believe his words
As I believe the sublime symbol of heaven.
He knows that he is my sole support down here;
He has read every page of the book of my life;
He knows that my heart, as pure as a lily.
    Has only beaten for him.

Oh, you who smile at this strange mystery,
Do not ask me my Angel's sweet name.
It is secret; my heart, henceforth calmer,
Will only speak it to God—but the mocking crowd,
The crowd that laughs at every dreaming soul
    Shall never know it.

XXIII. An Illusion Destroyed

After the hours of inspiration came the days of depression; reason reappeared as the sweet images vanished.

Poor Clarisse became anxious again.

Either it's someone who has got to Marguerite and is amusing himself frightening me in order to make fun of me, she said to herself, *which frightens me, or it's my imagination that is ill, in which case I'm going mad, which is terrible!*

That idea tormented her. She dared not tell her mother all that she experienced, for fear of making her anxious in her turn, but she was no longer seen to laugh; her poor soul was deeply troubled. She became pale; her beautiful complexion faded.

Madame Blandais, who attributed that melancholy to the marriage project she had favored, dared not mention it again. Tancrède, however, who knew its cause, took pity on her; he was frightened by the excitement to which he had given rise; he reproached himself for having played with an imagination that was too ardent—and in order to destroy the excessively dangerous effect of a dream, he summoned reality to his aid.

One morning, he hired a box at the Théâtre-Français and sent a ticket for the box to Madame Blandais, on behalf of the Comtesse de D***.

Clarisse wanted to question the domestic who had brought the ticket but he had already left. She was astonished that Madame de D*** had not written a note, but thought that she had probably instructed her domestic to offer an explanation that he had forgotten…and the other and daughter went to the Théâtre-Français, believing that they were going to Madame de D***'s box.

"Has the Comtesse not arrived yet?" Madame Blandais asked the usherette.

The usherette, who did not know to whom she was referring, replied: "No one else has come yet."

"It's early," said Clarisse. "Madame de D*** doubtless knows the play. She'll come later.

The play was *Angelo*, a drama by Victor Hugo, performed by Mademoiselle Mars and Madame Dorval.[63] It was a marvelous choice for a young woman from the provinces who had never been to a play.

Well, Clarisse did not listen to a word of the play. She forgot that it was by Victor Hugo. She did not see either Mademoiselle Mars or Madame Dorval. She did not see anything on the stage, and she did not see anything in the auditorium.

Nothing…except a phantom, a fantastic being the sight of whom gripped her with fear: an unknown man whom she recognized; a tall young man with a pale and melancholy face, who was standing at the entrance to the balcony and looking at her attentively.

It was the same man she had seen at Madame de D***'s house; the same one she had seen one evening in her mother's room; the same one she had seen one day in her mirror; the same one she had seen sleeping beside her bed.

The same one…O surprise! O joy…perhaps.

At that sight she remained motionless, paralyzed. She was so disturbed that she feared that she might be ill. The most various sentiments agitated her. First, she experienced a great joy at discovering that the man she loved in her dreams really existed; then a sentiment of dread saddened her; there is always something bitter in verity; on seeing her ideal being speaking, smiling like a gentleman, she mistrusted herself.

Yes, it's that young fop whose has made fun of me, she thought.

---

[63] Victor Hugo's *Angelo, tyran de Padua* was first staged in 1835. The widowed Marie Dorval (1798-1849), the actress who played Catarina, was Alfred de Vigny's mistress, and also—at least according to rumor and Vigny's fervent jealousy—George Sand's lover. Her great rival Mademoiselle Mars, who played La Tisbé, was then nearing the end of her long career.

And a frightful doubt seized her heart. She fell back into discouragement, and tears ran down her cheeks without her thinking of wiping them away.

Madame Blandais, fully occupied with *Angelo*, did not notice her daughter's emotion—which she would, in any case, have attributed to the misfortunes of Catarina.

For some time, Clarisse remained absorbed in the most ponderous reverie. When she looked up again, she perceived that he was looking at her through his opera-glasses: him, the handsome unknown, the deflowered ideal; for she experienced the opposite of what is ordinarily afflicting, when it is the reality that one regrets: "That which I believed to exist was only vain illusion..." In her case, it was the illusion she regretted; she was weeping for her cherished phantom; she was afraid that verity might take away all his prestige. She was afraid that she might not love him any longer.

During the entr'acte, seeking to calm herself down, she tried to triumph over her emotion and to fix her eyes on *him* in her turn, but she saw him quit the place where he was and leave the hall.

An inexplicable instinct warned her that he was coming to talk to her, and when she heard the door of the box open, she experienced a violent heartbeat.

She sensed that it was him.

It was.

Clarisse dared not look at him; she was trembling.

"Pardon me, Mesdames," he said, coming into the box. "Has Madame de D*** not arrived?"

"No, Monsieur," Madame Blandais replied. "That astonishes me."

"Perhaps she's not coming," Tancrède went on, in the most natural fashion. "I saw her this morning; she had several people dining at her home today; she'll doubtless only be free later."

And Tancrède sat down in the box as if Madame de D*** had asked him to wait for her there, and, in order to explain his presence better, he spoke about her as if he knew her intimately.

Madame Blandais sustained the conversation. Clarisse said nothing; she was listening to Tancrède speaking—his voice pleased her so much! His tone had something soft and honest about it, which reassured her.

"Madame de D*** is a charming woman," said Madame Blandais. "So beautiful, so gracious."

"She's delightful," said Tancrède, enthusiastically. "Full of intelligence and learning; she's a very distinguished person."

It amused him to say all that, because he knew nothing about her; he had only ever seen Madame de D*** on the day when he had entered her home fraudulently; he could call her beautiful, since he had seen her, but he could only praise her mind at hazard.

He was about to continue inventing further qualities for Madame de D*** when he looked at Clarisse; the painful expression of her visage stopped him; he understood the sentiment of jealousy that had caused her suddenly to go pale, and, in order to destroy the unfortunate effect of the eulogies he was lavishing on Madame de D*** he added: "Unfortunately, we shall soon lose her; she's returning to Italy next week."

Those words were magical; Clarisse's cheeks became pink with pleasure, and an involuntary smile brightened her features.

"It's bad news that you're giving my daughter," said Madame Blandais, who had not followed the mute drama. "Madame de D*** is her sole protectress in Paris; her absence will be a great loss to us."

"Mademoiselle your daughter can do without a protectress now," said Tancrède, in a tone that Clarisse alone would understand. Then he added, for Madame Blandais: "Her talent is already celebrated."

"Nevertheless," said Madame Blandais, "I regret Madame de D***; it's very unfortunate for us that she's leaving."

"Believe me," said Tancrède, "you no longer need her." Addressing Clarisse, he added: "Isn't it true, Mademoiselle, that you no longer need anyone else now."

He said those words so tenderly that Clarisse blushed. She lowered her gaze and did not reply.

"Say something, my daughter," said Madame Blandais. "You're like a child this evening; one can't get a word out of you." She went on: "Clarisse has never been to a play before, Monsieur; it's not astonishing that she should be so anxious on finding herself here. She's not timid, however; perhaps you were at Madame de D***'s house on the evening when Clarisse recited her verses?"

"Of course I was there," Tancrède replied, "and I shall never forget that day. For me, it was an evening of emotions and adventure; not only did I have the pleasure of hearing Mademoiselle's beautiful verses, and those of Lamartine, but I was greatly amused. I had bet one of my friends that I could keep my hat on my head all the time that Lamartine was reciting his verses, without anyone noticing."

On hearing that, Madame Blandais and her daughter looked at one another.

"And I won my bet!"

"You lost it!" said Clarisse, sharply.—and was then very confused, at having said it.

"My daughter is right," Madame Blandais said. "For I remember that when we returned home that evening, she mentioned to me, with astonishment, a young man that she had noticed because he was wearing his hat—whereupon I said that it was impossible, and that she was seeing things."

"Well, it was true; the most extraordinary things, you see, always end up being explicable."

Those words, which were addressed to Clarisse again, caused her to blush for a second time.

The curtain went up; the second act began. Madame Blandais turned toward the stage, and no longer thought about anything but the play and the actors.

Clarisse wanted to listen, but could not; sometimes she looked without seeing, sometimes she lowered her head and remained plunged in her reveries, overwhelmed by a profound emotion.

Noting her preoccupation, he said to her, smiling: "You don't like the play, Mademoiselle? But it's Mademoiselle Mars who is playing it."

"Oh, that's Mademoiselle Mars," she said.

"Yes—she's the one playing the role of La Tisbé. See, I'm not misleading you."

And Tancrède showed her a newspaper that he was holding, in which the names of the actors were listed.

Clarisse turned round to read the page he was holding out to her, but found herself so close to him that she hesitated.

She dared not look at him. Oh, how troubled she was then! She could see him: the man she had only ever perceived in dreams! He was there; he was speaking to her; he admitted his presence. How full of delights the moment was!

On seeing her so beautiful and so emotional, he forgot the role he was playing.

"Clarisse," he said, with the most tender emotion, "do you recognize me?"

She looked at him, utterly astonished. "I was afraid that I was mad," she said.

"He's a frightful man!" exclaimed Madame Blandais, revolted by the behavior of the tyrant of Padua toward his wife.

And from then on they only paid attention to *Angelo*.

XXIV. A Dream Realized

When the play ended, Tancrède said: "Since Madame de D*** has abandoned you, Mesdames, will you permit me to accompany you?"

Madame Blandais accepted Tancrède's arm, with all the more confidence because she believed him to be an intimate friend of Madame de D***, who had become an eccentric individual.

Tancrède took Madame Blandais and her daughter home in his carriage.

Having arrived there, he put on a semblance of leaving them, but he took his cane in his left hand and went in with them, invisibly, in order to discover what they were going to say about him.

"Well, you were right, my child," said Madame Blandais, as she went into her room. "That young man was at Madame de D***'s house."

"Oh, Maman, if you knew...!" Clarisse exclaimed. But she did not finish.

Facing her, she had just perceived Tancrède, who was signaling to her to be quiet.

She was disconcerted.

Noticing her agitation, Madame Blandais attempted to calm her down, saying, cleverly: "He's very handsome, that young man, but I think he's very stupid. I wouldn't be surprised if he were only amiable as a phantom. What do you think?"

"I believe, on the contrary, that he's very intelligent." And then she started laughing, because she thought Tancrède was probably still there, and able to hear what she had said to her mother.

The mysterious presence worried her, though. She dared not leave, and it was not until Madame Blandais said to her:

314

"Go to bed, my child; you don't look well; the play has made you ill," that Clarissa decided to retire to her own room.

She kissed her mother more tenderly than ever, and withdrew.

She waked slowly and pensively, but when she went into her room, how surprised she was to see Tancrède sitting at her desk! He seemed perfectly tranquil; he was sitting there like a brother waiting for his sister, or a husband waiting for his wife.

Clarisse's first impulse was to flee and go back to her mother, but a glance from Tancrède retained her.

"Have no fear," he said, in a softly respectful tone. "Come in, Clarisse; I need to talk to you."

Clarisse did not move.

"Come on, then, child—are you afraid of me? Since I've been coming here every day, you ought to have more confidence in me. Why be afraid? I don't deserve it."

The reproachful tone in which Tancrède spoke afflicted the young woman. She took a few steps toward him, and then stopped.

Tancrède was wounded by so much mistrust.

"You don't understand me," he said, sadly. "Adieu."

And he took the cane in his left hand.

Clarisse, no longer seeing him, emboldened by regret and absence, launched herself toward the place that he seemed to have quit, and found herself in front of him.

"What a prodigy!" she said. "Oh, I'm afraid!"

"Don't worry, Clarisse," said the visible Tancrède. "I'll explain the mystery to you one day. For now, I only want to occupy myself with our happiness. Tell me, frankly: Would you like to be my wife?"

"Me, Monsieur?" she said, embarrassed. "But...I don't know you."

"Clarisse, you're not telling the truth. That's bad. Are you seeing me today for the first time?" Smiling, he added: "Are you denying your guardian angel?"

"Oh no," she said. "It's really you!"

"It's really me that you love, isn't it?"

"Yes, but still, I don't know you. Tell me who you are, and by what mystery…?"

"Don't interrogate me; I can't answer you yet. Tomorrow, Clarisse, I shall come to speak to your mother; she shall know that I love you, that I want to marry you; but don't tell her anything about us—all that is a secret that she mustn't know."

"But what if she asks me where I've seen you?"

"In your dreams. In any case, haven't you already met me at Madame de D***'s house? By the way, about that young man to whom she wanted to marry you…"

"That was you?" Clarisse exclaimed.

"Me? No—you don't know him, then?"

"I've never seen him. I didn't want to go to Madame de D***'s house on the day when he was there."

"Very good," said Tancrède, laughing. "I'll tell your mother that it was me."

"But you'll explain the truth to me?"

"That's impossible. Don't ask me for a secret that isn't mine; it belongs to one of my friends; I'm not free to confide it, even to you. I'm obliged to keep silent."

"I can guess," said Clarisse, excitedly. "That friend is the owner of our house. I remember seeing him smile the other say when I met him in the garden; it's him who has betrayed us—he's given you the keys to our apartment so that you can get in."

Tancrède started laughing at that idea, but, as Clarisse had adopted it, he let her keep it. People who have imagination always act in that way; they furnish others with the ideas that might deceive them.

The duplicate keys, however, did not explain the sudden appearances and disappearances that had frightened Clarisse so much. She persisted…and Tancrède became annoyed.

"You don't love me," he said. "Love doesn't demand explanations."

"Well, just tell me: will you always be there without my knowing?"

"Ah! You're already afraid, Madame," said Tancrède, in jest.

"It's not that, but I'd rather see you." And Clarisse, as she said that, fixed her beautiful eyes on him with so much pleasure that it gave a great deal of verity to her words.

How beautiful she was then! Tancrède, who was affecting a coolness full of dignity, could not resist that gaze. He drew Clarisse toward him, and kissed her very tenderly.

"That's strange," she said. "It seems to me...one day...I dreamed..." Then she asked him, naively: "Is that the first time that..."

"That I've kissed you? No, but don't interrogate me. *Bonsoir*. Go to bed, sleep well—you won't dream. Sleep. Until tomorrow! Adieu, Clarisse, adieu, my wife."

And he left quickly, for he was afraid of himself.

Clarisse saw Tancrède go out through the door like a real being, no longer as a phantom. Her eyes followed him, lovingly.

As soon as she was alone she began to jump for joy, like a child.

"It's all true, then!" she exclaimed. And joy intoxicated her heart.

Before going to bed she looked around the room again, to see whether he was entirely gone...but he really was no longer there.

A month later he came back, no longer as an invisible being but as an adored husband, whom she was to see beside her always.

Madame Blandais was dazzled by the brilliant marriage, which she attributed to her daughter's talent, but which was entirely due to Monsieur de Balzac's marvelous cane.

Celebrity had only revealed the extent of Clarisse's nascent genius; the beneficent cane had revealed the purity of her life, the simplicity of her heart and the charm of her character. The cane, in fact, had repaired the wrong that celebrity had done her; she had learned from Tancrède that souls which conserve themselves pure in the world are those that live in illusions, and that, if celebrity is a torch that casts too much light on life, the slightest poetry is a holy veil that covers and preserves the heart.

Blessed are those who are poets! Woe betide those who are no longer.

Tancrède took his young wife to Blois, to his mother's house. Clarisse left Paris without regrets; she forgot the success that she might have obtained there; her wishes had been granted beyond her hopes. She had only come to Paris in search of glory, but she had found happiness.

What became of the cane, you might ask?

You shall know.

It has returned to the hands of Monsieur de Balzac, and *Les Héritiers Boirouge* will soon appear.[64]

---

[64] The projected novel in question, with Balzac mentioned to his great admirer Madame Hanska as well as to Madame de Girardin in 1836, was mentioned again as a project in 1839 and 1845, but never actually written. It remains on the extensive list of his phantom titles,

SF & FANTASY

Adolphe Alhaiza. *Cybele*

Alphonse Allais. *The Adventures of Captain Cap*

Henri Allorge. *The Great Cataclysm*

Guy d'Armen. *Doc Ardan: The City of Gold and Lepers*

G.-J. Arnaud. *The Ice Company*

Charles Asselineau. *The Double Life*

Henri Austruy. *The Eupantophone; The Olotelepan; The Petitpaon Era*

Barillet-Lagargousse. *The Final War*

Cyprien Bérard. *The Vampire Lord Ruthwen*

S. Henry Berthoud. *Martyrs of Science*

Aloysius Bertrand. *Gaspard de la Nuit*

Richard Bessière. *The Gardens of the Apocalypse; The Masters of Silence*

Albert Bleunard. *Ever Smaller*

Félix Bodin. *The Novel of the Future*

Louis Boussenard. *Monsieur Synthesis*

Alphonse Brown. *City of Glass; The Conquest of the Air*

Emile Calvet. *In a Thousand Years*

André Caroff. *The Terror of Madame Atomos; Miss Atomos; The Return of Madame Atomos; The Mistake of Madame Atomos; The Monsters of Madame Atomos; The Revenge of Madame Atomos; The Resurrection of Madame Atomos; The Mark of Madame Atomos; The Spheres of Madame Atomos; The Wrath of Madame Atomos* (w/M. & Sylvie Stéphan)

Félicien Champsaur. *The Human Arrow; Ouha, King of the Apes; Pharaoh's Wife; Homo-Deus*

Didier de Chousy. *Ignis*

Jules Clarétie. *Obsession*

Michel Corday. *The Eternal Flame*

André Couvreur. *The Necessary Evil*; *Caresco, Superman; The Exploits of Professor Tornada* (3 vols.)

Captain Danrit. *Undersea Odyssey*

C. I. Defontenay. *Star (Psi Cassiopeia)*

Charles Derennes. *The People of the Pole*

Georges Dodds (anthologist). *The Missing Link*

Charles Dodeman. *The Silent Bomb*

Harry Dickson. *The Heir of Dracula; Harry Dickson vs. The Spider*

Jules Dornay. *Lord Ruthven Begins*
Alfred Driou. *The Adventures of a Parisian Aeronaut*
Sâr Dubnotal *vs. Jack the Ripper*
Alexandre Dumas. *The Return of Lord Ruthven*
Renée Dunan. *Baal*
J.-C. Dunyach. *The Night Orchid; The Thieves of Silence*
Henri Duvernois. *The Man Who Found Himself*
Achille Eyraud. *Voyage to Venus*
Henri Falk. *The Age of Lead*
Paul Féval. *Anne of the Isles; Knightshade; Revenants; Vampire City; The Vampire Countess; The Wandering Jew's Daughter*
Paul Féval, *fils. Felifax, the Tiger-Man*
Charles de Fieux. *Lamékis*
Louis Forest. *Someone is Stealing Children in Paris*
Arnould Galopin. *Doctor Omega; Doctor Omega and the Shadowmen* (anthology)
Judith Gautier. *Isoline and the Serpent-Flower*
H. Gayar. *The Marvelous Adventures of Serge Myrandhal on Mars*
Léon Gozlan. *The Vampire of the Val-de-Grâce*
G.L. Gick. *Harry Dickson and the Werewolf of Rutherford Grange*
Edmond Haraucourt. *Illusions of Immortality; Daah, the First Human*
Nathalie Henneberg. *The Green Gods*
Eugène Hennebert. *The Enchanted City*
V. Hugo, P. Foucher & P. Meurice. *The Hunchback of Notre-Dame*
Romain d'Huissier. *Hexagon: Dark Matter*
Jules Janin. *The Magnetized Corpse*
Michel Jeury. *Chronolysis*
Gustave Kahn. *The Tale of Gold and Silence*
Gérard Klein. *The Mote in Time's Eye*
Fernand Kolney. *Love in 5000 Years*
Paul Lacroix. *Danse Macabre*
Louis-Guillaume de La Follie. *The Unpretentious Philosopher*
Jean de La Hire. *Enter the Nyctalope; The Nyctalope on Mars; The Nyctalope vs. Lucifer; The Nyctalope Steps In; Night of the Nyctalope; Return of the Nyctalope; The Fiery Wheel*
Etienne-Léon de Lamothe-Langon. *The Virgin Vampire*
André Laurie. *Spiridon*
Gabriel de Lautrec. *The Vengeance of the Oval Portrait*
Alain le Drimeur. *The Future City*
Georges Le Faure & Henri de Graffigny. *The Extraordinary Adventures of a Russian Scientist Across the Solar System* (2 vols.)

Gustave Le Rouge. *The Mysterious Doctor Cornelius* (3 vols.); *The Vampires of Mars; The Dominion of the World* (w/Gustave Guitton) (4 vols.)

Jules Lermina. *Mysteryville; Panic in Paris; To-Ho and the Gold Destroyers; The Secret of Zippeliu; The Battle of Strasbourg*

André Lichtenberger. *The Centaurs; The Children of the Crab*

Jean-Marc & Randy Lofficier. *Edgar Allan Poe on Mars; The Katrina Protocol; Pacifica; Robonocchio; Return of the Nyctalope;* (anthologists) *Tales of the Shadowmen 1-11*

Xavier Mauméjean. *The League of Heroes*

Joseph Méry. *The Tower of Destiny*

Hippolyte Mettais. *The Year 5865; Paris Before the Deluge*

Louise Michel. *The Human Microbes; The New World*

Tony Moilin. *Paris in the Year 2000*

José Moselli. *Illa's End*

John-Antoine Nau. *Enemy Force*

Marie Nizet. *Captain Vampire*

C. Nodier, A. Beraud & Toussaint-Merle. *Frankenstein*

Henri de Parville. *An Inhabitant of the Planet Mars*

Gaston de Pawlowski. *Journey to the Land of the 4th Dimension*

Georges Pellerin. *The World in 2000 Years*

Ernest Pérochon. *The Frenetic People*

Pierre Pelot. *The Child Who Walked on the Sky*

J. Polidori, C. Nodier, E. Scribe. *Lord Ruthven the Vampire*

P.-A. Ponson du Terrail. *The Vampire and the Devil's Son; The Immortal Woman*

Edgar Quinet. *Ahasuerus; The Enchanter Merlin*

Henri de Régnier. *A Surfeit of Mirrors*

Maurice Renard. *The Blue Peril; Doctor Lerne; The Doctored Man; A Man Among the Microbes; The Master of Light*

Jean Richepin. *The Wing; The Crazy Corner*

Albert Robida. *The Adventures of Saturnin Farandoul; The Clock of the Centuries; Chalet in the Sky; The Electric Life*

J.-H. Rosny Aîné. *Helgvor of the Blue River; The Givreuse Enigma; The Mysterious Force; The Navigators of Space; Vamireh; The World of the Variants; The Young Vampire*

Marcel Rouff. *Journey to the Inverted World*

Léonie Rouzade. *The World Turned Upside Down*

Han Ryner. *The Superhumans; The Human Ant*

Pierre de Selenes: *An Unknown World*

Angelo de Sorr. *The Vampires of London*

Brian Stableford. *The New Faust at the Tragicomique;The Empire of the Necromancers (The Shadow of Frankenstein; Frankenstein and the Vampire Countess; Frankenstein in London); Sherlock Holmes & The Vampires of Eternity; The Stones of Camelot; The Wayward Muse.* (anthologist) *News from the Moon; The Germans on Venus; The Supreme Progress; The World Above the World; Nemoville; Investigations of the Future; The Conqueror of Death; The Revolt of the Machines*

Jacques Spitz. *The Eye of Purgatory*

Kurt Steiner. *Ortog*

Eugène Thébault. *Radio-Terror*

C.-F. Tiphaigne de La Roche. *Amilec*

Louis Ulbach. *Prince Bonifacio*

Théo Varlet. *The Golden Rock. The Xenobiotic Invasion; The Castaways of Eros; Timeslip Troopers* (w/André Blandin); *The Martian Epic* (w/Octave Joncquel)

Paul Vibert. *The Mysterious Fluid*

Villiers de l'Isle-Adam. *The Scaffold; The Vampire Soul*

Philippe Ward. *Artahe ; The Song of Montségur* (w/Sylvie Miller) *Manhattan Ghost* (w/Mickael Laguerre)

MYSTERIES & THRILLERS

M. Allain & P. Souvestre. *The Daughter of Fantômas*

A. Anicet-Bourgeois, Lucien Dabril. *Rocambole*

A. Bernède. *Belphegor*; *Judex* (w/Louis Feuillade); *The Return of Judex* (w/Louis Feuillade); *The Shadow of Judex*

A. Bisson & G. Livet. *Nick Carter vs. Fantômas*

V. Darlay & H. de Gorsse. *Arsène Lupin vs. Sherlock Holmes: The Stage Play*

Séamas Duffy. *Sherlock Holmes in Paris*

Paul Féval. *Gentlemen of the Night; John Devil; The Black Coats ('Salem Street; The Invisible Weapon; The Parisian Jungle; The Companions of the Treasure; Heart of Steel; The Cadet Gang; The Sword-Swallower)*

Emile Gaboriau. *Monsieur Lecoq*

Goron & Emile Gautier. *Spawn of the Penitentiary*

Rick Lai. *Shadows of the Opera: Retribution in Blood; Sisters of the Shadows: The Curse of Cagliostro*

Steve Leadley. *Sherlock Holmes: The Circle of Blood*

Maurice Leblanc. *Arsène Lupin vs. Countess Cagliostro; Arsène Lupin vs. Sherlock Holmes (The Blonde Phantom; The Hollow Needle); The Many Faces of Arsène Lupin; The Island of the Thirty Coffins*

Gaston Leroux. *Chéri-Bibi; The Phantom of the Opera; Rouletabille & the Mystery of the Yellow Room; Rouletabille at Krupp's*

Richard Marsh. *The Complete Adventures of Judith Lee*

William Patrick Maynard. *The Terror of Fu Manchu; The Destiny of Fu Manchu*

Frank J. Morlock. *Sherlock Holmes: The Grand Horizontals; Sherlock Holmes vs Jack the Ripper*

Jean Petithuguenin. *The Adventures of Ethel King*

Antonin Reschal. *The Adventures of Miss Boston*

P. de Wattyne & Y. Walter. *Sherlock Holmes vs. Fantômas*

David White. *Fantômas in America*

Pierre Yrondy. *The Adventures of Thérèse Arnaud*

Victor Margueritte. *The Bacheloress; The Companion; The Couple*

SCREENPLAYS

Mike Baron. *The Iron Triangle*

Emma Bull & Will Shetterly. *Nightspeeder; War for the Oaks*

Gerry Conway & Roy Thomas. *Doc Dynamo*

Steve Englehart. *Majorca*

James Hudnall. *The Devastator*

Jean-Marc & Randy Lofficier. *Royal Flush*

J.-M. & R. Lofficier & Marc Agapit. *Despair*

J.-M. & R. Lofficier & Joël Houssin. *City*

Andrew Paquette. *Peripheral Vision*

Robert L. Robinson, Jr. *Judex*

R. Thomas, J. Hendler & L. Sprague de Camp. *Rivers of Time*

NON-FICTION

Stephen R. Bissette. *Blur 1-5. Green Mountain Cinema 1; Teen Angels*

Win Scott Eckert. *Crossovers* (2 vols.)

Jean-Marc & Randy Lofficier. *Shadowmen* (2 vols.)

Randy Lofficier. *Over Here*